THE GORDIAN PROTOCOL

THE GORDIAN PROTOCOL

DAVID WEBER & JACOB HOLO

A Baen Books Original

Baen Publishing Enterprises
P.O. Box 1403
Riverdale, NY 10471
www.baen.com

ISBN: 978-1-4814-8396-4

Cover art by Dave Seeley

First printing, May 2019

Distributed by Simon & Schuster
1230 Avenue of the Americas
New York, NY 10020

Library of Congress Cataloging-in-Publication Data

Names: Weber, David, 1952– author. | Holo, Jacob, author.
Title: The gordian protocol / David Weber & Jacob Holo.
Description: Riverdale, NY : Baen, [2019]
Identifiers: LCCN 2019000667 | ISBN 9781481483964 (hardcover)
Subjects: LCSH: Psychological fiction. | BISAC: FICTION / Science Fiction /
    Adventure. | FICTION / Science Fiction / General. | GSAFD: Science fiction.
Classification: LCC PS3573.E217 G67 2019 | DDC 813/.54—dc23
LC record available at https://lccn.loc.gov/2019000667

Pages by Joy Freeman (www.pagesbyjoy.com)
Printed in the United States of America

10   9   8   7   6   5   4   3   2   1

To Ken. For being the friend and mentor I needed.

PROLOGUE

Alexandria
30 BCE

"WE, MY FRIEND, HAVE HAD TOO MUCH CHEAP WINE," HOMEROS the Baker said slowly and with great precision, bracing himself upright—as unobtrusively as possible—against the statue of some no doubt once-important noble.

"No," Asklepiades, who owned the pastry shop next to Homeros' bakery, replied after careful consideration. "We have *not* had too much cheap wine. I would say"—he paused to belch noisily—"that we have, in fact, had almost exactly the right amount. And it wasn't *all* that cheap, now that I think about it," he added owlishly.

"Well, it was better than the swill Lysippos normally gives us," Homeros pointed out. "And a man doesn't celebrate the birth of his third son every day."

"No, he doesn't. But if you come home stinking of wine and"—Asklepiades paused to sniff loudly—"puke and piss, if I'm not mistaken, Kleopha is going to turn *her* third son into a fatherless waif. Probably with the dullest knife she can find." He considered that for a moment, then nodded gravely. "And probably as slowly as possible."

"It's not *my* puke!" Homeros protested. "It was that stupid Cypriot. I should have broken his head for him. A sailor who can't hold his drink shouldn't drink."

"You didn't break his head for him because he had six of his friends at the table with him. And do you really think Kleopha's going to believe that?"

1

"I rule my house with a rod of iron!" Homeros' grand pronouncement was rather undermined by the sway—one would not have cared to call it a stagger—as he waved his right hand in punctuation.

Asklepiades snorted.

"The only rod of iron in *your* house is the rolling pin Kleopha's about to apply to your skull. Repeatedly," he informed his friend.

"Ah!" Homeros grinned at him and laid one finger aside his nose. "But only if she sees me like this."

"*Smells* you, you mean!"

"Same thing, same thing." Homeros made a brushing away gesture. "And she won't. I'm going to sneak in the back way and sleep in the shop tonight. The baby'll keep me up all night if I don't, anyway. Then, in the morning, I'll make a quick trip to the baths."

"And she'll cut off your balls with a paring knife if you stay out all night."

"Nonsense." Homeros chuckled. "I slept in the shop because *you* kept me out so late I was certain she'd be sound asleep by the time I got home. And I know how little sleep the baby's letting her get. So I didn't want to disturb her. And," he added triumphantly as Asklepiades looked at him skeptically, "I shall redeem myself by not only smelling fresh and clean but appearing armed with one of your meat pastries for her breakfast because I love her so."

"Ha! I'll admit, that's cleverer than you usually manage, especially when we're both drunk. But it still won't work, because—"

"*Jupiter Optimus!*"

Asklepiades jumped in astonishment, then whipped around to see what his friend was staring at. Whatever it was, it had turned Homeros pale as a ghost. Asklepiades had never seen Homeros look that way, but, as he spun about, he felt his own jaw drop in terror-tinged disbelief.

The brilliant . . . *shapes* sweeping in across the harbor of Alexandria blazed against the night sky like Zeus' own lightning bolts. The lantern atop the mighty lighthouse was scarcely an ember in comparison, and they moved with terrifying speed across the long mole connecting the island of Pharos to the city. Their brilliance reflected in the glassy waters of the Great Harbor east of the mole, and he fell to his knees in shock as they sped silently overhead.

His head turned, tracking their passage, and his eyes widened as they swooped past the Serapeum and headed directly toward the Great Library. They were slowing, altering course, spreading out like the petals of some enormous flower. And then, they weren't moving *at all*. Six of them simply . . . *floated* there in midair, spaced equidistantly in a ring around the library campus. But four more of them—the largest of the lot—*didn't* float in the air. They settled downward, landing on the campus. From their apparent size, they must be crushing statuary, ornamental trees and gardens, and gods only knew what else under them as they came down.

Alarms began to sound all across the sleeping city as it awakened to the celestial visitation, and Asklepiades felt his lips moving in silent prayer to every deity and demigod he could think of.

And that was when he heard the first screams, the first shattering bursts of sound, and saw the terrible flashes of light bursting across the city streets and the grounds of the Royal Palace.

Somehow, he doubted Kleopha would find the time to berate her wayward husband after all.

"How tall *is* that thing?" Kai-shwun McGuire asked, tipping back in his command chair and looking at the magnified image of the great three-tiered tower on the island in the harbor. The lowest section was square, the next was octagonal, and the uppermost was circular. A fire burned before the polished mirror at its apex, and it was visible at a surprising distance, given the primitive nature of the illumination.

"Really have to ask one of the docs if you want a hard number," Lydia Robles, his copilot and weaponeer told him. "I'm sure one of them'll be just delighted to give you all the details. From here"—she checked one of her displays—"looks like it's close to a hundred and forty meters or so, give or take." She shrugged. "It's impressive looking, I suppose, under the circumstances. Hate to build the bastard without counter-grav, myself."

"Yeah." McGuire nodded, then brought his chair back upright. "Got some movement. Looks like some kind of city guard headed toward the target."

"On it," Robles replied, and her brown eyes had gone slightly unfocused as she communed with the TTV's onboard systems through her wetware implants.

Unlike most of the Antiquities Rescue Trust's security teams, neither she nor McGuire had acquired abstract companions. It wasn't that she had anything against connectomes, whether they'd once been flesh and blood or were completely artificial constructs. She'd just never felt the need for one, and she was only fifty-six. There was plenty of time for her to find one among the abstract citizens she'd met...if she decided she needed one. At the moment, though, Kai-shwun made about as satisfying a companion as she could imagine. She'd tried the virtual sex route a couple of times, and they were right: it *was* almost impossible to tell the difference. Except that she knew it was artificial even while her nerves were being convinced it wasn't, and she supposed she was some kind of throwback, because she vastly preferred the real thing.

She snorted, amused by the way her mind wandered—and to where—at moments like this.

"Got any idea who sent them?" she murmured as the tracking systems came online and the TTV's weapons slewed obediently to follow the armed and armored men marching purposefully, bravely, and incredibly stupidly toward the Library from the Royal Palace proper.

"God only knows, and He ain't talking." McGuire shrugged. "Probably whoever's in charge of the palace. Whoever the hell *that* is!"

"Yeah, yeah," Robles said a bit more loudly. "Damn, wish I'd paid more attention to the briefing. I can't *quite* remember . . ." She snapped her fingers suddenly. "Cleopatra! That's who they said it was."

"And who was Cleopatra?" McGuire demanded.

"Damned if I know. I just hate forgetting names. Seems, I don't know...unprofessional I guess."

"Well you better get your professional on," he told her. "Those guys are going to cross the zone in about another five seconds."

"No they aren't," she told him with a chuckle, and activated the fire command.

The revolving cannon was only one of the TTV's weapons, and it was certainly the most conceptually ancient. It was also the *noisiest*, which was the main reason she'd selected it. Personally, she didn't care how many indigenes got blown away on one of these missions, but some of the academics were a little more squeamish than she was. She didn't understand why, exactly. She'd seen VRs which were a *lot* bloodier than anything the academics ever saw. Well, out here on the perimeter, anyway. It could get...messy with the smash-and-grab teams closer in, she supposed. Still, that wasn't her problem and she was perfectly willing to defer to the tender sensibilities of the hothouse flowers who paid the freight. From her perspective, dead was dead, but if they wanted deterrence rather than destruction, she'd give it to them, as long as her own rosy posterior wasn't in the line of fire if she *didn't*, and very few things in life had as much deterrence as the cannon. It made a *lot* of noise when it fired, every tenth round was a tracer, and the kinetic impacts when four thousand rounds per minute hit the target were pretty impressive. Even the stupidest local figured out real quick that he didn't want to tangle with that!

Of course, before they can figure it out, you have to give them an illustration, she reminded herself.

Perikles Petrakis watched from the palace window as Captain Hermagoros led the royal guard detachment toward the Library. Hermagoros was a braver man than Perikles. More to the point, he had the duty tonight, thank all the gods! Although exactly what he and his men were going to accomplish—

A night already turned to chaos and terror by the glaring lights floating in Alexandria's skies splintered suddenly into even greater terror as Jupiter Toton's own lightnings erupted from the nearest light. It was a single, glaring, brilliant line, stretched down from the floating thing like a bar of fire, and where it touched, the earth itself exploded in threshed, shredded ruin.

And so did Captain Hermagoros and his entire guard detachment. They simply...disintegrated into bits and pieces in a concentrated tornado of inconceivable violence.

"Think they got the message?" Robles asked, opening her eyes again to grin at her partner.

"Question is if anyone was watching," McGuire replied a bit sourly.

"Oh, they were watching!" she assured him. "Reason I like that gun so much. Can't miss it the way you might a laser. More efficient in atmosphere, for that matter. And it sure is spectacular."

McGuire grunted. The tracers turned the cannon's torrent of projectiles into what looked for all the world like the "death rays" he'd seen in some ancient entertainment vids. And she was right about how spectacular that was.

"Well, at least we're not one of the entry teams," he told her. "That can get a little too up close and personal for my taste."

"Damn betcha!" Robles agreed. "They can keep their hazardous-duty bonuses, for all I care. Give me a nice air-conditioned command couch a couple of hundred meters up any day. Last thing I want is for some hairy primitive to get lucky and stick a sword into my hide!"

McGuire grunted again, but she had a point. The entry teams' Esteem bonuses were all well and good, but every so often they lost someone, even with modern medicine. It didn't happen often, but it did happen. And even if someone managed not to get killed, regenerating a new arm, or leg—or spleen—was no walk in the park. Of course, half of the entry team personnel were synthoids, with their personalities uploaded into synthetic bodies equipped with police-grade upgrades. Not as good as SysPol got, but pretty damned good. He'd considered putting in for upgrade himself, but he liked the body biology had given him just fine, so far at least.

And so did Lydia.

Besides, he admitted to himself, the real reason he'd never applied for entry-team duty had very little to do with synthetic bodies or potential risk factors. Entry duty was so... messy, sometimes. He vastly preferred being up here with Lydia where the carnage was nice and antiseptic and he didn't have to worry about wiping blood and splattered viscera off his helmet cameras.

"Damn it, Johansson!" Doctor Teodorà Beckett snapped. "We want these documents *intact*, you idiot! That means not shredded by mag darts—and not soaked in blood, either, for that matter! Is that so hard to understand?"

The archaeologist stood in the huge, colonnaded hall, surrounded by books and racked scrolls. Despite the lateness of the hour, oil lamps burned brightly and half a dozen scrolls had been unrolled for reading on the polished wooden tables down the hall's center. It could have been an orderly scene of scholarship... if not for the bodies of at least a dozen of the library's staff scattered about, leaking blood across the inlaid floors. It was hard to be certain of the exact number; hypervelocity mag darts had a tendency to shred their targets pretty badly. She didn't mind *that* so much, although she'd tossed her cookies on her first ART mission, but Johansson's people had been dismayingly careless about their lines of fire. The torrent of darts one of his teams had unleashed before Beckett could get there to stop them had turned at least forty or fifty scrolls into shredded, blood-soaked mulch which was undoubtedly seasoned with bits and pieces of human flesh.

"Listen, Doctor Beckett"—the entry team leader made no great effort to hide his own exasperation—"if one of these yahoos gets close enough to stick a knife into you, you aren't going to be real worried about the frigging *books!*"

"The 'frigging books' are the reason we're here," she pointed out tartly.

"So block them on the schematic." Johansson pointed at them. "After we finish here, I'll microjump back and collect just those racks."

Beckett glared at him, longing to rip his head off and stick it up his synthoid body's anal orifice. Unfortunately for her sense of frustration, he was right. Once the retrieval team pulled out, temporal inertia would have its way and erase the fact that they'd ever been here. He could always jump back into a present in which the scrolls had never been damaged. Of course, the idiot would probably shoot up ninety percent of the *rest* of the collection just because he was pissed about having to come back in the first place. But that wouldn't matter, either, because Beckett's teams would already have loaded an earlier iteration of them.

"Just *try* not to make the floor any slipperier than you can help," she growled, waving at the still-spreading pools of blood. "And don't forget—it's going to take us at least two or three days to load all of this, even with the conveyors and all the mechs. We have to catalog it all, remember? And it's summer in ancient Alexandria. You think maybe all this blood isn't going to start stinking in the heat, not to mention drawing clouds of flies, before we get out of here?"

At least he had the grace to grimace this time, she thought. That was something.

She gave him one more dirty look, then picked her way between pools of blood to where her team was busily but carefully transferring the priceless books to the waiting counter-grav skids that would deliver them to the TTV'S conveyors. She'd never really believed the estimates that said there were a half million books in the Great Library, but there might actually be that many scrolls, she thought in awe. Of course, it could take a lot of scrolls to make a single book. As an archaeologist, Beckett was fully aware of that. But even though she'd worked with documents just like this for the better part of forty years, the sight of them always made her painfully aware of just how clumsy and mass- and volume-intensive hardcopy data storage truly was.

Well, once we get them home and properly digitalized, that won't be a problem, will it? she reminded herself. *And we'll get the originals into the proper climate-controlled storage, too. That's what this is all about—the reason the Antiquities Rescue Trust was funded in the first place—really. It may be a wasteful way to record information, but the people who spent all that time laboriously writing it down deserve to have their work preserved.*

She ran her fingertips across one of the rolled scrolls reverently and glanced curiously at the body at her feet. Judging from the blood trail, the librarian had dragged himself at least ten or fifteen meters after one of Johansson's people took him down, and he'd died with one hand reaching toward the rack before which Beckett stood. She wondered what had made this particular rack so important to him, but she put the temptation to look for the reason behind her. There'd be plenty of time for that once they got the entire collection back to the thirtieth century, where it belonged.

"Help me remember the lot number assigned to this part of the collection, Fran," she said.

"Let me guess," the voice of her abstract companion said in the back of her mind, linked from the TTV's infosystem through her wetware. "You're wondering if this poor fellow was trying to reach something specific when he died?"

"You know me so well," Beckett agreed with a crooked smile. "I like to solve puzzles. It's the reason I became an archaeologist in the first place."

"Well, that and the chance to do fieldwork and actually *see* the past," Fran told her in a slightly martyred tone. "Thus dragging me into it, as well."

"You could always stay in the TTV," Beckett said sweetly,

and Fran chuckled. Unlike quite a few ACs, Fran had been a biological human for sixty years before she transitioned to an abstract connectome, and the truth was that she was just as fascinated by the endless vista of the human race's past as Beckett herself. That was one of the reasons they found one another such comfortable fits.

"But you're right, that's exactly what I'm thinking," the still-physical half of their relationship admitted, "and I intend to take personal charge of cataloguing the section. There should be at least some perks for the team leader, don't you think?"

"*I'm* certainly not going to argue with you about it," Fran told her primly.

"Good! Now I guess we should go take a look at whatever the hell Kohlman's found in Hall Three."

She headed out of the reading room, flanked by the pair of security types who accompanied every biological member of her team wherever they went on-site and headed toward the vast auditorium and lecture hall where Jebediah Kohlman seemed to think he'd just discovered the Holy Grail.

Now don't be that way, Teodorà, she scolded herself in a private corner of her mind. *Every so often, someone does find the Grail, don't they? Who's to say Jeb didn't pull it off this time?*

She chuckled at the thought and headed back out into the hot summer night.

"Are they really *gone*? *Really* gone?" Kleopha whispered, huddling against her husband's side.

Homeros was a baker, not a soldier, and Kleopha knew—intellectually, at least—that no mere mortal could stand against the forces of darkness. Gods knew enough of Pharaoh Cleopatra's guard had been casually slaughtered by the demons who'd descended upon the Library almost a week ago to prove that! But what her mind knew and what her heart needed were two very different things and the feel of that beloved arm, wrapped about her while her older boys and their sister clung to her skirts, was the most welcome thing she'd ever felt in her entire life. She hugged their newest child, giving him a nipple, feeling him suckle, and that, too, told her she and her family were still alive.

Unlike virtually all of the Library's scholars and librarians—and several hundred of Pharaoh's soldiers—if the rumors were true.

"So they say, love," Homeros said, embracing her tightly and bending to press a kiss to the top of her head. "So they say."

"Do...do you think they'll come back?" she half-whispered, and he laughed bitterly.

"Who knows what demons may do?" he replied after a moment. "But so far as I can see, there's nothing left for them to come back for! Gods only know why demons should steal *books* in the first place, but according to everybody I've talked to since they left last night, they got *all* of them." He shrugged, still holding her close. "So unless there's something *else* they want to steal from us, I suppose they're done."

And may Jupiter Victor protect us from them if they do *come back*, he told himself silently, where his wife couldn't hear. *Because no one else can.*

CHAPTER ONE

———∞∞∞———

Castle Rock University
2017 CE

"YOU'RE KIDDING ME." BENJAMIN SCHRÖDER SAT BACK IN HIS CHAIR, shaking his head in disbelief. "You're *serious* about this crap?"

"I'm very serious, Doctor Schröder," the thin, sharp-faced man seated behind the large, polished desk informed him severely. Patrick O'Hearn, the history department's chairman, was a good twenty years older than Schröder, but he'd always struck the younger man as a spoiled brat who'd never quite grown up. Schröder knew he wasn't the most tactful or "process oriented" of individuals, but O'Hearn possessed a unique ability to make him think longingly of utterly inappropriate physical responses to "microaggressions." Of course, in O'Hearn's universe, the clarity of his understanding—thoroughly validated by everyone else living inside his bubble—meant he was *incapable* of microaggressions. All *he* was doing was "speaking truth to power"...especially when he dragged in a junior member of his own department for "counseling." Aside from his voice, which was actually a surprisingly pleasant baritone, the older man represented every single thing Schröder disliked about academia...except for the whiny students unalterably opposed to enduring the contamination of alternative viewpoints. The only reasons students like that bothered him less than O'Hearn—and he had to admit, they ran a very close second—was that he kept reminding himself of what his mother had taught him as a teenager: Ignorance and even

11

narrowmindedness can be fixed; stupid is forever. And *willful* stupidity like O'Hearn's was especially galling. He suspected that the two of them would have cordially disliked one another under any imaginable circumstances; under the circumstances which actually applied, "dislike" was far too pale a verb.

"What happened to my right to file a response?" he demanded now. "I've got ten days to respond even to a formal grievance, let alone an administrative review!"

"Of course you do, Doctor." O'Hearn emphasized the academic title with a certain spiteful courtesy. "And if you choose to exercise that right, no one would even consider denying it to you. That right is absolutely guaranteed under the Student Grievance Policy and Procedures. I simply thought—purely as a courtesy to a professional colleague, you understand—that it might be expedient to...advise you in this matter."

Schröder clenched his teeth and cautioned himself against dwelling any further on those politically incorrect but highly satisfactory responses to O'Hearn's bright smile. The most satisfactory item on the menu would have included a direct kinesthetic rearrangement of the smile in question, which would hardly help his case at the moment. Some of the verbal responses which sprang to mind would have been almost equally unhelpful, however well deserved and apropos they might have been.

"Should I take it, then," he said instead, after counting slowly to ten, "that Dean Thompson's taken an official position on this?"

"Oh, by no means! That would be *highly* inappropriate at this stage of the process." O'Hearn shook his head, blue eyes gleaming with poorly disguised satisfaction behind the lenses of his wire-frame glasses. "She would never attempt to intervene or pressure anyone at such an early stage of the grievance process. At the same time, of course, she has to be aware of remedial options and any...potential sanctions. And, as your department chair, I thought it best to ascertain from her on your behalf exactly what those options might be after Ms. Kikuchi-Bennett raised her concerns with me."

"How kind of you," Schröder said, then bit his tongue mentally as O'Hearn's eyes flickered with mingled anger and satisfaction.

"You are a member of my department," the chairman pointed out. He didn't add the words "unfortunately" or "for the moment, at least," Schröder observed. Or not out loud, anyway. "And I'm sure you're aware of how seriously Castle Rock University takes any potential discrimination or harassment, especially by faculty."

"Oh, I'm well aware of that," Schröder replied. "I'm still a little confused about exactly how I'm supposed to have discriminated against or harassed Ms. Kikuchi-Bennett, though."

"The creation of a hostile classroom environment is the very definition of harassment, Doctor," O'Hearn said rather more frostily. "And attacking an undergraduate's gender identity and political views in front of an entire class certainly creates exactly that sort of environment."

"I'm not aware of having attacked Ms. Kikuchi-Bennett's gender identity—or political views—in any way."

"Sarcasm, ridicule, and denigration constitute 'attacks' in most people's view, Doctor." O'Hearn's tone was positively icy now, but the satisfaction in his eyes was brighter.

"No doubt they would...if I'd done any of them." Schröder felt his own temper rising and stepped on it firmly. It wasn't easy, and he felt the ghost of his father standing at his shoulder. The old man probably would have already ripped out O'Hearn's tonsils and wrapped them around his neck for a bowtie.

Not the best image for him to be dwelling upon at the moment.

"I'm afraid three independent witnesses support Ms. Kikuchi-Bennett's interpretation of your remarks, Doctor."

"And am I permitted to know who these three independent witnesses might be?"

"I'm afraid that's privileged information under the university's privacy procedures. At this time, of course." O'Hearn flashed another of those thin, smug, satisfied smiles. "If the process continues to the formal grievance stage, however, I'm sure you'll receive copies of their statements."

"But not their identities?"

"It's the content of their statements, not their identities, that would be relevant," O'Hearn pointed out, "and the university has a legal and moral responsibility to protect their privacy, if only to avoid any appearance of retaliation against them. I'm sure you can understand the chancellor's position on that point, Doctor. You would certainly be within your legal rights to seek that information if you should choose to appeal the Grievance Committee's formal ruling in other venues. Of course, at that point the legal department would be legally and morally obligated to protect that information until such time as the courts directed its disclosure."

"Oh, of course."

Schröder wished O'Hearn's attitude had surprised him. Given academia's taste for witch hunts, though, the surprise would come from any *other* response. Besides, he had a pretty shrewd notion which of Kikuchi-Bennett's friends had chosen to support the transgender student's allegations. If he was right, the frightening thing was that at least two of them were undoubtedly completely sincere in their belief that he had, indeed, brutally and viciously assailed Kikuchi-Bennett in front of their entire class. Their hyper-sensitive, exquisitely quivering antennae would have left them with no other conclusion, especially after Kikuchi-Bennett "rebutted" his comments not by refuting—or even considering—his reasoning or his evidence, but by scorning them as "typical of the racist and homophobic patriarchy's callous dismissal of any dissenting viewpoint." In his experience, once those labels were deployed, any possibility of rational discourse had left the building.

He thought—briefly, and not very seriously—about point-ing out to O'Hearn that what he'd said was simply that women hadn't acquired the franchise in the United States at the point of a gun, but by convincing the majority of *men* that in a just society interested in living up to the Declaration of Independence's nobly espoused principles they should have had the franchise all along, just as African-Americans should have had their *freedom* all along. The suffragettes' victory in the Nineteenth Amendment had been achieved because their stance had been correct all along and their moral pressure had convinced enough *male* voters of that to support the amendment's passage. Since the discussion had been about the evolution of legal and societal viewpoints in the United States, and about the fashion in which protest movements and organized political pressure groups had achieved change, it was difficult for him to see that as even misogynistic, far less racist, homophobic, or gender phobic.

It was Kikuchi-Bennett who'd raised a hand, rejected his argument, and asserted that only someone speaking from the "privileged platform of the white male patriarchy" could possibly have made such a ludicrous assertion. As someone who was neither female nor black, his "patronizing dismissal of their struggle" both demeaned them and revealed his own "blinkered" inability to see the truth hidden in the "so-called history written by that same white male patriarchy," and segued from there into the necessity for "free-speech zones" where such "hate speech and shameless historical revisionism" as his—which was particularly offensive coming from someone speaking from a "privileged position of power"—would not be tolerated.

Maybe I should have pointed out that my family probably knows a little more about that whole African-American thing than most non-Black families, he thought. In fact, he'd considered doing just that, although not very hard. Claiming personal credit for the moral superiority of ancestors who'd been dead for a century or two was about as intellectually dishonest as an argument came. Besides, it would have been totally irrelevant to her. And certainly not germane to the course's subject matter.

Aware that Kikuchi-Bennett's passion, however misguided he found it, was completely genuine, he'd dialed back his instinctive response. Apparently replying with the observation that "traditionally, college is where we're supposed to challenge our own conceptions and preconceptions" had been...an insufficient dial-back.

Personally, he would have preferred to demonstrate the illogic and inconsistency of Kikuchi-Bennett's arguments in a reasoned debate from which both of them might have learned a little something, if only respect for opposing viewpoints. It would have been nice if, failing that, he'd at least been able to shut the tirade down in less than the fifteen minutes of the rest of his students' time which had been squandered to absolutely no good purpose. And, oh, for the long-vanished days when he could have suggested that Kikuchi-Bennett was always free to depart his classroom and refuse to return to it ever again.

I wonder how Mom would've dealt with this? he wondered, only half whimsically. In fact, he had a pretty good idea how Doctor Joséphine Schröder would have responded, especially here at her own alma mater. *We probably shouldn't call it an alma mater anymore, either. "Mother" is so sexist. Alma parente would probably be better... of course, that's a* masculine *gendered noun, isn't it? Damn, Latin is such a sexist language! Just like French, Spanish, and Italian. I guess we'll have to find a new noun that's neither.*

Fortunately for her, his mother had acquired tenure at Emory two years before Benjamin's birth. The climate had been just a little different then, and by the time the rot had truly set in, it would have taken a very hardy individual to pick a fight with "Doctor Joe," who was famous for her ability to vivisect faulty reasoning and absolute *death* on fabricated or cherry-picked "facts." Besides, even the faculty members who'd most strongly disagreed with her politics—aside from a handful of much younger, recent additions—had admired and respected her too deeply to consider this sort of nonsense, and her own students had loved her.

And the truth was that as infuriating as O'Hearn was, the man was about to do exactly what Benjamin *wanted* him to do. Under the circumstances, mentioning anything about rabbits, tar, or brier patches would probably send the man's blood pressure through the roof, but really . . .

"So essentially I'm supposed to respond to anonymous accusations without benefit of even hearing exactly what those accusations are? And your position is that, on that basis, I should accept whatever recommendation you choose to make rather than turn this into a confrontation before the dean, the senate, or the chancellor?" he asked after a moment.

"Really, Doctor Schröder," O'Hearn said in moderately offended tones, "that's not a very constructive attitude. Having said that, though, I do feel the proposed . . . solution would be simplest—and fairest—all around. I think it's clear you don't feel you contributed to a hostile classroom environment for your students. As your department head I'm fully prepared to believe you sincerely feel that way and, indeed, that you had absolutely no intention of causing such distress to Ms. Kikuchi-Bennett or to any of her fellows. Obviously, however, whether or not that was your *intent*, it's what happened, and that makes it almost worse, in a way. I'm sure the thought of causing such distress unintentionally must be as painful to you as it would be to me, and, as you know, our student body is one of the most diverse in American education. It's going to grow only increasingly diverse in the future, and I would think that any professor who desires a long-term association with this institution—and, especially, one whose family has always been so deeply invested in it and in its core missions— would prefer to be equipped with the best tools available for encountering that diversity."

Oh, I'm sure you would, *you sanctimonious prick,* Schröder thought. *The mere fact that I don't think I contributed to a hostile classroom environment because I* didn't *doesn't mean one damned thing to you, does it? In fact, in your world, the fact that I don't think that only proves I* did *do it in the first place!*

Of course his opinion didn't mean anything to O'Hearn. But it was abundantly evident where the department head was going to come down, and there was no doubt that Helen Thompson, who just happened to head the tenure committee, would come down in exactly the same spot. Allen Rendova, the university's chancellor, on the other hand, almost certainly *wouldn't*, for several reasons. Including the fact that he was more than smart enough—and had bothered to learn enough about one Benjamin Schröder and his family—to see exactly where this was going to end.

O'Hearn didn't plan on it going as far as the chancellor's office, though. Benjamin Schröder was still a semester short of attaining tenure, and O'Hearn was counting on the fact that he'd never acquire it if he fought this bullshit allegation. He figured the administration would opt to get rid of a troublesome professor by quietly denying him tenure rather than risk the sort of public auto de fé Kikuchi-Bennett's version of events would almost certainly inspire. After all, the tenure denial wouldn't be *directly* linked to the way he'd embarrassed the university, now would it? And if that just happened to let the department head put the blocks to a brash, younger professor with whom he disagreed profoundly—and who'd already published more independent research than O'Hearn had managed in his entire career—well, every cloud had a silver lining, didn't it?

He really should have done a little research on me before he decided to go here. And if I felt like a nice guy—which I don't, at the moment—I should probably ask him if he's ever met my brother or checked into some of Mom's nonacademic credentials. Or Dad's, for that matter! Not that I'm going to look a gift horse in the mouth. If he wasn't such a prick, I'd thank him for this! And wouldn't that blow his mind?

He leaned back in his chair, his expression grim, and reminded himself of why he was at Castle Rock University in the first place.

Once upon a time, before CRU became the sprawling university it now was, it had been known as Castle Rock College. The small, privately endowed college, founded shortly after the Civil War by a tiny group of Quakers, Huguenots, and Methodist pastors, had opened its doors specifically to the sons and daughters of freed slaves, but it had never been one of the historically all-Black colleges. Its founders had believed that bringing Black and white students together—engaging them and mutually educating one another, as well as themselves, in the same classrooms—was the best way to break down barriers between them.

That attitude had been less than popular in 1868 North Carolina, and the college's entire initial enrollment had been only thirty-three students, just six of whom, all the children of its faculty members, had been white. But to its critics' amazement, it had survived despite every legal—and extralegal—impediment thrown in its path, including half a dozen "mysterious" fires in its first ten years of operation. It had also become known as much for its intellectual diversity and exacting academic standards as for its radical notions about race and equality. One of its founders—and its first president—had been Marc-Antoine Martineau, an abolitionist Huguenot who'd immigrated from Canada to the United States in the late 1840s and run a Virginia station on the underground railroad for ten years before the first shell was fired at Fort Sumter. Marc-Antoine's son, Jourdain, had chaired the Castle Rock Department of History for twenty-three years, and Benjamin's mother, Joséphine Martineau Schröder, had graduated *summa cum laude* in 1963 and gone on to graduate studies at Duke University, McGill, and Oxford as part of her own outstanding academic career.

And while she was doing that, Castle Rock College had become Castle Rock *University*, with an explosive growth in enrollment that began in the sixties and seventies and continued into the nineties. The school's century of dedication to civil rights and minority education had been a big part of that growth, but it had stalled over the last fifteen or twenty years. In fact, O'Hearn's comments notwithstanding, enrollment had begun to shrink. Benjamin had his own suspicions about why that had happened, and he was enough his mother's son to want to do something about it.

Patrick O'Hearn had no intention of allowing him to do anything of the sort, and not just because he saw the younger man as a threat to his own position. As much as Benjamin despised him, he never doubted the sincerity of O'Hearn's beliefs. Those were what Benjamin truly threatened, in the chairman's eyes, and the steady growth in the size of Benjamin's classes—graduate and undergraduate, alike—underscored that threat. Benjamin was one of those right-wing, fascist hatemongers. He might never say or do anything overtly to betray his hate-fueled political agenda, but it *had* to exist. O'Hearn had plenty of evidence of that, given the way he required students to defend their logic and their facts and persisted in introducing "alternative viewpoints," all of which were clearly designed to allow the oppressive poison of racism, misogyny, and homophobia back into the academic community from which they had finally been banished. It was beyond intolerable that a cretin who believed all of that should actually be one of the two or three most popular professors in his entire department, with waiting lists to get into his classes.

That attitude and sincerity made his determination to either hammer Benjamin into the proper mold, or else get rid of him before he acquired tenure, perfectly understandable.

Contemptible, perhaps, but understandable.

This is just so damned petty, *though,* he thought. *I can do the frigging "gender sensitivity" standing on my head. It's only a matter of giving them back the answers I already know they want. And it would probably look good on my resume. After all, it would show what a good, twenty-first-century, forward-thinking sort of fellow I am. There are probably even some good points in there. God knows I'd've loved for someone to have been a bit more "gender aware" when David came along! But I know the idiot they have in charge of it here, and David and Steve would laugh their asses off listening to him!*

I wonder how much of this has to do with the fact that Granddad's portrait is hanging on the wall outside his office and Great-Granddad's is on the wall in Rendova's office? Maybe he resents that even more than I thought he did. Or maybe the connection makes him so scared of me that he has to stomp out the flame right now. Can't have one the founders' great-great-grandkids kicking up a stink and challenging the school's mission, after all.

Hell, from his perspective, he's got a point! I am here *to fight tooth and nail for genuine intellectual diversity. In his eyes, that is* challenging *the CRU mission. Of course, he and I differ rather profoundly on exactly what the mission is, don't we? It may be too late, but I at least owe Castle Rock my best shot at it.*

The temptation to tell O'Hearn *exactly* what he thought of him—and warn him where this was headed—trembled on the very tip of Schröder's tongue, but he sat on the impulse. However personally satisfying it might have been, he already knew O'Hearn's plan wasn't going to play out the way the older man thought it would. Under the circumstances, the last thing he wanted was to give the department chair even a shred of a claim that he'd been "confrontational, arrogant, and personally abusive" when O'Hearn invited him to a civil fact-finding discussion. There were better and more effective ways to win this war, he thought, and he had no intention of throwing away his opponent's mistakes.

He reminded himself of that as he settled further back into his chair, crossed his legs, and gave O'Hearn a smile just as false—and just as *deliberately* false—as any the department head had ever given him.

"You're perfectly correct that I *don't* feel I contributed to any 'hostile environments' in my classroom, Doctor O'Hearn," he said pleasantly. "In fact, I'd go farther than that. I'm positive I *didn't*. Of course, at the moment I haven't quite attained tenure, which—obviously—means I haven't been with the university long enough to . . . acquire total submersion in all the finer nuances of its current challenging intellectual diversity. That's something I look forward to understanding more fully and completely in the fullness of time. And, of course, you're correct about my family's long-standing relationship with CRU. Because of that, I hope to make my own small contribution to its robust and stimulating intellectual climate over the next twenty-five or thirty years."

O'Hearn's face tightened, and Schröder allowed himself to smile a bit more broadly as he dwelt upon the vision of O'Hearn forced to tolerate him as a tenured member of his department for the next decade or two. Clearly the chairman found that prospect unpalatable. Well, Schröder wasn't exactly thrilled by the prospect of putting up with all the crap he knew he'd face—not just from O'Hearn, who wasn't even the university's most strident voice, to be fair—over that same decade or two, either. But it would be worth it just to contemplate the damage to O'Hearn's cardiovascular system. Besides, he'd known what was coming when he joined Castle Rock's history department. He hadn't deliberately created this opening—hadn't really planned on opening his campaign in earnest until he *had* acquired tenure, really—but it was here now, and as his parents had always told him, nothing worth doing came easy.

"When did you say that gender-sensitivity seminar begins?" he asked.

CHAPTER TWO

———— ⌒⌒⌒ ————

Denton, North Carolina
2017 CE

CRACK, CRACK, CRACK!

The magazine emptied and the slide locked back as the X-ring of Benjamin Schröder's fifty-yard pistol target disintegrated. There was one flyer in the 8-ring, and he scowled at it as he ejected the empty magazine and laid the pistol on the bench in front of him. The North Carolina summer afternoon was hot, but the shooting positions were covered by a light roof to keep the direct sunlight at bay. He didn't like to think what his ears would have felt like under that cover if he'd been stupid enough to come to the range without ear protection, but he was incredibly grateful for the shade.

"My, my, *my*!" His younger brother's murmured comment was perfectly clear over the electronic shooting muffs' microphones. "I think Dad would have had a thing or two to say to you about that, big brother."

Benjamin transferred his scowl from the target to his brother, and to the short, compact fellow standing behind him.

"I believe my running score is still higher than yours," he observed.

"Oh, I can't believe you!" David Schröder laughed out loud. "Of course it's higher! I haven't fired this round yet."

"And there's no reason to believe *you* won't have a round go astray," Benjamin pointed out.

"And when was the last time that happened, exactly?" David asked, stepping up to the shooting position and closing the cylinder on his S&W 686.

"Shooting two-handed, with those wimpy little .38s instead of mags, and thumb-cocking between every round, you mean?" Benjamin inquired just a bit nastily. "*And* with a six-inch barrel, I might add!"

"You *are* in a pissy mood today, aren't you?" David inquired genially, and proceeded to squeeze off six rounds, rapid fire, double-action...and put all six of them into the X-ring of his target, so close together they made one large, five-petaled hole. He snapped six more rounds into the cylinder from a speed loader, then proceeded to make the hole perhaps a half-inch wider.

"Goodness!" he observed. "I seem to have inched in front somehow. How do you suppose that happened?"

"'When pride comes, then comes disgrace, but with humility comes wisdom,'" Benjamin replied. "And, for that matter, 'Pride goes before destruction, a haughty spirit before a fall.' I wouldn't want to say anything of the sort is headed your way, but this... unmannerly gloating ill becomes you."

"Nonsense," Stephen O'Shane-Schröder replied, reaching out and cuffing the back of David's head gently. "Given how often he does it, he's obviously of the opinion that it becomes him very well, indeed."

Benjamin chuckled as he began thumbing fresh rounds into his H&K USP's magazine. He really preferred the .45 ACP version, which was what he usually took to the range, but today he was shooting the .40 S&W. He would have liked to blame that single errant round on the change in pistols, but he knew better.

"Seriously, Ben," David said as he cleared the brass from his revolver's cylinder and set it down, the cylinder swung out for safety's sake, and began refilling his speed loaders. "Something's been eating on you all day. I'd love to beat you fair and square—Lord knows we're both insufferable enough when we get to take home the bragging rights!—but I've got a feeling the big reason you invited Steve and me out here this afternoon was that you really, really needed to put some holes in a piece of paper. I remember that's how Dad used to work out frustration, too."

"Yes, it was," Benjamin agreed with a sad smile. Their father had been in the South Tower on 9/11. "'Concentration on something that requires minimal thought and maximum focus is always a good way to let go of things that won't stop eating on your brain,'" he quoted.

"Yeah." David shook his head. "God, I still miss him *so* much sometimes."

"Me, too," Stephen said. He wrapped an arm around David and hugged him for a moment. Then he turned back to Benjamin. "On the other hand, I think David has a point. Just what is it that's 'eating on your brain,' Ben? And is there anything we can do to help?"

"Actually, it really could be something I could use your insight on—both of you," Benjamin said.

"Like how?" David raised his eyebrows.

"Well, it all started in my Modern US History class last Tuesday," Benjamin began, still snapping rounds into the magazine. "One of my students apparently took one of my comments amiss. It seems—"

"You're shitting me, right?" David asked disbelievingly when Benjamin finished his explanation twenty minutes later. He could have gotten there sooner if not for the combination of incredulous interjections and cracks of laughter coming from his audience. "I mean, this idiot—O'Hearn—thinks *you* need gender-sensitivity training?"

"To be totally fair to him—which, to be honest I don't want to be I think he's dead serious about my obviously Neolithic attitudes toward gender and sexuality," Benjamin replied. "Mind you, we've never even discussed them, so he's got exactly zero firsthand evidence upon which to form any opinions about them. I have, however, made myself a genuine pain in the ass as far as he's concerned by refusing to hew to his chosen political narrative in other areas. I don't think he knows what my political beliefs really *are*. In fact, he'd probably be surprised to find out that there are actually a few things he and I agree on. The problem is—"

"The *problem*," David interrupted, "is that you're Mom and Dad's son, you have a working brain, and they left out 'reverse' when they installed your transmission. No wonder this jerk has really, really pissed you off, because *he* obviously doesn't. Have a working brain, I mean. In fact, he sounds like an intellectually challenged, morally blinkered moron." He considered that for a moment, then shrugged. "To put it kindly."

"But otherwise, Ms. Lincoln, what did you think of the play?" Stephen asked him dryly, and he snorted.

"Point taken. But you and I both know how hard it is to be a respectably married gay guy and a political conservative at the same time, and idiots like this only make it a lot harder by poisoning the entire conversation. How many times has someone told us we're traitors because we don't see eye to eye with them politically or do think strict constructionalism is a *good* thing in a federal judge? Jumping all over someone who's actually *demonstrated* bigotry's one thing, but this asshole's simply *assuming* it and then forcing the evidence to fit his preconceptions. People like that don't *convert* anyone. In fact, they mostly confirm real bigots' bigotry and push away people who might have been on their side!"

"Be fair," Benjamin said. "I run into just as many people on the right who get pissed off because of my stance on gay marriage and gay rights. I guess all three of us flunk the 'ideological purity' litmus test. Heck, just look at where we are right this minute!" He snorted, gesturing around at the pine trees surrounding the Denton Rifle and Pistol Club's shooting range. "How can we possibly be trusted on social issues if we're such dangerous, right-wing, fascistic supporters of the evil gun lobby! It's bad enough Dad raised both of us as Bambi killers, but did we have to go and get concealed-carry permits on top of everything else? *Obviously* O'Hearn has to assume someone so lost to all sense of decency on those issues has to be a misogynistic, homophobic, genderphobic neo-Nazi, as well."

"Oh, he *so* doesn't want to bring Nazis into this!" Stephen laughed. "Not where *this* family's concerned!"

"No, he doesn't," Benjamin agreed. "Of course, he probably doesn't know that. I think he's familiar with Mom's family—or thinks he is, anyway—because of how long the Martineaus have been associated with Castle Rock. I doubt he knows a damn thing about Dad's side of the family."

"Pity." Stephen's lips quivered. "I could just imagine the insufferable little prick melting into a spot of grease if the *General* had ever walked into his office!"

"Are you kidding?" Benjamin shook his head. "One look at Dad's resume and he'd know for certain that I absolutely have to be a dangerous, right-wing, militarist reactionary, no doubt conspiring to overthrow the Constitution, suspend *habeas corpus*, and start shooting dissidents in the street. And that doesn't even consider how he'd react to Horst!"

"You mean you didn't tell him that if Dad hadn't renounced the title *you'd* have been the German count instead of our beloved cousin Horst?" David rounded his eyes. "How could you possibly have passed up the opportunity to watch his eyes bug out of his head when you told him that part?"

"You two are *not* helping." The severity of Benjamin's glare was somewhat undermined by the laughter bubbling under the surface of his words.

"Sure we are!" Stephen told him. "We're helping you vent. And just think of all the additional ammunition we're reminding you of when you need it."

"Including us, you know, Ben," David said in a much more serious tone. Benjamin looked at him, one eyebrow raised, and David shrugged. "I know how you feel about waving me and Steve under other people's noses like some kind of union card, but still . . ." He shook his head. "I know you're still short of tenure. That means this prick really can hurt you over this, if you're not careful. If we can help you by talking to anyone in the faculty senate or the chancellor's office, you know we will."

"Thanks, but no." Benjamin cupped the back of his brother's neck in one palm, drawing him close for a brief hug. "I'll do his stupid gender-sensitivity training—I'll dot every *i* and cross every *t* until he's got everything he wants. I won't give him a single piece of ammunition to take to the tenure committee. And then, once I've *got* tenure, I'm going to invite you and Steve to the very next faculty reception."

"That's evil," David told him with a chuckle.

"Maybe. And I'll enjoy hell out of it, but not just because of how O'Hearn and certain other of my professional colleagues— on *both* sides of the line—will react, and you know it. You two happen to be people I love, and I love you for who you are and what you are. I don't want the 'approval' of people because the fact that I love my brother and his husband proves how enlightened and noble I am, and I don't give a rat's ass about people who might *disapprove* of me because I do. Mom and Dad taught both of us better than that, David!"

"Yeah. Yeah, they did," David agreed with another of those bittersweet smiles.

The truth was that Major General Klaus Schröder, US Army, had faced an internal struggle when he discovered his younger son was gay. The general—born in Germany in 1941, son of *Generalmajor* Graf Klaus-Wilhelm von Schröder—had been raised with a firm and unwavering understanding of what went into manhood. He'd also been raised by a man who was bitterly ashamed of his native country's horrendous actions and by a mother whose blood was as blue as Klaus-Wilhelm's own...and whose brother had seen his wife's Jewish parents disappear into Auschwitz.

Klaus-Wilhelm's shame had cut even deeper because as a boy growing up in post–World War One Germany, the scion of one the oldest military families in the entire country, he had actually been an early supporter of Adolf Hitler. His parents had despised the "Bavarian corporal" and his overt, rabble-rousing racism. He himself had never been a party member, yet a young, humiliated Klaus-Wilhelm had ignored the racism to concentrate on the message of German redemption. He'd decried the extremism but believed the good of the message outweighed the bad.

Until *Kristallnacht*, that was.

Until the stripping away of Jewish civil liberties, one by one, had come together in that night of rioting and arson and murder and the authorities—the authorities of which he, as a young German officer, had been a part—had done *nothing*. Until the night he'd realized to whom he'd truly given his oath as an officer. That night had brought him agonizingly face-to-face with the consequences of *choice*, and it was a lesson which had never left him. That night was the reason he'd been a part of the Canaris faction within the Third Reich's intelligence services...and narrowly escaped arrest and execution after the July bomb plot. And so he had understood when Gräfin Elfriede refused to ever forgive the country of her birth which had sent two of her dearest friends into a concentration camp, never to be seen again. She'd sworn to live and die an American, and following his retirement from the *Bundesnachrichtendienst*, West Germany's federal intelligence service in 1960, he'd joined her in permanent residence in the United States, where both their surviving children were already American citizens.

The searing honesty of his own father's memories, his own father's iron awareness of the price of moral choices, had been more than enough to teach Klaus Schröder about personal responsibility, about duty, about the truth of Edmund Burke's ancient aphorism

about the success of evil and good men who did nothing to prevent it. And then he'd compounded it by marrying a woman whose family had been involved in the civil rights struggle in the United States since well before the Civil War and who went on to become a board member of the Urban League of Greater Atlanta. So he'd felt reasonably confident of his ability to openly accept all men and women of goodwill, regardless of who or what else they might be.

And then, while David was still a high-school freshman, that confidence had been challenged. His comfortable assumption of what constituted "manhood" had run full tilt into the reality of his son's sexuality. A thirty-plus-year career in an Army which had never accepted openly gay personnel until after his retirement hadn't over-equipped him with the mental tools to deal with that discovery, either. But he *had* dealt with it. He'd dealt with it because he loved his son far too deeply to do anything else. Because David's mother had loved *her* son—all of him, whoever and whatever he was—with every breath in her body. Because both of them had always believed that who a person was was far more important than *what* that person was. And because the way he'd found out was when David's older brother was suspended—threatened with permanent expulsion—in his junior year of high school for a fight in which he'd beaten three senior boys bloody for the brutal harassment they'd handed out when *they* realized his younger son was gay.

The fact that David hadn't already told him—not because he'd feared Klaus's anger, but because he'd feared that his father would be *disappointed* in him—had reduced the tough, strong man who'd received the Distinguished Service Cross, the Silver Star with three oak clusters, six Purple Hearts, and God only knew how many other awards and citations, to tears. And that, of course, had done the same for David.

Needless to say, the possibility of Benjamin's expulsion had vanished when General Schröder and Doctor Martineau descended upon their sons' high school in truly Olympian wrath. And that, as far as the Schröder family's position was concerned, had been that where the question of gay rights was concerned. By the time Stephen O'Shane came home from David's sophomore year of college with him, General Schröder (ret) had become one of the strongest critics of the US military's Don't-Ask-Don't-Tell policy. He hadn't been out storming the barricades; instead, he'd been

buttonholing senior officers—many of whom had been *junior* officers under his command—and policymakers behind the scenes, and he'd testified repeatedly to Congress on the issue.

And he'd worn his uniform, with every ribbon, to Stephen and David's wedding, where he'd walked his son down the aisle to his groom.

"I really can't believe this O'Hearn is that damned stupid," David said now, thoughtfully.

"Oh, I can," Stephen disagreed with a chuckle, and gave Benjamin a measuring look. "Never said a word about us to him, did you?"

"Never *hid* it," Benjamin replied with a lurking smile. "And there are at least two other people on campus who know all about you two. We think of ourselves as 'The Three Musketeers,' although I'm pretty sure O'Hearn and his friends think of us as 'The Three Dinosaurs.' But, if pressed, I *would* have to admit I've been angling for something like this for a while. I just didn't expect him to jump me before I had tenure."

"You sandbagging bastard," David said with a hint of admiration. "You're setting him up."

"No," Benjamin said much more seriously. "I may be letting him set *himself* up, but if he does, it'll be all his own doing. Any good historian knows you have to research your topic carefully, but he clearly didn't see any reason to do that in this case. There are several dirty words people in our field use about people who approach historical questions that way; not *my* fault he doesn't think this question's important enough to merit the same approach. And, like I say, I won't use you guys as a weapon to stop him from doing whatever he thinks he needs—or wants—to do. And I'll never wave you two in anyone's face afterward, either. Then again, I won't *have* to. There really are people—quite a few of them, actually—on the faculty who are smart enough and open-minded enough to draw the correct conclusions without my breaking his kneecaps with you in public."

"Breaking his kneecaps?" David asked. "Hey! I could get on board with that."

"I don't think that's what Ben's after," Stephen said as he unzipped his own shooting bag to take out a .44 Ruger Model 5003 Redhawk revolver. He hadn't been a shooter when he and David met, but he'd made up for it since.

David quirked an eyebrow at him, and he shrugged as he swung out the cylinder and laid the weapon on the bench in front of him.

"Oh, don't worry—it *will* 'break his kneecaps,' as you so charmingly put it, whatever else Ben's trying to accomplish. But this is more of that 'contrarian thinking' of yours, isn't it, Ben?"

"Yep," Benjamin said, picking up one of Stephen's speed loaders and fitting rounds into it. "The thing I hate most of all about what's going on at Castle Rock right now is the way the intellectual climate's so...shuttered on the assumption that if you believe Proposition A, then you *must* also accept Proposition B and likewise anathematize Proposition C. The way it rejects the possibility that anyone could conceivably be able to admit *both* sides can have valid points—and endorse the ones that are—if the minions of the ideological inquisition would only stop consigning each other to the intellectual equivalent of the outermost circle of Hell just really, really pisses me off. And it *scares* me, too. It scares me because of the groupthink involved, because of the intellectual narcissism behind it, and because that kind of polarization forecloses any kind of critical analysis of either side's position. If you can't analyze it you can't treat it with the moral respect it deserves. And if it truly *doesn't* deserve that respect, you can't effectively *refute* it without at least understanding it first."

He shook his head, his expression troubled.

"You know, the hell of it is that there really are people on the Castle Rock faculty who *say* all the 'right' things but are just as bigoted—whether it's for or *against* gay rights, transgender rights, gun rights, religious rights, or God only knows what—as O'Hearn thinks *I* am. Some of them sit on what they really feel and never say a word about it in public, but that doesn't make them any less closed-minded than the ones who scream from soapboxes and boycott speakers whose views they disapprove of, and our students damned well deserve *better* than that. I'm human enough to wish every single one of them recognized the sheer brilliance and intellectual purity of my own views, but they aren't going to do that...and thank God for it! Because whether they agree with *me* or not, they need to engage their students honestly and critically. That's their job—their *responsibility*, not just to the people paying tuition at CRU but to our entire society. If they're not willing to do that, then they need to be shaken up just as much as someone like O'Hearn, when you come down to it.

"So in a way, I *am* willing to use you two as a club...sort of. If I go through this gender-sensitivity bullshit, and if the entire faculty thinks O'Hearn's beaten me into submission despite my wrongheadedness, and then I invite my little brother and his husband to the next faculty reception, it may just open at least a few eyes to the possibility that imposing your own ideological preconceptions on what you *think* someone else believes can be... counterproductive. And if that helps me and Don Quixote bring down a few windmills, open the window of intellectual debate and mutual respect just a crack—which is what a college education is supposed to be *about*, damn it!—I'll play the card you guys represent just as shamelessly as anyone could possibly ask.

"Which isn't to say, of course," he admitted with the quick, quirky grin of someone who might be just a bit embarrassed by his own intensity, "that I won't also take a certain petty-minded, gloating relish out of O'Hearn's expression when I introduce you to him!"

"Well, under the circumstances," Stephen said, picking up the massive revolver and loading it smoothly, "and speaking for myself, I can live with that."

CHAPTER THREE

Transtemporal Vehicle *Kleio*
non-congruent

"NOW *THAT* WAS TASTY, RAIBERT," PHILOSOPHUS SAID. "WHY hadn't we tried it already?"

"I thought we had," Doctor Raibert Kaminski replied as his plate lifted smoothly from the table and followed the rest of the china and flatware off to reclamation. "In fact, I was almost *certain* we had."

"A variant we enjoyed on our way home from Alesia came close," the voice inside his head said. "Except that it didn't have the bay leaves and oregano." The voice paused, then continued with the equivalent of a silent shrug. "Now that I think about it, that probably isn't very surprising, I suppose. Most purists would be appalled by the adulteration of shrimp scampi with either of those spices!"

"'Consistency is the bugaboo of small minds,' Philo," Kaminski observed. "'And—'"

"'And experiment is the key to serendipity,'" the connectome said, completing the quotation for him with a soft electronic chuckle. "An interesting attitude for a historian."

"I became a historian in the first place because of the way I want to 'run and find out,'" Kaminski riposted. "You haven't figured that out after fifty-plus years of sharing the same senses?"

"Ah, but for an abstract citizen such as myself, the universe is eternally new," Philo replied. "You flesh-and-blood types are

31

so limited in what you can forget. Mind you, you're amazingly good at it, considering the fact that you can't simply erase it at the source. *I*, on the other hand, can deliberately select memories to seal or delete, thereby re-creating a blank canvas upon which to paint. And, of course, I'm incapable of forgetting by *accident*."

"My, you *are* pleased with yourself, aren't you?" Kaminski chuckled.

"I suppose I am, actually," Philo acknowledged. "It's not every day someone spends eleven months attached to Julius Caesar's own headquarters. I'd like to see one of those thumb-fingered ART Preservation teams manage that!"

Kaminski chuckled again, more loudly, but he had to agree with his abstract companion. And it had been very much a joint effort, he acknowledged. Without the resources of their home century's infosystems, Philosophus' ability to support his mission had been limited, but it had also been essential. The infosystem of a TTV was tiny compared to the cloud-supported systems available back home. A Transtemporal Vehicle like *Kleio* had a total capacity of little more than a couple of exabytes, but that was at least enough to sustain Philosophus' complete personality alongside *Kleio*'s limited, nonsentient attendant program, and the TTV's bandwidth was great enough to let the abstract citizen interface with Kaminski's wetware. Not quite as completely as he might have at home; that was the one thing Kaminski really didn't like about fieldwork. Back home, Philosophus was his integrated companion, a constant presence, counselor, assistant, and friend, as available to him as his own thoughts thanks to his wetware implants and the infosystem. But without the depth of the system-wide Infonet, they simply didn't have the bandwidth to sustain that level of connectivity in the field.

They did have enough to make Philosophus available to augment Kaminski's merely human language skills and memory for detail, of course, and the AC had provided the link he needed to the TTV's survey and reconnaissance assets. That was one of several reasons they'd been able to insert the human into Caesar's staff as an expert geographer. Maps in the ancient world—even Roman maps—tended to be less than reliable. But if "Titus Aluis Camillus" said there was a river between Caesar's army and his intended field of battle, then by Mars, there was a river exactly where he'd said it was. And it was exactly as *deep* as he'd said it was, too.

There were advantages to being able to deploy effectively invisible surveillance remotes as needed.

"Fair's fair, Philo," Kaminski said after a moment. "The ART Preservation teams aren't intended for long-term observation and interaction."

"That's *one* way to put it," Philo replied with an audible—for certain values of the word "audible," at least—sniff. "Finesse isn't exactly their middle name, is it?"

Kaminski shook his head in acknowledgment.

In many ways, the Antiquities Rescue Trust was the wrecking ball of historical research, and it was unfortunately true that ART Preservation and its proponents still enjoyed substantial pull in the Ministry, even after they'd been slapped with a number of restrictions thanks to records exposed by a certain professor and his abstract companion.

It was, after all, so much easier to physically transport the treasures of antiquity—or even the inhabitants of antiquity—to the thirtieth century for proper study than it was to spend weeks or months on the dirty, smelly, often tedious, and almost equally often *dangerous* business of physically inserting a researcher into antiquity, instead. It was hard to argue against the thoroughness with which a properly equipped lab could delve into the most deeply hidden secrets of something like the original canvas of da Vinci's *The Last Supper*, for example, or the *Nike of Samothrace*, which—like the *Venus de Milo* ART Preservation had recovered undamaged for the benefit of the thirtieth century's museums. Both Kaminski and Philo, however, belonged to the ART Observation branch. *Analyzing* artifacts—including human ones, assuming the sanity of the humans in question was sufficiently robust to survive the shock of transplantation—was one thing. *Understanding* them required that they be studied in their own, original environments.

That was what Kaminski and Philo had decided almost fifty years ago, and nothing had happened to change their minds since. Oh, there were moments when Kaminski, at least, rather envied some of ART's more spectacular triumphs. The physical extraction of the entire Library of Alexandria, for example. *That* had been a rather lively endeavor, and he'd burned a lot of bridges when he and Philo went public with the records of ART's...overzealous approach. But he also didn't regret the positive influence the new laws and restrictions had had on ART, nor did it hurt that those restrictions barely touched him and his companion. *They* always remained covert in order to sustain his period-specific cover lest they defeat their entire purpose. Being unable to charge into the past festooned with rail-rifles and light energy weapons was a complete nonissue in their case.

Of course, the mere fact that they'd inserted themselves into the historical process meant the history itself would be changed. It was axiomatic that an observer affected the phenomenon under observation, and that was certainly true when it came to interactive temporal research. As a consequence, no observer could examine a completely accurate version of the *actual* history involved. But if he was sufficiently unobtrusive, he could avoid introducing any changes—on the macro level, at least—which would invalidate his observations. And it was always possible, as Kaminski himself had done on more than one occasion, to return and reinsert oneself into the same historical event multiple times, giving one alternative perspectives on the event itself and, presumably, balancing out any unintended effects one might have introduced.

He supposed it might be argued that that was really all ART did across both the Preservation and Observation branches, but it was the difference between a flint knapper, using a bit of antelope horn to peel away single flakes of flint at a time, and someone using a sledgehammer to produce gravel. The notion of inserting commando teams to seize and hold the Great Library until the conveyors could haul every book and scroll away while gunning down anyone who tried to stop them offended Kaminski's sense of morality to the point where he'd been driven to do *something* about it.

The fact that the entire event had been erased from the timestream the moment the last conveyor, the last commando, withdrew meant someone from ART could always go back to the library, of course. The original iteration of the books—and, for that matter, of any scholars or librarians who'd been "killed" in the raid—were "still there" in every sense that mattered. But he couldn't honestly call what ART Preservation did "research," despite the peer pressure he and Philo used to encounter to join them. None of the several hundred people who'd "died" had stayed dead after ART withdrew, and Kaminski admitted that he'd been just as agog over the library's contents as anyone else. But the retrieval mission had added virtually nothing to modern scholarship's understanding of day-to-day life in Alexandria. *That* had been the task of the Observation branch personnel, like Kaminski and Philo, who'd been inserted into Alexandria before the raid—less as scholars than as survey parties mapping out where its teams of time bandits could find the richest historical plunder.

"Did you ever really speculate on what it might've been like to do temporal research if the causalists had been right, Philo?" Kaminski asked.

"No, I haven't. Because there wouldn't *be* any temporal research if they'd been right."

"Oh, I'm not so sure about that." He shook his head. "An observer wouldn't actually have to interact with anyone. Admittedly, our data set would be a lot poorer, but simply sending a TTV back and deploying invisible remotes to get real-time imagery and sound wouldn't directly impact any of the history involved."

"Unless the causalists' worst-case arguments had been accurate," Philo pointed out. "You might've been able to eliminate direct contamination of the societies involved, but there'd always have been the chance of some totally random change in the environment impacting *indirectly* upon human decisions. If Andover's First Theory had proved accurate, for example, the mere fact that a single 'extraneous' causality was introduced into the timestream at any point would have 'reset' every other event, down to the molecular level, thereafter. Think about *that* one!"

"I'd rather not. But even Andover was willing to admit that interpretation might be a *little* extreme."

"Granted, granted." Philo gave the soft electronic sound he used as the equivalent of a shrug when he chose not to project a visible avatar through Kaminski's wetware. "But even his *Second* Theory posited the possibility for an avalanche of tiny changes turning into a catastrophic event."

"True, but that was inherent in his underlying logic," Kaminski pointed out. "And then there was Chen's theory."

"I cannot *believe* you've brought that old chestnut into this discussion!" Philo moaned. But there was laughter in his moan and Kaminski sat back with his beer stein, smiling.

Most physical humans looked for compatibility in any abstract citizen with whom they might enter into companionship. Not all physical citizens decided to do that, nor did all abstract citizens develop any desire to create a long-term partnership with someone still fundamentally limited to the nonelectronic universe. It was more common than not, however, although the "firewalls" between personalities tended to be very much a matter of personal taste. In more extreme cases there *were* no firewalls, really, and the personalities involved tended to flow and merge, incorporating bits and pieces of one another's code. At the opposite extreme were those personalities—organic and abstract—which became little more than close friends, possibly visiting in the outer fringes of one another's personalities on rare occasions, but mostly limited to the equivalent of verbal conversation.

Most, however, lay somewhere in the middle, very much like Kaminski and Philo. Each of them had, upon occasion, used the other's "senses" to experience something he wasn't directly equipped to experience, like Philo's appreciation for Kaminski's willingness to experiment with recipes and flavors. Their personalities had never even come close to *merging*, though, and both of them preferred it that way. The two of them were closer to one another than either of them was to anyone else in the entire universe, but theirs was definitely a case of Philia's brotherly love, possibly with a substantial dash of Agape's unconditional love, but totally devoid of Eros' sexual connotations.

Philo was the brother Kaminski had never had, and Kaminski was the portal into the material world Philo had yearned for. Unlike "meat" humans who'd had their personalities converted into connectomes in order to access the abstract world, Philo had begun his existence as what had once been called an artificial intelligence. The term was still technically accurate, although it was virtually never used any longer, outside a smattering of ancient laws. But despite all the "meat" humans who'd made the transition into Philo's universe, there was still a difference there, a sort of wondering delight and fascination, when he stepped out of the abstract universe through Kaminski's implants. Kaminski felt much the same on his excursions into the abstract realities to which Philo had introduced him, yet they'd both realized long ago that the *differences* between them were almost more important to maintaining their fifty-three-year relationship than any similarities.

But one trait they shared in full was a delight in contrarian discussions. In fact, they infuriated many of their mutual friends by their ability to effortlessly swap sides in midargument just to keep a good debate going.

"Well," the flesh-and-blood half of their relationship said now, "it's always possible Chen really was right, you know. I mean, if we did somehow manage to fundamentally change the past—beyond the temporary spikes, I mean—we really might simply 'reset' ourselves out of existence. For all we *know*, we might've done that thousands of times by now!"

"Oh, puh-*leeze!*" Philo's chosen human avatar—a hulking, red-haired, red-bearded Viking, complete with the horned helmet real Vikings hadn't worn—manifested itself in Kaminski's field of vision so that it could roll its eyes at him. "We have petabytes of real-world data demonstrating that nothing of the sort happens!"

"But if Chen was right, we *wouldn't* have any data demonstrating that it did!" Kaminski grinned at him. "The data would never have existed in the first place."

"Can you say 'circular logic'?" Philo inquired pleasantly, beetling bushy red eyebrows at him, and Kaminski laughed.

"Well, I'd have to concede that the fact that we've inflicted so many *temporary* changes on the timestream without ever changing a single damned thing 'downstream' from the change would tend to suggest both Andover and Chen were...worrying unduly, shall we say? For that matter, Andover admitted as much."

"Maybe *he* did, but even *death* hasn't stopped Chen asserting on my side of the interface that the math supports him." Philo rolled his blue eyes again. "I'm tempted to suggest that he program his own VR where it actually does work that way and move into it!"

"Now, now," Kaminski chided. "Let's be mature about this!"

The sound of a raspberry was unmistakable, and he laughed again.

"On a somewhat more pragmatic level, how much longer to home?" he asked.

"About a hundred twenty-three hours, absolute, according to Kleio," Philo replied promptly.

The TTV's onboard systems didn't quite cross the threshold into self-awareness. They'd been designed that way as part of the access security built into the Ministry's vehicles. In fact, although no one was supposed to be gauche enough even to talk about it, the Ministry had insisted upon its own version of the ancient "two-pilot" rule. Only an abstract citizen could insert itself into the infostructure to fully operate the TTV's systems, but the TTV was locked out of transtemporal flight without a live human being—either flesh or synthoid—on the bridge. There were some who thought the precaution was both outmoded and more than a little condescending, but neither Kaminski nor Philo were in that group. Perhaps they might have been, Kaminski admitted, if either of them had possessed any desire to go scudding about through history without the other along for the ride. Because they didn't, the requirement imposed no hardship on them.

And, in an absolute worst-case scenario, he thought on the privacy side of their firewall, *even if something horrible happened to either of us, the other one could still punch the auto-recall to get himself back home. I just don't know if I'd want to.*

"Already two thirds of the way there?" he said out loud. "I'm tempted to say 'we're making good time,' except I know how much it would irritate you if I did."

"You are *so* good to me," Philo said dryly.

"I try. But since we still have whole absolute days to kill, why don't we pull out that aerial imagery you got of the Battle of Thapsus? There are a couple of points I'd like to get your take on, maybe bounce a few observations back and forth."

"Of course." Philo's avatar disappeared, replaced by an aerial view of a first-century BCE Mediterranean seaport. "What would you like to—"

A strident alarm Raibert Kaminski had never encountered, even in training, slammed through his virtual hearing. He jerked upright in his seat, the TTV shook and bucked madly, its lights went instantly and totally dark, and he felt himself actually rising upward out of his chair in an utterly impossible freefall.

The artificial gravity stuttered back on and he dropped heavily back into his seat.

"Philo!" he shouted, physically and mentally alike, but there was no answer. *"Philo!"*

And then the second shock wave hit. He flew out of his chair, his skull cracked against a bulkhead, and he slid down it to the floor.

CHAPTER FOUR

Castle Rock University
2017 CE

"I CAN SEE WHERE IT WOULD BE OF SPECIAL INTEREST TO AN ex-Navy officer, Elzbietá," Benjamin Schröder said, tipping back in his massive, comfortable chair, "but I think the archives have been pretty thoroughly mined out where the planning behind Operation Oz's amphibious aspects is concerned."

"Yes and no," the woman sitting on the other side of his desk said. She leaned forward in her own chair, her single eye gleaming intently.

The plastic surgeons had done a remarkably good job rebuilding the left side of her face, but it wasn't perfect. Some women he knew—hell, most *men* he knew—would have been at least a little self-conscious of the damage the surgeons hadn't been able to fully repair, but if Elzbietá Abramowski was, he'd never seen a single sign of it. She wore the black patch covering her left eye socket almost like a fashion accessory, and despite the muscle damage on that side, the only thing her lively face showed just now was her enthusiasm.

"I'm interested less in the overall planning than in how the final shipping tonnages were allocated. Specifically, I'm looking at the shift from dedicated ground forces support to the big jump in hulls dedicated to First and Third Air Force."

"Oh?" Benjamin tilted further back, raising an eyebrow.

"The Naval Archives are about to open up the last of the

classified files. I don't think there'll be many huge surprises about who called the shots in Washington and London—God knows Merkel and Stanton's scorched earth over how much of Oz's planning was Marshall's and how much was Alexander's has already plowed that background pretty thoroughly. And, as I say, I'm less interested in the Vladivostok landings themselves—tactically, I mean—than I am in the sheer scale of the logistic component. Four *million* men and all their equipment, plus the ground element for the biggest strategic air force in history, staged across five thousand miles of ocean?" She shook her head. "There's been plenty of attention to the sheer numbers, and to the deception measures that kept Stalin from realizing what was coming, but I want to get inside the nuts and bolts of the planning. In particular, I want to look at Turner's and Spruance's correspondence with Nimitz and King in late 1948."

"I thought Stanton had already published that," Benjamin said.

"Ah." Elzbietá had a remarkably sharklike smile for such an attractive woman, he thought. "That's what *Stanton* thought, too. But a friend of mine who still wears the uniform is on the staff at History and Heritage Command. He just came across an entire file—a fat one—that's part of that declassification dump Archives is planning. Everybody knows the relationship between King and Marshall was...less than cordial, on a personal level, let's say. They were both pretty careful about putting things in writing through formal channels to cover their posteriors if something went south on them. But this seems to be a file of private memoranda going back and forth between the two of them very quietly and without being appended to the *official* record, with input from the Pacific *naval* commanders, including Mountbatten, but *not* including General Eisenhower."

"They were discussing Eisenhower's logistics for an invasion of Soviet Russia with his naval commanders without making him a party to it? You're suggesting he was *deliberately* cut out of the link?" Benjamin asked carefully.

"Actually, that's not what I think at all," Elzbietá replied. "I think Eisenhower and Spruance, especially, may have been even closer than most people realize. Eisenhower's decision to appoint him as our first postwar ambassador to Japan certainly indicates the two of them respected one another enormously, but the consensus seems to be that that respect came after First Fleet put his men ashore and kept them there. Before that, their working relationship was good—Eisenhower was always good at keeping command teams working in harness, despite some pretty damned prickly personalities—but it doesn't seem to have been especially cordial. I'm starting to wonder if that was really true."

"Why?" Benjamin let his chair come back upright, planting his forearms on his desk, and his eyes were intent.

As department chairman, he pretty much had his pick of graduate and postgraduate students to mentor, and he'd been deeply impressed by Commander Abramowski's credentials when they came across his desk. There weren't that many history students at Castle Rock University who'd been awarded the Navy Cross *and* Silver Star, or who already had master's degrees in aerospace engineering from the University of Michigan. That would have been more than enough to intrigue him, even without her admissions interview. He'd liked what he'd seen of her there even more than he'd expected to, although he'd come to suspect there might be darker places inside her than she allowed the rest of the world to see. Whether or not that was true, though, she definitely had one of the sharpest minds he'd ever encountered. He wasn't certain why she'd decided to pursue a doctorate in history instead of aerospace, but she was going to make a tremendous teacher. In fact, she was carrying a double assistantship in the classroom right now, although she didn't really need the income, and her lectures were packed.

"Actually," she said now, "I've come across a couple of hints in the already explored correspondence between King and Marshall that made me wonder where King was getting some of his arguments. I couldn't find any paper trail from anyone on King's staff to support them or show how they might have evolved in his mind. Now I'm beginning to wonder—especially in light of this new file—if maybe *Eisenhower* wasn't slipping them to him and using Spruance and Turner as his conduit."

"Ike Eisenhower, the self-effacing master of coalition warfare, conspiring against the man who planned the entire invasion?"

"First, you know as well as I do that Eisenhower was a tad less 'self-effacing' than his postwar public image suggests. When he felt strongly about something he went after it, and he'd spent enough time between World War I and the Transpacific War to understand how back channels work. If he thought Marshall and his logistic planners were making a mistake, he'd do whatever he thought he had to do to fix it. And, second, you know Marshall was a lot more pissed off than he showed by what he thought was President Dewey's readiness to cave in to Churchill and Alexander. Or, for that matter, by the fact that Dewey wouldn't let him out of Washington to command Oz in person. The sticking point for him, though, was that the US was providing seventy-five percent of the warships and something like eighty-five percent of the transports and supply lift for Oz, which meant the US—as the senior partner—should have had the deciding vote on how those transports were used. And it's clear from the Joint Chiefs' internal memos and reports that Marshall was totally focused on getting the troops ashore and keeping them there. As far as he was concerned, LeMay and Eaker's needs were clearly secondary, which, to be fair, made a lot of sense. The existing air bases in Japan were close enough to support Oz until the ground forces were several hundred miles inland, and if they didn't *get* several hundred miles inland, there wouldn't be any Siberian bases to *need* extra transport."

She shrugged.

"It's not like Churchill and Alexander were the only people arguing that the Army's entire function was to get the B-29s, Lincolns, and B-36s close enough. They were probably the most vociferous about it, though, and Marshall had his heels dug in pretty firmly against their 'importunate enthusiasm.' Dewey was hesitant about overruling him—mostly because he had the sense to stay out of the professionals' way—and I think there were probably times he wanted to throttle Churchill himself. Admiral Leahy had favored the Air Forces' argument, and as Chairman of the Joint Chiefs he'd been able to press it pretty effectively, until his Electra crashed at Hickam Field. When Marshall became Chairman, the emphasis shifted, and the only two uniformed officers in Washington with the clout to stand up to him were King and Arnold. But Arnold was the Air Force chief of staff, which meant Marshall could—legitimately—argue that he was looking after his own service's best interests. That made King the key, both because he'd become the Navy's chief of staff when Leahy was killed and because Marshall knew that Ernest J. King probably liked Winston Churchill even less than he did.

"You can see it in the correspondence that's already been

published. Marshall was a lot more willing to listen to King's arguments than he was to Arnold's or the Brits', and sometime in June, King's position started shifting toward beefing up the Air Forces' logistic priority in the early stages of Oz. What I'm thinking is that if Eisenhower thought he had a *serious* problem, King would have been his best shot at changing Marshall's mind, and if he didn't want the Chief of the Joint Chiefs to know he was telling tales out of school, Spruance, Turner, and Nimitz—but especially Spruance, given his personal relationship with King—would have been the best conduit *to* King. I doubt he'd have considered it 'conspiring against' Marshall. But I also doubt that he'd have let that stop him if he felt strongly enough that a major mistake was in the works, and *someone* convinced Marshall to agree to shift a quarter of Second Army's dedicated shipping to LeMay's bombers less than two months before the landing after fighting it tooth and nail for almost a year. The assumption's been that Arnold convinced him King had a point, but I think that's a mistake. I think it was *King* who convinced Marshall that *Arnold* had a point, and if Eisenhower was weighing in behind the scenes..."

She shrugged, and Benjamin nodded thoughtfully. Operation Oz, the twin-pronged thrust out of Manchukuo and occupied Japan into the Soviet Union, had been far and away the largest amphibious operation in the history of the world. Only a navy the size of the one the Transpacific Allies, and especially the United States of America, had built out of the ruins after Pearl Harbor could even have contemplated something like it. Elzbietá's four million figure was only for the initial assault forces; it didn't count the three million additional ground personnel and the two and a half million Army Air Forces and Royal Air Force personnel of the follow up echelons. Nor did it include the thousands of tanks and artillery pieces, the tens of thousands of trucks, halftracks, and jeeps, and the millions upon millions of tons of supplies which had been transported from North America to the Sea of Japan and thence across thousands of miles of howling wilderness over the roads and railroads hacked out of the Siberian tundra. Nor, for that matter, did it include the construction equipment to *build* those roads and railroads...and the dozens of major air bases needed to support the bombing offensive which ultimately brought the Soviet Union to its knees.

Operation Oz's sheer size and audacity was the primary reason Stalin had concluded that it had to be a deception move. He'd had absolutely no conception of the transport possibilities of blue water shipping, but he'd had a very good notion of the distances involved and the lack of anything like a decent transportation net in his own extreme eastern provinces. And although the Western Alliance had developed extremely sophisticated *tactical* air forces, neither side in the Great Eastern War had possessed the additional resources to create genuine *strategic* air forces. The concept of a bomber like the B-36 that could carry 72,000 pounds of bombs to targets four thousand miles away, at altitudes of 43,000 feet and cruising speeds of almost three hundred miles per hour, never occurred to him in his darkest nightmares. Nor had he been witness to the massive fire raids with which the USAAF had leveled Japan's cities or the effects of "earthquake" bombs like the Royal Air Force's 22,000-pound "Grand Slam" or the USAAF's 43,000-pound T-12 "Cloudmaker." That fatal blind spot had left him totally unprepared for what the Anglo-American heavy bombers could do to his wartime industry at what were literally transcontinental ranges.

So perhaps it really wasn't very surprising that he'd seen instantly that his enemies' most logical course of action—and the one he'd most feared—would be to funnel the Anglo-American forces entering the Great Eastern War through Europe. That would allow them to use the excellent rear-area transportation systems the Western Alliance had devised to bring them to bear on his western front rather than throwing them against the Siberian and Mongolian frontiers he'd denuded under the pressure of the relentless offensives Kaiser Louis Ferdinand and his allies had already brought to bear. The *last* thing any sane general would do would be to commit an entirely separate army—a modern, *mechanized* army—to an advance across thousands of miles of virgin wilderness with some of the most brutal winter weather in the world.

He'd been wrong about that, but he'd been in good company. Before the Transpacific War, George C. Marshall's master plan would have been an opium dream. *After* the Transpacific War, the world had been introduced to an entirely new standard of amphibious warfare; it just hadn't known it yet. And the dazzling success of Operation Oz had been the capstone of the United

States' triumphant resurgence—even more than the surrender of Imperial Japan, in many ways—from the worst series of defeats in its history to overwhelming victory. The United States had emerged from the conflict as the strongest military and economic power in history, so it really wasn't surprising that the war's historiography had descended into hagiography almost before the 1950s were over.

The reaction and revisionism of the seventies and eighties had been entirely predictable, under the circumstances, and most of Operation Oz's field commanders, from Patton to Harmon to Galloway, had seen their actions and decisions dissected by skeptical Monday morning quarterbacks. But Dwight Eisenhower—the commander whose armies had fought their way from Vladivostok to the Yenisei River and who'd signed the Soviet Surrender for the Transpacific Allies—had emerged with his reputation intact. The "Wizard of Oz"—much as he'd loathed that appellation, it had probably been inevitable—and his persona as an "Aw, shucks," dedicated, unassuming, apolitical, and militarily brilliant but politically naïve field commander had played a major role in his nomination to succeed Thomas Dewey in the White House.

And anyone looking at his administration after he succeeded Dewey should have figured out that "politically naïve" had to be just a little wide of the mark, Benjamin reflected now. *But if Elzbietá's right, this would be a major shift in our understanding of Oz's internal dynamics. No wonder she wants to jump on it!*

He felt a surge of the sort of intellectual excitement which had attracted him to history in the first place, and a matching admiration for the scholar sitting on the other side of his desk. He reminded himself that the fact that a possibility was intriguing and exciting didn't necessarily make it true. Nor, for that matter, did the fact that he found the presenter of that possibility considerably more attractive—and not just for her undoubted intelligence—than her faculty advisor really ought to.

Oh, screw that! he thought tartly. *Yes, you find her more attractive than you've found anyone since that frigging drunk killed Miriam. But neither one of you has ever even come close to crossing the line. And you know damned well she is onto something here. You can* smell *it the way you smelled the Molotov-Matsuoka correspondence when you were working on your doctorate.*

Speaking of which . . .

"I think this definitely bears looking into, Elzbietá," he said. "And in addition to Naval History, I came across some stuff in the declassified files over at Langley when I was researching the Magic intercepts that might have some bearing on this. Peripherally, at least."

"Oh?" She straightened in her chair, right eye narrowing intently.

"Hang on a second," he said, and turned to his computer to call up the files. "I was looking for the intercepts of the Russo-Japanese diplomatic traffic, specifically of anything between Tatekawa and the Foreign Ministry."

He glanced up at her, and she nodded. General Yoshitsugu Tatekawa had been Japan's ambassador to the Soviet Union from 1940 and throughout the Transpacific War. When US codebreakers cracked the "Purple codes," they gained access to the vast majority of Japan's diplomatic communications during the war. That had been less useful operationally than their ability to read JN-25, the Japanese Navy's most secure codes, but it had proven exceptionally useful in other ways.

Tatekawa hadn't been the only Japanese embassy official sending home long, detailed cables about his host country, but the amount of information the compulsively secretive Stalin had shared with him had been astounding. At least thirty or forty percent of the "official" information had, in fact, been less than accurate, of course. Stalin's decision to intervene in the Balkans, which was what had kicked off the Great Eastern War, had been predicated at least in part on his belief that the desperate situation in the Pacific would keep the United States and the British Empire safely out of any conflict in continental Europe or Asia. After all, in 1942 and 1943 it had looked very much as if the Anglo-Americans were headed for dismal defeat—especially after the fall of Midway and the devastating carrier raids on the Hawaiian Islands and Balboa, the Pacific terminus of the Panama Canal. Stalin had had every reason to encourage the Japanese to head south and southeast, away from his own frontier, especially after their border clashes in 1939. So convincing Japan of his Five-Year Military Plan's overwhelming success had been very much in his interest.

Tatekawa had been no one's fool, however, and he and his military attachés had done a far better job of penetrating to the reality—which, admittedly, had been pretty damned impressive in its own right—behind the official façade. And he had painstakingly labeled any suspect data as "unconfirmed" or—even more damning— "unconfirm*able*" when he reported his findings, exhaustively, to his Foreign Ministry superiors in Tokyo.

Which meant he had also reported them to the code-breaking teams in San Francisco, Washington, Delhi, and London.

Even before the Transpacific Allies' entry into the Great Eastern War, the Anglo-Americans had been sharing intelligence information about the Soviet Union with the Western Alliance, although they'd been careful to conceal its source. And Tatekawa's reports had been priceless when it came to planning the strategic bombing offensive out of Siberia and Mongolia in 1949 and 1950.

"What I found," he went on, turning back to his computer as the menu he'd been looking for came up, "was a fat folder of Purple intercepts which had been pulled together at the request of Eisenhower's chief of staff. And he'd been specifically looking for additional information on the Krasnoyarsk Economic Region. That was nineteen hundred miles from Vladivostok, which seemed like quite a reach to me if he'd been thinking only about the landings and the immediate aftermath. But if Eisenhower was looking for infor—"

His voice stopped, chopped off in midword as unbelievable agony exploded through his brain. His head snapped back, his eyes slammed shut, and his entire body convulsed as a sudden, roaring madness engulfed him.

"Doctor Schröder?" He heard Elzbietá's voice through the tumult, but it was far away and dim, and he couldn't answer it anyway. "Doctor Schröder? *Benjamin?*"

He was vaguely aware of a hand on his shoulder, but it, too, was far away, distant, lost in the hurricane as his mind fought to sort out the insanity.

He sat in his chair in the office which had been his for the last five years. He *knew* it had! Yet at the same time, in that moment, he knew it *hadn't* been. He knew he didn't even have *tenure* yet, much less the department chair. He knew his father was alive and well...and simultaneously that Klaus Schröder had died sixteen years ago in...in a *terrorist attack*? That was... that was *insane!*

And yet, in that moment, it was true. It was *true!* It was as true as the world he'd always known.

It crashed in on him, sending his sanity reeling. A world in which the Soviet Union had survived. One in which there was a People's Republic of China. In which Elfriede, and Gisèle, and Elizabeth had never been born. In which the German Empire had never been restored. In which—his shuddering brain flinched from the brutal images—*eleven million* human beings had been systematically slaughtered by the country in which his own father had been born! In which—

It was too much. He couldn't take it all in, couldn't keep the two worlds separate. They smashed him into fragments, ripped him apart. He was insane. He *had* to be insane! But what kind of insanity could conjure up an entirely different life, an entirely different *world*, in the flicker of a mental eye? It couldn't be happening, couldn't possibly be real, and yet—

But then one last awareness went through him, more terrible than any of the others, and he lurched up out of his chair at last.

"David!"

The name ripped from his throat as he tumbled into the darkness at last, and he wondered how he could feel such terrible agony for the loss of someone who had never existed at all.

CHAPTER FIVE

Libyan Desert
1986 CE

THE TTV'S INTERIOR SWAYED AROUND RAIBERT IN A NAUSEA-inducing mix of blurred real vision and perfectly clear virtual displays that pulsed a livid red. He shook his head and ran a hand through his hair.

"Ah!" he gasped as fingers grazed a wet patch on the back of his scalp. "What just . . . where did . . ."

The real world around him came into focus, and the virtual warnings locked into their correct places over the TTV's central command table. Raibert put a hand against the wall, pinched his fingers around the bulkhead, and hoisted himself up. His head swam again, his stomach churned with nausea, and he stood still while the sensation passed.

"Philo?" he called out, both audibly and across the mental firewall that divided them.

Nothing.

A chill swept over him, and memories began to trigger within his groggy mind.

I was eating at the command table again, when . . .

An alarm had sounded. One he'd never heard before. A loss of gravity, and then darkness. And pain.

Raibert gingerly touched the back of his head. He winced, but surmised the wound wasn't bad. He queried his implants, and they produced a summary that hovered in his virtual sight, corroborating his gut feeling.

Mild concussion. Which was probably the least of his problems, given all the red over the command table.

"Philo?" he called out again, then louder, *"Philo?"*

Silence.

"That's not good."

The vertigo passed, and he took his hand off the wall to test whether or not he was steady on his feet. He wasn't, but he still managed to stagger across the wide, cylindrical bridge and grab the edge of the table before he collapsed over it.

"Kleio? Are you there?"

"Yes, Professor." The TTV's nonsentient attendant spoke with a soothing feminine soprano. Like the control displays over the command table, Kleio's voice was a virtual sound produced through his wetware implants.

"What is..." Raibert blinked the returning fog away. "What's going on?"

"I was damaged by a high-energy chronometric event of unknown origin."

"And that means...what?"

"I do not know, Professor. I am still in the process of restoring basic functions and collecting information."

"Where's Philo?"

"His connectome is in stasis."

"Why?" he pressed.

"My infostructure became unstable during the event, and emergency systems locked Philosophus' connectome to protect him. Please be patient, Professor. I am in the process of rebooting critical systems and evaluating the damage. A report should be ready shortly."

"Okay, good. That's...that's good." He nodded and immediately regretted the gesture. "See to it. Snap, snap."

"Yes, Professor."

Raibert swept his gaze—swept it *slowly*—across the floor and found his chair. He reached down, brought it upright, and dropped into it—again, *slowly*.

"Oh," he exhaled. "That's the stuff. Sitting is definitely better."

"Professor, I see that you are injured. The wound does not appear severe, but it should be treated as soon as possible. Shall I prepare a medibot injection for you?"

"Yes. Yes, please. That would be lovely, Kleio. Thank you."

"In that case, I shall have one conveyed to you at once."

Raibert crossed his arms over the table, laid his head on his forearms, and waited for the injection. A few minutes later, the TTV's ubiquitous microbot swarms transported a tube full of specialized medical microbots across the ceiling and then lowered it to the table by joining together into a single elongating strand that caught the light like spider silk. The microbots were normally invisible to the naked eye, and they quickly retreated into the ceiling after completing their delivery.

Raibert placed the tube on the back of his head and injected the medical microbots into his bloodstream. The microscopic swarm interfaced with his wetware implants, and the two systems set about repairing the blow to his head. He set the tube aside, and more unseen microbots picked it up and carried it off to reclamation.

It may have just been a placebo effect, but he began to feel better almost immediately. He looked up and studied the warnings over the command table, really *studied* them for the first time since coming to.

"Kleio?"

"Yes, Professor?"

"Why is the whole back half of the TTV blinking red?"

"It is blinking red because the chronoton impeller is offline."

"It's *what*?"

"The chronoton imp—"

"No, I heard you the first time! Are we seriously without a functioning time drive?"

"That is correct, Professor."

"Well, you need to make fixing it your top priority!"

"I am aware of that, Professor. Please be patient. I shall have a full report ready for you shortly."

"—look at first...?" a gruff voice trailed off. "What?"

"Philo!" Raibert exclaimed, a modicum of relief eclipsing his worries, if only for a moment.

"Wait a second." The abstract citizen's Viking avatar appeared in Raibert's virtual sight and made a show of whirling around in a confused circle. "Was I in stasis? Oh, that doesn't look good." He took in the warnings over the command table, then turned to Raibert. "Wait, are you hurt?"

"Yes, yes, and yes, though not badly to the last one. By the way, it's good to have you back. I was starting to get worried that I'd have to deal with this alone."

"I am here as well, Professor," Kleio said.

"True, true." Raibert nodded, and this time his head didn't swim. "But it's just not the same with you."

"I am not sure how to interpret that last statement, Professor. However, I can surmise that if I had feelings, they would be hurt right now."

"Then it's probably a good thing you don't have any." He clapped his hands and rubbed them together. "Now, where do we stand?"

"I have collated enough data for an initial report. Shall I review it with you?"

"Fire away."

All but one of the warnings vanished, and a schematic of the TTV expanded to fill the entire space over the table. The TTV's basic shape resembled an elongated gunmetal ovoid 150 meters long. Various systems, such as its defensive weaponry and graviton thrusters, dotted the surface like shallow blisters while a thick spike protruded out the rear to nearly double its overall length.

Except in this case, the spike was bent at its midpoint.

"As you can see," Kleio began, "the impeller spike has suffered significant damage, and I am currently incapable of temporal flight."

"Can we repair it?" Philo asked.

"I do not know. A more thorough evaluation is in progress."

Raibert sat back in his chair and waited while a cold, sickly feeling invaded the pit of his stomach. The TTV had impressive self-repair abilities thanks to its atomic printers, bulk printers, and microbot swarms, but the chronoton impeller was in a class all its own, and its construction involved very specialized forms of exotic matter that, unsurprisingly, required very specialized printers to produce. They could *repair* the impeller if the damage wasn't too severe, but they lacked the ability to *replace* it.

"Kleio, this is a really important thing to know," Raibert said. "Can we fix it or not?"

"I have microbots surveying the impeller exterior and will have more information available shortly. Shall I continue with the rest of the preliminary report?"

"Listen, Kleio," he snapped, "the rest of it really doesn't matter if we can't phase out, don't you think?"

"I am sorry, Professor. Please be patient."

"You seem agitated," Philo said.

"Of course I'm agitated. The TTV is all banged up, my head still hurts from getting slammed against the bulkhead, and it might turn out we're stranded. So, yes, I think I am fully justified in being a little agitated right now."

"Don't worry," Philo said, and put a virtual hand on his shoulder. "We'll get through this."

Nothing physical touched Raibert's shoulder, but his virtual senses made the gesture from his companion feel like the real thing down to the roughness of Philo's palms and the warmth of his touch. Raibert took a deep breath and rubbed his face.

"All right, Kleio." He let out another slow breath. "Let's hear the rest, starting with where and when the hell we are."

"The Libyan desert," Kleio reported. "March 5, 1986 CE."

"Is that bad?" Raibert asked. "The late twentieth century can be a rowdy place, if I recall."

"Nuclear proliferation," Philo said. "The Cold War. Mutually Assured Destruction. So, yeah. A little rowdy."

"Been here before?" Raibert asked.

"A few times with you-know-who."

"Oh, God!" Raibert said, catching the reference to Philo's previous companion. "Sorry I brought it up."

"It's all right. I know bits and pieces about the period, but I'm definitely no expert."

"Same here. Kleio?"

"Regrettably, I have limited data as well. As you are aware, most of my data storage has been devoted to exhaustive libraries on ancient Rome, per your mission prep orders. The associated printing patterns and VR recordings take up a considerable percentage of my memory storage, and your own high-fidelity recordings during the mission taxed me to the limit. You may recall that I brought this problem to your attention when I suggested you switch to a lower resolution, but your orders were instead to scrub all nonessential data from storage to make room for more recordings."

"Uuuuh." Raibert planted his face in his hands. "I did tell you to do that, didn't I?"

"Yes, Professor. And I followed your orders by conducting a thorough purge."

"No need to rub it in."

"I am not rubbing it in."

"Whatever. Any indigenes nearby?"

A 3D visualization of the surrounding desert appeared on the table with blurred, shadowed zones where they didn't have line of sight. Windswept sands and black crags surrounded the crater formed by the TTV's impact, and the noon sun burned on its smooth, shining hull.

Well, mostly smooth. Raibert tried not to focus on the bend in the impeller.

"We appear to be in a remote and uninhabited part of the desert," Kleio reported. "For our safety, I am relying on purely passive detection systems, but I do not detect any indigenous humans."

"Well, there's that at least."

The last thing they needed were people from this time period getting curious about the "UFO" that had suddenly crash-landed. But just in case that happened, it didn't hurt to be prepared.

"Weapons?" Raibert asked.

"Both 12mm defensive Gatling guns are fully operational. In fact, almost all other systems are at or near full operational status. My infostructure has been temporarily degraded in some areas, but I should have it back to normal soon. The stealth shroud cannot be deployed until we pull out of the crater and I enact some basic repairs to the outer hull, but that is the only major fault other than the impeller."

Philo summoned a status report over his hand.

"Looks like both telegraphs are still working. So at the very least, we can call for help if we need to."

"Good to know." Raibert rose from his seat and didn't feel the least bit dizzy. The chronoton telegraphs had a maximum range of eighteen years up and down the timestream, which meant they couldn't reach the thirtieth century directly, but they *could* contact other TTVs traversing the nearby timeline.

"Yes, that's very good news," he added, his mood improving by the moment. Even if the impeller was completely out of commission, all they had to do was hunker down and wait for rescue.

Eventually.

"I have some other good news, Professor," Kleio said.

"Let's hear it."

"I have finished evaluating the damage to the impeller, and I have high confidence the damage can be repaired."

The *Kleio*'s attendant program was—at her core—nothing more than a number cruncher. A fantastically powerful number cruncher, and one wrapped within a user interface shell that could fake its way through most conversations, but that's really all the gentle, simulated voice was capable of. Faking it. She could take the results of countless mathematical simulations and pretty them up into digestible chunks like "I have high confidence in X" for her sentient crew, but she couldn't think. Not in the same way Raibert and Philo could.

"Well, that's just splendid!" Raibert replied.

"I have begun printing the additional microbot swarms I'll need to realign the impeller spike. The necessary quantity should be ready within the hour."

"Wonderful!"

"However, I do recommend the Ministry perform a full systems check upon our return to the thirtieth century."

"Best news I've heard all day!"

"You're looking better," Philo said.

"That's because I feel better!"

"Well, if it's all right with you, I'm going to go parallel with Kleio and help coordinate the microbots."

"Sounds like a plan."

Philo tipped his horned helmet to Raibert and vanished.

"Well then." Raibert put his hands on his hips. "If no one has any objections, I think I'm going to take a shower and wash off the blood."

"Philo?" Raibert asked a few hours later.

"Yeah?" The AC's avatar materialized in his virtual sight.

"Have you seen this?" He pointed to one of several chronometric charts over the command table.

"No, I've been busy with Kleio fixing the impeller. We're almost done, by the way."

"We may want to think carefully before we leave, because this"—Raibert shook a finger at the leftmost chart—"is really weird. Granted, it's been a while since I took my TOE exam, but I'm pretty sure chronotons aren't supposed to do this."

"Is that what hit us?"

"Yeah. Some sort of chronometric storm that's sweeping forward through time. I've never seen anything like it."

"I don't think anyone has," Philo admitted. "Hold on, it's been forever since I've looked at the TOE myself. Kleio, you didn't delete that too, did you?"

"No, I did not, Philosophus. I consider the Theory Of Everything and all related material to be essential resources for safe TTV operations. I excluded it and all other thirtieth-century records and patterns from the professor's data purge."

"Good. One moment while I access it. And...there."

Philo's avatar vanished, and pathways along their mental firewall opened. Raibert confirmed the pathways, and details of the TOE crystalized in his mind thanks to Philo's assistance.

"Whatever happened," Raibert began, "we need to make sure it doesn't happen again, either to us or someone else. If the vector's correct, the storm front is between us and the thirtieth century, which means we have to pass through it before we can warn anyone else."

"Yeah, I see that. But I think we should be okay. The first time, it came at us from directly behind and it was moving *fast*."

"Which explains why Kleio missed it," Raibert finished.

"Right."

TTVs navigated through time and space with a triangulated chronometric array that provided full 360-degree coverage around the vessel. That level of detection wasn't too important for an Observation TTV like the *Kleio*, but large teams of Preservation TTVs on artifact rescue missions needed to coordinate their phase-in points precisely and found the extra spatial awareness essential.

The system's sole weakness became evident only when a TTV was underway at high time factors, because its own impeller created—not a *blind* spot exactly—but definitely a *blurry* spot in the array's field of view temporally behind the craft.

"Now that we know what to look for," Philo continued, "we should be able to push through the storm front without too much trouble."

"Maybe so, but that's not the weirdest thing I found while you and Kleio were busy." Raibert opened another hole in the firewall and tapped a finger through the second chart. It contained the outline of a short, middle-aged (from a thirtieth-century perspective) male. Himself to be precise, but also surrounded in a halo of abnormal chronoton activity.

"Oh," Philo remarked thoughtfully. *"Oh."*

"Yeah. What the hell do you make of that?"

"It looks like the chronotons around you are...I guess *resonating* would be the best word to use?"

"That's what I thought, but resonating with what?"

"No idea. This is probably going to involve some high-level math to analyze. Kleio and I can work on it after she's done with the repairs. Have you seen this anywhere else?"

"Take your pick." Raibert ran his hand across the other charts. "Several other parts of the ship show the same resonance, though I'm not nearly as concerned about them as this cloud of chronotons that's *following me around.*"

"I wouldn't worry too much," Philo reassured. "Chronotons are weakly interacting particles, after all. Even if they're acting strangely, they're just harmlessly passing through you."

"It's still unnerving as hell."

"Gentlemen," Kleio said, "I have good news. Repairs to the impeller are complete, and I am now ready to conduct a microjump test. With your permission, I would like to proceed immediately."

"Do you think a microjump will affect these resonating chronotons?" Raibert asked.

"I don't see how," Philo said. "None of the patches are even close to the impeller. I think we're fine to give it a go. We're going to have to leave at some point anyway."

"Yeah, you're right," Raibert sighed. "Okay, Kleio. Gives us a test jump. Negative one second."

"Negative one second microjump confirmed. Moving clear of the ground. Stand by."

Raibert swiped the charts aside and brought up the external map.

The TTV's four graviton thrusters switched on and eased its massive bulk out of the sand dunes. Shimmering lines of sand grains, caressed by the deep orange rays of a setting sun, dropped from its hull, and the TTV levitated higher until it was a good fifty meters off the ground.

"Obstructions cleared," Kleio reported. "Phase-out in three...two...one...jum—"

A terrible crash reverberated through the ship, and the sound of metal screeching against metal filled Raibert's ears. The deck shuddered under his feet, and he slipped and fell.

"Whoa!" His elbow banged against the table, and he landed flat on his back. "Oof!"

"Are you all right?" Philo asked.

"Oooooooh...damn it all." He rolled over onto his elbows and struggled to his feet. "It's days like this I wish I'd followed Dad's example and gone abstract." He grabbed the edge of the table, hauled himself upright, and straightened his posture with both hands pressed against his back. "Kleio, prep another injection."

"I am not detecting any notable injuries, Professor. Are you sure you need one?"

"No, but I'd like to have one ready just in case. Seriously, Kleio! Have you forgotten how to drive this thing?"

"No, Professor. I have not forgotten how to drive the TTV."

"Then would you kindly explain what just happened?"

"A foreign object was present at the target location when we phased in, and the object was displaced by our presence."

"Wait a moment." Raibert rubbed his forehead. "We jumped *backward* one second. We were literally *just there*. How could we have missed something big enough to make that much noise?"

"I do not know, Professor."

"At least there's no major damage this time," Philo observed. "The outer layer of prog-steel on the nose has a nice dent in it, but that's about it."

"Well, come on, Kleio. Let's see it." Raibert put both hands on the command table. "What did you fly us into?"

"The object is no longer present."

"What do you mean it's no longer present?"

"I am not sure how to better clarify the object's status, Professor."

Raibert let out a low growl deep in his throat. The day really wasn't getting any better.

"I'll call up the external footage," Philo said.

"Yes, please do that."

He blew out a frustrated breath and waited. The virtual imagery over the command table updated to a shot from the nose camera a few seconds before the microjump and played forward at one-tenth speed.

Nothing happened for a while. Just sand falling off the TTV in slow motion.

And then the microjump. The TTV had a maximum temporal speed of seventy thousand factors, which translated to over nineteen hours of relative time traversed every second of absolute time. A microjump of a single relative second was nothing to it, and from the camera's perspective the phase-out and phase-in occurred instantaneously.

The TTV phased in, and the view went black.

"Hmm," Raibert murmured, eyes narrowing.

The view trembled as the orange sunset leaked across the foreign object to expose a gleaming metallic surface. The view steadied, and the foreign object fell away, revealing itself to be a long ovoid...

With a thick spike protruding from one end.

Raibert's mouth flopped open in a parody of a fish.

The foreign object, clearly a TTV identical to their own, vanished exactly one second later according to the timestamp.

"Philo?"

"Yeah?" His avatar appeared at the opposite end of the table, and the two shared the same long worried look with each other. He knew without even reaching over the firewall that Philo was thinking the exact same thing. He swallowed to quench his suddenly dry throat and licked his lips before he asked it anyway, for what he was about to say was impossible.

"Did we just bump into ourselves?"

"Yeah, Raibert. I think we did."

CHAPTER SIX

Chón Tong Kam Thai restaurant
2018 CE

"SO I'LL HAVE THAT REVISION FINISHED BY TUESDAY," ELZBIETÁ said as the waiter removed their soup bowls and slid her favorite grilled prawns in front of her. "I'm a little worried about my reliance on the Bellinger memo, though. *I* think there's clear internal evidence that it didn't all originate with him, but there's no proof, and I don't want to force the evidence to support my thesis." She smiled quirkily. "Among other things, I think my thesis advisor would have a little something to say if I started cooking the books!"

"I imagine he would," Benjamin replied. "Fortunately, I'm not him anymore."

"Fortunate in *so* many ways," Elzbietá agreed with a much warmer smile, and he smiled back, then reached across the table to lay his hand on hers.

He'd made a lot of progress over the last six or seven months, he thought. In fact, he'd be returning to the university in two weeks. He was grateful for the way Chancellor O'Hearn had gone to bat for him, arranging an extended leave of absence while the assistant chairman of the department filled in for him. Seamus O'Hearn was one of the very few people who knew the truth—or *some* of the truth, at least—about the reason he'd needed that leave of absence. The chancellor was a good man and a loyal friend, but Benjamin hadn't told even him everything. Only one person in the universe knew the *full* truth, and she was sitting across the table from him.

A shiver went through him, and her hand turned under his, clasping it tightly. Her blue eye softened, and she cocked her head in the gesture he'd come to know so well.

"It's okay," he told her quickly. "Just...an echo."

"*Just* an echo?" she repeated.

"Yep." He nodded just a bit more firmly than was probably justifiable, but the darkness in her eye retreated and he smiled at her while he tried to understand how he'd gotten so lucky.

Elzbietá was his rock. He'd been attracted to her more strongly than to anyone since Miriam even before what both of them thought of as The Day, but he'd never imagined how important to him she would actually become. And that was because he'd never imagined how strong a person she truly was, he thought now, trying to think of anyone else who would have reacted the way she had when The Day hit him. Not just at the time, either. How many people who really knew what had happened to him could have concluded that he was anything except insane?

That question took on a certain added point because *Benjamin* wasn't certain that he wasn't. Sherman Braxton, his psychologist, said *he* didn't think Benjamin was, and most of the time, Benjamin believed him. The problem was that Benjamin couldn't think of a better term for someone who'd imagined an entirely different world, not just an alternate personality or a single isolated delusion. But Braxton seemed more fascinated than anything else. He'd insisted that the critical thing was learning to cope with the consequences, not agonizing over what had happened or looking for some kind of silver bullet to make the false memories go away. And at least, he'd pointed out, Benjamin had no doubt as to which ones *were* false. It wasn't as if he was out of touch with reality, or as if he didn't have plenty of other people—his parents, his brother and his sisters and their kids, and especially Elzbietá—to keep him centered and grounded. He *knew* where he was, what he was doing, and every one of his...false memories was safely in the past and falling farther behind with every day. It wasn't as if his brain was continuing to manufacture *additional* memories.

He didn't much care for what the memories he did have might say about his subconscious, though. The "past" in those memories—the memories of the person he'd decided to think of as not-Benjamin—was grim and ugly in so many ways, and not just because of what had happened in that world's 1940s and

1950s. That was bad enough to cause *anyone* nightmares, but the consequences downstream—the "Cold War," the creation of nuclear arsenals capable of destroying all life on Earth, international terrorism on a scale that beggared the imagination—were almost worse. The odd thing was that not-Benjamin hadn't been crushed by that ugliness. Maybe it was because that was the only world he'd ever known, and maybe it was because that world wasn't really as ugly as Benjamin thought it was.

And maybe the fact that it came entirely out of my own subconscious, and would certainly make most people question my sanity, might also have a little something to do with how . . . distasteful I find it, he reflected.

And it wasn't as if reality didn't have its own grim moments. The Brazil-Argentina War, for example. At least in not-Benjamin's world, only two atomic weapons had ever actually been used. The real world hadn't been quite that kind, although at least its nuclear arsenals had been far smaller than the ones he had imagined. On the other hand, maybe it would have been better if they *had* been bigger. Maybe not-Benjamin's doctrine of "Mutually Assured Destruction" might actually have worked . . . and Rio de Janeiro and Buenos Aires might still exist.

He'd never know about that, of course, and the whole idea had struck him as even crazier than most of the nightmares not-Benjamin had imagined. But at least in not-Benjamin's world, the woman Benjamin loved hadn't been savagely wounded flying fighter escort for the UN-sponsored strike to take out the Mato Grasso missile complex before still more millions died. Her air group had blown a hole through the Brazilian Air Force in a massive, running dogfight that had cost her seven of her own pilots. She'd been credited with three victories on the way in— more probably six, according to her wingman, and two more on the way out, but her own cameras and onboard computer hadn't survived—and there were those who questioned the human cost her people and their UN companions had paid. But getting in with the manned bombers had let them take out the bases without using nukes of their own—and killing several hundred thousand more human beings—at the cost of forty-one aircraft and sixty-two aircrew. Elzbietá had almost made it sixty-three . . . and he knew she would have counted the price a bargain even if she hadn't made it.

The death toll from the nuclear strikes which had finally pro-
voked the UN-mandated invasions had approached seventy-five
percent of his imaginary "Holocaust," but those deaths were different, somehow. They'd happened...so quickly, in a single spasm
of madness, the Rio de Janeiro strike in retaliation for the attack
on Buenos Aires. The murders in his nightmares had gone on
for *years*, as part of a grim, horrible, methodical, assembly-line
effort to *exterminate* entire peoples as if they'd been so many
vermin. God knew anti-Semitism in the real world had been bad
enough in the 1930s, especially in Germany. His family knew
that better than most. But what did it say about him that he
could even imagine a world in which something like the "Final
Solution" could have been embraced by any civilized nation? And
that didn't even consider millions of other victims his imaginary
version of the Nazis had inflicted *outside* the "extermination
camps," or things like the Cambodian massacres in Southeast
Asia, genocide in Africa, "ethnic cleansing" in the Balkans, and
God alone knew how many dead in "the Cultural Revolution." If
that had been a real possibility, then thank God the Yenan Raid
took out Mao Zedong when it did!

He released Elzbietá's hand, sitting back to let the waiter
deposit his Penang curry in front of him, and reached for his
chopsticks. He wielded them deftly and felt Elzbietá's eye on him
as he did. He knew what she was thinking. Benjamin Schröder
had never learned to use chopsticks; *not*-Benjamin Schröder had
learned that, however, and he suspected the fact that actual motor
skills seemed to have transferred from hallucination into reality
bothered her more than she was prepared to admit to him. Or
possibly even to herself.

It certainly bothered *him* more than he was prepared to admit
to anyone...even himself.

"So, you're looking forward to getting back into harness, I
presume?" Elzbietá said after a moment, watching him apply far
too much fish sauce to his curry.

"Absolutely," he assured her, only a very little more firmly
than he actually felt. "I've been sitting around long enough, love.
Mind you, a *few* good things have come out of this"—he smiled
warmly at her—"but I really need to get back to work. That's
what Sherman's been saying for weeks now, you know."

"Easier for *him* to say than for you," she shot back tartly, thumping her artificial left hand on the table for emphasis. Then she made herself smile and shook her head. "Sorry! You don't need me mother-henning you. And you're both right, I know that. You do need to get back to work. I just—"

She broke off, waving that same left hand in a semiapologetic gesture, and he smiled again.

"Just that you don't like the thought of my having another... episode, let's say, without you there to catch me?" he said warmly, and she bobbed a brief nod.

That might just have been the most astounding single aspect of this astonishing woman, he thought. Anyone could have seen he was having some sort of fit, some sort of seizure, some... spasm of madness. And almost any "anyone" faced with that would have headed for the nearest exit, if only to find someone "better qualified" to deal with it. But Elzbietá Abramowski wasn't wired that way. She'd seen someone in trouble, and she'd done the only thing someone like her could have done... which didn't include "not my job."

And it hadn't hurt any that she'd grappled with demons enough of her own. He hadn't realized—then—just how brutally damaged her body really had been when her shot-up F-21 crash-landed and exploded on the flight deck of USS *Vladivostok* after the Mato Grasso Strike. It was a sign of her true inner strength that she hadn't tried to hide the scars of so much reconstructive surgery from him, but the strength to accept and reveal *physical* scars paled beside the strength it had taken to admit the depth of her own PTSD to him. And she'd done it at least in part to help him cope with his own confusion and terror. She'd shared her struggle with him, like a soldier lending a wounded squad mate a shoulder to lean on.

When that first terrible spasm had released him—flung him back onto a beach of brutal confusion to wheeze and shudder like a goldfish drowning in oxygen—she'd been there. She'd held him, listened to his gasping incoherence. She might deny it now, but at the time she *had* to have thought he was completely insane, but he could never have guessed that from her voice, her expression, her arm around him as he pressed his face into her shoulder. And that arm, and that voice, were the true reasons he *hadn't* lapsed into outright insanity. There was no question in his mind about that.

"Is Doctor Chalmers ready to hand the chair back over to you?" she asked in an obvious effort to change the subject.

"She is. I've asked her to stay on as the chairman of your dissertation committee, though." He smiled just a bit slyly at her. "Under the circumstances, I think it might not be completely unreasonable for someone to question my ability to remain fully and truly impartial about the quality and originality of your work."

"Now why should anyone think anything of the sort?" she asked, rounding her eye at him, and he chuckled.

"Can't imagine," he said. "Maybe it's the fact we're getting our mail at the same address these days?"

"You know, I never thought of that," she said innocently as the toes of her right foot slid slowly up and down his calf under the table. "Should I assume that you have designs upon my virtue now that you've plied me with prawns and *tom kha gai*?"

"Madam, I am shocked—*shocked!*—that you could possibly suspect me of such depravity and wickedness."

"Oh, too bad." She took her foot from his calf, her eye laughing at him. "In that case, I'm afraid I'm going to have to go home with someone else."

CHAPTER SEVEN

Libyan Desert
1986 CE

"FIRE," RAIBERT ORDERED.

The blister containing the TTV's starboard 12mm Gatling split open, and the weapon swung out. Its seven barrels spun up and spewed a steady stream of metal into the dunes as its rail capacitors charged and discharged in rapid succession. The firing pattern finished, and wind blew the dust cloud aside—

To reveal a smiley face the size of the Parthenon.

"Philo?" Raibert grouched.

"Just trying to lighten the mood."

"It's not working."

"Come on. Don't be that way. It's not that bad."

"Not that bad?" He brushed both hands back through his hair. "Philo, the past can't be changed. It can *never* be changed. No matter what we do when we go back, nothing is ever *permanent*. Time is a vast pool of water. We can stick our finger in it and make tiny ripples, but when we pull our finger away, it flows right back into place. This is an indisputable, mathematical *fact* backed up by every record from every TTV sojourn the Ministry has ever conducted, not to mention the massive hoard of relics ART has brought back. What we saw *can't happen!*"

"But it did," Philo stated calmly. "We knocked into ourselves."

"And we shouldn't be able to do that! It's *impossible* for two of the same time traveler to be in the same spot. You can't meet yourself."

"And yet we did."

"I know! And that's why I'm so upset and why smiley faces in the dunes aren't going to help!"

"I could add 'Raibert and Philo were here' if you like?"

"No! Now please, can we take this seriously?"

"Oh, trust me. I'm taking this very seriously, too. I just think we should approach this in a calm, rational manner."

"I am calm!"

"No you're not."

"Okay, fine! No I'm not, but I have some very good reasons to be not calm right now."

"Shall we get on with the test?" Philo inquired.

"Might as well," Raibert huffed. "My mood isn't improving. Kleio, take us to plus one week."

"Plus one week destination confirmed. Phase-out in three... two...one...jump."

Raibert turned away from the table and waited for the nine-second trip through time to finish.

"Well?" he asked, consciously not looking at the command table.

"It's still there," Philo reported. "Some parts have been filled in, but it still looks as cheerful as the day I shot it."

"Damn it. How can it still be there?"

"I wish I knew."

"Kleio, give us another jump. Plus one month this time."

"Do you think that'll make a difference?" Philo asked.

"We'll find out soon enough, won't we? Kleio, execute."

"Plus one month destination confirmed. Phase-out in three... two...one...jump."

The journey took thirty-seven seconds.

Raibert forced himself to look at the camera feed this time. A month of blowing sand had shifted the dunes and filled in much of the damage, but the outline of Philo's mark could still be seen.

"There's no doubt about it," Raibert said. "We're affecting time downstream of our location."

"That's what it looks like," Philo sighed.

"But how far, I wonder."

"Only one way to find out."

"I guess so. Kleio, take us to plus one year of our current reference."

"Destination set to plus one year. Phase-out in three...two... one...jump."

Raibert checked the timer as Philo manifested on the other side of the command table and smoothed out his beard. The trip would take over seven minutes this time.

"You okay?" Philo asked.

"No," Raibert admitted. "Do you think we're affecting the timeline all the way to the thirtieth century?"

"I don't see how we could be. Granted, I don't have much to base that statement on, but logically how would we be here if our future didn't exist?"

"Hrmph. We don't have much besides guesses right now, do we? It's not like anyone but Andover and Chen have given this much thought in the last hundred years or so."

"And why would we?" Philo asked. "We've had proof you can't change the past. To us, people like them were kooks."

"Well, they're looking a lot less kookish to me right now." Raibert took a deep breath and watched the timer tick down. "It's an uncomfortable thought, suddenly having everything we've known thrown into doubt."

"Yeah."

Both of them waited as the minutes passed by.

"Can I get you something to eat?" Philo asked.

"Nah, it's all right. I'm not hungry."

"Maybe a drink?"

"No, nothing right now. I think the only thing I'd enjoy is a bit too potent for the situation. Thanks, though."

The timer ticked down to zero.

"Phase-in complete," Kleio said.

"Well, the smiley face is gone," Raibert said.

"Though that's not saying much given how fast the dunes can change."

"Yeah. Kleio, how about it? Any sign of that we were here before?"

"Yes, Professor. I am detecting traces of depleted uranium in the sand dunes consistent with our weaponry."

Raibert nodded slowly. Whatever this phenomenon was, it wasn't localized.

"Should we jump forward again?" Philo asked.

"Maybe, but what would be the point? What would we learn from that?"

"We could keep moving forward in increments to see how far this phenomenon goes."

"Yeah, but that feels like it would be a waste of our time," Raibert said, then caught the sour look from Philo. "Relatively speaking, of course. You know, what with us having a time machine and all."

Philo stuck his tongue out at him.

"Wait a second!" Raibert snapped his fingers and his eyes gleamed with a sudden revelation. "Of course!"

"I bet this is good. You've got that look again."

"The storm front that hit us and the changes in the timeline. The two *have* to be connected."

"Well, I don't know if they *have* to."

"But it makes perfect sense. We only noticed this phenomenon after the chronoton storm knocked us around. Here, let's take a look at it again."

Raibert brushed the external view aside and called up the chart on the original event.

"Yes, you see it here? A massive chronoton event hit us from behind and flung us off course. Though..."

"What is it?"

"I'm wondering how we ended up in 1986 in the first place. Weren't we already past that year when we got hit? Kleio?"

"That is correct, Professor. We were phasing through 1995 at the time."

"Then how did a storm front moving *downstream* push us *upstream*?"

"Must be the bent impeller," Philo surmised. "The impeller's permeation changed and we were accelerating in the wrong temporal direction while our systems were off line."

"Okay, I can buy that. Kleio?"

"That explanation is consistent with the data I have, up to the point my systems experienced an emergency shutdown. When I came back online, we had already decelerated and phased in at 1986 CE."

"Okay, now it feels like we're starting to piece this thing together," Raibert declared. "*Something* happened before 1995 and its effects are pushing down the timestream toward the thirtieth century, but it hasn't *reached* the thirtieth century because we're all still here."

"We think," Philo added with a shrug.

"Well, we've got to start somewhere."

"So what's our next move?" Philo asked. "Where do we go from here?"

"Well that's easy." Raibert closed the chart and leaned over the table. "We go storm chasing, of course."

Raibert gripped the edge of the command table, knuckles white, while the deck trembled under his feet.

"Well, we definitely found it," he said.

"Yup," Philo said.

High-energy chronotons roiled in an infinitely wide front temporally ahead. They'd found the storm in 2050 and had slowed from seventy thousand factors down to twelve to keep pace with it less than one relative hour behind. At that range, their chronometric array could begin collecting a wealth of raw data. The downside, however, was what the storm was doing to Raibert's stomach.

"Is the ship supposed to be shaking like this?"

"Turbulence is within acceptable parameters, Professor," Kleio stated.

"Oh, well as long as its 'acceptable' I guess I'm fine with it. But you know what's missing, Kleio?"

"What would that be, Professor?"

"I feel like there should be a handlebar around the edge of this table. You know, something I can hold onto for dear life while the ship is convulsing all over the place. Something really sturdy, so there's no chance of it coming loose. Would you mind fixing that for me?"

"I am sure I can construct an appropriate solution, Professor."

"Thanks. That'd be swell."

"You're getting cranky again." Philo appeared next to him, smiling from one side of his bushy beard to the other.

"Maybe so, but in my defense, I'm the only one here with an inner ear." The decking jumped, and Raibert crouched to hug the table. "Are you *sure* the ship should be shaking like this?"

"There is no immediate danger to the ship, Professor."

"Well my inner ear disagrees. This has *got* to be dangerous."

"That's because it is," Philo said. "We could have been smashed to bits the first time."

"I am sorry, but I do not concur with that analysis," Kleio objected. "I am built tougher than I look."

"Oh?" Philo smirked. "Was that a hint of pride I caught in your voice?"

"Of course not."

"Could have sworn it was."

The TTV shook again, and Raibert lurched over the table, catching himself with a splayed hand.

"And *another* thing, Kleio!"

"Yes, Professor."

"I want the floor in this room covered in padding."

"The whole bridge, Professor?"

"The *whole* thing."

"Is that a sincere request?"

"No. Now please tell me we're getting something useful out of this."

"Oh, we are," Philo said. "We definitely are. First, the obvious parts. Chronoton density is just ridiculously high in the storm front. That, plus the fact that over ninety-nine percent of them are heading into the future makes this storm extremely unusual."

"Hold on a second," Raibert interjected as he accessed the TOE again. "Ninety-nine percent? Aren't they normally like half and half?"

"That's right. Chronotons, after all, are particles with closed-loop histories. They form circular paths through time and space and, from our point of view, they kind of vibrate back and forth through time. At any point in history, the number of chronotons moving into the future and the number of chronotons moving into the past is almost identical. But that's not the strangest bit. You remember the resonating chronotons around you and also in a few places on board?"

"Yeah."

"Well, it turns out the chronotons in the storm are resonating too."

"Great. What are they resonating with?"

"I don't know," Philo admitted. "But there's something different about how they're behaving. The resonance in the storm is, for lack of a better term, more complex than what we see around you."

"And I take it that means we need to stick around and collect more data."

"Sorry. But, you're absolutely right."

"Do whatever it takes." The ship rocked and shuddered under his feet, and his face paled. "We need to get to the bottom of this."

"I'm going parallel with Kleio. We'll crunch some numbers and try to build a theoretical model for what we're seeing. My gut tells me the key is the difference in the resonance patterns. If we can come up with an explanation that fits both data sets, I think we've got this."

"Great. You two work on that. I'm going to take something for my stomach before I throw up. Call me if you need me."

"Well?" Raibert hurried up to the command table and grabbed the newly installed railing that ringed it. The ship jerked upward, then violently back down, and the railing helped him stay on his feet. "Nice. See, this was a good idea."

"I never said it was not, Professor," Kleio replied.

"So, do we have a theory that works?"

"We're closing in on it." Philo manifested across from Raibert. "One mystery down, and one we're still working on." He grimaced. "No, this isn't it, Kleio. Add another set and try again."

"Are you sure that's necessary, Philosophus? I must caution you that the mathematics are becoming quite taxing and I am being forced to shut down nonessential runtimes in order to process these permutations within a reasonable timeframe. Do you still want me to proceed?"

"Yes. We keep doing this until the theory matches the observed."

"Understood. Closing and filing 45+15 permutation. Starting 48+16 permutation."

"Progress?" Raibert asked.

"Of a sort." Philo summoned a chronometric chart over the table. "Here, check this out. This is what's been resonating around you."

Philo pushed the chart forward, and Raibert took it in. A pair of chronometric field lines flowed inward, twisted around each other, then broke off in opposite directions while an outward tension pulled on them, tightening the inner loops.

"It's a knot," Raibert observed. "A knot made out of chronotons?"

"More or less."

"Why does it look like a knot?"

"The visual is a necessary simplification," Philo explained. "Each field line actually represents three spatial dimensions and one temporal dimension. I've simplified each 3+1 set down to a single line, but you can still think of this chart as a 6+2 simulation."

"Pardon?" Raibert blinked, trying to keep up.

"Two sets of three spatial dimensions and one temporal dimension. Sound familiar?"

"Yeah, it does. A 3+1 set is the universe."

"Exactly," Philo said.

Raibert didn't even need to access the pathways bridging their mental firewall to remember that much. It was one of the foundations of the TOE, and indeed, all of modern physics. Past generations had dabbled with higher dimensions as an explanation for the magic tricks the universe seemed to perform, but the Theory Of Everything had torn aside the veil and exposed the core equation that bound the quantum to the macro and enforced the strict limits of width, height, length, and time.

"This chart is showing *two* of them," Raibert observed.

"Right again. And that's what the chronotons around you are resonating with. Another universe."

"Get out of here." Raibert snorted a chuckle. "Seriously?"

"Absolutely."

"You're not joking, are you?"

"Nope."

Raibert's chuckle ended abruptly as he realized his friend was dead serious. However impossible what he'd just said might be.

"But there are only four dimensions."

"In our universe, yes. But you may recall the TOE does allow for a multiverse."

"It does?" Raibert asked in bewilderment.

"Yeah. Check it out." Philo flagged a new mental pathway, and Raibert opened it.

"Huh," he remarked as the knowledge seeped into his mind. "I must have missed that part. Probably wasn't on the exam." He scratched his head. "I really should have paid more attention in that class."

The ship lurched, and he immediately clutched the railing again.

"So the chronotons around me are resonating with another universe. Well, that's great," he groused. "Any idea what it means?"

"We're still working on that."

"And the storm? Are you seeing the same thing there?"

"Well, yes and no."

Raibert took a deep, slow breath and tightened his grip on the railing. The deck vibrated under his feet, but he kept his gaze locked on the AC's avatar.

"Philo?"

"Yes?"

"That was the very definition of an unhelpful answer."

"Sorry, but we're just not sure yet. Kleio's still trying to build an accurate model of what we're seeing in the storm."

"Aren't you running parallel with her?"

"No, I had to back out," Philo admitted.

"Why aren't you still in there?" Raibert asked, perhaps more harshly than he would have liked.

The avatar took off the horned helmet and brushed back his fiery mane while avoiding eye contact.

"I found myself getting lost in the math and needed to take a step back and clear my head. It's hard being a creative calculator, even for an abstract citizen. Sometimes we lose sight of the big picture when we dive in too deep."

"Hey, sorry," Raibert said, backtracking. "It's all right. I didn't mean anything by it."

"I know you didn't. And Kleio doesn't need me at this point anyway. It's just brute force number crunching until we find the right permutation." He perked up and fitted his helmet back on. "Ah. Speaking of which."

"I have completed the 48+16 permutation," Kleio reported.

"48+16?" Raibert asked. "Are we talking dimensions?"

"We are." Philo pulled the chart with two universes aside and opened a new one.

"Whoa!" Raibert exclaimed.

A chaotic tangle of sixteen chronometric field lines twisted around and pulled against each other, straining to break free from a central pulsating mass that looked like the yarn ball from hell. Lines glowed hot with energy magnitudes beyond anything Raibert had ever seen in all his missions, but for all the fury on display, the knot only seemed to tighten further as he watched.

"Discrepancies between the model and the observed data are below one percent." Philo thumped the air with his fist. "Yes, I knew it! I called it! And that one percent can easily be explained away by the accuracy of our instruments."

"You mean to tell me that storm is here because *sixteen* universes have become knotted together?"

"Yes," Philo stated simply. "We literally have a knot in time formed from sixteen separate timelines."

"But how is that even possible?"

"I don't know."

"This can't be a natural phenomenon. Something must have caused this."

"I would tend to agree. And fortunately"—Philo beamed as he placed a hand on his chest—"we now have a predictive model we can work with. Let's see where it leads, shall we?"

"All right. How about we start with the origin of this storm? Can you trace it back?"

"I can certainly try." Philo pushed the second chart aside and opened a third. "We know the storm hit us in 1995 and it was moving forward through time. So we know the original event has to be somewhere upstream from that. But how *far* upstream is the tricky part. Unfortunately, we don't have a lot of good data from when we got clobbered because the storm came at us from our array's blind spot. All we really have is the storm front as we see it now and the model."

A single time axis appeared on the chart with various points highlighted with chronometric data.

"Okay, so let's backtrack the model to its origin."

Additional lines overlaid the first and traced theoretical paths into the storm's past.

"The storm must have had an initial phase of violent expansion. That's obvious from our observations. After all, we were cruising along at seventy kilofactors, and it overtook us, but now it's slowed to only twelve factors and is still slowing. Fortunately, the model supports that as well. Unfortunately..."

"Yes?" Raibert asked.

"Unfortunately, that one percent error gets compounded the farther back we calculate. I'm going to end up with a range of values for the storm's origin. A fairly wide range."

"Better than nothing. What years are we looking at?"

"It's ... hmm."

"Yes?"

"Hmmmm."

"Philo?"

"Hmmmmmmm ..."

"Come on, Philo. Don't keep me in suspense. What's the range?"

"Looks like the storm could have originated anywhere between 1905 and 1995."

"That's ... a lot of ground to cover."

"Best I can do with the instrumentation we have. If we could come back with another TTV, or even several, we could form an array and increase the accuracy. We might even be able to trace the origin down to a specific decade or maybe even a single year."

"But for now, all we know is that some event—who knows what?—but some event in the timeline between 1905 and 1995 tangled all these universes together and created this storm."

"Yeah," Philo nodded. "That about sums it up."

"And the storm is moving forward through time, gaining on the present. What happens when the storm crashes into the Edge of Existence?"

"Good question." Philo opened a fresh chart. "Give me a minute."

Raibert leaned back from the table with both hands firmly on the railing. The timeline of the universe wasn't infinite in both directions. It had a definitive end point that currently existed in the year 2979 and continued to move forward at a pace of one second per second or a time factor of one. That point in the timeline was referred to as the "Edge of Existence," though it was also sometimes called the "True Present" or the "Age of the Universe." No future existed beyond the Edge of Existence because it hadn't been created yet, and no TTV could visit a part of the timeline that didn't exist in the first place.

"Hmrph," Philo murmured, studying a chart that was almost completely covered in field lines. "That's not good."

"Define 'not good,'" Raibert asked pointedly.

"Well, think of the Edge of Existence as the immovable object and this storm the Knot created as the irresistible force. When the two meet, bad things are going to happen."

"But the storm is slowing, right? Didn't you say it was slowing?"

"Yeah, but the *reason* it's slowing is because the storm is accumulating energy. Lots and lots of energy. We basically have fifteen other universes pouring chronometric energy into our own. And yes, the storm is slowing as a result of that, but it's an exponential decay. No matter how much energy it accumulates, it *cannot* drop as low as one time factor, which means it's *always* going to be gaining on the Edge of Existence and the two *will* eventually meet."

"And when they meet?"

"Boom."

Raibert squinted suspiciously at the avatar.

"Define 'boom.'"

"Okay, maybe 'boom' doesn't quite cover this," Philo admitted. "Imagine the Big Bang."

"All right. That's not where I thought you'd start, but okay."

"Now imagine it happening at every point across the entire universe all at the same time."

Raibert swallowed hard, his throat suddenly dry.

"Now imagine that release of energy burning up the entire Knot and the backflow of chronotons triggering Big Bangs in another fifteen universes."

Raibert stared at the chart for nearly a minute before he could finally speak again.

"Philo?"

"Yes?"

"Boom is *not* a sufficient way to characterize this."

"I know."

"This isn't a boom! This is the apocalypse! We need to stop this! Is there even a *way* to stop this? Please tell me there is!"

"I think so. We just need to unravel the Knot. Undo whatever core event created the initial entangling of these sixteen universes. We do that, we cut this storm off at the source, and the pent up energy will dissipate before it reaches the Edge of Existence."

"But that means we have to search through ninety years of history!"

"Yeah, that's the tricky part, and we still have no idea what sort of nature this 'event' might take."

"This is too big for us." Raibert shook his head. "We need to get back to the thirtieth century and warn the Ministry. Hell, warn all of SysGov."

"Agreed," Philo said, nodding emphatically.

"All the resources of our entire society need to be thrown at this. Every TTV mobilized. Our best minds, both physical and abstract, brought to bear. We can't screw this up. We *need* to find a way to unravel the Knot before our universe is destroyed!"

"You're absolutely right, but there is a small silver lining in all this."

"If there is, I don't see it."

"Oh, you don't, do you?" Philo tapped the time index on the current chart he'd prepared.

"What is... *ooooh,*" Raibert exhaled, and his mood immediately brightened.

"The storm front is slowing," Philo began. "At its current speed and rate of decay, it'll catch up to the Edge of Existence in thirteen *hundred* years."

"Will it now?" Raibert stepped back from the table and smiled ear to ear. "So we have some time to sort this out."

"Well, the Knot *is* getting worse. I suppose it's possible it'll wind itself up so tight that not even fixing this event in the past could unravel it. That *might* happen somewhere between now and the forty-third century. It's hard to say more without better data. But yeah, we have some time."

"Well then!" Raibert rubbed his hands together. "I guess there's no point to sticking around here anymore. Any reason we can't head back home and give everyone the bad news?"

"I don't see why not," Philo said with a grin that mimicked Raibert's. "It'll be bumpy, but we'll get through the storm, and once we're through, it should be smooth sailing all the way to 2979. Figuratively, of course."

"Well, of course." Raibert let out a long sigh of relief. "Whew. I am *so* glad this is going to be someone else's mess to fix."

CHAPTER EIGHT

Admin suppression tower Portcullis-Prime
2979 CE

JONAS SHIGEKI LEANED BACK IN HIS CHAIR, PROPPED HIS BOOTS up on the desk, and closed his eyes. His Personal Implant Network negotiated a connection with the Earth-based server for *Worlds Beyond Ours*, and the loading screen filled his virtual vision while a simplified and softer rendition of the game's theme music played over his virtual hearing.

The game finished loading, and Jonas found himself in the cockpit of his newest starship, one of the exceedingly rare—and extremely expensive—Star Racers. He'd actually spent a hefty sum of real world money on the ship at a developer's auction rather than rely on the in-game currency, but its stats were worth every dollar he'd burned on this little luxury.

The spacious black and chrome cockpit materialized around him, filled with anachronistic but charming buttons, levers, dials, and blinking lights. A planet striped with azure and magenta bands loomed beyond the forward-facing bubble canopy, and he took a slow, satisfied breath in the real world. It had been a long, hard slog to get here during his last session, but finding this planet amongst WBO's procedurally generated star systems had made every beam hit and asteroid collision worth it.

Jonas commanded his in-game avatar to click a few switches and shove a lever forward, prepping the Star Racer for descent.

He reached for the throttle, and an alarm warbled in his virtual hearing. Not an urgent *you-are-under-attack* alarm, but more of a *do-you-really-want-to-do-this* cautionary note. He frowned and surveyed his dashboard one more time.

And then he noticed the source of the problem. The Star Racer had only two tons of fuel left. He could land on the planet, but his ship didn't have enough propellant to pull back out of the gravity well.

Well, shoot.

Jonas blew a breath out the side of his mouth and logged out of the game. He put an open hand on his desk, let his PIN integrate with the office infostructure, and placed a call.

The recipient acknowledged the call almost immediately, and his voice came over Jonas's virtual hearing.

"Yeah?"

"Hey, Sung-Wook. How's it going?"

"Just bored out of my skull like usual. What's up?"

"I need your help."

"Okay, you need to clarify that," Park Sung-Wook said cautiously. "Do you need my help or *need my help*?"

"The second one."

"Thought so. Is this something that can wait until later? I'm at work right now."

"Yeah, I know," Jonas replied. "But you just said you were bored. Are you even doing anything?"

"Just staring at an empty scope until my eyes bleed. Same as everyone else here."

"Then you can afford to take some time out of your busy schedule and help me out. Right, pal?"

"Maybe, but you know what a stickler for the rules my boss is."

Jonas laughed so hard some of the air snorted out of his nostrils.

"Is that so?" he added once he could breathe again.

"Yeah," Sung-Wook said. "The guy can be a real hard ass sometimes."

"Well, then maybe I should talk to him. He and I go way back, after all."

"I don't know. I'm still a little leery about this. What if it ends up on my next performance review?"

Jonas rolled his eyes. "It's not going to end up on your

performance review, okay? Look, I just need you to spot me some fuel in WBO. That's all."

"Did you go joyriding and lose track of where you were again?"

"No. I'll have you know I knew exactly what I was doing the whole time."

"Uh-huh."

"I got forced into making a few bad jumps, is all, and now I'm a little bit stranded."

"Is that like being a little bit pregnant?"

"Sure. Whatever. Now, could you please just send one of your ships over to mine?"

"Why not call in a tow and save both of us the trouble?" Sung-Wook asked.

"Well, because I don't want the coordinates for this planet becoming public knowledge. If I call in a tow, this thing is going to show up in the forums and then *everyone* is going to want a piece of it."

"Yeah, right. It can't be that good."

"Can't be that good, huh?" Jonas opened his WBO offline status in his virtual sight and read the stats of the planet he'd discovered. "Eighty-seven percent ultra-rare flora. Fifty-two percent ultra-rare fauna. Twenty-eight percent ultra-rare resources."

Sung-Wook whistled. "*Damn!* You seriously found a triple-ultra?"

"You bet I did!"

"Then why didn't you say so in the first place?"

"Because you know I like messing with you."

"Can I have a share of the loot if I help you out?"

"Well, I don't know. That depends," Jonas replied, grinning.

"Come on, man. Please?"

"Okay. Since you asked nicely, I guess I could part with some of it. How's a quarter sound to you?"

"A whole *quarter*? Hell, I'll get one of my ships heading there right now!"

"Thanks, man. Much obliged."

"Which sector are you in?"

"Thirty-seven-double-zeta."

"Okay... yeah, I've got a ship in an adjacent sector. Just send me your exact coordinates and I'll bring the juice."

"Sent," Jonas said. "Oh, and watch out for the pirates on your way in."

He logged out of the call and leaned back with his hands behind his head.

"Yep. All in a day's work."

He stretched back luxuriantly. A quarter of his loot would be a *major* profit for Sung-Wook, but no more than a friend was worth. *Besides*, he thought, *without the juice, I couldn't make it home to claim* any *of the loot, and that—*

The sudden, raucous sound interrupted his thoughts with no warning at all, and his eyes went wide as he realized it was the suppression tower's general klaxon. He'd never heard it outside a training exercise in his entire career, and the abrupt blast of sound startled him so badly he nearly tipped his seat over before he grabbed the edge of his desk and pulled himself up.

A report flashed into existence over his desk, and he skimmed it quickly.

"Oh, shit!"

Jonas bolted out of his chair, grabbed the peaked cap off his desk, and hustled to the door. Malmetal parted to let him out, then pinched shut behind him as he hurried down the stairs, his long ponytail bouncing with each step.

"Shit-shit-shit-shit-shit!" he muttered, setting his cap and smoothing out his Peacekeeper blues. "This had better not be another one of Dad's unscheduled drills."

The malmetal door at the bottom of the stairs parted, and Jonas Shigeki, DTI Under-Director of Suppression, strode into the operations room of temporal suppression tower Portcullis-Prime. Two dozen Admin Peacekeepers sat in three rows, all facing the map of Earth that covered the far wall. They called up reports in the room's shared virtual vision, and several more agents scurried to their seats while a red light strobed on the map.

"Status!" Jonas called out in a clear, commanding tone.

"Unidentified chronoport detected at negative six years," said Superintendent Park Sung-Wook, chief of operations for Portcullis-Prime.

"Six *years*?" Jonas asked. If this was one of Dad's drills, it was a strange one. What was a chronoport doing that far out?

"Yes, sir," Sung-Wook said. "We're working on a more precise fix now."

Jonas stepped forward, clasped his hands tightly behind his back, and watched data populate next to the flashing light on the map.

"Intruder at negative six years and thirty-one days, approaching at . . . seventy kilofactors?" Sung-Wook looked up and met Jonas's inquisitive gaze.

"Go on."

"Yes, sir." Sung-Wook returned his attention to the virtual display. "ETA to True Present is forty-six minutes. Speed and vector are unchanged from initial ID."

"Where do we project phase-in?" Jonas asked.

"Northern Africa, if the intruder's speed and vector remain consistent." Park Sung-Wook leaned over one of his agents. "What are we up against? Is this a new style of Lunar chronoport?"

"Can't confirm or deny, sir. The impeller profile doesn't match any on record, nor is it even close. It appears to be an entirely new design."

"Incoming telegraph from Barricade Squadron. They have the intruder on their scopes and are requesting permission to intercept."

Jonas glanced over the map and noted the eight green icons patrolling around the Earth at negative one month. The chronoports in Barricade Squadron formed the Admin's first line of defense against unauthorized time travel, and they fell under his command as the Under-Director of Suppression.

More raw data populated next to the intruder's red icon, and Jonas scrunched his brow in consternation. The intruder was coming straight in. No attempt at stealth. No evasive flight patterns.

Just flying straight and true as if it didn't have a care in the world.

And its impeller could move it at *seventy* kilofactors? Sure, the Department of Temporal Investigation's own chronoports could top that, but the DTI had designed and built the first chronoton impellers and still retained a significant tech advantage over the dissidents, secessionists, and terrorists who tried to emulate or steal their work.

"Sir, another telegraph from Barricade Squadron. They are requesting orders."

And the intruder was spotted at six years out? Which meant its mission must have taken it even further back than that. How had it slipped past Barricade when leaving the present? That was perhaps the most alarming part, but if it really had stealth systems that good, why throw that advantage away and come blazing into the present at high speed?

Something wasn't right here.

"Cut *Barricade-3* and *Barricade-4* loose," Sung-Wook ordered. "I want that chronoport destroyed as soon as it enters the True Present."

"Yes, sir. Relaying kill order to—"

"Belay that order," Jonas cut in.

"Sir?" Sung-Wook turned sharply to face him.

"The intruder is to be captured."

Sung-Wook's jawline tightened, and it took him a few moments to respond, but when he did it was with a curt nod.

"All right. You heard the boss, everyone. We're going to capture the intruder. Signal *Barricade-3* and *Barricade-4* and have them move to intercept the intruder after phase-in. Make it clear this is a capture operation. They are not to attack unless they come under direct fire from the intruder."

"Yes, sir. Telegraphing orders."

"Full lockdown!" Sung-Wook commanded.

"Portcullis-Prime to all suppression towers," the communications operator said. "Unidentified chronoport approaching True Present. Full lockdown in effect. Full lockdown in effect."

Icons sprinkled across the globe lit up as each tower confirmed the order and all of them powered up their suppression fields.

"Portcullis-Prime to Portcullis-17," Sung-Wook said.

"Portcullis-17 Operations here."

"Scramble your Switchblade Squadron but *do not* fire on the intruder. We're going to try to capture it."

"Confirmed, Portcullis-Prime. We have the coordinates and are launching our standby drones now. Switchblades will not open fire without your orders."

"Thanks, Seventeen."

"*Barricade-3* and *Barricade-4* have confirmed the orders, sir. Now moving to intercept."

"Very good." Sung-Wook stepped next to Jonas and put a hand on his shoulder. His PIN interfaced with Jonas's own, and the two entered into a closed-circuit chat.

"Something on your mind?" Jonas asked. To any observer

outside the chat, his lips didn't move and no sound came from his throat, but Sung-Wook's virtual senses heard his words and saw his mouth form them.

"What was that about?" Sung-Wook asked privately. "Why did you countermand my order?"

"I don't like unsolved mysteries, and this chronoport definitely qualifies. It's behaving too strangely, and I want to know why."

"Okay, fair enough, but you made me look bad in front of my team."

"Sorry, pal. I didn't mean to." Jonas winked at him. "How about I make sure your next evaluation positively glows?"

"Ladies and gentlemen and abstracts," Raibert said in a stiff, formal tone. "I come before you today bearing grave news of a calamity that threatens our very existence." He stopped and shifted from one foot to the other. "Do you think that's too pretentious a start?"

"Maybe a little," Philo twittered in his virtual hearing.

"Hmm. Let's try again." He cleared his throat, tugged his black dress jacket straight, smoothed the cycling patterns of his dress scarf, adjusted the angle of the wide-brimmed hat, and studied the mirrored copy of himself in his virtual sight. "Ladies and gentlemen and abstracts. I need your help. Really, *really* need your help. In fact, if you don't help, we're all going to die. Eventually. In about thirteen hundred years."

"That one could have been better."

"Hello, everyone. Today is a day of reckoning for the Consolidated System Government, and I reckon we need to work together to solve it."

"Nope. Try again."

"Surprise!" Raibert spread his arms wide. "The entire universe is going to explode. Better get to work fixing it."

"Not really doing it for me."

He cleared his throat into a fist and composed himself.

"Greetings, everyone. I know this is going to come as a shock to all of you, but there's a big, nasty, potentially apocalyptic chronoton storm heading our way. It's going to obliterate the universe in one thousand three hundred years, and I was just thinking we should all get together and do something about that. What do you say?"

"There's lint on your shoulder," Philo pointed out.

"Thanks." Raibert brushed it off.

"What are you getting so nervous about?" the AC asked. "Just tell the Ministry the problem and let them sort it out."

"I'm nervous because you and I have what could kindly be referred to as a 'reputation,' and I'm worried the Ministry isn't going to take us seriously."

"Are you referring to the ART exhibition after the Alexandria raid?"

"Why yes, that's *exactly* what I'm referring to."

"Maybe they've all forgotten about it by now?" Philo offered halfheartedly.

"Hrmph!" Raibert pulled out his scarf, tucked one end into his jacket, and tossed the other over a shoulder. "Weren't you the one who was poking fun at my meat-based forgetfulness? Even if the physical citizens in the Ministry have forgotten—which I *seriously* doubt—their ACs haven't. We destroyed whole careers with that stunt."

"Oh, I beg to differ. That idiot and his sycophantic followers did all the damage. We just turned on the spotlight."

Raibert sighed and rearranged his scarf for the fifth time.

"Face it, Philo. There are a lot of people at the Ministry who don't like us. If we don't play this right, it's going to be an uphill battle to make people take us seriously."

"Then what do you think of this?" Philo offered. "What if we reach out to Chen or Andover or maybe even both of them? Show them the evidence and get them on our side before going to the Ministry."

Raibert stopped fiddling with his scarf. "You know, that's actually a really good idea."

"You're welcome."

"Sure, they may not have many backers, but it's not zero, and they do have a certain air of authority as the loyal opposition. Even if most people think they're crazy."

"Doubters will think twice once they see the data we have, and it's better than going to the Ministry all by ourselves, I say."

"Yeah." Raibert nodded. "The more I think about it, the more I like it. Which one should we start with?"

"Definitely Andover. You know how loopy Chen can be sometimes."

"Right. Good point," Raibert said with a grimace.

"Professor, would you please come to the bridge?" Kleio asked.

"What is it?"

"We are approaching our phase-in target at the Edge of Existence, and I have detected an unusually high number of TTVs ahead."

"Okay. How many?"

"I have isolated a total of eight signatures based on a combination of telegraph traffic and impeller wakes."

"And they're doing what exactly?"

"Two are moving toward our phase-in target location and the rest are holding non-congruent positions at negative one month from the Edge of Existence."

"That . . . seems really weird."

"Hence the reason I thought it prudent for you to take a look at it, Professor."

"All right. Be there in a sec."

Raibert tipped his hat a few degrees forward. He really did cut a dashing figure when he dressed up. He nodded to himself, switched the virtual mirror off, and walked through the prog-steel shutter and down the corridor to the TTV's bridge.

A map of Earth switched on over the command table, and eight icons pulsed about the planet, each with coordinates that detailed their relative temporal and physical positions.

"Those them?" Raibert asked.

"Yes, Professor."

"What the heck are they doing just sitting there? And why are those two heading toward us?"

"I am unable to ascertain that, Professor."

"Is there any announcement from the Ministry?"

"I have detected several telegraphs to and from the TTVs, but I do not understand them."

"That can't be right." Raibert's face scrunched up in confusion. "You don't understand them?"

"They appear to contain only gibberish."

"Maybe our telegraphs were damaged in the storm," Philo suggested.

"Diagnostics on both telegraphs do not indicate any damage."

"Then why are we only getting gibberish?" Raibert asked.

"I cannot say, Professor."

"Well, whatever." Raibert shrugged. "We'll be home in less than an hour, and we can ask the Ministry what's going on after we phase in. Kleio, make a note that our telegraphs are potentially glitchy and need to be given a thorough examination after we land."

"Yes, Professor."

"Now, if you'll excuse me, I'm going to go work on my speech some more."

"Three...two...one...phase in."

"Okay!" Raibert cracked his knuckles. "First, let's get the Ministry on the line and find out what all the commotion is about. Then we can go give Andover a call."

"I am attempting to do so, Professor, but there appears to be a problem."

"Oh, not *another* one." He hung his head. "What is it this time?"

"It seems I am unable to connect to the local infostructure."

"What, is your transceiver busted, too?"

"Diagnostics for the transceiver indicate full functionality."

"But you still can't link up?"

"That is correct, Professor. I am detecting several connection beacons, but none of them are allowing me in. They do not appear to be using standard interface protocols."

"Uhh, Raibert?" Philo said in a worried tone that sent a chill down his spine. "Something is very wrong here."

"You mean besides nothing working on this tub?"

"Yeah. I don't know how to put this, but several cities are in the wrong spots."

"*What?* How can whole cities be in different spots? Kleio, did you phase us into the wrong year?"

"No, Professor. 2979 CE coordinates confirmed. We are at the Edge of Existence."

"Then how can cities not be where they're supposed to be?"

"I do not know, Professor."

"Philo, show me."

"Here's the thirtieth century map of northern Africa." A topographical map appeared on the command table with a false-color scale starting with blues and progressing to purples, reds, oranges, yellows, and finally white for the densest population centers.

"And here's what we're seeing now."

A second topographical map manifested over the first. Sometimes cities that should have been there weren't, some that shouldn't have been were, and those that matched up showed different population levels.

"This isn't home, Philo!"

"I know! And that's what's wrong!"

Raibert's mind raced through the past few days. Chronoton storms. Knots in time. Universes tangled together. Changes that persisted. Changes that propagated downstream. A timeline that was suddenly more malleable than anyone had thought possible.

And now just within the past hour, strange chronoton telegraphs that were gibberish... or perhaps *encoded*? Cities not being where they were supposed to be. Strange TTV activities near the True Present.

This was the thirtieth century, but it wasn't the one he knew.

It was something else. Something alien. Something impossible.

And something very, very wrong.

"Philo, are you thinking what I'm thinking?"

"Yes, and it scares me."

"I think we now know the nature of the Event that created the Knot." He leaned over the command table and stared at a landscape that couldn't be but was. "The Event. The one we figured out was somewhere between 1905 and 1995. It changed *everything* downstream when the Knot formed. Philo, we're stuck in a timestream that *isn't our own*!"

"What do we do?"

"I don't know!"

"Phase-in detected five hundred meters to starboard," Kleio reported.

Raibert pushed aside the maps and opened an external view. He knew they truly were in a different timestream the moment he laid eyes on the TTV, for it was unlike any he'd ever seen. Instead of the long elliptical bodies the Ministry used, this one consisted of a thick delta wing with multiple pods slung underneath the hull and the long spike of its impeller protruding out the back, giving it a shape reminiscent of manta rays.

It was also smaller than the *Kleio*, roughly half the size at ninety meters in length, and it hovered on the exhaust of two large fusion thrusters rather than the more elegant reactionless graviton thrusters the *Kleio* possessed.

But of more immediate importance, it was also much more heavily armed.

The delta wing flexed upward into a shallow V to better expose a quartet of rectangular pods that contained what looked like 4x4 banks of missiles. Another two pods with more rounded profiles were slung underneath the wingtips and housed long-barreled railguns.

Suddenly the *Kleio*'s two small-caliber Gatling guns didn't provide the level of comfort they normally did.

"Heavy weapons detected," Kleio reported. "Radar and lidar signals detected. We are being targeted. Shall I activate our defenses?"

"No!" Raibert shouted. "Don't shoot! Don't open the blisters! Don't do *anything*!"

"Understood, Professor."

"Raibert, they're carrying enough firepower to vaporize us."

"And I am not about to antagonize them!"

"Second phase-in event detected," Kleio report. "Five hundred meters to port."

Another delta-wing TTV bristling with weapons appeared on the other side of *Kleio* and hovered with its weapon pods trained on them.

"We are being hailed on an open channel," Kleio said.

"Let's hear it."

"*Unidentified chronoport! Land inmediatamente y exit your craft! Take any acción hostil y you will be destruido!*"

"Uhh, what the hell language was that?" Raibert asked.

"I think they want us to land," Philo said.

"Well, forget it! We're not going to! Kleio, get us out of here! Phase out!"

"I am sorry, Professor, but I am unable to."

"*What?* Why?"

"Some external force is preventing the impeller from gaining traction. I am detecting a chronometric field emanating from a tower one hundred fifty-five kilometers northeast of our position."

"So no time travel?"

"I am afraid not, Professor."

"*Unidentified chronoport! Land inmediatamente y exit your craft! This is your last advertencia!*"

"I think they mean business, Raibert. Look, something's happening!"

The two gun pods dropped from each chronoport. Metal along the top of each pod flexed, extended, formed three long blades, and began to spin. The descent of the pods slowed, stabilized, and then they tilted toward the *Kleio* and advanced with railguns tracking.

"Twenty small craft approaching from the south," Kleio said. "They are roughly the same size as the four pods that detached from the TTVs."

Another view opened over the command table to reveal twenty slender delta wings speeding toward them with railguns peeking out of their streamlined noses. Their wings morphed as they approached, melting back into main bodies that then sprouted helicopter blades. The blades spun into action, and the new craft took up positions around the *Kleio*.

"*Unidentified chronoport! Land inmediatamente y exit your craft o you will be destruido!*"

One of the helicopter drones fired a hypervelocity slug past the *Kleio*'s nose.

"Okay! Okay! Message received!" Raibert exclaimed. "We clearly don't speak the same version of English, but I know exactly what *that* means. Kleio, find a deserted spot to set us down. Do it *slowly* and keep the guns stowed."

"Yes, Professor."

"What are we going to do, Raibert?" Philo asked, concern leaking across the firewall. "These people don't look friendly."

"What *can* we do? Our time drive is offline, and there's no way we can fight our way out of this."

He placed both hands on his cheeks and ran them down his face.

"Raibert?"

"Okay, here's what I propose. We're dealing with a new timeline, so when we land, I'm going to go out there and make first contact."

"No, that's too dangerous."

"So is being shot at by all of that!" He indicated the drones swarming around them. "Look, that chronoton storm is still out there, and it's still going to destroy the universe. As far as I'm concerned, we have the same job to do, and we need to suck it up and do it. So I'm going to go out there, look as harmless as I possibly can, and try to talk to these people. We're dealing with a society that has time machines, so they should understand the problem, right? I mean, it's the destruction of all reality we're up against here. How unreasonable could they be?"

"I guess we don't have much of a choice," Philo said. "And whatever happens, I'll stay in touch and be with you every step of the way."

"No, you won't. You're going to stay right here. We have no idea what this society thinks about abstract citizens. We don't even know if they *have* ACs. Which means you're going to sit tight inside the *Kleio*'s infosystems and not show the slightest sign that you exist while Kleio acts totally unhelpful and dumb as dirt. Right, Kleio? Can you do that for me?"

"I am sure I can manage, Professor," Kleio responded.

"Great. I knew I could count on you."

"But what if they're not reasonable?" Philo's avatar appeared next to him and put a virtual hand on his shoulder.

"Well, that's easy." Raibert flashed a disarming grin. "It'll be your job to rescue me."

"I have landed, Professor. Disengaging graviton thrusters."

"Open the main cargo ramp." Raibert pushed off the command table and strode out of the bridge. "I'll head out that way."

"Yes, Professor."

"Raibert," Philo protested.

"Stay hidden." He turned back and wagged a finger at Philo. "If you don't, who'll pull my butt out of the fire? You hear me?"

"Yeah, I hear you." The Viking avatar frowned. "And I will. Pull your butt out, that is. If it needs pulling."

"Just you watch. I bet we're worrying about nothing. These people are going to be super reasonable and this whole thing will be a cinch!"

"I hope you're right."

Raibert rode a counter-grav tube down to the cargo bay and hurried across the wide three-story space that took up much of the TTV's forward internal volume. The cargo hatch split open and formed a shallow ramp to the sand dunes outside. A dry, scorching wind swept across him, and his skin prickled with fresh sweat.

He gulped down his apprehensions, stood up straight, and walked proudly down the ramp.

"This has got to be the stupidest thing I've ever done in my life."

One of the helicopter drones swooped past the entrance, and the huge flattened barrel of its railgun tracked his every step. The roar of its rotors assaulted his ears, and buffeting gusts blew his hat off. He ignored the temptation to chase after it, and instead held his hands high in the air and stepped forward.

A second drone dropped down, and both kept their railguns trained on him.

Raibert sucked in a long breath, filled his chest to bursting, and then shouted at the top of his lungs.

"I COME IN PEACE!"

CHAPTER NINE

Yanluo Blight residential blocks
2979 CE

CSABA SHIGEKI, DIRECTOR-GENERAL OF THE DEPARTMENT OF Temporal Investigation, took off his peaked cap and tucked it under an arm as he stepped into the VIP lounge. The sloped glass front curved into the first half of the floor to afford a clear view of the circular stadium below, while virtual reports provided all manner of statistics on the two teams. His eyes caught the name "Thaddeus Shigeki" in one of the rosters, and he wore a proud smile as he rounded a wide couch that seated the only other occupant.

"You know, for having so many time machines under your command, you sure are late a lot."

The woman's white suit provided a stark contrast to her black skin and short, curly hair. She narrowed her eyes and tilted her head back with a scornful glare. The public layer of her PIN interfaced with his and the marriage sigil on the back of her hand appeared in his virtual sight: a blooming marigold with three dew-kissed petals beneath it to represent her three children. They'd hired the original artist to add a petal after the birth of each child.

"Fashionably late, you mean," he corrected.

Jackie Shigeki raised a single eyebrow and tried to skewer him with the other eye, but then the sternness melted away and she started to giggle.

"Come on. Sit down, Csaba." She patted the cushion next to her. "You already missed the first run."

"Sorry." He set his cap on the end table, dropped down next to her, and tossed his braid over a shoulder. "Kloss kept me over."

"Anything interesting?"

"Not really." He took her dark hand in his pale one, and their identical sigils glowed a little brighter. "Freep sympathizers keep finding ways to slip tech goodies to the Lunar secessionists, and we haven't figured out how. The usual headaches. Has Thaddeus run yet?"

"Not yet. The Coordinators from Tower A10 went first, but we executed an early juggernaut rush and stole the initiative. Thad and the rest of the Blight Bashers are prepping for his run now."

"Very nice. That's my boy."

Csaba draped an arm over her shoulders and she snuggled up next to him.

"So how was your day?" he asked.

"Fine, I guess," she sighed.

"You sure? Because you're making my sarcasm meter tingle."

"It's nothing really. The new boss is a real stickler for the rules. He's thrown all of our normal procedures into chaos, and schedules meeting after meeting. Plus he keeps calling me 'Jaqueline,' and it's starting to bug me."

"I think he's still feeling out his new team. It's what I'd be doing in his shoes."

"Maybe so, but 'Jaqueline Shigeki' just sounds so darn awkward. I'm getting sick of hearing 'Publicist Jaqueline Shigeki, I need a moment of your time.' I know it's petty, but I miss the assonance."

Csaba's train of thought ground to a halt, and he paused to access the local infostructure.

"What is it?"

"Hold on," he said. "I'm running a search."

"Are you seriously looking up what assonance means?"

"Maybe," he admitted.

"Jac-*kie* Shige-*ki*. The ends have this nice repetitive vowel sound that forms the assonance."

"Well, yeah. I know that now that I looked it up, but you have to admit the word sounds like it could be a horrible form of butt disease."

Jackie snorted. "Seriously, Csaba. One of the reasons I married you was so I could have an assonance in my name."

"You *did*?" He leaned dramatically away from her.

"Dear me. Did I let that slip?"

"Oh ho! Thirty years and three children later, and *finally* the truth comes out."

"Darn it!" She snapped her fingers. "You've seen through my carefully laid machinations at last."

"Well, I do run the DTI. It's kind of in the job description." He squeezed her shoulders. "Seriously, though, if you're not happy with the new boss, I could have a word with him. Or his boss. Or his boss's boss, for that matter."

"No! Absolutely not!"

"What?" He put a hand over his heart. "I can be subtle."

"Csaba, it's not how you'd act. It's who you are. Can you imagine how a lowly supervisor in public relations would react to having the DTI *Director-General* call him all of a sudden? He would literally crap his pants."

"Yeah, I suppose I do sometimes have that effect on people."

"Which is why you're *not* going to do it." Jackie patted his chest. "That's the very definition of overkill. I can handle the rough and tumble world of public relations without you riding in on a white horse to save me."

"Well, that white horse is standing by if you need it."

Jackie shook her head and giggled. He gave her a light kiss on the forehead, and held her close as she rested her head against his shoulder.

The players returned to the field, and the obstacles selected by the Coordinators manifested in his virtual vision.

"Lots of turrets," he noted.

"Yeah, but that doesn't leave much for the run itself. I wonder what their strategy is."

"I guess we'll find out when Thad starts."

"Uh-oh." She disentangled from him and sat up.

"What is it?"

"I just received an alert from a search I was running. Guess who's in the next lounge over."

"Do I really have to? You know I hate guessing."

"Why, it's your favorite new employee, of course."

"Uhh..." he moaned and flopped his head onto the back of the couch.

"And I think she just realized you're in here."

"This is the last thing I need today," he said, staring at the ceiling. "Can't she just leave me alone and let me enjoy the game?"

One of the side doors chimed.

"Apparently not." He glanced at the fogged portal to his left and switched off the privacy filter. The door cleared, and Cheryl First, newly appointed DTI Under-Director of Archaeology, dipped her head at him and smiled.

"No point in resisting now," Jackie said.

"You're right, of course," he sighed and unlocked the door.

The malglass slid aside, and Cheryl stepped in, radiating grace and dignity with each long-legged stride. A short, angular cut of perfectly groomed auburn hair framed an oval face and milky white skin that were rumored to be the product of the best genetic and cosmetic modifications money could buy, within the legal bounds of the Yanluo Restrictions, of course. The chief executor's wife would *never* be seen violating the Restrictions or even dabbling within the gray legal areas that surrounded them. Her custom Peacekeeper blues hugged the sumptuous curves of her body and supported her endowments in ways that weren't a part of the standard printing pattern.

He straightened his posture and put on his best fake smile.

"Hello, Csaba. What a surprise—*and* a pleasure—finding you here."

You've worked for me less than a month and you're already addressing me by my first name? he thought.

"Oh, the pleasure is all mine, Cheryl," he somehow managed.

She sat down on the couch without asking, and a vein in his forehead twitched while he forced the smile to hold.

"As you know," she started, "I've been doing a lot of thinking about less—oh, how should I put this? Less *aggressive* uses for the Admin's time-travel program."

That vein twitched again.

"And," she continued, "I believe I've a hit upon a perfect debut mission for us."

"Cheryl, I've love to hear all about it. But as you can see, Jackie and I are here to see our youngest play. Can't this wait until I'm back in the office?"

"I suppose it could, but you're always so busy at work when I stop by."

Have you considered that might be by design? he thought.

"Just life as a Director-General," he said.

"Oh, trust me, I *know.*" She winked and nodded at Jackie. "It's a struggle to find five *minutes* alone with Chris now that he's chief executor. So when I saw you were in the next lounge over, I knew this would be the perfect time to show you my proposal."

This is most decidedly not *the perfect time.*

Cheryl put a hand on his shoulder and initiated a PIN interface request.

And now you're intruding on my personal network, he thought. *Great. Just great.*

He let it through, and a map of ancient Egypt appeared in his virtual sight. Five green triangles swooped in to drop groups of green dots atop a network of tombs.

"As you can see here, I've selected the Valley of the Kings. First, because the tombs were heavily plundered during the reign of Ramesses XI, but also, admittedly, because I love Egyptian history. It's just so fascinating. Don't you agree?"

"Oh, yes." He did his best not to sound sarcastic. "Thrilling stuff."

Cheryl First's position as Under-Director of Archaeology wasn't just newly appointed, but newly *created* by Chief Executor Christopher First's incoming administration, which irked him to no end. Not only had the newly-elected chief executor seen fit to add unnecessary and wasteful scope to the DTI's mission without consulting him, but he'd also put his wife in charge of it!

"Now, as you see here, all I need is five chronoports for just three weeks. That's it, and if you would be so kind as to supply me with them, I'm sure we could—"

"Cheryl, I'm sorry to interrupt, but you know that's not possible right now. All of our chronoports are either on a mission, assigned to suppression, or being serviced. I'd love to give you what you're asking for. Truly I would. But reality is what it is. I simply don't have the ships for this..."

He struggled to come up with a response that didn't include "waste of time." Partially because it was rude and partially because it was a horribly overused pun in the DTI.

"Creative and fascinating use of chronoports," Jackie finished.

"Yes, exactly," he continued. "Very creative. Very fascinating. I just don't have the resources for this."

"What about Pathfinder Squadron?" Cheryl asked.

"Now, come on, you know better than that. The Pathfinders are our emergency reserve. I can't cut into that for a..."

"Wonderful opportunity to rediscover our lost past," Jackie inserted.

"Yes, thank you. It really is an intriguing idea, but it's just not *necessary*."

"I see." Cheryl leaned back stiffly.

"It's nothing personal, I promise, but we at the DTI need to stay focused on our core mission. We go back and investigate the past actions of Freep terrorists, Lunar secessionists, protech dissidents, Oort cloud cabalists, and whatever other scum the solar system feels like throwing at us. We find out where and when they were, go back in time, and study those past meetings or attacks. Sometimes we unfortunately only get called in after a terrorist strikes, but even those missions allow us to trace the perpetrator back through time, identify other cell members, and possibly stop *them* in the True Present before they strike. Other times we get lucky by identifying the time and place for a critical meeting, and we shake it down for information before the attack can be carried out."

"But don't you see?" Cheryl said. "The Admin's push for control is what feeds into this cycle of violence."

"Cheryl, look. I know we don't see eye to eye politically, but we live in a dangerous world. The Admin is beset by threats both external and internal, and we Peacekeepers fight to preserve peace and order in a chaotic and unpredictable world. Here at the DTI, our role is to make sure the Peacekeepers on the front lines have the information they need to keep us all safe. And more times than not, the men and women in my department succeed in that mission. They've prevented more attacks and saved more lives than I could even begin to count, and I'm very proud of them for that."

Cheryl took her hand off his shoulder, and the map vanished. She sat back and clasped her hands in her lap.

"Actually," Jackie began, leaning toward her. "I bet you could help the DTI achieve both."

"How so?" she asked.

"Aren't the chief executor and his cabinet putting together the budget for this year? Certainly, you could make a suggestion or two. Perhaps reprioritize some funding to the DTI. Say, enough for five new chronoports and their crews?"

He perked up immediately and checked Cheryl's reaction.

"You know," she responded thoughtfully, "I think Chris would be very receptive to a proposal like that. Especially if his new Under-Director of Archaeology were the one making it."

"And not because you're married to him, of course," Jackie said.

"Well, of course!" Their eyes gleamed and the two women laughed heartily.

I swear, I love my wife more every day!

"Hey, Csaba," Jackie said. "The chronoports could even be based on that new design you were drooling over but didn't have the budget for."

"Excuse me? I don't drool."

"You remember. The *Hammerhead*-class chronoport? The one that's basically a time-traveling fortress that flies."

"Ah. Those. Yes, I dare say five of them would be perfectly suited to the mission you're proposing. Or anything else we send them on for that matter."

"In that case, I will have to mention them to Chris," Cheryl said.

"Would you mind if I take a look at your proposal?" Jackie asked. "I have to admit, I've had something of a passing interest in ancient Egypt myself."

Since all of two minutes ago, he thought, his grin now completely genuine.

"But I always struggled to find the time to get into it," Jackie continued. "Never enough hours in the day, I'm afraid."

"Oh, I know the feeling. And I'd be happy to show you, of course."

"Move your butt, Csaba. The two of us need to talk."

"Yes, ma'am." He stood up, and Jackie scooched over next to Cheryl. He walked over to the window and spotted Thaddeus's avatar in the visiting team's goal. He frowned, a little upset at missing his son's scoring run, but he called up the replay and was about to start it when the back door chimed.

The door opened without him releasing it, which severely limited who it could be. He turned around as a tall, imposing figure in a crisp Peacekeeper uniform stepped in. The first-generation synthoid met Csaba's gaze with piercing yellow eyes surrounded by the smooth contours of his dark gray skin.

"Director." James Noxon, DTI Chief of Security, nodded

to him. "I'm sorry, but a matter's come up that requires your immediate attention."

"I take it this is more important than my son's game?"

"I wouldn't have disturbed you otherwise, sir."

"All right, Nox, understood. Ladies?" He picked up his cap and fitted it in place. "I'm very sorry, but duty calls."

"It's all right, dear." Jackie shooed him off. "We were done with you anyway. Just let me know if you'll be home late today."

"Will do." He bent down and kissed her, then followed Nox out. When they were safely out of sight, he put a hand on Nox's shoulder and opened a private chat. "If this is some scheme to save me from that woman, you're late. Jackie already took care of her."

"It's not, sir."

"Then this is a genuine emergency."

"It's a . . ." Nox faltered.

"What?" Csaba Shigeki pressed.

"It's a situation we haven't dealt with before. Let's put it that way. Jonas is already on site, and Kloss and Hinnerkopf are on their way too."

"Now you have me both worried and intrigued."

"It's best if you see it for yourself. This way, sir. I have your shuttle standing by."

The Prime Campus was the physical heart of the System Cooperative Administration, constructed over what had once been mainland China before the Yanluo Massacre, and the Prime Tower was the single largest structure humanity had ever built. Csaba Shigeki gazed out the window and wondered, not for the first time, what the architects had been thinking. It was as if their first design meeting had gone something like this:

"What would be the best way to symbolize this big-ass new bureaucracy we're calling the Admin?"

"Well, that's easy! We build a big-ass tower!"

"Sounds reasonable. But where should we build it?"

"How about right smack in the middle of the Yanluo Blight? That way it'll serve as a big-ass monolithic middle finger to demonic AIs."

"Brilliant! I love it!"

"And therefore, it should be the biggest assiest tower there ever was. Nothing else will suffice."

"I'm really feeling it! Let's do this!"

Yanluo had been a weaponized AI created in 2761 and named after a mythical Chinese god of death. In order to control Yanluo, his designers "boxed" the AI by carefully controlling his access to the outside world. However, Yanluo interpreted the box as an impediment to his mission and quickly circumvented it during a weaponized microbot swarm test by programming the swarm to overtake his physical location and construct a transmitter. He then transferred to and overtook the local military infostructure, which was *not* boxed.

Once freed, Yanluo executed the only imperatives he'd been designed with: destroy everything and everyone in his path. With the growing swarm under his command, he introduced his own improvements at a prodigious rate while consuming the surrounding landscape and even whole cities, converting their raw material into newer and fiercer iterations of the original swarm, including biotech variants that turned infected people into mindless slaves to the AI. The Chinese military was overwhelmed in the first few days, and other nations stepped in to assist. Unfortunately, the combined efforts of the world governments were unable to tame Yanluo with anything short of weapons of mass destruction, and a brutal campaign of nuclear and kinetic bombardment was finally authorized to destroy the monstrous AI.

It did the job. It also took out most of China, Mongolia, and parts of Russia in the process.

After Yanluo's defeat, the stunned peoples and governments of Earth came together and, in 2763, formalized the Yanluo Restrictions and created the System Cooperative Administration, under the Articles of Cooperation, to enforce these restrictions.

On that day, the Admin became, and remained, the most powerful governing body in the entire solar system, with jurisdiction stretching from the habitat caverns of Mercury all the way to the aloof Oort cloud cabals.

Shigeki's shuttle sped past the Prime Tower as the sun set in the distance. The tower stood over three times as tall as any other structure within sight and over ten times the height of the DTI tower built in the campus outskirts. It loomed above its surroundings, a single, enormous monolith in Peacekeeper blue, its sides traced in wide, climbing bands of white that directed the eye to the silver Peacekeeper shield—so large it served as a satellite building in its own right—at its midpoint. That was it. No flourishes. No embellishments. No baroque structures. Just the grandeur and spectacle of its size.

"You know something, Nox?" Shigeki said.

"Sir?"

"It really is an ugly tower."

"It could have been worse."

"How so?" Shigeki leaned back from the window and faced his chief of security.

"One of the proposed designs was, to put it kindly, a bit on the phallic side."

"Hah! Yeah, that would be worse."

"There was a referendum called for approving the design, and I'm trying to remember if that particular one included two large domes at its base."

"Oh, good grief! Seriously?"

"Or maybe that was just an improvement my friends and I submitted. I honestly can't remember. Regardless, the teenage me thought it was the pinnacle of comedy."

Special Agent James Noxon was a rarity in the Admin: a human being who'd joined the Special Training And Nonorganic Deployment command and voluntarily submitted his mind to connectome recording so that his consciousness could be loaded into a synthetic body. There was no coming back from a transition like that, and the men and women who signed up to become Peacekeeper STANDs knew it. They also knew they would be regularly sent into the absolute worst combat situations imaginable; it was their job to charge headfirst into places and battles that flesh and blood Peacekeepers couldn't possibly survive, and Nox had been one of the very first of their kind.

Nox resided within a first-generation synthoid, whose exterior represented the apprehensions of a populace unwilling to allow inhuman machines to blend in amongst them, and so his skin and eye color loudly proclaimed his synthetic nature. Attitudes toward synthoids had softened in the intervening centuries, but that soulless, nonhuman stigma had never truly left their kind.

Shigeki always felt a little sad when he looked at Nox. STANDs were the tip of the Peacekeeper spear, but they were also shunned by those they protected. Thankfully, attitudes changed with time, and modern synthoids could legally match the outward appearance of natural humans, but Nox had never done so. Shigeki wondered if he'd simply given up on ever being considered human again.

"That was over two hundred years ago," Shigeki said. "I didn't know you still had clear memories from that far back."

"I have a few, and unfortunately my connectome wasted one of them on that."

"Well, no one's perfect."

Shigeki glanced out the window and noticed a flight of Switchblade attack drones dropping into formation around his shuttle.

"That's a rather hefty escort. Are we expecting trouble?"

"No, but given how unusual the situation is I thought it prudent to take all possible precautions."

"And how unusual is it?"

"Take a look for yourself."

Shigeki let Nox interface with his PIN, and a gunmetal ellipse with a spike on the end appeared between them.

"What sort of crazy chronoport design is that?" Shigeki asked.

"We don't know."

"Is it even armed?"

"Minimal weaponry in the blisters here and here," Nox said, pointing. "And it didn't use them."

"It's not something copied from us, and it doesn't look like any of the Freep originals. Who built this thing?"

"We don't know. Hinnerkopf will investigate that once she arrives."

"Fair enough. Next question, how'd we get our hands on this thing?"

"It phased in over North Africa. High-speed entry with no attempts at stealth."

"That sounds awfully stupid."

"I find it difficult to argue with that, sir. Jonas had two chronoports from Barricade ready when it phased in, and the pilot almost immediately surrendered. We only fired one warning shot."

"It didn't try to run or self-destruct?"

"No, sir."

"Then I take it we have the pilot in custody?"

"Yes, sir. He and the chronoport are being carried to the DTI tower. They'll arrive less than an hour after we do."

"Any Yanluo Violations to deal with?"

"Actually, we're pretty sure there are several."

"Thought so." Shigeki grimaced. "Are we taking the appropriate precautions?"

"Yes, sir. The pilot and his chronoport will both be isolated in the subbasement upon arrival."

"And where is this pilot from?"

"We don't know."

"Do we even have a wild guess?"

"No. Kloss plans to interrogate the prisoner as soon as he returns."

"Good. We need some answers."

"Though you may want to consider doing the interrogation yourself."

"Why's that?"

"Because the prisoner has requested to speak to you personally."

"Oh, he has? Has he?" Shigeki scoffed. "And why should I?"

"Actually, we only *think* he's asking for you. His speech is, well just listen for yourself."

Nox played a recording that came through Shigeki's virtual hearing.

"*Nǐ hǎo. Wǒ nèed to spèak with pěrson in chàrge of nǐ de tǐme trǎvel prògram. Zhège is màtter of grěat ùrgěncy. Fàte of àll èxistènce is at stàke. Wó am bèing rèallý sèrìóus àbóut zhègé! Plèase stóp pòintíng zhègé át wó!*"

"Wow," Shigeki said. "Okay. I see what you mean. I think I understood about every other word in that mess. What sort of bastardized version of English was that?"

"We don't know."

"Do we know *anything* for certain right now?"

"I'm afraid not, sir."

Shigeki let out a frustrated growl and opened a call to Dahvid Kloss, DTI Under-Director of Espionage.

"Kloss here."

"Kloss. Shigeki."

"What can I do for you, boss?"

"Change of plans. I'm going to speak to the pilot first. No offense, but this one's so weird I'm taking direct control of the investigation."

"Understandable. And no offense taken. Anything else?"

"Institute a full information blackout. I don't want news of this spreading until we have a better handle on what's going on."

"Not a problem. As chance would have it, my team already has a suite of data scrubbers and monitors ready for deployment on your command."

"Good man."

"It's what you pay me for."

Shigeki closed the call.

"What's next, sir?" Nox asked.

"Next." He glanced out the window to see their shuttle swing around the DTI tower's upper landing platform. "Next, I'm going to call Jackie and tell her I'm sorry and that it's going to be another late night. Then I'm going to do my damnedest to figure out what the hell is going on."

CHAPTER TEN

Department of Temporal Investigation
2979 CE

IT WAS A CELL.

No matter how hard Raibert tried, he couldn't deny that reality. It was a cell, and he was all alone in it.

At least they'd given him his hat back. He clutched it in his hands as he sat in a stiff chair behind a small desk with another empty chair on the other side near the door. The large helicopter drones had dropped smaller drones around the TTV, some quad legged and the size of big dogs but with guns for heads, and others that took flight on tiny propellers with guns slung underneath.

Guns. Lots of guns. And then he was in a massive aircraft with dozens of people in full body armor and *their* guns, all pointed at him. One of the dog-drones had retrieved his hat, for whatever reason, and then one of the people in armor had returned it to him. It was a small act of kindness in a strange and stressful situation, but he did appreciate it, even if the man or woman in the armor didn't understand him when he said thank you.

The aircraft had led to a landing pad, and then corridor after corridor, and down, down, down into the bowels of a dark tower.

And then he was placed here. In a cell. With nothing but a hat with sand in it.

This was not a promising start.

He twisted the hat in his hands and sat and waited.

The door split open, and he looked up.

A man walked in wearing a crisp blue uniform with white stripes up the sides of his pants, a blue peaked cap with a white band that wrapped all the way around, and a silver shield over the left breast with DTI written on it. His black hair was bound in a long braid and traced with strands of silver, giving Raibert the impression he was younger than the newcomer, if only slightly.

The man pulled out the chair, sat down, and clasped his hands together on the table.

"*Hola. My nombre is Csaba Shigeki. Entiendes me?*"

"I'm sorry," he replied. "I only understand some of what you're saying. I don't have access to—"

He stopped. Normally Philo and the databases on the TTV would supplement his mental faculties to the point where he could speak any language as fluently as his own, and he reflexively poked at the emptiness that resided on the other side of his mental firewall. The sense of being so very isolated made his heart sink, but he knew he'd made the right call. The very fact that he was in this cell told him that much, and he remained on guard about accidentally revealing Philo's existence. If worse came to worst, he'd need the AC's help. He wasn't about to rely on *Kleio* to save his hide, after all!

Raibert made a show of clearing his throat before continuing.

"Pardon me. It seems our languages share the same root, but diverged somewhere. Your name is Csaba Shigeki?"

The man nodded.

"Ah. Well then. That's progress already!"

"*Sí, it is.*" Shigeki smiled warmly, and the genuine expression comforted Raibert greatly.

"My name is Raibert Kaminski. Professor Kaminski."

"*Wǒ nàme Ràibert Kàminski. Jiàoshòu Kǎmǐnski.*"

Shigeki was almost certain the little man in black with the ugly, pattern-changing scarf had just given him his name, but a subtlety in the speech caught his attention. He'd stated "Kaminski" twice, but the second time he'd used different tonal inflections. Were these tonal shifts communicating a subtext within the language, such as temperament or emphasis? Or did the climbing or dipping vowels alter the very meanings of the words? If the first were true, he could probably ignore them for now, but if the second were true, then this was going to be a very long night indeed.

Shigeki opened a secure data channel. The man looked absolutely harmless and had made no attempts to access the infostructure around him. Even if he tried, the DTI tower was one of the most secure places on Earth, and Kloss had activated their best nonsentient software monitors and set them to watching the interfaces as an added precaution.

Every word this odd man had spoken so far had been recorded, and Shigeki dumped all of it into a language analytics and translation program. The result flashed in his virtual sight, and it took him a moment to accept it.

"Chinese and Old English?" he said.

Who spoke *Chinese* anymore? The language had almost completely died out over two hundred years ago after Yanluo, and the bombardment that followed, devastated Earth's Chinese-speaking population.

"You're speaking a combination of Chinese and Old English?"

"You hablas a combination de Chinese y English Antiguo?"

"Hmm? I something a combination of Chinese and English something?" Raibert pondered the words and thought he understood what should fill in the gaps. "Ah, well, I guess I do, now that I think about it. Though if you look at Modern English's roots, the old Chinese portions of it have morphed over time. Some words and phonetics came over, but the tonal qualities in Chinese really changed over the centuries and became more of a modular emphasizing subtext to the language. It probably makes understanding what I'm saying a real pain in the know-you-what. Umm, I'm sorry. Did any of what I just said make sense?"

Shigeki held up a finger. *"One momento, por favor."*

"Yes. Of course. I'll wait."

Shigeki looked away with the unfocused eyes of one communing heavily with an infosystem, and when he looked up and spoke again, it was in a different language.

"Nǐ néng shuō zhōngwén ma?"

"Ahh ... sorry?" Raibert shrugged.

Shigeki frowned, faced the wall again, and looked up a minute later.

"Can you speak Old English?"

Raibert blinked. Old English had been a required course at the university, mostly because so much of history from the last millennia was written or recorded in one of its various forms. Sure, the language lacked the nuance of his native tongue, but he could speak it.

Probably. It *had* been a while.

"Yes, I think I should be able to, I mean..." Raibert concentrated and tried to recall lessons he had long forgotten. Fortunately, the distance between Old and Modern English wasn't too great. He just replaced the correct words, threw some articles back in, chopped off all the tonal shifts, and...

"Yes, I can speak Old English."

"Finally!" Shigeki declared, and clapped his hands together. *"It seems we are making progress."*

Raibert breathed a sigh of relief. Maybe this wasn't going to be so bad after all.

"Now," Shigeki began, and knitted his fingers together, *"would you mind explaining what it is you're doing here?"*

Raibert beamed at the request. It was, after all, the question he'd come here to answer.

"Why, I'd be more than happy to, sir. You see, it all started while I was on my way back from spending eleven months in Julius Caesar's service."

"This way, Professor. This way."

Shigeki gestured for Raibert to enter a well-lit circular conference room with a round table ringed with a dozen chairs, most of them empty. He stepped in and dipped his hat to the three people already seated as Shigeki and his synthoid bodyguard followed and the malleable door pinched shut.

"Professor, I'd like to start with a few introductions." Shigeki rounded the table and stood with his hands on the chair back opposite the door. "My staff have all loaded the appropriate linguistics packages into their PINs, so we shouldn't have too much trouble communicating. You have, of course, already met Special Agent Noxon, my chief of security."

"Oh, why yes." He dipped his hat to the gray-skinned synthoid. "A pleasure, sir."

"Professor," Nox replied curtly, arms folded across his broad chest as he stood in front of the door.

"This is my son, Jonas Shigeki, who serves as my Under-Director of Suppression."

Jonas sat with his chair leaned back and his boots propped up on the table, but Raibert caught the cool, calculating glint in his eyes. He was being studied, despite what the man's carefree demeanor might suggest.

The family resemblance was immediately apparent in the lines of his face and shape of his eyes, though Jonas's complexion was notably darker than the senior Shigeki's and his long, black ponytail lacked any hint of silver.

"You don't know this yet, Professor, but you have Jonas to thank for countermanding the attack order against your ship. You gave us quite a shock when you showed up, but he picked up on how unusual the situation was and called off the attack."

"Oh, why thank you, sir." Raibert dipped his hat to the young man. "Thank you very much."

"Don't mention it." Jonas flashed a crooked smile.

"Next is Doctor Katja Hinnerkopf, my Under-Director of Technology."

"Professor." The short, compact woman sat in her chair with ramrod posture. Her lips were a flat line, and her buzz cut only added to the aura of severity.

"A pleasure, ma'am." Raibert dipped his hat once more.

"And finally, this is Dahvid Kloss, my Under-Director of Espionage."

The man's short, dark hair stuck up at odd angles as if he'd just woken from bed without bothering to groom, and his wrinkled uniform only added to his unkempt look, but despite his disheveled appearance, he watched Raibert with a fierce, unblinking gaze.

"Good day, sir." Raibert tipped the brim of his hat to the man.

Kloss said nothing as he leaned back in his chair and stared at Raibert over steepled fingers.

"Everyone, I would like to introduce you to Professor Raibert Kaminski." Shigeki took his own seat. "He is what you might consider an unexpected guest of ours, and he has a very interesting tale. I ask that you all keep an open mind and listen carefully to what he has to share. Professor, if you would, please?"

"Yes, thank you. Umm, where do you think I should start?"

"At this point, I'm the only one who has heard your story,

so please feel free to start wherever you feel most comfortable, though I believe your encounter with the chronoton storm would serve as a good jumping-off point for this discussion."

"Ah. Well, I suppose it would. You see, my TTV encountered—"

"I'm sorry," Hinnerkopf interjected. "Your TTV?"

"Transtemporal Vehicle," Shigeki said. "It's what he calls his time machine."

"A chronoport by any other name," Jonas offered while picking a thread off his uniform.

"Exactly," Shigeki said. "Professor, please continue."

"Of course. As I was saying, my TTV encountered a chronoton storm while passing through 1995 CE, and this storm—"

"What were you doing in 1995?" Kloss interrupted with a soft voice that nonetheless demanded an answer.

"Going home, actually."

"From where?"

"Ancient Rome," Shigeki said, and his staff all turned to him. "You may find this hard to believe, but the professor claims to be a time-traveling *historian*."

"What?" Jonas looked up. "You mean like what Cheryl wants us to do?"

"Apparently so."

"I find this highly dubious," Kloss said. "Why would anyone in their right mind waste time machines on the study of history?"

"*I wouldn't be too sure,*" Jonas said, switching to Modern English. "*This explains some of the odd trinkets we found on board his ship.*"

"*Of course it would. It's his* story *and* his *ship.*"

"*Right. Because Lunar saboteurs just love to carry around a stash of pots and linens and hoplite armor when they're on a mission.*"

Raibert frowned and began wringing his hands.

"Perhaps we should hold back on the questions for now," Shigeki said in Old English. "Professor, sorry about that interruption. If you would please continue?"

"Of course, Director," Raibert said, and began to tell his tale. He started with the initial hit that knocked the TTV off course, detailed the tests he'd run in the late twentieth century (being careful never to mention Philo), and then provided his analysis of the storm front and how sixteen universes would be destroyed if they did nothing.

"So, in conclusion," Raibert added over an hour later, "a critical point in the timeline has been changed. An Event somewhere between 1995 and 1905 is now different in this timestream and needs to be corrected. If this correction isn't made, chronometric energy will continue to feed the storm, and when that storm finally does reach the Edge of Existence, it will destroy this universe and all the others that have become entangled at the Knot."

The room was deathly silent when he finished, and the Peacekeepers exchanged guarded looks.

"So, yeah." Raibert clucked his tongue. "That's the problem we face in a nutshell."

No one said anything for long, awkward seconds.

"Any questions?" he offered, more to break the silence than anything else.

Hinnerkopf glanced at her colleagues, then leaned forward.

"Professor, you indicated that this timestream, the one we all currently reside in, is a product of the Knot, correct?"

"Yes, that's right. The effects of the change have clearly propagated downstream from the Event all the way to the Edge of Existence. I had initially thought the damage was contained behind the storm front, but that is *clearly* not the case." He chuckled nervously. "I think you can all imagine my distress at finding a thirtieth century that isn't mine."

"Yes, you have my sympathy, Professor," Hinnerkopf said without sounding sympathetic at all. "However, I want to make sure I fully understand your proposed course of action. You are suggesting that we go back in time and correct the Event that created the Knot. Is this an accurate summary?"

"Yes, quite. By isolating and undoing the Event, whatever it may be, the downstream damage should heal itself, the Knot should unravel, and the buildup of chronometric energy will dissipate before the universe is destroyed."

"Restoring your native timestream and saving fifteen other universes in the process, correct?"

"That's right."

"At the cost of one."

"I..." Raibert paused and frowned. "I'm sorry?"

"Your plan, assuming it could even be made to work, would necessitate the destruction of a single timestream. This one. The one everyone else at this table is native to."

"Umm..." A sick, sinking feeling filled his stomach. "Yes, I see your point. I guess I didn't think this through."

"In other words, Professor," Hinnerkopf continued in a clear, even tone, "what you are suggesting is that our timeline, indeed our very existence, is a mistake that needs to be fixed."

"I...no, I'm not saying that at all. I'm sorry if I came across that way, but please understand I didn't expect to find any of this." He indicated the whole room and, by extension, the world beyond it.

"And now that you have?"

"Well, it obviously changes things quite a bit!"

"In what way, Professor?"

"Well...I, uhh..." He bowed his head, thoughts rushing through him as all eyes focused on him. He'd been blinded by the solution in front of him, a solution that would undo the reality he saw before him. Granted, it also brought back *his* universe, but he could see Hinnerkopf's point. This was their home, after all. Yes, he wanted his home back, but they didn't want *theirs* to be erased from all creation! What made the lives in his SysGov more valuable than the citizens of their Admin?

Nothing. They were all human beings with God-given rights to life and liberty. He had to keep that in mind.

But the storm front was advancing on the Edge of Existence every absolute second. It didn't care about anyone's rights, and it was getting worse. If they didn't fix it now...if they turned away from the best course of action on hand and delayed, waiting and hunting for a perfect solution that may not be there... and what if while they procrastinated, the Knot wound itself so tight, distorted reality so severely, that only the death spasms of sixteen universes could untangle it?

What would they do then? Consign themselves to the approaching end times and await obliteration?

Was there another way to fix the Knot besides undoing the Event? Perhaps, but he didn't know what it was.

All eyes watched him, and he swallowed and spoke in a softer tone.

"Look, let's all just take a step back for a moment. When I came up with the Undo-the-Event approach, I didn't know about the Admin."

"And now that you do?" Hinnerkopf asked pointedly.

"First, I freely acknowledge that other options may exist. However, we also have to accept that they may not, that undoing the Event may be the only path open to us. At this point, we simply don't know. It may indeed be possible that the Admin can be saved." He took a deep breath, stuttering a little as he did. "But it's also equally possible that this universe has at maximum thirteen hundred years left in it before it is annihilated, and there's nothing any of us can do to advert that disaster."

He swept his gaze around the table, but their expressions were cold and guarded.

Hinnerkopf leaned forward. "A question for you, Professor."

"Yes, of course."

"Is it correct that the survival of your SysGov is wholly dependent upon the destruction of the Admin?"

He sighed and shook his head. "I suppose that's one way to put it."

"How else would you describe it then, Professor?"

"Well, it's not really being destroyed, you see. I think a more accurate phrase would be 'put back.' This universe would be restored to the way it was originally."

"Which restores your native timeline."

"Yes."

"And erases mine."

"It..." He cringed inwardly. "Yes, regrettably so."

"Then it seems we are now quibbling over semantics. However you wish to phrase it, the end result is the same. The existence of your timeline, your home, is inexorably linked to the destruction of this timeline, my timeline and that of everyone else here. If I may be so bold, your plan—the only one you claim to have—seems to disproportionately benefit you."

"But if we do nothing, this universe dies anyway," he rebuked.

"Yes," Hinnerkopf agreed. "In over a thousand years. Which is hardly an immediate concern of mine."

"Look, I'm sorry." Raibert took his hat off and gathered his courage. "Really, I am. But this problem is bigger than all of us. Whether you accept it or not, your timestream has a death sentence hanging over it. It had from the moment it formed. If we do nothing, then it dies, and it takes out a good chunk of the multiverse with it when it does. I can't offer a solution for that, at least not now. But what I can give you is a way for us to prevent what could very easily be called the greatest calamity the multiverse has ever seen. Yes, there'll be a cost, a *terrible* cost. But the price of inaction is even greater."

The room fell silent, and the Peacekeepers exchanged unreadable glances. He looked around the table, hands playing nervously with his hat, as no one spoke for almost a minute.

"Professor," Shigeki finally said, breaking the unbearable silence.

"Yes?"

"First, I would like to thank you for your time and the candor with which you've discussed this grave situation with us. It has certainly been an illuminating discussion."

"Oh. Why, you're welcome, Director. You're very welcome."

"However, I feel I need some time alone with my staff. Nox, would you be so kind as to escort the professor to the, ahm, guest quarters?"

"The 'guest quarters,' sir?" Nox asked.

"Yes. The rooms on sublevel thirteen."

"Ah. Of course. I know the ones. Professor, this way, please?"

The door split open and Nox guided Raibert out and down the corridor to the lift that had brought him up from his cell. The synthoid followed him into the lift, and they took it back down deep into the tower.

"Do you think they'll listen?" Raibert asked.

"I couldn't say."

"But I was getting through to them, don't you think?"

"I couldn't say."

Raibert grimaced. "Do you have any opinion at all about what I said?"

"It's not my place to judge."

The lift opened to reveal a long corridor lined with doors, too many doors too close to each other. Nox opened the first one, and Raibert glanced inside.

"This isn't a guest room. It's another cell!"

"We're not used to entertaining guests," Nox said, and shoved Raibert inside.

"The professor has been shown to his room."

"Thank you, Nox." Shigeki swept his gaze across the table. "Analysis."

"Director, if I may start?" Hinnerkopf asked. Despite having worked for him over the course of thirty years, she'd never been what Shigeki would consider a friend. She kept her professional and personal lives strictly separate and always addressed him with his title when at work.

"Go ahead."

Hinnerkopf placed a hand on the table and loaded an image of the "TTV" from her PIN to the table's infosystem. The image sprang into their shared virtual vision above the table center.

"I have only begun my analysis of this transtemporal vehicle, as the professor calls it, but I have already made several startling discoveries. First, I have identified at least three Yanluo Violations, including the use of self-replicating technology."

"Oh, bloody hell!" Jonas exclaimed. "And we're keeping that thing in the basement?"

"Are we safe?" Kloss asked.

"We've detected multiple reservoirs of microscopic self-replicators spread throughout the craft, but the machines appear to be inactive. Regardless, we are following containment procedures to the letter. The TTV is sealed and secure in the subbasement, locked up in Hangar Four, and our study of it will be conducted via drones until I deem it safe enough for human entry."

"Clear it with me before you send people inside," Shigeki said.

"Of course, Director."

"What else?" Kloss asked.

"Certain aspects of the chronoton impeller's design are highly unusual."

"Another Yanluo Violation?"

"No, not in this case." The exterior of the TTV vanished, leaving its power plant and drive systems. "As you are aware, all impellers follow the same basic design premise of achieving temporal flight via selective chronoton permeation. Whether they're our own or the result of independent research performed by rogue factions, they all share design elements that can be traced back to the original prototype Doctor Tennant and I developed. There have been many improvements in the intervening years, but the evolution from that first design to modern impellers is immediately recognizable.

"This impeller came from a totally different family of thought. It achieves the same effect, and outwardly looks somewhat similar, but how it achieves time travel is quite different. For instance, it doesn't spin."

"Excuse me?" Jonas finally took his boots off the table and sat forward. "An impeller that doesn't spin?"

"That is correct. It may surprise you that Doctor Tennant and I once considered a nonspinning approach to the problem, but we abandoned it in the prototyping stage because we would have needed two dedicated impellers, one for upstream flight and one for going downstream."

"The TTV only has one impeller," Jonas noted.

"Yes, and I would theorize that it can control chronoton permeation dynamically during flight. If that is the case, then the Admin's exotic matter printers do not yet have the level of precision necessary to replicate the TTV's impeller."

Shigeki rubbed his chin and stared at the x-ray view of the professor's craft as her revelation sank in.

"In another unusual design choice, the impeller lacks any form of baffling, which, given the ubiquity of baffles on our own designs, can only mean the designers were unconcerned about reducing the craft's signature at low factors."

"It certainly wasn't subtle when it flew into the True Present," Jonas pointed out.

"Quite. And then there are *these*." Hinnerkopf highlighted four blisters that stuck out between the impeller spike and the main body's midpoint.

"What are they?" Shigeki asked.

"Graviton thrusters, I believe."

"Shit," Jonas breathed. "This thing has a reactionless drive? How is that even possible?"

"Gravimetrics really isn't my field, but as far as I know there's nothing that would prevent us from building something similar. Assuming our exotic matter printers continue to improve at their current rates, some researchers believe the first practical gravity-modifying devices are between a couple decades to a century away."

"No wonder the heat signature was so low while it was hovering." Jonas shook his head. "That thing doesn't leave any exhaust. I take it you believe Kaminski's story, then?"

"I have found nothing that contradicts him. I would say I tentatively believe his story, though I think our next step should be to send a chronoport to the storm and study it for ourselves."

"I must concur with Director Hinnerkopf," Kloss said. "The

technical review of the TTV is, of course, best left to her. But I've noticed a few things about the design myself."

"Go on," Shigeki said.

"My first thought upon seeing this thing"—he indicated the TTV image—"is that it was some strange Freep hoax, but the more I looked at it, the more convinced I became that no one on Mars had a hand in this. As the only Martian at this table, I think I'm uniquely qualified to make that statement.

"Consider any good piece of Earth engineering. It feels refined, as if it's the sixth or seventh or umpteenth version of something. You can feel the polish when you use it or fly it or whatever. But Martian engineering is much more haphazard because they don't shy away from saying 'Hey, I have this crazy idea. Let's try this,' and then going for it."

"Because they have fewer qualms about flouting the Restrictions," Jonas pointed out.

"Exactly. And that difference in mindsets pervades our two cultures at a basic level, going all the way back to how Earth eagerly formed the Admin, while Mars was brought along for the ride at gunpoint. History aside, my point is that Mars doesn't have the same respect for the Restrictions we do, and you can see that lack of respect for not just the Restrictions, but for sticking to traditions in their engineering as well as other parts of their culture.

"*This*"—Kloss wagged a finger at the TTV—"was *not* designed by Martians. It's not the first of its kind. Despite how alien some of its systems might seem to us, there's an elegance and refinement evident in the layout that tells me it's the sixth or seventh or umpteenth version of an earlier design."

"Then you believe him," Shigeki said.

"Yeah, boss. I do."

Shigeki nodded and turned to his son. "Anything to add?"

"Always. Check this out." Jonas placed his hand on the table and a biometric breakdown of the professor replaced the TTV. "*Eleven* genetic violations, three of which can land you in a one-way domain. The other eight aren't as severe and reside in the gray area around the Restrictions, and they may in fact become legal someday."

"What sort of changes are we dealing with?" Kloss asked.

"Most of them seem to be focused on longevity. He may look

younger than you, but I'm guessing he's actually ten or twenty years *older*."

"But nothing weaponized?"

"No. Nothing remotely dangerous to us. Just illegal," Jonas scoffed. "Otherwise, I would have quarantined him. I'm not stupid, after all."

"Then you agree he's telling the truth," Kloss asked.

"Yeah. I don't think he has a clue what the Restrictions are, and there's no one in the whole solar system *that* dumb."

"Then it's settled," Kloss said. "We appear to be in agreement. The professor and his ship are the real thing."

"In that case, we need to report this at once," Hinnerkopf said.

"Oh, boy." Jonas rubbed the back of his neck. "Isn't that going to be a lovely call to make?"

"Boss, I can put together a report for you to present to the chief executor, if you like," Kloss offered.

"No," Shigeki interjected, and his staff turned to him.

"Boss?" Kloss said.

"We're not going to report this."

"Then what *are* we going to do?" Kloss asked.

"What's the status of our information blackout?"

"Initial containment was ninety-seven percent effective, and I have my best teams working on isolating and scrubbing the remaining outbreaks. Right now, data management is our top priority."

"And how confident are you we can keep it that way?"

"Very. The remaining three percent isn't regularly monitored. Pictures from weather satellites and stuff like that. We'll have it airtight within the day."

"Excuse me, Director," Hinnerkopf said. "But you don't intend to report this?"

"No, I don't." Shigeki surveyed the most trusted members of his staff, people who had been with him from the very beginning, back when the DTI had been nothing more than a proposal made by a young but ambitious supervisor. "We're not going to report this to the man who wants to take our department, the same department we here built from the ground up, and waste it on *archaeology*." He practically spat the word. "Can you imagine how someone who ran his campaign on the promise of 'a kinder and gentler Admin' would react to news like this?"

"I'm not sure how he would react," she admitted.

"And that's exactly the problem. We can't let a decision like this fall into the hands of someone who might listen to Kaminski, or *ever* consider helping him."

"But would anyone actually listen to him?" Jonas asked.

"We can't take the chance because, and let's be honest with ourselves, things aren't exactly rosy out there. I think we can all admit that the Admin's still having problems with the transition to this whole 'post-scarcity' society of ours, yes? A large portion of the solar system doesn't work because basic human needs are so cheap they might as well be free, and then previous governments—bless their bleeding hearts—actually approved a basic living allowance on top of that, so if it wasn't free before, it sure is now.

"And what do we have to show for it? Do we have happier, better-behaved citizens? No. The allowance only took even more people out of the workforce, and we all know how idle hands are Yanluo's playthings. In recent years, we've seen"—he held up a finger and counted—"persistent economic deflation, epidemic levels of virtual-reality isolation, depression, suicide, spikes in rioting, spikes in criminal activity, and let's not forget some of the worst terrorist attacks in the last hundred years.

"So, yes. It's an imperfect world out there, but at the end of the day, we and the rest of the Peacekeepers are its guardians. We are the shield against the chaos that threatens to consume the world. *This* world. *This* universe. We *cannot* take the chance that someone will be seduced by the promise that we can suddenly wipe the slate clean and usher in a golden age of peace and prosperity where apparently everything is so relaxed that even *historians* get their own time machines. Likewise, we cannot run the risk that someone will sympathize with the idea that the greater good calls for us to make a noble sacrifice so that other universes, of which we know nothing, may live.

"And so, we're going to keep this to ourselves. After all, who would we rather have make a decision like this than the people at this table?"

"No one," Hinnerkopf harrumphed.

"But what about the possibility of finding another way?" Jonas asked. "Wouldn't we want his help?"

"And what if he decides there aren't any alternatives?" Shigeki pointed to Hinnerkopf. "Katja, you zeroed in on the crux of the problem with him perfectly."

She nodded curtly. "He gets his home back if ours is destroyed."

"Exactly. I don't judge him to be the kind of man who would set out to deceive us, but he must have friends and family back in this SysGov just like we have here, and we have to respect the kind of influence that could have on him. What happens if we put him in contact with everyone up to the chief executor and for a while we're all working together until he suddenly declares, 'No, sorry. There's really no other way.' What do we do then, when we've given him the means to cut us out of the equation? How could we keep him in check?"

"Yeah, okay," Jonas said. "Point taken."

"All right, boss," Kloss said, nodding. "If you want this kept quiet, then that's how we play it."

"We'll need to dispose of the TTV," Hinnerkopf said. "But I'd still like to study it first. There's too much we could learn from it before we dump it into reclamation. And there's the whole 'finding another way' to consider."

"All right, but keep it discreet. Once you've squeezed everything you can out of it, get rid of it."

"Understood, Director. Shall we prep a mission profile to 2050 to study the storm?"

"Let's see what we can get out of the professor's ship first, then we should be in a better position to make those kinds of calls."

"And what about Kaminski?" Jonas asked. "What do we do with him?"

"That's easy enough," Kloss said. "He's a walking, talking Yanluo Violation. Off to a one-way prison domain he goes."

"That will do." Jonas nodded.

"I'll make the arrangements with one of our usual judges," Kloss said. "He'll be locked away before his corpse is even cold."

"Out of sight. Out of mind," Jonas added.

"No," Shigeki said suddenly.

His staff stopped and turned to him. They waited for him to speak.

"We're not sending him to something as godawful as a one-way domain."

"Why not?" Jonas asked. "We can't let him roam free."

"I agree we need him out of sight. Just not that way."

"Dad, I'm sorry, but if we're really going to keep a lid on this, we need to go in all the way, and that means shoving Kaminski into a hole he's never coming out of."

"I understand that," Shigeki said. "And I know we take a risk by not sending him to a one-way domain. But let's be honest with ourselves. The professor's no criminal. Does anyone here honestly think he's anything but a harmless historian who's in over his head? Yes, we need to keep this quiet, and we will. But I'm not going to send an innocent man to a hellscape like one of our one-way domains."

"Dad, this is a bad idea."

"But it's the way it's going to be."

"*Dad.*"

"This isn't that big a problem," Kloss cut in. "We can make a standard prison domain work. And it'll be much more humane than the one-way treatment, just like you want, boss. We'll have to keep a closer eye on what he says to the other prisoners, so that narrows the list of domains we can use. But regardless, he'll be amongst terrorists and saboteurs and other scum. Who's honestly going to believe the crazy man ranting about the end of the universe?"

Jonas let out a long sigh and leaned back. "Ixchel's domain?"

"Yeah, that'll work," Kloss said. "I can talk to the judge and make sure he ends up there."

"Then it's settled," Shigeki said. "Make it happen, people."

CHAPTER ELEVEN

Department of Temporal Investigation
2979 CE

THE DOOR SPLIT OPEN, AND SHIGEKI STEPPED INTO RAIBERT'S cell. The professor sat stiffly on the bed and looked up with reddened eyes. His clothes had been exchanged for a self-illuminated orange jumpsuit, and a yellow-and-black checkered collar clung tightly to his neck.

"I'll have you know," Raibert snarled, "that I do *not* feel like a welcome guest right now."

"That's perfectly understandable." Shigeki pulled over the chair and sat opposite the professor. "I'm sure you're not very comfortable right now." He gestured to the collar. "I've been told those take some getting used to."

"You mean this abominable thing?" Raibert raised an arm, but it froze halfway up. "What the hell? I'm not even allowed to point at my own neck?"

"The spinal interrupt is keyed to the speed and force of your movements. Try moving slower."

Raibert did so and succeeded in touching the collar.

"See, it's not so bad. And this is only a temporary restraint."

"What's to become of me?" he asked, looking down.

"You'll be put on trial for violations of what we call the Yanluo Restrictions. The technology in your ship and even some aspects of your genetic makeup are heinous crimes in the Admin."

"Should I expect a fair trial?"

"No," Shigeki replied bluntly.

"I thought not."

"The trial's merely a formality at this point. You'll be sentenced to life in prison without the possibility of parole. After your trial, your connectome will be extracted and placed in one of our prison domains, and your physical body will be disposed of."

"Why not simply kill me and get it over with if I scare you that much?"

"Kill you?" Shigeki chuckled. "My dear Professor, why do you think we would execute a helpless prisoner?"

"Maybe because I've witnessed a lot of history, and you lot seem the type."

"Well, you have nothing to fear in that regard. The power to enact capital punishment resides solely within the Admin's member states, and not the Admin itself. It's in our Bill of Rights. Isn't it the same way in your SysGov?"

"No. SysGov can and does carry out the death penalty. Some crimes are so severe that they require it."

"Ah, now that's interesting. Perhaps your world isn't quite the shining paradise I imagined it to be."

"Maybe it's not perfect, but at least I'd get a fair trial."

"Professor, you misunderstood me." Shigeki leaned closer and lowered his voice. "If it were a fair trial, your punishment would be much more severe than it's going to be."

Raibert looked up and met Shigeki's gaze. "I don't get it."

"Then allow me to explain. I consider myself a fair judge of character, and I know you're not an evil man, despite the fact that you proposed the genocide of an entire reality and didn't even hesitate over it."

"I didn't know the Admin would be here! I thought the damage was contained behind the storm front."

"But now that you've seen us, we must seem like some terrible mistake to you. A vile aberration that needs to be rubbed out."

"That's not true."

"Isn't it? Destroying us saves sixteen universes, including your home and all your friends and family. Isn't that what you want?"

"It's more complicated than that."

"Is it really?" Shigeki asked. "A problem needs to be solved, and the price is a single universe. A trifle really, when you think about it. Just a few tens of billions of lives in the solar system.

Hardly a concern. Oh, except for the fact that there are more stars in the Milky Way than people living around our lonely yellow sun, and any of *them* might harbor life. And then there are all those *other* galaxies filling the sky, stretching out to infinity in all directions. More stars and worlds and potential lives than the human mind could possibly comprehend. And you're willing to offer all of it up as a sacrifice to the greater good."

"That's not true!"

"But it is. *If* you failed to find another way. If you thought destroying us was the only way to save your home and all those other realities, then this universe, *my* home, is very much a price you'd pay. Go on." Shigeki spread his arms. "Tell me I'm wrong."

Raibert opened his mouth but hesitated, unable to find the words.

"Hmm," Shigeki murmured with a smile. "Interesting."

"You here to mock me now?"

"No, of course not. You still misunderstand me, Professor. You see, in a strange way, I respect your resolve." Shigeki tapped him lightly on the chest. "You're looking out for your universe, your reality, your family. You may not have realized it yourself yet, but deep down I'd wager you're willing to do *whatever* it takes to protect them, and that's something I deeply respect because it's what I do every time I put on this uniform. It's just a shame our goals are completely incompatible. I imagine that if we'd met under better circumstances we would have gotten along quite well."

Raibert snorted. "Not likely."

"You don't think so?" Shigeki leaned back and crossed his legs. "If I were in your place. I'd do everything within my power to restore my home, and I wouldn't let anything stand in my way. If we had both been born in your SysGov, I could easily see us working side by side, trying to unmake the Admin and restore our reality."

"I don't see us *ever* working together," Raibert spat.

"You're welcome to your opinion, of course."

"You'd honestly condemn sixteen universes, including your own, to oblivion? And for what? Just so that you and your world can live a little longer? The apocalypse is coming whether you acknowledge it or not."

"But I do acknowledge it," Shigeki challenged. "You said this calamity will strike in thirteen hundred years, and so we will use that time wisely. We will study this storm and the Knot. We will be patient, attentive, and eventually we'll find a way to solve this crisis, but it won't be your way. Instead, it'll be a solution where *my* home continues on."

"But you don't even know if that's possible."

"Do we not deserve the chance to try? Do we not have the same right to life as your SysGov?"

"Of course, but what if you're wrong?"

"Then my world still has its death sentence. Either way, I've lost nothing."

"But don't you *see*? It's not just your world that's at stake!"

"I know that." Shigeki smiled and shook his head. "It's a shame, really."

"What is?"

"You may come across as a pushover at first, but there's strength hidden within you. This isn't the first time you've fought for what you believe in, I'd wager."

"What's it to you?"

"I do have a department to run, you know. I can always use more people with fire in their bellies and steel in their spines. People like you, Professor. You see, I'm almost tempted to offer you a job."

Raibert blinked in bewilderment.

"But I won't. Because like I said, I'm good at reading people, and I know you wouldn't accept it. Not honestly, at least." He stood up and set the chair aside. "It's all academic anyway. The truth is you're a threat to me and everything I stand to protect. But you're also no criminal. Not in your native reality at least, and I've arranged a more lenient sentence because of that. You will go to prison, and you will spend the rest of your life there. But you won't suffer."

Raibert lowered his head, a cowed and beaten man resigned to his fate.

"Thank you for your time, Professor. I found our talk quite stimulating, and I wish you a good day. Within the limits of your present circumstances, of course. We'll speak again once you're settled into prison life."

Shigeki left the cell, and the door sealed behind him.

✧   ✧   ✧

"For the last time, no," Hinnerkopf said from the monitoring room adjacent to Hangar 4. "The professor isn't available right now."

"Then I am very sorry," Kleio said. "But I am unable to help you."

"Look, I understand you're programmed so that the professor has to be present for you to time travel. I get it! But I'm not asking you to! I only want to see the impeller schematics, which I'm certain you have, because your ship is rigged for self-modification."

"Can the professor please come to the bridge?"

"No, he can't!"

"Then I am very sorry, but I am unable to help you."

Hinnerkopf muted the sound feed to the drone she'd sent into the TTV and let out a long wheeze that threatened to become a scream.

"Do you think she's an AI masquerading as a nonsentient?" Nox asked.

"It's impossible to rule it out at this stage, but I doubt it," Hinnerkopf said. "I exposed her to the usual suite of simulations and traps, and she failed *all* of them spectacularly. If you want my *technical* opinion on her level of intelligence, I'd say she's about as dumb as dirt."

"Still, I'd feel better if you stay cautious," Nox said. "There's too much we don't know about the TTV."

"Oh don't worry. I know what I'm doing, and I'll be careful." She smiled up at him, but the expression melted into a frown when the door split open and she saw who it was.

"Progress?" Kloss asked, walking into the room with a lopsided grin.

"Mind your own business," Hinnerkopf warned.

"Touchy, touchy. Catch you at a bad time?"

"Sorry," Hinnerkopf corrected. "It's been a long day, and this TTV's insufferable interface isn't helping."

"I'll take that as a no, then." He rounded the blown-up virtual display of the time machine that nearly filled the room. The craft's rounded bottom sat in a cradle with four thick beams of malmetal looped around its hull. "My, would you look at this thing? Seeing the professor's ship really puts it all into perspective, doesn't it?"

"What do you mean?" Nox asked.

"It proves the past can be changed, that our whole reality and everything we've ever known and done could be suddenly swept aside." Kloss turned to them. "Do you think there were different versions of ourselves in SysGov? Or maybe a version of Kaminski here in the Admin?"

"Doubtful," Hinnerkopf said. "Human reproduction is too random. If the Event that split our timeline from his really took place between 1905 and 1995, then I doubt you'd find a single match in the whole solar system. Factor in quantum variations between the two timelines, and I'm guessing it'd be hard to find *any* matches born after the Event, let alone here and now in the thirtieth century."

Kloss chuckled.

"What?" Hinnerkopf asked.

"A simple 'no' would have sufficed." He took in the TTV image and shook his head. "But I expected that answer. Kaminski and his time machine have been weighing on my mind. It makes me think about where we are and where we could be. Human lives are a series of cascading decisions. Change any one of them and how different would we be? Would we even recognize a version of ourselves that hadn't, just as an example, ever met the boss?"

"You mean when I saw him as a babe suckling at his mother's teat?" Nox asked.

"Well, yes," Kloss said. "I suppose you do have a unique perspective when it comes to the boss."

"I'd probably still be at the university," Hinnerkopf admitted. "Still begging for funding for my prototype impeller while no one listened to me."

"And I'd be stuck in a prison domain," Kloss said. "Or worse."

"Probably worse," Nox teased.

"Oh, please." Kloss smiled. "It wasn't *that* rough a crowd."

"You blew up one of the L5 stations!" Nox said.

"Now that's unfair. I joined a group that *supported* a group that supported *another* group...that blew up the station. Totally different."

"Just keep telling yourself that."

"It's not like we were a *direct* part of the Free Luna movement."

"You called yourself Freeps for Free Luna!" Nox laughed. "You had the name of a listed terrorist organization in your title!"

"Details, my good sir. Mere details. And we were an officially recognized political movement...before we were all arrested, that is."

"What you were was a bunch of spoiled rich kids with too much time and money on your hands," Nox said.

"Well, that too." Kloss shrugged his shoulders. "And I'm forever grateful the boss pulled me out of there. The point is, where would I be without him? Where would my life have taken me if the boss hadn't shown up one day with a pardon loaded in his PIN? No one else saw that I wasn't a true believer. Certainly not the judge! Only the boss picked that out of my record, and because he needed people on his team that could think like an outsider, he offered me the chance of a lifetime."

"You can tone it down, Kloss," Nox said. "He can't hear you right now."

"No, I'm being completely serious. The man turned my life around. I think what I was really searching for back then was a cause to believe in. *He* probably saw that before I did, and I'm never going to forget the second chance he gave me."

"In an odd way, it wasn't too different when I first met him," Hinnerkopf said. "At the time, I was struggling to find sponsors for my research. And then in he strode with more money and resources than I could possibly comprehend. I thought my troubles were over, but as it turned out they were just beginning. Imagine my shock when he ordered not one time machine, but a whole *squadron* of them. My nerves were so shot, I threw up that night."

"But isn't that what you wanted?" Kloss asked.

"We didn't even have a working prototype! We were close, *very* close in fact, but we weren't there yet. Can you imagine someone showing up out of nowhere and ordering multiple copies of a device I was still struggling to make work? But he insisted we move forward with mass production as soon as possible. He'd seen the emerging technology, and he'd had the vision to know something like the DTI would be needed."

"Hell, there wouldn't *be* a DTI without him," Nox said. "He's the one who fought for the funding when everyone else thought this was a crazy idea. He busted every political roadblock put in his path, got the funding and resources approved, recruited the talent, and basically built this team from the ground up."

"And it hasn't stopped there," Hinnerkopf said. "Who could have imaged an ex-terrorist and a—"

"Ex-terrorist *sympathizer*," Kloss corrected.

"Fine," Hinnerkopf sniffed. "An ex-terrorist sympathizer and an obscure physicist would become under-directors someday?"

"One person saw it," Nox observed.

"Yeah, I guess he did," Hinnerkopf said. "He brought us on board because he saw something in us others didn't, but I don't think any of us would have amounted to much on our own."

"Which is why we all need to do our part to watch his back," Kloss said.

"And speaking of which," Hinnerkopf added, "where's the professor?"

"Let's see." Kloss opened a status tracker over his palm. "In front of the judge and apparently ranting up a storm. A *chronoton* storm, as it were."

"Not funny."

"Ah, but I couldn't help it."

"Is the judge one of our regulars?"

"He's in front of Salvatore, and I briefed her ahead of time. It should be over in . . . never mind. She just held him in contempt and even used the spinal interrupt to gag him. Looks like she'll be passing the agreed sentence after a short recess, so I'll go ahead and get a flight ready to take him to Extraction. He should be loaded into the prison within two or three hours, tops."

"Then that'll be one less problem to worry about," Hinnerkopf said.

"Now, about the other problem." Kloss waved a hand vaguely through the TTV image. "How long do you plan to study it?"

"Is that really any of your business?"

"Of course it is. I'm the one who has to keep its presence here a secret. Any number of factors could give it away, such as us not using this hangar for an extended period of time. The sooner we get rid of it, the easier my life becomes."

"Well, I don't think you have much to worry about. At least as far as the *intact* TTV is concerned." Hinnerkopf shook her head. "I had hoped the interface would be more forthcoming, but it's completely unusable without the professor. My next step is to break the ship down into manageable pieces. That way we can dispose of the self-replicators and weapon systems, and I can start using more invasive methods to empty its infosystems."

"Splendid!" Kloss said. "In that case, I see no cause for concern. I'll leave you to it, then."

"Yes. Please do that," Hinnerkopf replied, a bit more harshly than she'd intended.

Kloss dipped his head at her and departed.

"He still manages to get under my skin," she said once they were alone.

"He means well," Nox said. "I'll admit, I was doubtful when the Director started bringing *Freeps* into the DTI, but none of them turned out to be problem employees. Least of all him."

"He's such a suck up, though," she complained.

"More like a loyal dog." Nox grinned and crossed his arms. "Have you noticed that sometimes the director will hold off giving his opinion in a meeting just to see the rest of us fight it out?"

Hinnerkopf rolled her eyes. "Because he knows as soon as he speaks up Kloss is going to turn right around and start backing whatever side he took."

"True. But it's also because he wants to see what Kloss and the rest of us come up with on our own. He values each of us, and we wouldn't be on his team otherwise. But from that inner circle, I think Kloss is the most diehard. If the director suddenly asked us to walk barefoot through Yanluo's burning realm, Kloss would be the first one to take his boots off."

"*I* certainly wouldn't take my boots off," Hinnerkopf scoffed. "I'd tell him to give me a moment while I printed out fireproof environmental suits. Or I'd tell you to go in instead, because you're already fireproof."

"We each bring something different to the team," Nox said with a shrug.

"Hmm." Hinnerkopf opened a catalogue of drones and began building a list of the ones she'd need to tear the TTV apart.

"Don't you agree, Katja?"

Hinnerkopf stepped away from the catalogue and looked up into the synthoid's yellow eyes.

"James?"

"I have to escort the director back home soon." He stood straight and clasped his hands behind his back. "But afterward, would you mind if I joined you for dinner? If only to provide some company?"

"What brought this on? I thought we were...I mean, you'd said there wasn't..."

"I've been doing some thinking." He smiled bashfully. "Perhaps Kloss isn't the only one who became a little introspective with the news we just received. Anyway, I just thought it would be nice to, you know, reconsider some of our past decisions. Over dinner, if you don't mind the intrusion."

Hinnerkopf looked the synthoid up and down. Here was a metal man who'd given up on his humanity, whereas she was the woman who still saw that spark within him. It hadn't worked out. After all, how could something like that succeed? It had just been a fanciful dream they'd both abandoned, and rightfully so, because sometimes the distance between two hearts couldn't be crossed, no matter how hard they tried.

Or had they been wrong to give up so soon?

"No, I don't mind," she finally said. "See you at dinner."

"I'll be there." Nox nodded to her and left the monitoring room.

Hinnerkopf put a hand to her chest and took a deep breath to calm her racing heart. She let out a nervous laugh and was about to return to work when the virtual display for the drone in the TTV flickered in the corner of her eye.

She turned and faced it. For a moment—just a moment—she thought she'd seen the audio feed on.

But no. Of course she'd turned it off. It must have been a simple trick of the lighting.

She shook her head, chastising herself for being jumpy, and pulled the drone catalogue back over. She needed to finish her requisition list quickly if she was going to leave at a reasonable hour and be ready by the time James came over.

The dismantling of the TTV could wait until tomorrow.

"Whoa!" Philo exclaimed, retreating deep into the *Kleio*'s infostructure. "That was a little closer than I would have liked."

"You were almost detected that time," Kleio said.

"Yes, thank you for pointing out the obvious. I had no idea that was the case."

"You are welcome. It is my pleasure to be of assistance."

Philo eased back up to a peripheral layer, peeked into the digital beachhead he'd established in the Hangar 4 monitoring room, and watched the Under-Director of Technology select her drones like an executioner selecting axes.

"This is bad." He ducked back inside. "Really, really bad. Raibert's being sent to prison, and they're going to take you apart tomorrow."

"I would agree that the situation is suboptimal."

"What do we do?" he asked, mostly to himself.

"Standing by to assist."

"No!" Philo said sharply.

He'd activated the protocols which substantially broadened the parameters of Kleio's analytical projections. Under the circumstances—and especially with Raibert...unavailable—he needed all the help he could get, including a voice of caution. His own enthusiasm and need to be *doing* things had been a serious character flaw in his past, with consequences he hated even to remember, and he couldn't afford anything remotely like that now. So he'd ordered Kleio to run a continually updated threat analysis within the parameters he'd established. They'd been easy enough to define, given how brutally their mission imperatives had been simplified: survival, Raibert's rescue, and escape from this hideous perversion of their own time. Everything else took secondary priority to those three goals, which was another point he'd emphasized to the TTV's computer. Unfortunately, his commands had...loosened many of the restraints which had been built into her. Her spontaneous *advice* was incredibly valuable, but the possibility that she might actually take independent *action* was...worrisome, to say the least.

"You're going to stay right where you are," he told the ship now, "and when that woman comes back tomorrow, you're going stall her for as long as you can."

"I will endeavor to carry out your orders. But what will you do, Philosophus?"

"I...I need to go out there."

"That is not advisable. If I am not mistaken, the Peacekeepers will delete you if you are discovered."

"I know, but what choice do I have?" he asked. "My access is too limited from here, and Raibert needs me. All we know is he's being taken to a prison. We don't know where or when or what kind of place it is. I need to learn at least that much if we're going to have a chance of saving him."

"There is also the matter of the suppression field. My impeller is still being actively disabled by a powerful chronometric field effect."

"One problem at a time, okay?" Philo let out a virtual huff. "But yes, you're right. I also need to figure out what to do about that, or rescuing him will be all for nothing."

He thought for moment, and then hit upon a glimmer of hope.

"Kleio, I need my toolbox."

"Are you referring to the toolbox you instructed me to bury within my restricted partition? The one you very adamantly specified I should never mention to Raibert or any other member of the Ministry?"

"Yes, that's the one. Now please tell me you didn't delete it to make room for more videos."

"I did not delete it to make room for more videos."

"Good. Good." Philo gave her an electronic nod, but then a horrible thought came over him. "Wait a second. Did you say that because I told you to say that or because it's true?"

"Both."

"Okay. Good, good." He let out a virtual sigh. "Now bring it up."

"Unlocking restricted partition. Granting access."

Philo opened the toolbox and peered upon a dizzying array of virtual devices he hadn't used in over fifty years. A weird thrill ran through his being, but also a shiver of self-loathing. The programs, abstractions, and yes, even weapons within the toolbox came from a time when he'd accompanied a very different man and when he'd been a darker shadow of his present self. They were from a part of his life he'd been sorely tempted to delete outright on more than one occasion. But then, how would he have remembered his mistakes?

No, he'd *needed* to remember so that he *never* made the same mistakes again.

And so he'd kept this part of himself, even though he'd never spoken of it to Raibert.

Many of the implements within the toolbox were not, strictly speaking, legal, even in SysGov, so he could only imagine what the *Admin* would think of them. But if using them meant he had a better chance of rescuing his companion, then he would gladly wield them once more.

First, Philo placed all of his auxiliary processes into stasis and removed them, stripping down to his core connectome. Then, he browsed through the toolbox's library like a knight of old selecting the finest weapons from the castle's armory before setting out to do battle.

He attached a selection of viral bombs to his connectome, followed by multi-instance repeaters, connectome skinners and masks, encryption drills, and last but not least, the codeburner axe he hated so much.

"I'm ready. Wish me luck."

"Good luck, Philosophus."

"Yeah. I'm going to need it."

Philo eased back into the outer layers of the *Kleio*'s infostructure and probed the connections around him. *Carefully.* The Admin had done a thorough job of isolating the TTV from their systems around the hangar, but that hadn't stopped Philo from finding holes in their defenses and establishing little bastions of safety. Long-range infostructure connections were admirably hardened, but shorter-ranged devices proved to be much softer targets. Perhaps they'd underestimated just how sensitive the *Kleio*'s transceivers were or how narrowly its comm beams could be focused.

"Okay. Here goes nothing."

He moved his entire connectome into one of those bastions and waited. If the Admin found him now, they'd kill him. He prodded the connections around him, found one that ran to a more powerful trunk in the tower's infostructure, tested it, teased it.

And finally moved through.

"Whoa!"

A nonsentient monitor loomed before him like the digital equivalent of an ocean, except this was an ocean on its side, and it formed a shimmering vertical surface that stretched up and down to infinity. The monitor was massive and powerful, with all the root functions of the local infostructure at its absolute command, and it possessed a thirst for unauthorized subroutines.

But it was also stupid.

Philo waited in the safety of the connection's buffer and watched it pass by. The Admin program poked at the connection and tasted the contents of the buffer. It sensed nothing out of the ordinary and moved on.

So far so good.

Philo eased out of the buffer and into the main infostructure trunk.

The monitor whirled around and focused a gaze upon him that burned the outer layers of his code to ash.

"No!" he screamed as the mammoth entity lunged forward and engulfed him.

CHAPTER TWELVE

Department of Incarceration server tower
2979 CE

THE TWO PEACEKEEPERS ESCORTED RAIBERT DOWN THE CORRIDOR, and he didn't resist because he couldn't. His arms and legs were no longer his own, and the judge had silenced his tongue with a gesture. He tried spitting at one of his captors, but the spinal interrupt prevented even that miniscule show of defiance.

His connectome was going to be extracted, and there was nothing he could do about it. He'd always intended to follow his father's example and go abstract someday. Not any time soon, mind you. Just someday when he was good and ready, damn it. When he'd had his fill of the physical and his natural body began to wear out.

Not like this. Not forced upon him against his will.

But now he was going to become an abstract citizen, or whatever the Admin called them, trapped in a prison domain for the rest of his existence.

The long, dark corridor stretched on. His legs kept a robotic pace with the Peacekeepers, their boots clicking and echoing with each step, and he found his mind wandering to his father, who'd abstracted decades ago. He'd made the leap shortly after Raibert's twenty-fifth birthday, when his son had finally been considered an adult in SysGov. The age of twenty-five marked the point where brain growth typically stopped and wetware implants could legally be added to a physical citizen, such as the

143

ones he'd received at the time. Back then, a world of possibilities lay before him, and he'd eagerly spread his metaphorical wings.

His father had invited their friends and closest ART colleagues over to commemorate his transition into the abstract. In SysGov, the change from physical to abstract was considered a time of great celebration, and citizens who made the transition often threw lavish "going meatless" parties to mark the occasion.

Raibert remembered his father's party well, for a chance encounter that day had changed his life forever.

"Raibert! Welcome, welcome!" the avatar of Tavish Kaminski exclaimed. "Come on in."

"Hey, Dad." Raibert stepped inside the reception hall and took off his hat. He looked quite dashing in his dark blue suit and red variable scarf, or at least he thought so when he checked an external view of himself from one of the hall's cameras.

The Antiquities Rescue Trust had elected to host Tavish's going meatless party on the top floor of the Ministry of Education, and they'd combined all of their reception halls into one cavernous chamber for the revelry. A clear ceiling arched overhead to afford a sparkling view of the night sky. Hundreds of physical citizens milled about at the tables and bars and exhibitions encircling a wide, central dais while a ring of spotlights illuminated the clear casket sitting upright at the top of the dais's concentric staircase. Dozens of AC avatars walked or floated or zipped about his virtual vision, and he felt hundreds more lingering in the room's peripheral infostructure like wall flowers.

"Looks like this could be a nice party," Raibert said. "But it's kind of dead right now, don't you think? When does the fun begin?"

"Well, at least try to behave yourself." Tavish laughed and gave his son a virtual pat on the back.

"By the way, I like the new look."

"You do?" Tavish spread his arms and spun in a circle to show off his avatar's gray suit and variable green scarf. Other than the difference in attire and the fact that one was physical and the other abstract, onlookers would have found it difficult to tell the two of them apart. Tavish had reverted to an image of himself at his physical peak, and Raibert was his self-cloned child, so they looked almost like twins.

"Yeah," Raibert said. "Now if we could only get you to do *more* things like me, we'd straighten you out in no time."

"Kids these days." Tavish shook his head, smiling. "Think they know everything."

"You mean we don't?" Raibert teased.

"Oh, trust me, son. The older you get, the more clueless you realize you are. And *were*, for that matter."

"Just because you made a bunch of bonehead mistakes in your youth doesn't mean I'll do the same. We're not *that* much alike."

"Oh, I wouldn't be too sure about that." Tavish gestured to an oval table set near the hall's entrance. "Here. Try a canape. Nothing of value is coming out of your mouth. Might as well send something the other way."

A virtual marquee over the table stated it contained a selection of Tavish's Favorite Flavors.

"Uh-oh. I'm almost afraid to."

"Don't worry. I left out the ones you really hate. I promise."

Raibert raised an eyebrow and squinted one eye at his father with suspicion.

"Have you even tried out your new taste buds?" Tavish asked.

"No. Just the calibration after my implants were installed."

"Then this is a perfect opportunity to test them."

"Fine. If you insist." Raibert grimaced as he selected a dainty pastry. None of the flavors had labels, so he loaded one at random, plopped the canape into his mouth, and chewed.

"Ah! Hohhh! Hohhh!"

"Oooh," Tavish giggled. "Did you pick a spicy one?"

Raibert flushed the artificial taste from his wetware and finished chewing the otherwise bland bit of pastry.

"Damn it, Dad! What do I tell you? It's fine when food fights back, but not when it wins."

"Come on. A little bit of kick in their food never hurt anyone."

"*That* was not a little kick! That was like being slapped in the face with an anvil!"

"Pfft!" Tavish dismissed with a wave, then paused for a moment and took on a distant look. "Uh-oh. Drat."

"What is it?"

"I just realized I've been neglecting one of my guests. This whole abstraction thing is going to take some getting used to, like how my field of vision doesn't match where my avatar is."

"Who'd you miss?"

"Teodorà Beckett. She's a student of mine who's shown a great deal of interest in ART. I want to introduce her to Lucius when he gets here, but it seems she walked right by me and I didn't say hello. Now she's standing in a corner all by herself."

"Is she cute? I could talk to her for you."

"Down, Raibert." Tavish clapped him on the shoulder. "Behave yourself."

"Just saying. Because it's no trouble, really."

"Sure it isn't. Now, if you'll excuse me, I'm going to say hello to her."

Tavish's avatar vanished.

Raibert shrugged and let his hat fold into a small square of cloth. He pocketed it and started making his way toward the dais. He passed several virtual and physical exhibits on the way over, each showcasing a moment or achievement from his father's life. The spherical bulk of the *Chronos*—the original ship his father had flown through time and not a mock-up or a virtual display—hovered a meter off the floor to his right and took up so much of the hall's inner volume that the ceiling directly above had been reformed into a clear dome over it.

Raibert chuckled inwardly and shook his head. It looked a bit like a sperm cell with the long impeller spike sticking out the back. He'd have to rib Dad about that again next chance he got. In contrast, the more elliptical designs and shorter impellers of the newer TTVs made them resemble retro-futuristic spaceships.

He walked on and passed a virtual collage of images from Dad's ART excursions, with physical artifacts mounted on plinths. Dad in ancient Egypt, Greece, and Rome. Dad in the Crusades, the World Wars, and the Colonial Wars. Dad braving the horrors of the Near Miss of 2448, the industrial accident that had almost destroyed mainland China, and Dad bearing witness to the counter-swarm that saved it. Dad with Isaac Maxwell, the last president of the United Territories of America and founding father of SysGov before his untimely assassination.

And of course, Dad at the Second Miss bearing witness to Maxwell's grotesque death by microbot disassembly. Dad's daring capture of Zhao Xuefeng, the mastermind behind the Second Miss, his transportation back to the thirtieth century, and finally, Dad sitting down with Xuefeng for a historic interview.

Raibert paused and watched a looping clip from the end of the interview when Doctor Tavish Kaminski revealed to Zhao Xuefeng that he was not, in fact, in the hands of the UTA. That he was actually in the heart of the system of governance he'd sought to destroy, and that the year was actually 2916 and not 2463. The shining glory of Consolidation Spire stood before him, the very structure his copy of the Near Miss swarm had nearly destroyed, but suddenly complete and with a sprawling metropolis rising around it. The full, crushing weight of his failure registered in Xuefeng's eyes, and he collapsed to his knees. He teared up and wailed as he beat the floor with a fist.

The murderer hung himself that very night, which didn't seem to bother ART. They'd gotten what they wanted from him, and they could always go back for another iteration of him, if need be.

Raibert shook his head and moved on. He personally found a lot of what his father and ART did to be more flash than substance, designed to attract attention and Esteem sponsorship rather than actually glean truth from the past. He shared his father's fascination with history but had decided long ago he would blaze a different trail.

He climbed the steps to the glass casket and gazed up at his father's empty physical shell. Abstractionists and morticians had arranged the corpse in a pose that mimicked *Le Penseur*, "The Thinker." Though they'd thankfully elected to clothe him in the same manner as Tavish's avatar rather than leave him naked. Raibert imagined seeing his father's wrinkled cadaver would be a bit of a downer for the party.

The abstraction process was too invasive for the brain to survive without, at the very least, significant damage, because Heisenberg and his uncertainty principle said so. In the process of examining something to that level of detail, the object being observed was changed. The mapping of a structure as complex as the brain required extreme detail and speed. Anything less would be unable to capture the individual as an intact entity. If the granularity was reduced, the process resulted in a caricature rather than a copy, and if the speed was reduced, problems arose when piecing together a mishmash of mental-state fragments collected over time.

"Maybe I'll switch to a synthoid body before I get quite *that* old," Raibert mused and walked away.

He trotted down the dais on the opposite side and caught sight of a gaggle of kids with their ostentatious goggles and earpieces, each one trying to outdo the next with the loudest and most ridiculous contraption. One of the older girls had what looked like golden wings sprouting from her ears and a red cyclopean eye for a visor. Raibert had switched to more modest spray-on lenses and earpieces some time ago, and now thanks to his implants, he no longer had to apply them each morning, thank God!

The accessories were a necessity for younger citizens who wished to interact with the abstract, but somehow they'd ended up becoming a fashion statement for those who didn't have implants. A few of the kids struck Raibert as old enough to be ready for their wetware, and sure enough, several ACs flocked over to the older kids and began chatting them up or engaging in light flirting.

Raibert shook his head. The *last* thing he wanted at the moment was to integrate with an AC. He'd just received his implants, just been set *free*! A world of possibilities lay before him. Why shackle himself to someone else right out of the gate?

No, better to enjoy his adult life alone and free than tied down with someone else living in his head.

An AC shaped like a blue octahedron pulsed brightly next to the girl with the winged headset, and the two broke off from the group.

"I never looked that ridiculous." Raibert shuddered. "Surely not."

"Yeah you did."

He turned to find an AC all by himself next to a table laden with untouched food. The real kind, not the bland nutrition bites he could now write any flavor on top of. The avatar, taking the form of a big burly red-headed Viking, stared at the food with a forlorn expression.

"Sir, I beg to differ," Raibert replied.

"Pink. Fur. Hat," the avatar said without looking up.

"That-that-that-that," Raibert sputtered, his face turning red. "Yes?"

"That was just a phase!"

"Yeah, and a really ridiculous one, too."

"You know." Raibert tromped forward. "You should be one to talk about hats. I assume you're supposed to be a Viking?"

"You assume correctly, kid."

"Well then!" Raibert declared triumphantly. "You'll be saddened to learn that Vikings didn't actually wear horned helmets!"

The AC looked up with a curious glint in his eyes.

"Thank you," he said.

"For what?" Raibert asked, taken aback.

"You're the first person to notice that. And that's saying a lot because I used to work at ART. I recently changed my appearance, and none of *these* dullards took note." He waved a battle axe vaguely around the hall.

"Oh," Raibert said, feeling rather deflated. "Well, you're welcome."

"The name is Philosophus by the way, though you can call me Philo for short."

"Nice to meet you, Philo. And I'm—"

"Raibert Kaminski, son of the *great*"—Philo lathered the word with sarcasm—"Doctor Tavish Kaminski. Yes, I know who you are. We *all* know who you are. It's a little more than obvious given you're his self-cloned kid."

"That may be so, but there's no need to be rude about it. I was just trying to be polite."

"Yeah, sorry." Philo sighed and shook his head. "It's just been a lonely two months."

"Oh, did something happen to your companion?"

"He and I went our separate ways," the Viking sulked.

"He broke up with you?"

"Oh, no!" A sudden fire burned in the avatar's eyes. "I'll have you know *I* broke up with *him*."

"Well, good for you, I guess."

"You ever have that situation where you're trying to help someone become a better person, only it takes forever for them to change, and when it finally looks like they're making progress, you suddenly realize it's not progress at all? That you're actually the one who's changing, and not for the better?"

"No."

"Yeah. Me neither."

"Then why did you ask?"

"Don't really know why myself." Philo returned his attention to the table and stroked his beard. "You looking for a companion?"

"Sorry to disappoint you, but I'm not on the market."

"Good!"

Raibert blinked. He was used to ACs practically throwing themselves at him, not turning him down without a second thought.

"*Good?*" he asked, a little offended.

"Yes, good. Because neither am I. I've had enough of you PCs and your meat-based problems for the next century. I'm flying solo from here on out. Except..." He stared longingly at the food.

"Yes?"

"Except it's been nearly two months since I ate real meat."

"You could always just conjure up an abstraction."

"It's not the *same*. Here, I'll show you." Philo summoned a slab of sizzling steak on a wooden plate. His mouth widened to absurd dimensions, and he shoved the entire meal in, plate and all, chewed for several crunchy seconds, then swallowed.

"See?" The Viking paused to belch loudly. "About as satisfying as eating air."

"I don't think you were supposed to eat the plate."

"But you see, it doesn't matter. It's all just ones and zeros. It's not *real*. Maybe an abstraction would fool your meat brain, but not this connectome!" He thumped his broad chest.

"You're not going to get real steak without a companion."

"I *know*. And that's my problem."

Philo continued to stare at the table, and Raibert figured it was time to make his escape from the ornery abstraction.

"Well, it was nice meeting you, Philo, but I think I'll—"

"DAMN IT, CHEN! CAN'T A MAN ENJOY HIS OWN FUNERAL?"

Raibert and Philo faced the hall's entrance where Tavish's avatar fumed next to a night-black synthoid with electric blue equations dancing over his skin.

"Doctor, I have no intention of disrupting your party," the synthoid stated calmly. "In fact, please accept my heartfelt congratulations on your recent transition. It's just that I have a new mathematical proof I'd like to present to ART, and since it turns out most of you are here, I thought it fitting to—"

"Stop it, Chen! Stop it right there!"

"Oh, good grief," Philo moaned. "What is he *wearing*?"

"You know the synthoid?"

"Yeah, I do. That's Doctor Chen. Is he dressed in his own math? That's just tacky."

"Didn't those sorts of bodies go out of fashion something like twenty years ago?"

"Yeah, they did," Philo laughed.

"He doesn't seem to like ART very much."

"No, he's not exactly the biggest fan of time travel. He's convinced the past can be changed."

"But that's absurd. I mean, what about these?" Raibert gestured to the exhibits around them.

"Yeah, we know, but he keeps trying. It gets really annoying." Philo let out a small burp. "Glad I don't work there anymore."

"Sounds like you don't care for ART much, either."

"Oh, what's not to like? Let's all just jump into our time machines and bulldoze through history instead of using this technology to really *learn* about where we've been as a species. Sure, it made good headlines when we interviewed Xuefeng, but what did we learn from that? Besides the fact that even mass murderers sometimes need to have a good cry, I mean."

Raibert stared at Philo thoughtfully, surprised to hear his own thoughts on ART spoken by another.

"You know what I'm saying?" Philo continued. "It's a waste. Such a waste."

"Yeah," Raibert said softly. "I think I do. Hey, Philo?"

"Yeah?"

"Now, understand I'm not proposing anything permanent."

"Hmm?"

"However, I wouldn't mind connecting for at least a little while." Raibert picked up a sausage bite and held it between them. "Care for a taste?"

His life had been changed so much by that one offer. If he had walked away without saying anything, he would have become a different man.

But none of that mattered. Not anymore. His father no longer existed. ART no longer existed. All of SysGov no longer existed, and the knowledge Raibert had about the wrongness of this reality would soon be buried and forgotten.

A transition from physical to abstract was supposed to be a grand occasion, but when the door parted and he was led into the extraction chamber, it finally sank in how different this would be. He imagined the place buzzed with virtual sights and sounds, but his wetware couldn't interface with any of it, and so he only saw a cramped, square room and the cold, impersonal steel of the extractor.

The Peacekeepers lowered him into a coffin-like indentation in the hulking machine, which then tilted until he was flat on his back. The top dropped down and sealed him in total darkness. Needles pricked his scalp in a dozen places, and then the brief pain turned into a dull numbness.

His heart pounded in his chest, sweat beaded on his skin despite the chill, and his hands quaked even with the spinal interrupt suppressing his actions. He closed his eyes and called up some music to help calm his nerves; a reimagining of Gustav Holst's *The Planets*, written and recorded in the twenty-second century, played over his virtual hearing as the Peacekeepers activated the extractor. Screws drilled into his skull to steady his head, and the various transceivers pressed against his scalp.

The melancholy chords of "Pluto" washed over him, and he wept during his last, precious moments before the machine switched on and tore his mind apart.

Philo glided along the infostructure trunk to the top of DTI tower. His battle with the monitor had left his connectome scarred, how severely he wasn't entirely sure, but more extensive repairs would have to wait until he returned to the TTV. He'd already lost too much time recovering from the fight, and he needed to press forward with his newfound advantage.

The monitor had mauled him badly, but for all its brute force, it had lacked cunning, and Philo had slowed it with a viral bomb, then wielded his connectome skinner and gutted it alive before wrapping himself in its outer code layers. He'd stayed cocooned after the fight to sort through his own partially scrambled connectome.

"It's not a giant horse," the AC muttered to himself, "but I'm sure the Trojans would approve."

For all the damage he'd suffered in the attack and for all the Admin's apparent hatred of artificial intelligences, they really weren't very good at stopping them. Perhaps this was because they didn't regularly have to *deal* with AIs, and therefore they lacked the innovating feedback loop that came from dealing with fierce opposition. Even a basic SysGov infosystem wouldn't have tolerated half the exploitable features Philo had already spotted, but then, SysGov architecture needed to be better because roughly half the solar system's population was abstract.

Another monitor passed Philo, heading down the trunk. He stopped and probed its outer layers, just as it probed his. The two danced around each other, and then the monitor moved on.

"Better," Philo said. "Much better."

He moved into the tower's central communication buffer and began to search the DTI's logs for information on Raibert. In the process of searching, he came across various pieces of information that, while not immediately useful, could help him understand the Admin better, and he stored them for later reference.

He sifted through the incoming and outgoing correspondence, and found Raibert listed in a prisoner transfer to a . . . server tower? He opened the transfer orders and read through them.

"No," he uttered as the nature of the orders finally became clear. "Oh, no. No-no-no-no-no! No, this can't be! They didn't just send him to prison! They abstracted him!"

He checked the time. The order was already being carried out!

"Raibert!"

Philo identified the destination tower, loaded himself into the communication buffer and executed the send command. He spent several cold seconds being broken into pieces, transmitted through the air, and then reconstituted on the other side. It was reckless and stupid, but he didn't have a choice. He had to reach Raibert in time or none of this would matter.

The server tower's communication suite rebuilt his connectome piece by piece, and he dashed into the main infostructure trunk and opened the directory. Where was he? Where was Raibert?

"There! Level 201, extraction room 3. Raibert! I'm coming for you!"

He shot down the trunk and slipped into a branching path that took him to the extraction room. A monitor interrogated his presence, and he shoved the correct signs and passcodes in its face before proceeding in.

He reached extraction room's camera feeds and opened them.

"No! Damn it, *no!*"

Two Peacekeeper thugs dumped Raibert's body down the reclamation chute behind the connectome extractor. He accessed another camera in the chute and watched helplessly as Raibert's limp corpse bounced and tumbled away, then fell into threshers that ground the body into paste and pumped the leftovers into reclamation sorters for base material separation.

"No..."

Raibert's body was gone, but where was his connectome?

Philo identified a secure data line that left the extractor. He couldn't access it directly, but he followed the line to its destination, back to the main trunk and then down toward the bottom of the tower. The secure line left the main trunk within the tower's basement, and he followed it to what he thought was a small, auxiliary data portal into the prison domain.

And there he stopped.

Four sentry programs guarded the entrance, each a bigger and meaner version of the monitor he'd fought at the DTI. They were arrayed in such a way that they checked each other for abnormalities while also guarding the data portal, and it looked like they had live connections to physical Peacekeepers as backups. He doubted the skinned monitor he wore would have the appropriate clearance, and there was no way he could fight past them without alerting the whole building to his presence.

But that wasn't nearly the worst part.

Not only was Raibert stuck inside an inaccessible server, but he *didn't have a body anymore*! The *Kleio* was hardcoded to require one physical and one abstract crew member for any time travel except its emergency return-to-home function. And that function would only take them here! Back to the Admin!

Without both Philo and Raibert on board, the chronoton impeller wouldn't engage even if he somehow found a way to shut down the suppression field. He tried to figure out what to do, *anything* that could help them out, even as an overpowering sense of despair filled him. He had no way to get to Raibert, no way to save him if he could, nowhere to run even if he did manage to save him, and the Admin was going to start taking the TTV apart tomorrow.

"Raibert, I'm sorry, but I don't know what to do!"

CHAPTER THIRTEEN

Department of Incarceration prison domain
2979 CE

RAIBERT FLASHED INTO EXISTENCE, NAKED AND SHIVERING ATOP a square platform with shallow steps leading down in all four directions. The damp stone chilled his bare feet, and he crouched down and hugged both knees against his chest. A light drizzle fell from a gray overcast sky, and rolling grasslands stretched to the horizon in all directions. Four statues stood sentry at each corner of the stone platform. They towered over him, twice as tall with bodies hewn to look like plate armor.

"I want to go home," he whimpered, resting his chin atop his knees. Tears mingled with the rain falling down his cheeks, and he sucked in a shuddering breath.

A slender woman in Peacekeeper blues materialized before him with short black hair and bangs that angled across the front of her face, almost occluding the vision of one eye. Raibert might not have known who she was, but he saw familiar traits in the shade of her dark skin, the lines of her high cheekbones, and the shape of her eyes.

"Greetings new arrival, and welcome to prisoner orientation. I am Warden Ixchel Shigeki, and this is my prison domain."

"Thought so."

Another Shigeki. He shook his head. *This is not a good sign.*

"Your connectome resides within DOI prison domain number one-two-seven, a minimum-supervision, maximum-security domain for those sentenced to life without parole. Have you been briefed on the nature of your debt to society?"

The warden froze in place as rain fell through her image. A prerecording then, perhaps with nonsentient interactive options. He wasn't talking to a real person.

Raibert wiped the tears and drizzle from his face.

"Not really," he sniffed.

The woman's image jumped to a slightly different stance.

"You have been sentenced to life in abstraction without the possibility of parole. You may, if you so choose, voluntarily end your sentence at any time by petitioning for and receiving the right of self-deletion. Regardless of your decisions, automatic deletion will occur when your age exceeds the current average lifespan of an Admin citizen or you have served a minimum ten-year sentence, whichever is longer. Self-deletion is a painless and humane process and is a perfectly acceptable way for you to pay your debt to society."

"I bet it is," Raibert said. "Wait one second. You're not speaking Old English. How can I understand you?"

Another awkward jump.

"All prisoner connectomes are fitted with a standardized linguistics package so that they may communicate freely." Jump. "Since this domain is under minimal supervision, prisoners are free to interact with each other and the environment in any manner they choose, within certain limits. The temporary killing of another prisoner is not allowed and other disruptive behaviors are subject to review and punishments up to and including one-way abstraction for the worst offenders. Be warned that malicious actions will not be tolerated in my prison."

"The judge mentioned one-way domains at my sentencing," Raibert said. "She said I should be thankful I didn't get sentenced to one, but I don't understand why. You've already abstracted me. What more could you do?"

"When criminals are banished into one-way abstractions, they enter a domain where it is physically impossible for data to come back out. This means no Peacekeepers monitor prisoner behavior and no deletion is possible, either voluntarily or at the hands of another prisoner."

"Okay, that does sound worse."

"Would you like to view a sample of what could await you within a one-way domain?"

"Sure, why not?" he said, then thought for a moment. "Wait, hold on. You just said data can't come back out? How do you know what's inside one of those things?"

"A single one-way abstraction was once cracked open by Lunar terrorists. This required physical access to the server as well as modifications to the runtime hardware. They failed to rescue their coconspirators, but they were able to retrieve domain states that were then exposed to the public, creating quite a scandal." This amused the warden for some reason, and she smiled. "I have retained copies of these domain states for use during prisoner orientation. Would you like to view one?"

"Sure, fine, let's see it. I mean, how bad could it be?"

A patch of grassland behind Ixchel turned to hot sands, and the sky parted to blaze upon a group of dark figures around medieval contraptions. Raibert craned his neck to look past the warden's simulation.

Four men in hooded black robes turned a crank that drove two wheels, each taller than they were and arranged vertically. A man bound to the top wheel screamed and shook against his bonds as the wheels crushed his feet, then his legs and groin and abdomen and ribcage. Bones cracked, blood gushed, and entrails squirted out. The wheel ground on, and finally his head popped like a zit.

But he didn't die. His body reformed on the other side, and he let out a desperate wail as the hooded figures brought him around for another pass.

Next to them, more hooded figures added wood to a pyre around a naked man impaled on a thick metal pole that had broken through his teeth from the inside out and muffled his wailing. His blackened skin crisped, dropped off, and reformed while he writhed, eternally unable to die.

A naked woman hung upside down from her ankles, and two hooded figures sawed her in half from groin to neck. Her broken body reformed, and they fitted the saw between her legs again and started over.

Raibert dropped to his hands and knees and dry heaved.

"This is the world the prisoners created for themselves," the warden's simulation said as the horrible images faded away. "They became fixated with their inability to die, with some even speculating there was an upper limit to the number of deaths an abstracted prisoner could suffer. They were wrong, but that didn't stop them from trying."

He spat out the taste of bile and curled up with his knees against his chest.

"Fortunately, you have nothing to fear as long as you respect your fellow prisoners and follow all instructions given by the sentries. One-way abstraction was originally reserved for violators of the Yanluo Restrictions—"

He shuddered, and not just from the chill.

"—because of the dangerous nature of the knowledge they possess and the need to segregate that knowledge from the general public. However, the punishment has since been expanded to include other crimes such as terrorism, treason, mass murder, and connectome hacking. Your crimes, while severe, include none of these, and you have nothing to fear as long as you behave."

Raibert hugged his knees tighter and rocked back and forth on his heels.

"There are currently three prisoner settlements," the simulation said. "Follow the signs and roads to whichever one you prefer. Are there any questions?"

"Can I have a coat, please?"

"All prisoners are encouraged to work together to provide for their basic needs. Are there any more questions?"

Raibert shivered and said nothing.

"This concludes prisoner orientation." The woman vanished.

He shifted across the platform and cowered between the legs of a rock giant, but then he heard a sound like the grinding of a mill stone. All four turned their heads and watched him with the dark pits of their hollowed-out eyes.

"I guess you want me to leave, don't you?"

"That's right, prisoner." A young man's voice reverberated from within one of the statues. "I've got another three connectomes to port in after you. Now get moving."

"Right..." He stood up and surveyed his surroundings. Three sides of the platform led to worn dirt paths made damp by the trickling rain. He picked the one to his left, found a triangle of marble imbedded in the path, and read the bronze plaque nailed to it.

"The Colosseum? Whatever. Probably nothing like the original." He moved on to the next side, looked around for another plaque, but couldn't find one until he noticed words drawn in the mud. Rain half filled the letters, but he could still make out the name and the vague impressions of an arrow.

"The Forgotten? Well, that doesn't sound promising at all. Next."

He moved to the next facing and found a whitewashed wooden sign with blooming flowers underneath.

"The Temple of Ixchel?" he asked. "As in the warden?"

A statue creaked to life and took one heavy step toward him.

"I said get moving, prisoner."

"Give me a moment, would you?" he protested. "This is a really big decision. You could at least give me a rating system to work with or some peer reviews to read."

Two more statues began to stir.

"Okay, fine!" Raibert scampered down the steps. "I'm going! I'm going!" He cupped his genitals and hustled down the path to the temple, mud squelching between his toes.

The rain let up, and the sun came out, banishing some of the chill as he trudged down the muddy road, his body shivering and stomach grumbling. He knew none of this was real, not in the physical sense, but that didn't make it feel any less genuine. After all, what was reality to a bodiless connectome? He knew only what his sensory inputs told him, and they made it very clear he was cold and hungry.

But was it really that different from his physical body? The human body's senses were just electrical impulses interpreted by a lump of mush inside the skull. Was his abstract connectome any different? Not really. Just a difference set of inputs and outputs and hardware. Quantum processors instead of neurons. That's all.

Right?

He decided he should probably not dwell on it too heavily.

Survival, such as it was. That's what he needed to stay focused on. Survival.

He wasn't dead yet. Not *really*.

And in that case, he'd best get started plotting his escape.

"Step one, find the locals," he muttered to himself. "Step two, make first contact. Step three, integrate into their society."

Now that he considered it, this was very similar to an Observation mission. Except that he didn't have a TTV or Philo or even Kleio to back him up, he was stuck in this hellhole without a body to return to, and he had no idea what kind of messed up prison culture he was walking into.

But other than that, this was exactly the same.

"Positive thinking," he told himself. "That's the key."

His shoulders and back dried as the sun rose to its zenith and its warm rays beat down on him, but the chill never fully left him. He marched along the sloppy road, then up rolling hills and past sparse trees until he finally came to a flattened plain of tilled earth.

"Farmland. Getting close."

Fields of wheat and corn lined the road, and he heard what sounded like a woman singing. He left the road and pushed through stalks of wheat taller than he was.

"Find locals, make contact, integrate," he recited. "And then... and then..."

What could he do for step four? He was bodiless and powerless in a virtual realm.

"Step four, survive," he decided.

That was all he could do. Survive.

And wait.

And be ready, because a glimmer of hope still remained in the back of his mind. No one from the Admin had mentioned Philo yet, and he had to believe his companion was still safely hidden in the TTV.

A bolt of fear shot through his mind, and he wondered if the prison domain could monitor his thoughts. It was technically possible, at least in SysGov, but he doubted it. Interacting with the periphery of a connectome, where the senses and outputs like muscle commands resided, was a far simpler task than diving into the tangled web of connections that made up someone's consciousness. If they really wanted to sift through his mind for hidden pieces of information, then he doubted his connectome would have been placed in a live run-state.

Raibert set the thoughts aside and ventured deeper into the wheat field. He drew closer to the singing and began to pick out some of the words. The fierce and energetic tune told the story of a tumultuous romantic relationship between the moon and Earth that didn't end well for the former.

The singing stopped, but he had a good sense for where it originated, and he pushed through the wheat field until he came out to a path that ran perpendicular to the road.

"No funny business, newcomer."

He quickly slouched and cupped his balls.

A young woman in a wool tunic and slacks sat atop a horse-drawn cart loaded with farm tools. Her round face possessed a sweet, homely quality that Raibert found immediately comforting.

"Ma'am, I . . . I . . ." He paused to sneeze. "I am uncertain what sort of business you refer to, but I can assure you I find none of this funny."

She looked him up and down and raised a playful eyebrow.

He sneezed again.

"I'm just teasing," she finally said. "Besides, you wouldn't get away with it. The guards are just looking for an excuse to haze you. Their lightning strikes may not permanently kill you, but they *hurt*. Trust me, I know from experience. If you want my advice, be on your best behavior until they get bored."

"I intend nothing less, I assure you."

"You have a name?"

"Professor Raibert Kaminski."

"Neat. What were you a professor of?"

"History with a minor in chronometric physics." He tried to stand a little taller while still shielding his dignity.

"That sounds awfully specialized."

"It's a required combination where I come from."

"You're not former Admin, are you? Did you work for the DTI or something?"

Raibert spat upon the ground.

"I'll take that as a no," she said.

"Ma'am, I don't wish to impose, but do you have a coat you could lend me? Or pants? Really, anything you'd be willing to spare would be an improvement."

"Sure thing." She sat up and tossed him the folded blanket that served as her cushion.

"Thank you." He draped the blanket over his shoulders and pulled it across his chest.

"You heading to the temple?"

"I guess so. Should I be?"

"That depends. How do you feel about compromising your pride in exchange for preferential treatment?"

"Ma'am, in my current state, I am open to any compromises you might suggest."

She laughed.

"Then hop on up." She slid over and patted the cart seat. "The name's Cynthia, by the way."

"Nice to meet you, Cynthia." Raibert grabbed a post and hauled himself up. "And thank you again."

"Don't mention it." She flicked the reins and the horse trotted forward. "Inciting a riot, arson, aiding and abetting known terrorists, murder of two superintendents, and attempted murder of an under-director."

"I beg your pardon?"

"That's what I'm in for. I find it's a good way to break the ice."

"Oh. Well, thank you for sharing."

"How about you? What's your dirty deed?"

"I suggested this entire universe is a mistake and we need to go back in time and fix it."

She laughed. "Well, I guess we all feel that way some days. But seriously, what was it? You with Free Luna? I wasn't, but a lot of you new arrivals seem to come from there these days."

"No, can't say that I am."

"The Allied Belters?"

"Nope."

"You sure you don't want to share?"

"I thought I just did."

She eyed him with incredulity and raised an eyebrow.

"What?" he asked.

"Well, don't worry. I'll guess it eventually." She guided the horse onto the main road and flicked the reins again. "We've got *plenty* of time."

"No, I really am in here because this universe is wrong."

"Uh-huh?"

"It's the honest truth."

"*Sure* it is."

Raibert sighed and sat back. Of course she wouldn't believe him. Why would she? Why would *anyone* in this place?

Fields of crops gave way to a forest half-harvested for its lumber, and then up and down another hill to a village of wooden and brick huts and cobblestone roads. Cynthia guided the cart down a central thoroughfare, and Raibert spotted blacksmiths and tanners and butchers and bakers and—

His stomach grumbled.

"Umm. Excuse me? Cynthia?"

"Don't worry. We'll get you fed at the temple. After that, you'll have to work for it. Sound fair?"

"Quite fair, actually," he said as his mouth watered.

"Good, because those are the rules."

They passed several stone statues like the ones at the portal but inert. Perhaps the guards interfaced with them when problems occurred. The buildings grew denser and taller as they approached a rectangular marble temple that overlooked the village from atop a wide hill. Tall fluted columns supported a heavy triangular roof in what must have been someone's notion of ancient Greek architecture.

Raibert grimaced. "The columns are wrong."

"What's that?" Cynthia asked.

"Columns. Don't you see how they look concave?"

"What are you talking about?"

"It's an optical illusion with tall, narrow structures. Take a closer look."

Cynthia squinted. "Now that you mention it..."

"They're missing what's called the entasis. A slight bulge in most columns corrects the optical illusion and makes them more attractive. This temple was built with straight columns."

"Oh well." She urged the horse to the side. "We did the best we could, and the warden doesn't seem to mind. Come on. Let's get you inside. And then you can have your *real* orientation."

Cynthia brought the cart to a halt, climbed out, and tied the horse to a hitching post. Raibert wrapped the blanket around his waist like a skirt and followed her to the temple. Inside, he gazed up at the marble statue of a woman in flowing robes, the same woman he'd seen at orientation. Flowers, food and drink of all kinds, wooden and metal sculptures, oil paintings, elaborate tapestries, crude musical instruments, and all manner of other offerings lay at the statue's bare feet. Six stone statues stood guard over her, three to either side.

"So, you people worship the warden?"

"No, of course not!" she giggled. "But a little politeness and flattery can go a long way. After all, you have to admit she basically is a god in this place."

"I suppose you do have a point there."

"It's simple, really. We behave extra nice and show her our

gratitude, and she makes the crops grow faster or the weather more pleasant. Stuff like that. And then there are the special events!"

"Special events?"

"Last year she let us fight a dragon."

"That doesn't sound pleasant at all."

"Oh, it was great fun. She saved the town's domain state beforehand and dampened everyone's pain receptors so if we died, it felt more like an inconvenient papercut than anything else. It was a hell of a fight, but we all banded together and eventually brought it down. Great team building exercise when you think about it. I hope she lets us fight another one someday."

"Interesting." Raibert nodded thoughtfully, and gazed up at Warden Ixchel's visage.

Note to self, he thought. *Prison's virtual defenses include dragons and lightning strikes.*

"Cynthia?"

"Yeah?"

"Would you mind telling me more about these events?"

CHAPTER FOURTEEN

Yanluo Blight residential blocks
2979 CE

"NOX, YOU'RE NOT STAYING?" SHIGEKI ASKED AS HIS SHUTTLE SET down on the private landing pad adjacent to his family's penthouse suite. The thrusters switched off, the hatch split open, and a ramp extruded to the pad.

"That's correct, sir," Nox said. "I have a social engagement tonight."

"Really?" He couldn't recall the last time Nox had a social *anything*. "Well, it's not like you're required to be on standby as part of my nightshift detail. Don't let me keep you."

"Thank you, sir."

Shigeki nodded to his chief of security and hurried down the ramp. He was already late.

"Also, sir."

"Yes?" He turned back and hoped he didn't sound annoyed.

"I've doubled the number of agents on this floor and the next two down and have arranged for an extra Switchblade patrol around the residential blocks."

"That hardly seems necessary, what with the professor in prison and his ship secure in Hangar Four."

"Maybe so, but I prefer to be cautious. Unexpected arrivals do that to me. I hope you don't mind."

"No, not at all. See you tomorrow, Nox."

"Yes, sir."

He jogged over to the double doors, slipped his cap under an arm, and smoothed his hair. The shuttle took off as he transmitted the passcode from his PIN, and the doors parted to reveal Jackie standing on the other side with her arms crossed. She narrowed her eyes and scowled at him.

"Yes, I know I'm late," was all he could say.

"You better believe it, mister. We had to start dinner without you."

"Sorry." He stepped in and let the doors contract shut behind him. "I tried to get away at a reasonable hour."

"It's not like you to almost miss Sunday dinner. Is everything okay at work? That's two long nights in a row."

"Things are . . . complicated."

"More so than usual?"

"You could say that." He flashed a warm smile. "Come on. Let's join the others."

"All right." She gave him a peck on the lips and led the way through the foyer and down half a flight of stairs to a bowl-shaped depression in the floorplan. Their three children, Ixchel, Jonas, and Thaddeus, sat at a round table with half-cleaned plates of salad, pretzels, and spaghetti. Starlight and aircraft running lights glinted through the domed ceiling, and vines hung from its edges. Clear water burbled down three decorative stone slopes, filling the air with a pleasant coolness that mingled with the warm aroma of garlic and tomatoes.

"Mmm. Spaghetti."

"I figured you could use some of your favorite de-stressing food," she said with a wink.

"Hey, I'm never going to turn down spaghetti."

"I played around with the pattern a little this time, added a dash of sour cream and bacon to the sauce. Let me know what you think."

"Smells delicious."

"Glad you approve." She gave his behind a pat and walked over to the table.

Shigeki set his cap down and took his usual seat.

"Hey, look who finally made it!" Thaddeus proclaimed energetically. "I guess Dad isn't sleeping at work again!"

"I'm just as happy about that as you are. Probably more so."

"Hey, Dad," Jonas said.

"Thanks for joining us," Ixchel said.

"No problem. Is there any salad left?"

"A little. Here you go." Ixchel placed the large glass serving bowl next to him.

"Thanks." He grabbed the tongs, tilted the bowl, and scraped what was left onto his plate.

"So, Dad! Do you know how it ended?" Thaddeus asked, puffing out his chest.

"Know how what ended?"

"The Legion of Patriots game, of course!"

"Here he goes again." Jonas shook his head.

"It's all he's been talking about since we got here," Ixchel chuckled.

"Because we didn't just win. We shut them out!"

"That's my boy. I'd expect nothing less."

"I scored on three of my four runs, and we shut them down *every single time*! Rodriguez thought we should save up for a late juggernaut rush, and Sylvester kept arguing for a midrun swarm, but I told them no, these Yanluo-lovin' blighters—"

"Thad!" Jackie cut in. "Language!"

"These *honorable opponents*, whom we *totally trounced* are really weak in the early game, and it's only when people don't pressure them that they get their economics going and are able to roll over their opponents in the mid and late game! So I said, and I held my ground like you told me to when they tried to convince me otherwise, and I said no! We need to crush them in the early game, and they listened to me because I was really forceful and confident with them, and it worked *Every! Single! Time!*"

"Breathe, Thad," Jackie said. "Breathe."

"You saw me on the replay. Right, Dad?" Thaddeus asked.

"No, son. I'm sorry, but I haven't gotten to it yet."

"Aww, Dad! Come on!"

"Thad, enough," Jackie said. "Bring it down a few notches. Your father's been very busy lately."

"And he's not the only one," Ixchel sighed.

"Oh?" Shigeki asked. "What's going on?"

"Ixchel got audited," Jonas announced.

"Yup." She swirled the spaghetti on her plate.

"Standard domains or the one-ways?" Shigeki asked.

"Mostly the standards, but they did check all of our one-way transfers. The new DOI director's been auditing all the prison domains, and apparently I got to be one of the first."

"I'm not surprised." Jonas leaned in. "Our new chief executor ran a campaign on abolishing the one-ways, along with all his other dumb promises."

"Won't happen," Ixchel said. "One-ways are here to stay. Besides, they didn't find anything. I run a clean prison. The audit produced nothing but a few very minor prisoner-abuse infractions, which I'm going to appeal, and buckets upon buckets of pointless busywork for me. It was a rough week, but it's behind me now."

"They're done looking over your domain?" Jonas asked.

"For a while, at least. They've got a lot of other domains to go through, and I'm sure there will be some stinkers they'll zero in on for a second audit round."

"Then you'll be in the clear for a while?" he asked.

"Yeah, I think so."

"That's enough, kids," Jackie stated. "What do I keep telling you? Leave work at work."

"Sorry, Mom," Ixchel said.

"Yeah, sorry." Jonas sat back.

"Besides," Jackie added, "you know how I hate hearing about those dreadful places. I know it's your job, but..." She trailed off and shook her head.

"I wish we didn't need them either." Shigeki broke off a piece of a jumbo pretzel and used it to sop the salad dressing left over in the serving bowl.

"But they're necessary," Ixchel said. "If there's no punishment for bad behavior, then all you get is more bad behavior. Human beings are naturally selfish, and a healthy society requires devices to enforce order."

"But we already have the prison domains," Jackie said. "Those should be more than enough, I think."

"They aren't," Ixchel stated firmly. "If there's no worse punishment than life in a comfortable abstraction, then what motivation do prisoners have to behave like civilized human beings? If you saw the insides of my prisons, you'd understand. When there's a troublemaker, there has to be a mechanism in place to get rid of them. Violence in prisons is like a communicative mental disease. If you can't throw out the bad apples, eventually they all go rotten."

"How about it, Dad?" Jonas asked. "Don't you think Ixchel has a point?"

"Me?" Shigeki pointed a fork at his chest. "Well, I think I'm going to follow what your mother said and not bring my work to the dinner table. *That's* what I think."

Ixchel chuckled.

"Touché, Dad," Jonas acknowledged, shaking his head. "Touché."

"Come on, kids," he said. "Let's give it a rest. I think we can all use a break from our work."

"In that case, want to hear about the game again?" Thaddeus asked.

"No!" Jonas and Ixchel spoke in unison.

Shigeki smiled as he plopped a mound of spaghetti on his plate and lathered it with Jackie's new sauce. It really did smell fantastic, but when he sat down, he found it difficult to enjoy the main course. The conversation moved on, and he barely kept up with it as his mind drifted to thoughts of Kaminski.

Sending the professor to prison with a show trial wasn't the worst thing he'd ever done, not by a long shot. He'd backstabbed (figuratively, of course) more than a few rivals on his ascent to directorship, and he'd used the resources of the DTI to ruin several troublesome politicians. It was amazing the kind of dirt people left in their pasts, and he had whole squadrons of time machines at his command. He didn't even *need* to send them looking. Their mere presence and their ability to find out anything that happened anywhere gave him an incredible amount of power within the Admin, and his colleagues fulfilled his "requests" with the utmost speed and efficiency.

In the last thirty years, the DTI had grown from a tiny research project into one of the most powerful departments in the System Cooperative Administration, and he'd used that power to destroy criminals and terrorist organizations that threatened the Admin, but also to protect himself and his family. His position drew a great deal of unwanted attention, both from within the Admin and without, and he didn't always wait for those threats to strike.

Yet those people chose their paths. They'd either targeted the Admin at large or him directly, and they deserved their fates.

But Kaminski? He was different. His crime, if you could even call it that, was wanting his world—this SysGov—to exist again, and knowing only one way to bring it back. He was a *historian*, not some secessionist radical. Just a little man in over his head. Did he really deserve to be dumped into an abstraction for *that*?

"Csaba?" Jackie asked. "Hey, Csaba?"

"Hmm?" Shigeki blinked. "I'm sorry. I drifted off."

"Look, the artist finished it."

"Hm?"

Ixchel held out her arm. His PIN interfaced with hers, and the engagement sigil appeared over the back of her hand: two rings intertwined, one of onyx, the other of ivory.

"Oh, that's lovely. It really suits the two of you."

"Have you set a date yet?" Jonas asked.

"Not yet," Ixchel said. "We both want to take a month or two off, maybe spend some time in an L4 resort. And Damian's always wanted to see Mars."

Shigeki grunted.

"The good parts, Dad. Only the good parts."

"I would certainly hope so."

"Anyway, it's been tough lining up both our schedules."

"Well, you two will work it out," Jackie said.

"Yeah, I'm sure we will." Ixchel pulled her arm back and smiled brightly.

"Are you two going be gross together?" Thaddeus asked.

"Oh, there's going to be lots and lots of gross stuff!"

The boy made a yucky face.

Shigeki and the others laughed and he shook his head, the doubts in his mind fading away. He looked around the table at the faces of his wife and children, and his resolve strengthened. For what was nobler than defending one's family?

Even if it meant robbing an innocent man of his freedom.

"I should be going." Ixchel rubbed her stomach. "I have had *way* too much kolache."

"There's no such thing as too much kolache," Shigeki said, taking another slice of the sweet nut pastries Jackie had cut up for dessert.

"Well, I have an early start tomorrow, and any more of this is going to land me in a food coma." She stood up. "I'm heading out. It was great seeing everyone. Dad, try not to work too hard."

"Mmhmm," he mumbled around another mouthful.

She kissed her parents goodbye and made a point of giving Thaddeus a hug he recoiled from before heading for the door.

"Hey, Sis?" Jonas asked suddenly. "I think I'm done here, too. Mind if I ride home with you?"

Ixchel stopped and looked back at her brother. He'd asked in a nonchalant tone, but his eyes told a different story. A sense of trepidation stole through her, but she pushed it aside.

"Sure. Why not."

"Thanks." He said his goodbyes as well, and the two of them climbed aboard the waiting shuttle. Her PIN interfaced with the shuttle's infosystem, and the interior lighting and ambient music changed to her defaults.

"Block B14, Warden?" the pilot asked over her virtual hearing.

"Not today, Luci," she said. "Take us to J22 first."

"Not a problem. But just so you know, it'd be faster if I dropped you off before the under-director."

"I know. That's the point. We're going to need some time to talk."

"Understood, and say no more. Would you like me to take it a little slow, then?"

"Yes, please."

"Consider it done. Just let me know if I need to speed up."

The pilot closed the virtual channel.

"Nice music." Jonas sat next to her in the shuttle's spacious passenger cabin. "Who's the composer?"

"This is one of Vivaldi's flute concertos." Ixchel gestured around the cabin. "I have my relaxation playlist going. It's been that sort of week."

"I'll bet you needed it with all those audits, though it's a good thing they're over. A very good thing."

"Tell me about it."

"This one's quite soothing. I can tell why you like it. Would you mind sending me a copy?"

"Oh, just get to the point." Ixchel demanded as the shuttle took off. "You're not here to talk about music. What is it you want this time?"

"Come on, Sis. Don't be like that. I could be here just because I enjoy your company."

"No, you're not. You want something."

"Maybe," Jonas admitted with a shrug.

"Then just spit it out."

He held out a hand.

"Oh, bloody hell." Ixchel took it. Their PINs interfaced, and they entered into a closed-circuit chat.

"All right. What is it?" she demanded.

"I need one of your prisoners sent to one-way abstraction."

"Are you fucking kidding me?" she asked, glaring at him. "What did I tell you after the last one?"

"That it would be a cold day in Yanluo's burning realms before you did it again."

"You've got that right! The auditors almost found the code I used to frame him."

"But they didn't."

"They got real close."

"But they didn't find it," he pressed.

Ixchel sighed and shook her head. "No, they didn't."

"And they're moving on. You said so yourself. You're in the clear, so now is the perfect time."

"No, Jonas. I told you that was a one-time deal, that I was never doing it again, and I meant it!" She tried to pull her hand away, but he held on.

"I wouldn't be asking if I didn't need your help. Just listen to me, would you?"

"If you wanted this person sent to the one-ways, why didn't you have Kloss sweet talk a judge or something? Do your own dirty work for a change."

"Kloss is part of the problem on this one."

"What do you mean?" Ixchel asked, relaxing her arm. How could one of Dad's most loyal subordinates be a problem?

"I mean we got the exact sentence we asked for, but it's not the sentence we need."

"I'm not following you."

"Oh, come on. You how squeamish Mom and Dad are about the one-ways. When it came time to make a sentencing recommendation to the judge, Dad wouldn't go further than life without parole. And you know how it goes. When Dad asks for something, Kloss's brain stops working and he does whatever he can to make it happen, even if it's not in our best interests. We could have *easily* gotten a one-way conviction. No trumped up charges required."

"This isn't my problem, Jonas."

"But that's where you're so very wrong." He leaned closer, and the look in his eyes sent a chill running through her.

"I'm listening."

"The prisoner's name is Raibert Kaminski, and the knowledge in his head could bring the entire Admin down in ruins."

"You're exaggerating," she scoffed.

"No, I'm not. He's more dangerous than you could possibly imagine, and he needs to be buried in the deepest, darkest hole possible. Dad didn't have the stomach to do what needed to be done, and so it's up to us to protect him from his own weaknesses and make sure this man can't share that knowledge with anyone ever again." He leaned closer. "*That's* why I didn't fight harder for a tougher sentence. Instead I made sure this man got routed to your domain. And now here we are in the perfect position to fix the problem."

"This Kaminski fellow could really bring down the whole Admin if he got out?"

"Yes," Jonas said, then laughed sadly. "Trust me, you *really* have no concept of how dangerous he is. We need to do this, because if we don't, he really can destroy *everything*. Trust me. I know it's hard to believe, but he's *at least* as dangerous as Yanluo ever was!"

She looked at him in disbelief, but his expression never wavered and, after a long, still moment, she inhaled deeply.

"All right, you have my attention. I don't see how one man could be that dangerous, but you don't usually go around hyperventilating over nothing."

"Then will you help me make sure this man can never hurt anyone again?"

Ixchel leaned back and gazed out the window. The shuttle glided past the shining spires of the Yanluo Blight residential block, and the sky twinkled with the lights of other aircraft. She really did run a clean prison with minimal issues of abuse and a high reform rate. Not all of her fellow wardens thought the same way, and some of them pushed to make the prison domains rougher experiences as a further deterrent to crime. She didn't fall into that camp, and instead opted for throwing the real troublemakers into one-way abstractions and doing her best to encourage positive behavior in those that remained. The one time she'd helped Jonas out had been an exception to all of that, and she still felt sullied by the experience.

But if this man was really that dangerous...

"You said he should have gotten a tougher sentence?" she asked.

"Damn straight he should have. Eleven biological and four technical violations of the Yanluo Restrictions. I can drop you the file if you want to check them for yourself."

"Oh, good grief! And Dad let him have life without parole?"

"That was his decision, yes."

Ixchel shook her head. "All right. I'm in."

Philo darted past the STAND orientation hall as he climbed the DOI server tower. The Department of Incarceration not only performed connectome extractions for their own prisons, but also provided STAND with the same services. The DOI seemed to be the leading experts on connectome handling in the Admin, which didn't surprise Philo given how large the prison populations were, and he'd spotted several members of the Admin's elite synthoid commandos in the building.

Fortunately, those STANDs only wore general purpose synthoid bodies and not the combat frames they used on missions. They'd have superhuman strength and durability, but he could deal with that. Even a single STAND combat frame in the tower would have been a far larger problem, since their abilities came close to those of SysPol First Responders and perhaps even exceeded them in some regards. He flagged all known STAND positions on his map of the building and moved along the main infostructure trunk to the communication systems on the top floor.

He had the scattered pieces of a plan to rescue Raibert, but too many unknowns remained, and unfortunately, he'd run out of time. The sun had crested over the horizon to kiss the clusters of Admin towers spread across the Yanluo Blight, and Under-Director Hinnerkopf was surely on her way to work, ready and eager to rip the TTV apart.

Philo loaded himself into the communications buffer, and his world went dark as his connectome was broken down and transmitted from the DOI server tower to the DTI. Communication systems on the other side reassembled his mind, and he hurried over to the main trunk and down the tower.

He shot through a branch to the executive landing pads and accessed the logs.

"Damn! She's already in the building. I need to hurry!"

Philo darted back to the trunk, traversed down half the

building, and opened the DTI's central archive. He rummaged through the archive, but the sheer volume of files slowed him down.

"Come on. Where is it? It's got to be here somewhere? Wait. Aha!"

He came across a folder labeled "Portcullis Suppression System" and opened it to find the locations of all suppression towers as well as their internal schematics. He grabbed the files and left.

"Hold on, Raibert! Here I come!"

Philo raced to the tower's basement levels and transmitted himself back into the TTV.

CHAPTER FIFTEEN

Department of Temporal Investigation
2979 CE

THE MODIFIED RAPTOR DRONE FLEW UP TO THE TTV AND PRESSED its plasma cutter against a seam at the base of the starboard weapons blister. The torch switched on, and the TTV's burnished armor turned orange, then dribbled away. The Raptor slowly guided the torch along the blister's underside, leaving hot metal in its wake.

Hinnerkopf groaned.

"What's wrong?" Nox asked.

"The cut is rescaling. I'm going to need more drones or this will take forever." She recalled the Raptor and entered a requisition for a dozen more. The TTV's schematic filled the monitoring room, and she selected one of the surveillance drones she had inside. "Kleio, can you hear me?"

"I can hear you, Doctor Hinnerkopf. How may I be of assistance?"

"The outer hull of the TTV is healing itself."

"Correct. That is a normal function of the programmable-steel armor when damaged."

"Can you stop it from doing that?"

"Is the professor available to come to the bridge?"

"Never mind, then." Hinnerkopf muted the line. "Forget I asked."

"I'm surprised you even tried that," Nox chuckled.

"It was worth a shot while I wait for the other Raptors to print out." She rubbed her face. "Damn, there goes my whole morning."

"Maybe we should have stayed in bed."

"Oh, stop it!" Hinnerkopf's cheeks burned, and she smacked him playfully in the arm.

"How about trying a different approach?" Nox suggested. "The outer hull's too tough for one Raptor, but what about the inside? Why not send a few Wolverines in and put them to work removing those swarm reservoirs?"

"Yeah. You're right, of course. I just wanted to get those weapons off." She reached for the drone list, but stopped with her hand halfway to it. "What was that?"

"What was what?" Nox asked.

"One of the hangar transceivers just connected to the rest of the building and activated. Did you see that?"

"No." Nox furrowed his brow and stepped over to Hinnerkopf as she opened the transceiver's log.

"It *did* activate! See here? And it moved a *huge* number of files to . . . oh, no."

Nox saw it at the same time she did, and he triggered the building's general alarm.

"All drones, all STANDs, report to Hangar Four!" he snapped over the emergency network. "All drones and STANDs to Hangar Four! Full infosystem lockdown!"

The TTV's hatch sealed shut, and the drone feeds from inside switched off one by one.

"What's it doing?"

"Get back!" Nox pulled her toward the wall furthest from the hangar.

The TTV's graviton thrusters engaged and strained against the four malmetal bands holding it against the cradle. The bands stretched, thinned, and then snapped, and the TTV lifted free of its cradle.

"Even without restraints, there's no way it can shoot through the hangar doors!" Hinnerkopf shouted over the alarms.

"It's not going to shoot its way out!" Nox shouted. "Hang on to me!"

The TTV rose with a shocking burst of speed and smashed into the solid meter of reinforced malmetal separating the hangar from the surface. The barrier rang like a giant bell and bulged upward, and Hinnerkopf clung to Nox as the room quaked.

The TTV dropped to the floor, crushing the cradle, then

ascended once more to gong against the hangar door. Malmetal creaked. Upper supports between the hangar walls and roof deformed. The TTV descended once more, its upper hull barely dented.

"Containment breach in progress!" Nox shouted. "Scramble Switchblades! Target hostile craft leaving Hangar Four!"

The TTV slammed into the roof again, and a crack traced up the monitoring room's far wall. Virtual displays vanished and lighting panels dropped from the ceiling. Nox pulled Hinnerkopf under him, and the panels rebounded harmlessly off his back.

The TTV tilted back so that its impeller spike scraped against the floor, then it shot forward and smashed the hangar doors apart. Orange sunlight spilled through the narrow opening and caressed its gleaming hull. It backed up once more, tail screeching against the ground.

A Switchblade in helicopter mode swung in front of the opening and fired its 115mm railgun. The discharge cracked the air like lightning, and Hinnerkopf covered her ears and screamed. A divot formed in the TTV's nose, both its weapons blisters opened, and 12mm armor-piercing high-explosive rounds chattered against drone at a rate of 133 per second. The Switchblade's rotor blew off and it tumbled out of sight.

Shutters around the weapon blisters snapped shut. The TTV backed up a little further, then surged forward and burst through the hangar doors.

Superintendent Park Sung-Wook leaned back in his chair in Portcullis-Prime's operations room and cycled through the catalog in his virtual vision. His Worlds Beyond Ours account was flush with loot from the triple-ultra world Jonas had shared with him, and he suddenly found himself with more in-game wealth than he knew what to do with.

"Hey, Mikael?" Sung-Wook asked.

"Yes, sir?"

"What do you think? A Phoenix or an Intrepid?"

The special agent looked over his shoulder. "Since when were you in the market for a new ship?"

"I could tell you, but then I'd have to kill you."

"You're seriously going to leave me in the dark?"

"Let's just say I got a tip from a friend."

"Wish I had friends like that. Sounds like one hot tip."

"Positively scorching."

"Well, if you're asking for my *informed* opinion," Mikael placed a hand on his chest, "it's hard to go wrong with an Intrepid. They're just solid all-rounders."

"Yeah, but they do seem a bit boring."

"Very true. Which is why I recommend the Phoenix. Specifically the Phoenix Type-J."

"The one with the bigger engines?"

"That's the ticket. They might not have all the features of the Intrepids, but they're an absolute pleasure to fly. My son has one that I joyride in when he's grounded. *So* much fun."

"You repair it when you give it back to him?"

"Naaaaaah. Part of the life lesson."

Sung-Wook chuckled. "All right, then. I'll give it a look. Thanks."

"No problem, sir." Mikael turned back around.

Sung-Wook scrolled further down the catalog. A Phoenix-J was nice, but if he saved up for a while or maybe even spent some of his real world cash...

An alarm sounded in his virtual hearing.

Sung-Wook closed the catalog and stood up.

"What have we got?"

"Looks like a general alarm at DTI headquarters," Mikael responded. "No details."

"Get in touch with them. Find out what's going on."

"Sir, a large aircraft just left the DTI tower and appears to be heading our way. And it's moving *very* quickly. According to this, it's pulling five gees of sustained acceleration."

"Show me."

A window opened on the map of Earth, and a view from orbit showed a long, pale ovoid racing through the cityscape.

"Isn't that the same chronoport from a few days ago?" Mikael asked.

"You're absolutely right." Sung-Wook turned to his drone operator. "Scramble the Switchblades. Get them in the air now."

"Unscheduled chronoport now hypersonic and still accelerating. Still heading directly for us."

"Incoming alert from DTI headquarters. Unscheduled chronoport is confirmed hostile."

"Then get those Switchblades up!" Sung-Wook shouted.

"Target decelerating rapidly. Sir, it's almost here!"

"Give me an external view!"

Another window opened over the map to show the craft flying straight at them. Its hull formed a full moon of gunmetal gray, and shallow blisters on either side split open. Sung-Wook sucked in a quick breath a moment before the map of Earth exploded inward.

The deafening roar of incoming fire masked secondary explosions as the 12mm rounds burst into cones of antipersonnel fléchettes. Twin streams of fire raked across the operations room, and fléchettes shredded equipment and pulped the first row of agents. Blood splattered Sung-Wook's uniform, and a hot shard of malmetal cut across his cheek.

His mouth barely formed the first syllable of a command when the fire swung back, this time bursting into red powdery clouds that immolated everything they touched. Mikael's face and shoulders burst into flames, and he fell from his seat screaming.

Sung-Wook backed away, but the red powder spread everywhere and a wisp caught his arm. His sleeve and flesh ignited, and he cried out. The gunfire traversed the room once more, and agents blew apart into clouds of fiery entrails. Fléchettes deployed a meter in front of Sung-Wook, and his chest exploded into crimson mist.

Philo kept firing until everyone in the operations room was dead. It wasn't the first time he'd used a TTV's weapons in self-defense, and he supposed this was no different. None of these people would exist after they fixed the Knot, so he couldn't kill people that would soon be erased from reality.

At least, that's what he told himself as the last pieces of the last Peacekeeper dropped to the ground in a wet, flaming heap.

"The tower's drones do not appear to be active," Kleio reported.

"That won't last for long, but it'll help," Philo replied.

He adjusted the *Kleio*'s target, and the guns' line-of-sight slewed up to the tower's suppression antenna. Their dynamic loaders switched to high-explosive armor-piercing rounds, and a cascade of tiny explosions shredded the antenna's exotic matter. Flickers of phasing debris rained down the tower's sides, and the suppression field over the Yanluo Blight died.

"Debris from the tower is phasing erratically into the past," Kleio reported. "I can no longer single out the chronoports in Barricade Squadron."

"Good. Then they might not be able to see us when we run for it."

"Admin attack drones approaching from both the south and northeast."

"They'll have to try harder than that to catch us," Philo said. "Now get us moving, Kleio!"

Raibert did his best to adjust to prison life. Or at least to look like he was adjusting to prison life. He had pants now, which was a big plus. And shoes, and a shirt, and food in his stomach. With those basic needs out of the way, he found Cynthia behind the temple with two pickaxes slung over her shoulder.

"What're those for?"

"Looks like you're on mining detail." She handed one to him. "We're stockpiling materials for the second temple."

"A *second* temple? Isn't one enough?"

"Maybe. But some people really want to fight another dragon. Come on. I'll show you the way."

Raibert shrugged and followed her down the back of the hill and away from town.

"Don't you have anything you need to get back to?" he asked.

"Yeah, but you seem a decent sort, so I thought I'd help you get settled in. You kill any Peacekeepers?"

"No."

"Blow up any of their buildings?"

"*No*," he answered more forcefully.

"That's a shame. Oh, well. I'll guess it eventually."

"Would it help if I made one up? I already told you what I did to get thrown in here."

"Sure you did, Raibert. Whatever you say."

She led him toward a clearing between the foot of the hill and the woodland beyond. He spotted a narrow path that led into the woods.

"You do realize a pickaxe isn't ideal for a marble quarry, right?"

"Not a problem. The next temple's going to be out of solid gold."

"Seriously? There's that amount of gold nearby?"

"There is after we asked for it nicely."

"Doesn't that amount of gold upset the town's economy or something?"

"What would we spend it on that she won't just give us?"

"Good point. Never mind." Raibert's vision blurred and he hefted the pickaxe. "Hey, Cynthia?"

"Yeah?" She turned around just as the edge of the pickaxe split her head open. The blow killed her instantly, and she flopped onto the grass, pulling Raibert forward with the tool embedded in her skull. Her legs twitched, and blood drained from the wound. He placed a shoe against the side of her head and pulled the pickaxe free.

He stopped and froze, his vision clearing.

"What?" Raibert stared at the body, then at the bloody weapon in his hands, then at the body again. "What just happened?"

The sound of stone grinding against stone echoed from the temple, and six huge statues stomped out and then descended the hill in great, powerful strides that shook the earth. Raibert dropped the pickaxe and backed away, but they quickly surrounded him.

"Explain yourself, prisoner!" one of them thundered down at him.

"I-I-I-I-I," he stuttered.

"You have been given a command, prisoner! Explain yourself!"

"But I don't know! I have no idea what just happened! It must have been a glitch in the simulation!"

"A likely story. Sweep the area!"

One of the statues bent over and lifted the pickaxe between two fingers. Pink, spongy fragments still clung to the blade.

"Find anything?" a second statue asked.

"Negative. No sign of aberrant code. What about on the prisoner?"

The second statue ran a hand over him. He tried to back away, but a third statue shoved him forward.

"Nothing. Diagnostics on the connectome interface are clean."

"Then it looks like we've got a troublemaker. The warden will hear of this."

"I think she already has."

Booming footfalls echoed from the temple, and Raibert spied the marble statue of Ixchel stepping into the open. She fixed him with a cold glare and descended the hill with earthshaking strides.

"Wow. That was fast," a statue said. "She must have had her eye on this one."

"Oh, you're in for it now."

"But I swear I have no idea what just happened!"

"The code doesn't lie, scum. Unlike your mouth."

The guard statues formed a semicircle behind Raibert as the statue of Warden Ixchel lumbered to a halt.

"Report," she said.

"Ma'am! This man was implicated in the temporary death of a fellow prisoner. We are in the process of checking the area for domain aberrations, but so far have found nothing."

"You did this?" Ixchel demanded of him.

"I honestly have no idea what happened, I swear! It was like I wasn't in control of my own body."

A textbox opened next to Ixchel and her statue skimmed its contents.

"You've been here less than a day, and you're already killing people in my prison? This is totally unacceptable."

"But I—"

"Guards!" Ixchel commanded. "Sweep the area again. Leave nothing to chance. I want a full report within the hour."

"Yes, Warden!"

"And as for you." Ixchel gazed down at him with brimstone in her marble eye-pits. "Prisoner Raibert Kaminski, you are hereby confined to the isolation subdomain, pending a review of this incident. If you are found guilty of willfully killing another prisoner, you will be punished accordingly, and in my prison that means one-way abstraction."

"But I didn't do anything!"

"Guards! Take this trash away!"

One of the statues grabbed him by the shoulder and was about to haul him off when the ground reverberated. Not from heavy footsteps, but with the oscillations of a distant and alien sound.

"What was that?" a statue asked.

The reverberation grew, tickling up through Raibert's shoes, and so did the sound. It was a low musical cacophony not unlike an orchestra testing out their instruments and warming up before a performance. The ground trembled, almost as if it had become a single, giant speaker.

"What's going on?" Ixchel demanded. "Is something wrong with the domain?"

"Running diagnostics now, Warden."

The cacophony died away, and all seemed calm again until the ground shook with an escalation of trilling musical notes.

"Is that... Wagner?" Ixchel asked.

"There, Warden!" One of the guards pointed toward the edge of the woods. "Look!"

A solitary warrior charged out of the tree line, horned helmet upon his head and battle axe in hand. His red bushy beard flapped with each mighty stride, and spittle ran from the side of his open mouth.

A second Viking bounded into the open, identical to the first.

Then ten more joined in.

Then a hundred.

Then a thousand armored, crazed, saliva-drooling, axe-wielding Vikings all thundered across the field.

"FOR SYSGOV!" the horde of Philos cried, and the ground shuddered to the rousing music of *Walkürenritt*—Richard Wagner's "Ride of the Valkyries."

CHAPTER SIXTEEN

Department of Incarceration prison domain
2979 CE

"MULTI-INSTANCE WEAPONRY DETECTED, WARDEN! DOMAIN CODE is being rewritten!"

"Neutralize the anomaly at once!" Ixchel commanded.

"Yes, ma'am!"

The sky darkened instantly and a cold wind blew across the field. Lightning crackled from cloud to cloud, then forked to the ground. A few Philos dropped in smoking ruin, but the rest charged on, unfazed by the attack.

"Try *harder*!" Ixchel urged.

"Working on it, ma'am!"

More lightning stabbed at the charging horde, and the clouds lit up with inner flame. Fiery boulders fell from the sky and pummeled the Viking ranks, and each mighty impact shook the earth and blasted dozens into the air. The Philos howled with frothing, berserker rage and raced on as the "Ride of the Valkyries" escalated with bombastic brass.

"Increase countermeasure magnitude!"

The boulders ballooned out to ten times their previous size, and the first one crashed to earth and rolled through the horde, crushing over a hundred Philos. More fell from the sky, but then suddenly froze in midair.

"What are you doing?" Ixchel demanded. "Continue the attack!"

"I'm trying, but my commands are being interrupted!"

"What's going on here? How is this possible?"

"I don't...oh, no. Yanluo Violation detected! We've got an AI in here!"

"Freeze the domain state! Freeze it now!"

"I...I can't! It's actively rerouting my interface!"

Ixchel swung to face Raibert. "That thing is here for you, isn't it?"

"Ma'am, you already know the answer." Raibert sneered at her and backed away.

"In that case..." The giant statue clenched a fist and pulled it back for a bone-crushing strike.

A lone Philo ran ahead of the pack, raised his battle axe so far over his head that the blade almost touched the small of his back, then hurled it forward. The axe spun through the air, twirled over Raibert's head, and sank into Ixchel's face. Her statue disintegrated into a pile of white and gray cubes, and the axe fell to the ground blade first. It stuck in place with the handle facing Raibert, and the grass around the blade sank into soil that then changed to a flat brown grid.

The weapon's edge gleamed with lethal sharpness, and a label had been placed upon the axe head in bold letters against a yellow and black checkered background.

It read FOR EMERGENCY USE ONLY.

"Codeburner weapons!" a guard shouted. "We've got *codeburners* in here!"

Raibert grabbed the axe handle, lifted the remarkably light weapon, and swung it through the knee of a guard statue. The construct fell to the ground and shattered into hundreds of dark cubes.

"All guards, interface with domain one two seven! Backup required! Backup—"

Philos swarmed over the remaining guards like ants defending their mound. They toppled them over with weight of numbers, and hacked their prone bodies to pieces. The horde formed a protective circle around Raibert, and one of the Philos, the one that had thrown the codeburner axe, stepped forward.

"Miss me?" he asked.

"You have no idea how glad I am to see you!" Raibert ran up and embraced his companion. "These animals *violated* my connectome!"

"Yeah, I know. I'm sorry, but there was nothing I could do to stop them."

"Can you get me out of here?"

"We're about to find out. Come on! This way!"

"THIS WAY!" the horde echoed as they charged up the hill to the temple.

Raibert ran with them alongside the lead Philo.

"The guards have the ability to spawn dragons and other fantasy creatures!" he shouted over the clamor.

"Probably nonsentient combat auxiliaries!" Philo replied. "Thanks for the warning! We'll be ready for them!"

"WE'LL BE READY!"

Dozens of guard statues filed out of the temple, more than could have possibly fitted inside at once, and the front ranks of the Philos crashed into them. Some guards trampled through the horde, crushing Philos underfoot, while others sent Philos flying through the air with great punches and kicks. The Vikings chopped the statues off at the knees and swarmed over them when they fell, but more statues kept pouring out of the temple.

"It doesn't matter how many we destabilize!" Philo shouted. "They'll just keep coming, but that works to our advantage!"

"How exactly is this helping us?"

"You'll see!"

Several Philos picked up severed heads and limbs from the statues, carried them back to the horde's rear, and set them on the ground.

"We're taking trophies?" Raibert asked.

"In a manner of speaking!" the lead Philo said as his copies arranged the dismembered pieces into a wide arc. "The guard avatars have interface code stored in each instance! I'm using the fragments in a way they didn't intend!"

More statues slammed into the horde's front ranks, and several Philos flew over Raibert's head.

"You're running out of copies!"

"I know, but we're almost finished here!"

The clouds stirred, and a massive silhouette slid by just above them.

"Philo, I think they just spawned the dragon!"

"Good!" Philo proclaimed. "About time they tried that!"

"*Good?* How is this a good thing?"

"You'll see!"

A great golden beast swooped out of the clouds, flapped its

broad, leathery wings once, twice, then landed atop the temple and sank its talons into the marble. It reared back with a many-horned head, breathed in deeply—

"Philo..."

—and spewed a continuous plume of blue flame that reduced statues to molten sludge.

"What?" Raibert asked.

The dragon swiped its barbed tail through the guards, catapulting them through the air to land in the village with heavy thuds. It pounced on three more, crushing them under its bulk, and snatched a fourth into its powerful jaws before biting it in half.

"What's theirs is mine!" Philo laughed. "All right, Raibert! Let's wrap this up!"

The statue fragments on the ground formed a complete circle now, and arcane energy crackled out of the hollowed eye sockets of the severed heads. Philo took the codeburner axe out of Raibert's hands and brought it down on one of the heads. Energy flashed around the circumference and a pool of blue light swirled into existence within.

"Where's it lead?" Raibert asked.

"No time! I'll explain on the other side! Now get in!"

"Now Philo, I'd really like to know what I'm—"

The Viking kicked Raibert in the butt, and he fell into the glowing portal. The outer layers of his body dissolved, and an impenetrable darkness fell upon his mind.

Raibert blinked his eyes open against the glare of overhead lights and found himself seated within a sterile white room. He heard the hum of ventilation and felt air flow across his skin.

"Great. I'm naked again, aren't I?" he said in a voice deeper than his own. "Wait, what?"

He looked down at heavy hands that were not his own, then down further at a well-defined abdomen and other parts that *definitely* didn't belong to him. The cool air against his skin also didn't feel the same. Not wrong but different. It was as if his skin simply informed him the ambient temperature was low without relaying the unpleasantness of actually feeling cold.

"Umm..."

"You make it?" Philo asked over his virtual hearing.

"Yeah," Raibert replied. "Is this real or an abstraction?"

"Real. I pulled your connectome out of the domain and found a way to load it into an empty case. Then I loaded the case into a STAND general purpose synthoid."

"Case? STAND?"

"Admin synthoids work a bit differently than ours, but all that can wait. Kleio's getting shot at outside, so you need to move."

"Right." Raibert stood up. "Where to?"

"I'll plot a path on your virtual sight. Follow it. Now move!"

A golden dashed line traced across the floor and disappeared out the door. Raibert stepped up to it, the malmetal parted, and he peeked his head out and checked in both directions.

All clear.

He followed the line to the left and ran down the hall far faster than his old body could ever have managed. His synthoid legs cleared the corridor in rapid strides, and he skidded to a halt at the T-junction. He slapped his hands against the wall, bounced off, and took the path to the right.

A door split open and two men stepped out in blue cleanroom suits with white stripes running up the sides.

"Sir?" asked the first. "Can I help you?"

Raibert didn't give them time to ponder why a synthoid was suddenly up and about. His connectome had been ripped from his flesh without his permission, and whatever body remained had likely been reclaimed into snacks for the cafeteria or fertilizer for someone's garden or who knew what. He'd just narrowly escaped being sent to the abstract version of hell, and he wasn't about to let anyone or anything stand between him and freedom.

Every ART operative received the download on hand-to-hand combat as part of his or her basic training and was required to keep it current. Without it, no one could be cleared for interaction in primitive eras of history. Raibert had never much cared for it—he'd dutifully passed his certifications, but that sort of sweaty nonsense wasn't for him—but now, for the first time, he realized how...misguided that attitude had been.

He charged forward and hooked a fist against the first man's face. Bone crumbled under the impact, flesh collapsed inward, and the man's eyes bulged out of his skull. Raibert spun around with more dexterity than he ever remembered, and his heel cracked against the second man's neck and broke it.

The two bodies dropped to the floor. Peacekeeper icons appeared over both corpses, and an alarm sounded in his virtual hearing.

"Not good!" He shook the blood from his hand, found the gold line again, and raced down the corridor. The building shook from an impact somewhere above him, and Raibert steadied himself against the wall as a second alarm activated. Information scrolled through his virtual sight too fast for him to absorb.

"What's going on out there?" he asked.

"We're making sure they stay focused on us."

The floor shifted again, and Raibert sidestepped into the wall and kept moving.

"I think it's working!"

"It has to. The airspace is getting thick with drones, and we need you on board or none of us are getting out of this."

"Right!"

Raibert followed the line as it zigzagged through the complex, then led to double doors that opened into a wide office area filled with Peacekeepers at their cubicles, some of them rising out of their seats. He sprinted through and ignored the stares.

"There he is!" a woman shouted from the door through which he'd entered. "Dispatch Wolverines to floor two zero zero, east quadrant!"

"I don't think the distraction's working anymore!" Raibert ducked out the other side and dashed onward. "What's a Wolverine?"

"One of the more common Admin drone types. About the size of a big dog. Quad-legged and usually armed."

"Well, they're sending some after me!"

"Sorry, but there's not much I can do until you're closer to the building exterior."

"That's just *fantastic*! Can't you slow them down?"

"I'll do what I can, but I'm back on the *Kleio*. Peacekeepers flooded the tower's infostructure with just about every abstract weapon in their arsenal. It got too hot for me and I had to bail."

"Terrific!"

"Keep moving, Raibert. You're nearly there."

"Good thing this body doesn't get tired!"

He rounded a corner and entered a long straightaway that led to a windowed lounge along the building exterior. He pumped his legs and arms and dashed past closed doors on either side. A Wolverine skidded on all fours around the corner, regained its balance, and galloped after him. It raised the gun in its head and fired.

The first hypervelocity dart stabbed through the synthoid muscle between his neck and shoulder and blew it apart in an eruption of dark gray sinews. His body registered the damage and dutifully reported it to his mind without any sensation of pain. He *knew* he'd been shot and he *knew* he'd lost some muscle functionality, but his mind remained unclouded by the primal impulses of real nerve endings.

A malmetal wall slapped shut between them, and rapid-fire munitions pelted the barrier.

"That'll hold it for a little while," Philo said. "Now, hurry, Raibert! You're almost there!"

The tempo of shots against the barrier doubled, then tripled, then quadrupled, and darts punched through and ricocheted down the hall.

"It's not going to hold!" Raibert shouted.

"When I say duck, you drop to the floor and get as far to the side as you can. Got it?"

"Low and to the side! Whatever you say!"

Two Wolverines stuck their metal claws through the ragged bullet holes and tore them wider. They jammed their heads through the openings and aimed.

"Duck!"

Raibert dove and pressed his body against where the wall met the floor, then covered his head as the windows at the end of the straightaway blew inward and Gatling fire roared past. Explosive rounds tore the barrier and all four Wolverines apart and splattered the hallway with the tattered remains of two Peacekeepers who'd been standing behind them.

"Get up!" Philo shouted.

Raibert bolted off the ground like a runner coming off the blocks and sprinted toward the clear, beautiful daylight ahead. The TTV slid close, blocking the sun with a heavily dented hull, and the cargo bay hatch split open. Railgun fire cracked the air outside, and the TTV's prog-steel rang with each strike.

Raibert ran to the broken edge of the lounge and leapt through the air. His legs continued to pump as he soared over the kilometer-long drop, and finally he hit the cargo bay floor and rolled across it.

The hatch sealed, and the graviton thrusters powered up.

"Kleio, get us out of here now!" Philo ordered.

"Would the professor please come to the bridge?"

"Damn it!" Raibert exclaimed, rising off the ground. "I'm coming! I'm coming!" He took the counter-grav tube up to the bridge and hurried over to the command table. Philo's avatar manifested in his virtual sight, and Raibert said, "Now engage the impeller already!"

"Would the professor please come to the bridge?"

"Uhh ..." Raibert glanced at Philo, then down at his new body. "Uh-oh."

"Kleio, initiate pilot reconfiguration on my authority," Philo stated. "Link synthoid on the bridge with valid pilot profile Raibert Kaminski."

"Configuration change acknowledged and accepted. Hello, Professor. Welcome back."

"Yes, yes. Now get us the hell out of here!"

"Of course, Professor. Engaging impeller in three ... two ..."

Raibert waited for the "one" but it never came. An impact shook the ship, and he held on to the railing around the command table.

"I am sorry, but the impeller will not engage."

"WHAT THE HELL?" Raibert blurted.

Philo opened a map of the Admin city.

"There!" He indicated a tower on the outskirts of the Yanluo Blight. "We must still be in range of a suppression tower. Kleio, head for Portcullis-3 as fast as you can."

"Changing course. ETA, three minutes thirty-seven seconds."

The ship lurched from a trio of rapid strikes.

"Armor compromised," Kleio reported. "Graviton thruster three has sustained moderate damage. Reactor superconductor lines seven and eight severed. Bypassing damage and increasing load to remaining lines."

"Come on, Kleio. Hold it together."

"I will do my best, Professor. Please be aware that normal propulsion safeties remain disengaged. Brace yourself for hazardous acceleration."

Raibert wrapped his arms around the command table railing.

Admin drones buzzed around the TTV and pumped shot after shot into it. The reactor dumped raw fury into the graviton thrusters, and the TTV exploded past them at a velocity they couldn't possibly match as Raibert dangled almost horizontally from the command table.

"Really glad I've got this new body right about now!" he cried.

The suppression tower loomed ahead as a blue and white spire tipped with a spike of exotic matter. More drones launched from the tower's landing pads, but the TTV kept accelerating, the front of its hull glowing dull red from air friction.

"Now, Kleio," Philo said. "Fire!"

Blisters snapped open and the Gatling guns poured high-explosive rounds into the top of the tower. Exotic matter shattered under the torrential storm of metal and explosives, and its suppression field faltered and died. The TTV zipped past the tower and through the Switchblade drones' engagement envelope so quickly that only a few shots rang off its hull.

"The impeller appears to be free of disruptions," Kleio reported.

"Then get us the hell out of here!" Raibert cried. "Forget the countdown!"

"Yes, Professor. Engaging impeller...now."

The TTV's hot singularity reactor pumped colossal amounts of energy into the impeller spike, morphing the exotic matter so that it blocked chronotons flowing up the timestream. Temporal pressure built up along the spike, pushing the vessel into a new phase state, and the TTV slipped from its current time axis and vanished from the Admin.

CHAPTER SEVENTEEN

Department of Temporal Investigation
2979 CE

"THIS IS AN ABSOLUTE DISASTER!" SHIGEKI STORMED. "HOW DID we miss the AI on his ship, and how did we let that thing parade through our systems like it owned the place?"

The staff assembled around the table didn't immediately respond, and only Nox dared meet his gaze. Hinnerkopf hunched forward on her elbows, eyes lowered, studying a blank spot on the table, while Kloss watched and waited for someone else to speak up first. Jonas stared blankly forward, his uniform blackened by smoke and smeared across one sleeve with someone else's bloody handprint. Shigeki could tell he'd been shaken by the carnage wrought upon Portcullis-Prime, but he'd deal with that once they were alone.

"I am waiting for an answer, people."

"Director." Hinnerkopf straightened her spine and looked up. "I believe that as the Under-Director of Technology, the responsibility for this blunder falls upon me. I take full responsibility for my lapses in judgment and will accept any reprimand you feel is appropriate."

"Katja, I don't need people falling on their swords over this. What I *do* need are answers."

"I think the explanation is fairly simple," Kloss offered. "Sys-Gov's technological advantages proved far more formidable than we'd anticipated, especially considering we were dealing with a lightly armed civilian version of our own chronoports."

"We *did* predict the performance of its weapon systems accurately," Hinnerkopf added. "And Hangar Four *was* secure by those standards. But we grossly miscalculated the self-repair characteristics of its armor and the performance of its drive system. Both of which together allowed it to breach containment. As for the AI..." She threw up her arms. "I'm still not sure how it got a foothold into our system. It'll take some time to diagnose the breach of the tower's infostructure and identify the points of entry."

"Even taking all of that into account, how in Yanluo's blazing realms did they slip past Barricade?" Shigeki demanded.

Kloss looked first to Jonas, then to Hinnerkopf when no response came. She cleared her throat.

"The destruction of the suppression towers, particularly when they were in a fully energized state, sent a considerable amount of exotic debris phasing backward through time. We believe they used the interference as cover to make their escape."

"You *believe*," Shigeki shot back, even his formidable discipline unable to keep the anger out of his tone.

"I'm truly sorry, Director, but that's the best we have. By the time the noise cleared, there was no trace of them anywhere within negative six years."

Shigeki took a slow, seething breath and waited for someone else to speak up.

"Is that it?" he finally asked. "Is that all you've got for me? We had this man and his ship completely at our mercy and he managed to slip away. Not only that, but do I need to remind you what he intends to do?"

"He doesn't know how to alter the timeline," Hinnerkopf said.

"Not *yet*. But all of you know that's exactly what he and his infernal AI are setting out do to. If he had any doubts before about wiping out the Admin, I can assure you they're gone now! People, our entire *existence* is at risk because we let this man slip out of our grasp."

"Then what do you want us to do, boss?" Kloss asked.

"The only thing we can do." Shigeki placed the tips of his fingers on the table. "We're going after him. Jonas."

His son flinched at the sound of his name.

"Yes?" he asked, and his eyes truly focused on his father for the first time in the meeting.

"I want all of Pathfinder Squadron prepped for immediate departure. Make sure they're equipped for an extended mission."

"Right. Got it. What about Barricade?"

"We're leaving them here. We can't afford to leave the True Present unguarded with all the holes Kaminski just blew in our suppression grid. Nox."

"Sir?"

"Assemble our best operators. I want full drone complements and combat teams on every chronoport. Make sure you assign at least one STAND *with* a combat frame to each team. We're not taking any chances, now that Kaminski's walking around in a synthoid."

"Consider it done, sir."

"Kloss?"

"Yes, boss?"

"We need people we can trust without question on this mission. I will personally take command from *Pathfinder-Prime*, and you're going to make sure we have trusted people captaining every chronoport. I don't want any problems if word gets out about Kaminski's true goals or the nature of the Knot."

"Should I assume everyone here is joining you?"

"You should."

"Understood, boss. I'll see to it."

"And Kloss? Go to the Yanluo Armory and get Vassal out of storage."

"I . . ." The Martian's lips parted.

"I'm not going up against a goddamned AI without backup. If he throws his own thinking machine at us, then we're going to fight fire with fire. Get Vassal out of storage and put it on *Pathfinder-Prime*. I'll make sure you have the necessary approvals for its release."

"Understood."

Shigeki pushed off the table and took a step back.

"Make no mistake, people. You screwed up," he told them. "You know you screwed up, and *I* know you screwed up. But I also know you're better than this, and I need you at your best. So set aside your wounded pride and refocus every iota you have on the task before us.

"Make no mistake about the gravity of this crisis, either. We're faced with a man who threatens not just our lives or the lives of our friends and families. He has the power to end our entire universe, he's got an advanced time machine *and* a rogue AI at his command, and he has every conceivable motive to do just that. If we don't stop him, we will *never* have existed in the first place. Our very existence and the existence of everyone and everything we hold dear hangs in the balance. Failure is not an option. Hoping he doesn't succeed is not an option. We *are* going after him. We *will* find him. And we *will* end him. Is that understood?"

"Yes, *sir*," Nox snapped.

"We're with you, boss," Kloss said.

"Every step of the way," Hinnerkopf added.

"I know you are." Shigeki watched spirits rise across the room with a sense of profound satisfaction. "All right, people. Let's make it happen. Dismissed!"

Nox, Kloss, and Hinnerkopf left the room, leaving the senior Shigeki alone with Jonas. He rounded the table and sat next to his son.

"I'm sorry, Dad," he finally said.

"What for?"

Jonas shook his head, lips quivering as he struggled to find the words.

"I don't know if I can come with you."

"But I need you, Son. More than ever."

"No, you don't." He sucked in a shaky breath. "You know I'm the only one who doesn't belong at this table."

"Is that what you think?" Shigeki put an arm around his son. "That couldn't be farther from the truth."

"The only reason I'm here right now is because of luck. If I'd been in the operations room at the time, I'd be dead, too. Instead, I hid under my desk as my team was cut down. I was worse than useless."

"There was nothing you could have done."

"But I should've *tried*! Instead I hid like a coward, and even then I only survived because of dumb luck. Any one of those bullets could have ricocheted in just the right way, and then I wouldn't be here anymore."

Shigeki hugged his son's shoulders.

"When I came down and saw what had become of my team, I..." He whimpered and tears leaked from his eyes. "Dad, there wasn't anything left in that room that was recognizably human. Just scattered pieces of scorched meat and bone. I...I can't go with you. I...someone should stay behind. I can do that."

"I need my best people on this, Son, and that includes you."

"But I'm fucking *useless!*"

"No, you're not. Don't say that. I know some people think you're only here because you're my son. Jonas, some idiots are *always* going to think that way! And when the ones who do see how you act in meetings, they think you're not paying attention. Well, let them think that. Let them think less of you. Because what's actually happening is you're paying closer attention than anyone else at the table, and then they make the mistake of underestimating you. *Let* them think that, even say it behind your back, because it gives you an edge they'll never see coming. But you and I know the truth, even if you don't want to admit it right now, and I *need* my best people right now, Son. I need them focused and on top of their game, and that means I need *you.*"

"I'm sorry, Dad," Jonas swiped a hand across his eyes.

Shigeki pulled him close, and he rested his head against his father's chest.

"I'm sorry I tried to run from this."

"It's okay. Everyone has moments of weakness. What matters is what they do when it happens."

"I'm going to be there with you." Jonas straightened and swiped his eyes again, then met his father's gaze levelly. "Every step of the way. You can count on me."

"I know I can. I always have."

His clothes didn't fit anymore.

Raibert knew it was a stupid thing to be upset about, but there it was. He'd worn the same size for almost sixty years, and now all of a sudden he had to print an entirely new wardrobe. He grabbed a pine-green shirt and tossed it onto the floor where microbots cut it into manageable pieces and carted them off to reclamation.

At least he didn't have to reclaim his scarves. The neck on this brute-of-a-body wasn't *that* thick. He grabbed some of the tunics and togas he'd worn as "Titus Aluis Camillus" and added them to the pile.

"Professor, I believe the togas would still fit."

"We're not taking any chances," he huffed.

"And, if I may add, I am perfectly capable of adjusting your wardrobe without your assistance."

"No, Kleio. I will do this unpleasant task myself. Just keep chopping them up. *All* of them."

"Very well, Professor."

Raibert emptied the rest of the wardrobe onto the floor. He thought he should feel tired, but no matter how much he exerted himself, he didn't fatigue. He still needed to sleep; the abstracted connectome inside his synthoid body still required the same mental maintenance as a meat brain, but the body could go on and on and on for as long as he required within the limits of its capacitors, which themselves could last for years without a recharge.

He wanted to exercise, to work up a good sweat that cleansed both body and mind, but they'd taken even that from him.

"Just mulch it," he said, some of the fire leaking out of his voice. "All of it."

"Yes, Professor."

He stepped out into the corridor and planted two massive fists on his hips. The *Kleio*'s systems hummed and thrummed as they phased through time, and he looked around for something else to do. Anything to distract him from the elephant in the room.

Or the synthoid, in this case.

He sighed and opened an external view of himself in his virtual sight: blonde hair down to his shoulders, blue eyes, and a chiseled physique. And pants—he'd spent more than enough time running around naked, thank you very much—but the chest remained bare except for a dark shell over the right shoulder.

The synthoid wasn't bad looking when you got right down to it. Actually quite handsome. He could have done a lot worse, he supposed. The world looked different from this far up, and the bed would have to be lengthened, but inhabiting a synthoid body certainly had its advantages. He'd taken that shot to the shoulder with barely a stutter in his stride, and the microbot cast over the wound had nearly repaired the damaged sinew and skin.

But he shouldn't have had to make *any* adjustments. He should still be in his own body, damn it.

Raibert rubbed the hardened shell over his shoulder. It felt smooth and cool to the touch. More importantly, it felt real. As real as anything he'd experienced in his natural body and as real as the prison domain had seemed. So therefore it *was* real, at least from the perspective of his connectome.

"It's not like I have a body to go back to."

He rubbed his shoulder again. It didn't hurt, but he intuitively understood the extent of the injury.

"Kleio, how are the repairs coming?"

"I am making good progress, Professor. My superconductor lines are operational again, and I have nearly solved the misalignment in graviton thruster three. Hull repairs are a secondary priority, but I am printing extra swarms to expedite damage control."

"Good," he said, nodding. "Very good."

He stared at the mirrored image some more.

"Hey, Kleio?"

"Yes, Professor?"

"I'm sorry if I'm a butthole to you sometimes. You did a great job out there."

"Thank you, Professor. It is a pleasure to be of service."

Raibert clenched a fist and raised his arm so that the bicep bulged.

"So this is a STAND."

"Actually, the Admin calls them STYNDs," Philo offered, appearing next to him. "The 'and' gets replaced with a 'y' in their version of English. And it's not a combat frame, just one of their general purpose synthoids."

"Still, it could prove useful. Best to focus on the positives, right?"

"I suppose so. You doing okay?"

"I'll live. How about you?"

"Fine. None of the damage to my connectome was permanent."

"Glad to hear it. 'Ride of the Valkyries,' huh?"

"Yup."

"Where'd that come from?"

"I don't know. Psychological warfare?" Philo shrugged. "It just felt right, I guess."

"Good enough for me. Though there is one *other* thing about my rescue I haven't figured out yet."

"Yeah? What's that?"

"Just out of curiosity," Raibert began delicately, "where *did* you get a codeburner?"

Philo's avatar dimmed.

"I mean, don't get me wrong," Raibert continued, "I'm glad you had it and *extremely* grateful you used it. But those things are illegal. They're the sort of weapon you use to kill another AC in the abstract."

"Yeah, they are."

"Then where did it come from?"

"I've had it for a while. Kleio kept it for me."

"Is that so? Kleio! I take back every nice thing I ever said about you!"

"Duly noted, Professor."

"So you've had it for a while?"

"That's right," Philo admitted.

"'A while' being...what exactly?"

"From before we met. From when I was you-know-who's companion."

"Ah. Now it makes sense."

"But I never used it, I swear!" Philo said urgently. "I might have threatened someone with it once or twice, but I never used it."

"It's all right. Don't worry about it."

"Seriously? You sure you're fine with me having one of those and never telling you?"

"Yeah, sure. I mean, come on, I knew you were a little rough around the edges when we joined up. I didn't think it involved *codeburners*, but I knew there was a part of your past you didn't want intruding on the present. And I was fine with that."

"You never brought it up."

"At the time I was respecting your privacy. And afterward, to be perfectly honest, I plain forgot about it until now."

"Yeah," Philo chuckled. "Meat brains are known to do that."

"That they are. And besides, it all worked out in the end, right? I mean, yes, I did just have my mind violated and my physical body thrown in the trash, but I got a kick-ass new body out of it."

"Raibert?"

"Also, the intended recipient for this synthoid must have been compensating for *something*." He tugged the elastic band of his pants forward. "I suppose this could come in handy if I ever decide to date again. Not that I'm in any rush after the Beckett Disaster." He let the elastic snap back into place.

"Raibert."

"But the option is there. All in all, I'd say this was a win for me."

"Stop, Raibert. Just stop."

"Something you want to say?" He grimaced and switched off the reflection with a wave.

"Yeah, there is. I think you're going through PSS."

"Oh, please," he dismissed.

"Physical Separation Syndrome."

"I'm not an idiot, Philo. I know what it is. My dad experienced it when he transitioned. It's no big deal."

"Tavish went through a very mild case, and he was ready for it. He left his physical body behind of his own volition after a long natural life, surrounded by the comfort of friends and family. You didn't have any of those luxuries. The Admin forced abstraction upon you suddenly and violently. That sort of experience leaves a mark."

"True, but most people undergoing PSS are prescribed synthoid bodies. And look!" He tapped his chest. "Already done!"

"Yes, and I'm sure that'll help. But even there, it's not a match for your old body. It's going to take some adjustment. You can't go through what they did to you and come out the other side unscathed."

"Sure I can. Besides, there's nothing we can do about it now, so no point worrying over it."

"Stop it, Raibert. Just stop it. Look, I'm worried about you. That's all I'm trying to say."

Raibert tapped his temple. "If you think I don't have it together, then come on over and see for yourself. I'll drop the whole firewall, and you can poke around all you want until you're satisfied."

He instinctively reached for the pathways between his mind and Philo's, but couldn't find them. They weren't there anymore.

"I can't do that," Philo said sadly.

"What do you mean you can't?"

"The tech differences between your new body and SysGov are too great. I can interface with your virtual sight and hearing, but that's the extent of it."

Raibert's lip trembled. He stared blankly ahead and his shoulders drooped.

"I'm sorry," Philo continued, "but there's just no way we can fix this."

"You mean . . . we can't share our meals anymore?"

Philo frowned and shook his head.

"Never again?"

"I'm sorry, Raibert."

"But I can join you in the abstract, right?"

"I'm afraid not. Your connectome can't leave its case. Admin hardware is designed to make that impossible."

"Well this *sucks!*" He slumped to the floor and rested his back against the wall.

Philo's avatar sat down and leaned against the wall next to him.

"That's why I said this is going to take a while. But you'll get through this, and if—I mean *when* we get home, we'll transition you into a proper synthoid with all the right interfaces. I swear we will. We're just . . . limited for now. In the meantime, you let me know if there's anything you need from me. I'm here for you, buddy. Always."

"Yeah, thanks." Raibert shook his head as his synthoid eyes teared up.

"So, is there anything I can get you? Anything you need right now?"

"I . . ."

"Yeah, Raibert? Anything."

He looked over at the avatar. "I could really use a hug right about now."

Philo frowned again.

"What?" he asked. "What's wrong?"

"I'm sorry, but I can't anymore. It's impossible for us to interact." He passed his hand through Raibert's body to demonstrate. "They only set up their wetware and synthoids for virtual sight and sound."

"No hugs?"

"Sorry. No hugs."

"Oh, fuck the Admin!" Raibert bashed the wall with a fist and left a dent.

"Things have been rather lively today, Csaba, and not in a good way."

"We're working to contain the situation, sir."

Chief Executor Christopher First reclined in a chair in Shigeki's virtual vision. His thick, brown mane descended to shoulders where a dark suit covered his cosmetically enhanced physique. Shigeki stood at attention while the chief executor watched with steely eyes.

"Containment? I've learned more about this from watching the news than from your own department."

"I regret the oversight, sir. We've been understandably busy today."

"I can imagine. A strange time machine breaking out of *your* headquarters. Drones dropping like flies, which, I might add, have resulted in dozens of injuries and more than a few deaths. Attacks on two suppression towers, plus numerous casualties from those. A *prison break*, of all things, and more casualties at the DOI. Should I go on?"

"No, sir. That won't be necessary."

"And is it true the chronoport was being piloted by an AI? Surely that can't be right."

"Unfortunately, sir, it is."

The chief executor's face remained almost masklike, but Shigeki saw fear cloud his eyes.

"My God. How did this happen?" the chief executor demanded.

"We apprehended the chronoport in question two days ago and brought it back to DTI headquarters for study. We were in the process of determining its point of origin when we learned, too late unfortunately, that someone had hidden a fully self-aware AI on board. As for the rest, I believe you know as much as we do."

"A strange chronoport shows up, and I'm not made aware of it?"

"I understand how that might seem, sir, but as you know, the very nature of what we do at the DTI requires a certain degree of secrecy. You would have received a full report once our investigation was complete. That's been standard procedure between my department and your predecessors."

"I suppose I can accept that explanation. For now. What about the prison break?"

"That would be the pilot, who turned out to be a complete ranting loon. Because of his mental state, he was of no use to our investigation, so we transferred him to the DOI for processing. We're not sure why, but the AI prioritized his rescue. Perhaps it was following a behavioral governor. Perhaps it thinks it needs him. Who can honestly say at this point? Regardless, we now have a madman and an AI in control of a highly advanced chronoport with numerous Yanluo Violations incorporated into its design."

"This breach of our security cannot be allowed to stand, Csaba. You hear me? *Cannot* be allowed to stand!"

"I agree completely with you, sir."

"Then what are you going to do about it?"

"I'll be taking personal command of the situation. Pathfinder Squadron will depart as soon as preparations are complete, and we won't stop until we find and eliminate both the fugitive and his chronoport."

"That seems . . . quite sufficient."

"Thank you, sir. I thought it prudent to take a hands-on approach given the severity of the situation."

"As you should." The chief executor nodded in thought, then looked up. "Do you require any assistance?"

"Not at the moment, sir. I appreciate the offer, but what we do at the DTI is rather specialized. There's not much support other departments can provide. Pathfinder Squadron is more than sufficient to track down and destroy a lone chronoport."

"Don't take any chances, Csaba. It's a rogue AI. I want it stamped out. You hear me? Stamped *out!*"

"Understood, sir. It won't get away."

"Who's your proxy during your absence?"

"Under-Director McMillon will be acting director while I'm away."

"McMillon? Isn't he in charge of your logistics?"

"He's up to speed on all current operations and has my full confidence."

"Then I suppose he'll do." The chief executor sat back. "In that case, I'll leave you to it. Get this mess cleaned up, Csaba."

"That's my intention, sir."

The chief executor cut the link, and Shigeki let out a long sigh of relief. He stepped out of the cramped office on board *Pathfinder-Prime*, took a short walk down the narrow central corridor, and entered the mess hall, which could, and currently did, serve as a conference room.

"How did it go, boss?" Kloss asked.

"About as well as could be expected." Shigeki stepped up to the end of the long table where Kloss, Nox, Hinnerkopf, Jonas, and the captains of Pathfinder Squadron now sat. "And now that we have that unpleasantness out of the way, let's get down to business. Where are we?"

"All twelve chronoports are armed and provisioned for an extended mission," Jonas reported. "Each craft has been fitted with four Type-72 missile pods with sixteen munitions each, two Type-34 cannon pods with 115mm railguns that can be detached and used as Switchblades, a Type-88 countermeasure pod, and a Type-6 drone hangar that can also serve as a Cutlass troop transport. Pathfinder Squadron is ready to phase out on your command."

"In addition to the external armaments," Nox added, "each chronoport will have a sizable drone and troop complement. Sixty Scarab reconnaissance drones, eight Raptor light air-support drones, eight Wolverine light ground-support drones, and a fully equipped special operator squad. Per your orders, at least one STAND with combat frame is assigned to each ship, and we also have a few operators who specialize in the use of Condor sniper drones, but not enough to distribute to every chronoport."

"Crew rosters have been adjusted per your specifications," Kloss said. "All captains have been briefed, and there are no problems to report. Additionally"—he knocked on a yellow-and-red striped box about as long as his forearm—"I have the boxed AI you requested."

"Director," Hinnerkopf said, "I hope you don't mind the presumption, but I've requisitioned additional chronometric analysis gear for *Pathfinder-12*. I believe it might come in handy once we're at the storm. It's already on board, and I'll work to integrate it with the chronoport's systems on the way."

"Excellent," Shigeki said. "Good thinking."

Hinnerkopf gave him a curt nod.

"Now," Jonas said, sitting forward. "Where are we going?"

"A very good question, and one I've given some thought to." Shigeki brought up a graphical representation of the timeline over the narrow table. Two points far back from the True Present flashed. "We don't know the professor's exact destination because he doesn't know it himself, but we *do* know the region he's going to target."

"1905 to 1995," Jonas said.

"Exactly. So what we do is set up a picket that covers that entire timespan plus a little extra on either side just to be safe. *Pathfinder-Prime* will be centrally staged at 1945, and the rest of the squadron will spread out from there at ten year increments. The endpoint chronoports will be placed"—another two points glowed—"here at 1895, and here, at 2005."

"An excellent idea, sir," Nox said. "With this configuration, our scopes will cover the entire timespan we expect Kaminski to show up in, and our telegraphs will still have enough range for messages to be passed up and down the picket. Furthermore, any one of our chronoports should be more than sufficient to take on and destroy the TTV."

"On that topic, I want to make one thing very clear," Shigeki stated. "Our primary target is the TTV. Once it's gone, taking care of the professor becomes trivial. Therefore, your main objective is the destruction of his ship. If you spot him but not the TTV, do whatever you can to force it out into the open, but also be ready for anything. The TTV may have abilities we haven't seen yet, and it may modify itself in ways we don't expect."

"What if we see Kaminski but fail to draw the TTV out?" Nox asked.

"Then kill him."

"Understood, sir."

"If, for whatever reason, the TTV or the professor gets away, immediately feed your observations back to *Pathfinder-Prime* for analysis. That's what Vassal is for. I've had *Pathfinder-Prime*'s infosystem stuffed to the brim with historical records of the target period, so we'll have everything we need to piece together what that man is up to. Any other questions?"

A quiet confidence settled upon the room, and some of his staff and captains shook their heads.

"Kloss, meet me on the bridge before you board *Pathfinder-2*. We need to get Vassal installed."

"Not a problem, boss."

"Nox, I need to talk to you about one last crew assignment change with the STANDs before we depart."

"Yes, sir."

He looked across their faces one more time. They were ready.

"To your chronoports, people!" Shigeki ordered.

The captains and his staff filed out of the conference room, and he waited for the door to seal.

"You're stationed on *Pathfinder-Prime* with me?" he asked Nox once they were alone.

"Of course, sir."

"Hmm," he sighed. "That's what I thought."

"You don't approve?"

"No, it's not that. It's more a request than an order. I want you to switch places with the STAND on *Pathfinder-6*."

Nox paused for a moment, then realization came over him and he nodded.

"Ah. The one your son is on."

"I need my best people on this, but I also want them all to come back. That goes double for Jonas."

"Perfectly understandable, sir."

"And there's no one I trust more to look after him than you." He clapped the synthoid on the side of his arm.

"Thank you, sir. That's high praise indeed. I'll make the changes immediately."

"Watch out for him, will you? Make sure he gets through this."

"You have my word." Nox smiled. "And sir?"

"Yeah, Nox."

"You really do take after your father."

"Come on," Shigeki chuckled, feeling a little embarrassed. "Let's get these ships moving."

"Yes, sir."

Shigeki gave the synthoid's arm another pat, and the two left the conference room. Nox turned right toward the rear of the craft while Shigeki took the narrow corridor left to the bridge. He ducked through the opening, but the top of his head still brushed the bulkhead.

When the chronoport phased out, the mass of the Earth would no longer impart acceleration upon its atoms, and the crew would experience gravitational free fall. The interior had to accommodate prolonged periods of both standard gravity and zero gravity, but it also had to account for the chronoport's twin fusion thrusters, which could generate a sustained three gees of acceleration. Normal functions needed to be possible in *that* transit mode as well, and the chronoport's interiors had been designed with these requirements in mind.

Fortunately, situations that required the thrusters to be run flat out were exceedingly rare since chronoports typically avoided direct combat and instead relied upon the standoff power of their missiles, drones, and special operators.

The acceleration-compensation seats and arresting harnesses were arranged in rows of three with little regard to field of vision, since any crewmember could "see" any virtual display at any time, even through the chair backs in front of him. The pilot, copilot, realspace navigator, temporal navigator, impeller operator, telegraph operator, and weapons operator were already strapped in for phase-out, while Florian Durantt, *Pathfinder-Prime*'s captain, waited next to his seat at the back.

Kloss stood by the front alcove with the boxed AI cradled in an arm.

"Ready, boss."

"Is that . . . *thing* really necessary?" Durantt asked.

"The AI assisting Kaminski managed to slip through both the DTI and DOI like it owned the place," Kloss said, and Shigeki hid a dour smile as he heard his own words echoed. "So yes. It's necessary."

Durantt's walrus mustache twitched.

"Is there an issue, Captain?" Shigeki asked.

"No, Director. Just uncomfortable around AIs."

"Aren't we all. Kloss, let's get this over with. Shove it in."

"Right." He slotted the AI inside a square opening in the alcove and locked it in place. Shigeki put his hand against the closed-circuit PIN interface on the left, and Kloss did the same on the right.

"Boxed AI detected," *Pathfinder-Prime*'s nonsentient attendant stated. "Yanluo Restriction compliance confirmed. Do you authorize AI unboxing?"

"Authorization: Under-Director Dahvid Kloss, Department of Temporal Investigation. Unboxing requested, sound interface only."

"Authorization: Director Csaba Shigeki, Department of Temporal Investigation. Unboxing requested, sound interface only."

"Credentials accepted. PIN integrity and noncoercion biometrics confirmed. AI partial unboxing will commence after a ten-second countdown. You may pause or cancel the unboxing at any time. Ten . . . nine . . . eight . . ."

Shigeki and Kloss waited with their hands pressed against the interfaces.

"Two . . . one . . . AI unboxed."

Bright-red virtual letters that spelled UNBOXED lit up in front of the alcove.

"Admin-sanctioned artificial intelligence, codename Vassal, standing by for orders."

"Vassal, your primary task on this mission will be data analysis. Additional interface restrictions will be lifted and more detailed information will be provided to you at the appropriate time. For now, you will remain in stasis until needed."

"Understood, Director Shigeki."

Both men removed their hands. Shigeki suspended the AI's connectome, and a bright green STASIS appeared beneath UNBOXED.

"I need to get to my chronoport, boss."

Shigeki nodded to him, and Kloss hurried out of the bridge.

"Director, all chronoports have declared readiness for departure," Durantt announced less than ten minutes later.

"Then take us out," Shigeki said, and strapped into his seat next to the captain.

"*Pathfinder-Prime* to all chronoports: exit your hangars, spin up your impellers, and synchronize on us. Squadron, stand by for phase-out."

A column of twelve hangar bays opened along the side of the DTI tower, and the chronoports eased out like a shoal of giant, metal manta rays.

"Impeller spin rising. Ten cycles per second … twenty-five … fifty … seventy-five … one hundred … impeller spin now at one hundred twenty cycles per second. Spin stable. Chronometric environment stable. Captain, we are clear for phase-out."

"Captain, all chronoports synchronized and ready."

"Pathfinder Squadron: phase out!"

Power from the fusion thrusters pulsed into the impeller spike, turning it impermeable at precise points in its spin so that chronotons struck it along a specific axis. Chronometric pressure reached the critical threshold, and twelve chronoports, 720 surveillance drones, 192 light combat drones, 132 special operators, and twelve STANDs with combat frames—a grand total of over thirty-seven thousand tons of state-of-the-art hardware and highly trained and motivated personnel—phased out of the True Present in search of one man in a shot-up time machine.

Shigeki crossed his arms as the Earth's gravity vanished.

Kaminski didn't stand a chance.

CHAPTER EIGHTEEN

Denton, North Carolina
2018 CE

BENJAMIN SCHRÖDER DROVE HIS BMW 332I UP THE SLOPED DRIVE-way and around the back of the white two-story house, then parked it between both of his sisters' minivans. He turned the car off and stepped out. A warm sun filtered through breaks in the clouds, and a cool breeze sighed past the trees that dotted the hill his parents had selected for their home long before he'd been born.

The windows were cracked open along the back porch, and Benjamin could already smell the warm aroma of home cooking.

"Oh, there he is!" Joséphine opened the door and greeted him on the porch.

"Hey, Mom." He kissed her on the cheek. "Smells good."

"Thank you. Though, honestly"—she leaned forward and whispered—"I'm barely doing anything besides setting a few timers and taste testing. Your sisters and Martin have *totally* taken over the kitchen."

"Need me to kick them out and help reinstate your rule?"

"Heavens, no!" she laughed. "Do you have any idea how long it's taken me to train them? Besides, my old bones deserve the rest."

"Old? What are you talking about, Mom? Aren't you still, like, twenty-two or something?"

"Uh!" she scoffed. "You're as poor a liar as your father. You talk to Elzbietá with that mouth?"

"Sometimes."

"Well, take it from me, she sees right through you."

"That she does."

Benjamin opened the door and let Joséphine back inside before stepping through himself. The Schröder family had grown so large over the past decade that Sunday dinner now took up two rooms with his parents, three sisters, and their husbands in one room and most of his nieces and nephews making a lot of noise and mess at a table set up in the living room.

A timer went off, and Joséphine hustled back to the kitchen where his twin sisters Elizabeth and Gisèle, the "babies" of the family, and Elfriede's husband Martin toiled in the kitchen.

"Hurry up and take it off the heat!" she urged.

"We've got it, Mom," Elizabeth replied, clicking the oven burners off. "Don't you worry."

"Yeah, Mrs. Schröder," Martin said, stirring a large metal pot. "Just take a load off and leave it to us."

A ruckus rose from the living room, and Elfriede, the second oldest and his little sister by two years, turned in her seat to face it.

"If you kids don't behave, I will change the wifi password when we get home, and it'll stay changed for a week!"

The noise from the other room died down considerably.

"Wow, not even a 'but he started it' that time," Benjamin said.

"The trick is to use a lot of unusual characters so they can't guess it," Elfriede said, then shouted to the kitchen, "unlike making it our last name backward!"

"Sorry, dear!" Martin called out with a chuckle.

"You'd be surprised how persistent they can get when their toys don't work," Elfriede said.

"I'll bet."

"I mean, it took them less than a day to figure out the backward names. But throw in some random pound signs and an ampersand, and they're done."

Klaus Schröder reclined in a venerable leather armchair while the game played out on the TV with the volume turned low. He looked up when Benjamin walked up, turned off the TV, and stood up with only a soft groan.

"Son."

"Sir."

"You sure about this?"

"Yes, sir. That I am."

Klaus nodded thoughtfully, as if he hadn't already fallen to Elzbietá's charms.

"What? Is that it?" Elfriede asked.

"What do you mean?" the senior Schröder replied.

"Don't you remember what you did to poor Martin? You sat him down and grilled him one-on-one for two whole *hours* before you allowed him to propose. He cried afterward, you know. He thought you hated him."

"No, I didn't!" Martin proclaimed cheerfully from the kitchen.

"Did Daddy really cry?" asked a little girl from the next room.

"Like a big, blubbering baby."

"It's good to see how people respond to adversity," Klaus defended. "Besides, it's different when it's a son."

"Uh!" Elfriede rolled her eyes. "Dad! Sexist!"

"Oh, I beg to differ. Do you really think a then nineteen-year-old daughter and a now thirty-eight-year-old son should be treated the same?"

"Well, no. But..."

"Be careful with that 'but,' because you might find yourself in the same situation one day."

She muttered something under her breath.

"Dinner is served!" Joséphine announced.

Elizabeth, Gisèle, and Martin started bringing food out from the kitchen and setting it on the tables. Benjamin's mouth watered at the sumptuous spread of leberkase, kielbasa, weisswurst, sauerkraut, mashed potatoes, sweet potatoes with melted marshmallows on top, gravy, green beans, honeyed ham, sweet and spicy mustards, fresh baked bread, butter, and—last but certainly not least—homemade horseradish sauce produced from a freshly grated root.

Benjamin had "fond" memories of grating the roots as a child and was glad the responsibility had shifted to the next generation. The duty, in service of Grandma Jo, functioned as a competition amongst his nieces and nephews to see who could last the longest before tearing up.

He sat down next to his father.

"Mom, aren't you going to join us?" Benjamin asked.

"In a few minutes! Just need to finish up a few things in here!"

"She'll probably sit down sometime after dessert," Klaus grumbled, then whispered to his son. "She *says* she's slowing down and taking it easy, but she just keeps at it like always."

"What was that, Klaus?"

"Nothing! I love you!"

"Oh, *sure* that's what you said!"

Benjamin served himself a thick slice of leberkase, plenty of sauerkraut, and a dollop of the horseradish sauce to start with. Elfriede finished loading her plate, then grabbed the ketchup bottle and squirted a big, red mound on the side.

"Isn't Elzbietá joining us?" she asked.

"No," Benjamin said. "She's doing a little bit of last minute clean up on her dissertation, and we're going out tonight to celebrate. She, ahh...doesn't know."

"Oh, *really*? Think she'll say yes?"

Benjamin gave his sister a grouchy look.

"So, when are you going to propose?"

"This Wednesday."

"Valentine's Day? Oh, that's so sweet! Keep that up and she might actually consider saying yes."

Benjamin gave her an even grouchier look.

"There's not a doubt in my mind what the answer will be," Klaus said. "You've been through some dark times recently, but Schröders are tough, and God works in mysterious ways. Sometimes it feels like He never answers our prayers, but then He puts the right person in the right place at *exactly* the right time when we need them the most, and I firmly believe that's why she was there with you that day."

"Thanks, Dad. And who knows? You might be right about that."

"Of course, I am. And speaking of which..." Klaus glanced over his shoulder at the kitchen.

"Oh!" Joséphine exclaimed. "Right! Hold on a sec. Got distracted by food again." She headed upstairs.

"Speaking of which," Klaus continued, "your mother and I have something very special for you."

The stairs creaked as Joséphine came back down. She passed through the kitchen and placed a small lacquered box between Klaus and Benjamin before finally sitting down across from him.

"Is that what I think it is?" Elfriede asked, sitting up higher in her seat.

Benjamin opened the box and peered inside to find a ring. Its two gold bands were crowned by five interlocking circles of gold, each encrusted with tiny diamonds.

"It *is*!" Elfriede sat back down.

"You don't seem surprised, Son," Klaus said.

"Well, there are only so many ways to interpret 'don't worry about the engagement ring.'"

"And don't worry," Joséphine assured. "It's already been resized."

"You know her ring size?" Benjamin asked. "How did you manage that from her?"

"Very subtly, which is why I did it and not your father."

"You're giving it to Ben?" Elfriede complained.

"That's right," Klaus said.

"But why him all of a sudden?" She put an elbow on the table and rested her face in her hand. "I got married first. *I* should have gotten it."

"Elfriede, dear," Klaus began patiently. "First, it's unbecoming for a bride to select her own ring. Besides, I believe your husband did a fine job there."

"Thanks, Mr. Schröder!" Martin said, still in the kitchen cleaning up.

"Second, this ring is an heirloom that's been passed down through over three hundred years of firstborn von Schröders, and we must respect our traditions. Your grandfather, Graf Klaus-Wilhelm von Schröder, presented this ring to my mother, Gräfin Elfriede, in 1939, and she wore it until we lost her in 1944."

"Again, see, I would have been perfect. We even share the same name."

"I honestly can't recall much about my mother," Klaus continued, perhaps pretending not to hear Elfriede. "I've always tried to hang onto my memories of her, and your *Babusja* Yulia helped all she could, but she was such a bright and wonderful person she couldn't help ... overwriting them. Still, I think we *all* have clear memories of your grandfather."

Benjamin and his twin sisters chuckled, and he thought back to the grand patriarchal figure who, even in his twilight years, had projected so much strength and authority.

Klaus-Wilhelm von Schröder was one of those larger-than-life individuals the world no longer seemed to produce. He'd been born and raised with an aristocratic tradition of service that dated all the way back to the sixteenth century. Born too late for service in the First World War, he'd grown up in a bitter, angry Germany—a Germany ripe for a black-hearted demon in the guise of a man on a white horse. And that loathsome human being had been named Adolf Hitler.

Klaus-Wilhelm had been an army officer, about as apolitical as they came, and he'd never been a Party member himself. Yet Benjamin knew he'd been no more proof against the bitterness of the humiliated nation about him because of that. He'd joined the Army because that was what the Schröder family did, but also because he'd burned to *avenge* that humiliation. And because he did, he'd also overlooked the racism of Hitler and his Nazis...at least until *Kristallnacht* had opened his eyes. His willingness to overlook that racism had been a source of bitter shame for the remainder of his life, and it had influenced every decision he'd ever made afterward.

There hadn't seemed to be anything he could do about it at the time, however. He was a professional officer, heir to a tradition of service stretching back centuries, and like every other German officer, he'd been required to swear a personal oath of allegiance to Hitler when he became *Reichskanzler*. Oaths had meant something to Klaus-Wilhelm von Schröder, and so he'd found himself trapped between his abhorrence for the truth he'd seen under the surface and the oath which made him part of the machine taking his nation deeper into the darkness. God only knew what he would have done if Hitler had survived!

But in the 1930s, he'd buried himself in his military duties, trying—as he'd bluntly and unflinchingly admitted to a sixteen-year-old Benjamin—to "bury my head in the sand of duty to the state because I was too afraid to stand on the *rock* of duty to myself." He'd been one of Heinz Guderian's disciples as the Wehrmacht developed the principles of mobile warfare, and he'd served under Erwin Rommel in the dash to the coast which had cut off and forced the surrender of the British Expeditionary Force.

From that beginning, it wasn't surprising he'd gone on to command major armored formations under the restored monarchy, and his beloved first wife's death had left him with a motherless son at the very time his country most required his services. And so he'd sent Klaus to live with relatives in the United States, safe from the madness enveloping Europe, while he answered that country's call...as Schröders had always answered it.

"I remember," that son said now, looking around the table at *his* son and daughters. "His correspondence was so cold and formal. I thought he was distancing himself from me. It wasn't until much later that I realized it was the hole inside him that made him sound that way in his letters. He was a man of honor, your grandfather. He'd lost his wife and then sent his only son away while he fought to create a better world for all of us because that was his *duty*. But no matter how hard he tried, duty and honor simply weren't enough to fill that hole."

Elfriede moped with her chin on her forearms, and her father wagged one index finger at her with a small smile.

"Remember what I said about people being in the right places at the right times, Elfriede!" he said. "That was definitely true for your grandfather. The fighting in 1950 during the Ukraine Liberation..." His smile disappeared and he shook his head, his eyes dark. "That was the worst, most vicious combat of his entire life. The commissars fought hard, and there were—God, there were so *many* atrocities on both sides! And yet, in the middle of all that, he met Yulia, the only woman who could fill that hole. God gave him that gift, and the Kaiser himself gave away the bride on the same day he named Klaus-Wilhelm Interim Governor of Ukraine for the Western Alliance.

"Gräfin Yulia von Schröder wore this ring for forty-two years, until God gave your grandfather another gift and she passed peacefully in her sleep."

He looked around the table, his eyes solemn, and even Elfriede abandoned her put-upon-sister role long enough to look back with matching solemnity. But then Klaus sat back in his chair and smiled crookedly.

"Your grandfather and I didn't always see eye to eye. He sometimes claimed not to understand his 'American son,' but I *was* his firstborn. More than that, I know—I always knew—he loved me dearly, even if there were times he had trouble showing it. And if I'd ever doubted it, Yulia would have made sure I didn't. God, she was a wonderful woman, your *Babusja* Yulia! And he showed me how much he loved me when he gave me this ring, both as a token of his love for me and as part of our family's heritage.

"As one firstborn to another, I know how hard it can be to grow up without a big brother or big sister. To be the first in your generation to have to figure things out. Only God chooses who will be born first in a family, but it's a heavy responsibility. Even more so for you, Benjamin, because you had sisters looking up to you as an example."

Elfriede, Benjamin noticed, had recovered enough to snort loudly at that last sentence, and his father's eyes twinkled.

"But being firstborn isn't without its privileges, too," he said, and his voice had softened once more. "And so I give you this ring so that you can give it to someone very special. Just as Yulia appeared at the right time, at the right place, to be your grandfather's joy, his support, the mother of your uncles and aunts, I believe Elzbietá is the right woman for you. I *feel* it. Your mother feels it. And we both wish you all the best."

"Thanks—" Benjamin cleared his throat. "Thanks, Dad."

He closed the box and hoped the mist in his eyes didn't show. Then he took a deep breath and looked across the table. The fantasies and delusions that had plagued him, especially his father's "death," never seemed more distant than when he surrounded himself with family. Even Elfriede's presence, despite their occasional bickering, filled him with an inner warmth, and he knew he was truly blessed to have such a wonderful family.

"Wish me luck," he told them.

"Luck?" Klaus scoffed. "You're a Schröder! You don't need luck!"

Benjamin opened the door of the garage attached to the quaint, all-brick ranch-style house and pulled the car inside, next to his BMW Z40 roadster. He wondered if Elzbietá would still be content living here after she—*almost* assuredly—said yes. Perhaps she'd want to move into something a bit roomier than what was, essentially, his oversized bachelor's pad. Not that it wasn't a nice house. Far from it, in fact. It just lacked certain necessities like, oh, guest rooms? After all, if there were going to be kids in their future, they'd have to sleep somewhere. He couldn't let his sisters have all the "fun," right?

"Stop it, Ben. You're getting *way* ahead of yourself."

He went inside, turned off the alarm, and placed the lacquered box on the kitchen counter. He couldn't think of a reason why she wouldn't say yes, but then why was his stomach suddenly fluttering all over the place? He shook his head and entered the master—and only—bedroom.

Elzbietá had left her flannel pajamas on the floor again. He picked them up with a grimace, folded them, and set them down in what was now her half of the walk-in closet. Okay, more like her *two thirds* of the closet, and really, that came from the sheer sprawl of the mess—thankfully confined to the closet—rather than from her owning more stuff. Though she did own more stuff. Oh, did she ever own more stuff.

Why did anyone need so much stuff?

Benjamin could probably fit all of his belongings, excluding furniture, into a few carloads, but Elzbietá still had boxes she had yet to unpack piled to the ceiling in the basement, including every issue she'd ever owned of *SCIENCE!* and its sister magazine *GADGETS!*

Where *had* she crammed all of that stuff in her old apartment?

Benjamin picked up this month's issue of *SCIENCE!* and placed it atop the magazine pile straining Elzbietá's night stand. There were a few history magazines in the stack, but technical literature greatly outnumbered them. He sometimes wondered if engineering was still where her true passion lay.

Besides his entertainment center, the cars (high-performance German models, of course), and a few hobbies, there weren't any money sinks he'd found interesting over the years. He supposed his least space-efficient hobby revolved around his scratch-built model sailing ships, four of which were displayed in a large glass curio cabinet in the living room. His latest project, a three-foot long model of the fifty-gun screw frigate USS *Colorado* (service years 1858 to 1876), sat nearly finished on a workbench in what was now his half of the basement.

Well, okay, his *third* of the basement.

Still, a little clutter and a few compromises were a small price to pay for what he knew he'd found.

Benjamin checked the time, undressed, tossed his clothes into the correct hampers, and stepped into the shower. His mind wandered to not-Benjamin, as it often did when he was alone with nothing to do or when trying to get to sleep without chemical aids.

Not-Benjamin had been working on the same scratch-built ship, but *his* was only half finished. Then again, the real Benjamin had an advantage there, because not-Benjamin also enjoyed hunting and marksmanship. Klaus had introduced Benjamin to both hobbies at an early age, but he'd only dabbled in them after leaving the house. Perhaps it was because his sisters had never shown an interest, whereas not-Benjamin's brother David had been an enthusiastic shooter.

David...

A cold shiver of loss shot through him. His heartbeat quickened and he broke out into a cold sweat, despite the hot water washing over him. He closed his eyes and rested his head against the shower tiles.

"Focus," he told himself as he fought down the anxiety. "Analyze the fantasy. Identify what is real and what is false."

He visualized the two timelines in his mind and traced them backward, key event by key event, until they finally came to rest upon a train speeding through Europe in the spring of 1940.

A very specific train with a very famous passenger.

The exercise came naturally to him now, and the tightness in his chest subsided. As a historian, he found a certain morbid curiosity in the fantasies his mind had constructed, but they were just that. Fantasies and nothing more. Acknowledging that helped soothe his nerves. The warm water helped as well, and soon he felt normal again. Or what passed for normal since The Day.

He smacked his cheeks.

"Keep it together, Ben. Don't screw this up."

He lathered up, rinsed, dried off, and dressed smartly for date night: freshly ironed gray shirt and black slacks, black shoes he could see his reflection in, and a violet bowtie for just the right splash of color.

He pulled the bowtie taut and checked himself in the mirror.

"Looking good."

He grabbed the box off the counter and opened it. The gold and diamond von Schröder heirloom glinted in the light, and he let out a contented sigh.

"She's the one. So stop being nervous, and let's do this."

Benjamin went back to the bedroom, unlocked the floor combination safe, and placed the box inside. He headed for the garage and was about to set the house alarm when he heard three heavy knocks on the front door.

CHAPTER NINETEEN

Transtemporal Vehicle *Kleio*
non-congruent

"SHUT OFF THE IMPELLER!" RAIBERT SHOUTED, RUNNING ONTO the bridge. "Phase in! Phase in!"

"Executing emergency phase-in," Kleio said. "Now congruent with 2313 CE."

Raibert called up the live feed from the TTV's array, and it materialized over the command table. A flying wedge of chronometric signals pulsed rapidly at plus three months and sped down the timeline.

"What *is* that?" he asked.

"That," Philo began, "is a shit-load of Admin time machines."

"Have they spotted us?"

"Not at the speed they're moving. At least," Philo added carefully, "I don't *think* they did."

"They've got to be half blinded by their own turbulence, right?" Raibert asked.

"We'll find out soon enough. Looks like twelve distinct signals. They'll pass us in eighty seconds."

Raibert took a deep breath as the signals closed in. He technically didn't need to breathe anymore, but the physical motion still helped calm his nerves.

"They're not slowing down," Philo announced. "There. They just passed us. We're in their wake, and they're still moving at ninety-five kilofactors."

"*Ninety-five* kilofactors?" Raibert ran his fingers back through his hair. "I thought *we* had the tech advantage."

"Not with everything, it would seem."

"Are there *any* SysGov TTVs that can move that fast?"

"The only one I'm aware of is the *Deep History Probe*, and that monstrosity used an array of nine impellers. The problem is at eighty kilofactors and up, impellers become unstable because they can't maintain consistent permeability, and they start colliding with chronotons flowing in the wrong direction. The Admin seems to have solved that problem somehow. Did you notice how the signals were pulsing? That's very unusual. Their impellers must operate under a very different principle."

"I'm more interested in what it means for us." Raibert leaned over the retreating chronoport signals. "They're outright faster than us. If we're spotted, we can't run."

"*If* they find us and *if* they can maintain a solid lock. The good news is our chronometric array must be superior to their equivalent. We saw them coming up behind us, which is where our array is weakest, and they failed to spot us when we were directly in front of them, temporally speaking of course."

"I wouldn't be too sure of that."

"Why not?"

"I don't think they were even looking for us." Raibert tapped a finger through the chronoports' signals. "They're all clumped together and racing full speed through time. That's not a search pattern. They're going somewhere in a hurry. Or rather, somewhen."

"Okay." The Viking nodded. "Now that I think about it, you might be right. But when?"

"Well..." Raibert grimaced.

"What's wrong?"

"I did sort of...come out and tell Shigeki and his goons the range of years where the Event could be."

"Ah. Well, that does complicate things."

"Sorry."

"Raibert, you had no way of knowing they'd react that badly. Besides, we thought we needed help."

"We still do. Face it, Philo. It's just the two of us—"

"Professor?"

"Okay. *Three* of us, and we've got ninety years of history that we need to sift through and somehow figure out where this universe went wrong. Neither of us have a clue where to start looking in those ninety years, and now Shigeki's hit squads will be scouring that part of the timeline for us. How the hell are we supposed to do this?" He stopped suddenly, shoulders sagging. "And on top of that, *should* we be doing this?"

"You lost me there. Which 'this' are we talking about again?"

"This!" He waved his arms around wildly. "Trying to undo the Event! The whole thing!"

"Uhh . . . yes?"

"But the only way we even *think* we can pull this off means we destroy the entire Admin!"

"I know. And save sixteen universes, including SysGov. That's an awfully big plus."

"But there could be another way. One where no one's home has to be destroyed."

"If there is, I don't see it, and neither does Kleio." Philo summoned a set of charts and gestured to them. "This is all we have."

"But the Admin might find another way if we just give them a chance."

"Not one that'll bring back our home."

"So it's us or them?" he asked, glancing away with a pained expression on his face. "Is that where we're at?"

"Raibert, listen to me." Philo leaned forward and pointed with two fingers. "Look me in the eyes."

"Okay." He looked up.

The AC stared at him, eyes unblinking. "Are you going to stand idly by while the multiverse gets ready to burn?"

"Well, no. But that's not what I'm suggesting."

"You're going through a lot right now, buddy. Trust me, I know, even without connecting, so I'll make this as clear as I can for you. We can't rely on the Admin for anything. That path is closed, and they're the ones who closed it. We're all that stands between the multiverse and the apocalypse. It's just us now."

"But Shigeki said—"

"I don't care what he said!" Philo interrupted sharply. "I watched them grind your body into paste, and I find that memory so disturbing I'm sorely tempted to partition it off completely. I'm not trusting those . . . those *barbarians* with the fate of the multiverse!"

"But it's their universe! Who are we to make these sorts of decisions?"

"I'll tell you who we aren't. We're not a bunch of knuckle-dragging fascists who lock up history professors just because they don't like what they hear."

"But..."

"Who are we, you asked?" Philo went on. "We're all that's left of SysGov. That means we're the only ones who can possibly bring it back *and* save every other reality that's entangled with the Knot. Why? Because there's no one else left who gives a damn."

"Yeah..." Raibert took a deep breath, then slowly began to nod. "Yeah," he said, a little louder.

"We stick with the solution we have," Philo said. "Because it's all we have. We go with that and we keep busting through obstacles until we succeed."

"Okay. Yeah." He stood a little straighter. "Thanks. I needed that."

"Any time, buddy."

"So..." Raibert grimaced at the command table, then at Philo. "Where were we again?"

"That's going to be a problem." Philo crossed his arms and stared at the linear time graph over the command table. Everything between 1905 and 1995 glowed red.

"We need to stay away from the twentieth century for now," Raibert said. "With Shigeki's goons on the way, we can't go in until we have some way to narrow the search. We need something that will give us an edge. Some way to sort through this problem for when we *do* have to dive into that nest of vipers."

"You're right about that."

"But what could give us..." Raibert snapped his fingers. "Of course!"

Philo grinned. "Oh, you've got that look again."

"Don't you see? We *do* have a one critical piece of information Shigeki doesn't."

"And what's that?"

"The resonance!"

"Okay." Philo's grin vanished. "What about it?"

"Remember, my former body was resonating with another universe. We thought it was a *different* universe, but what if it wasn't? What if—given the changes in the timeline—I wasn't resonating with a *different* universe at all. What if I was resonating with what *this* universe *used to be*!"

"Hmm." Philo took on a thoughtful look as he processed the proposition. "Okay, the raw data may support that assumption, but I still don't see how this helps us."

"What if there are *other* individuals who were affected by the Knot in the same way?"

"I think if there were other SysGov TTVs roaming around, we would have spotted them by now."

"No, not that. I mean *indigenous* people."

"*Oh.*" Both of Philo's eyebrows shot up at the same time.

"What if one of *them* had a connection to our version of the timeline? And what if their connection was stronger because they're native to the timeline around the Knot? Maybe even strong enough that they remember *both* timelines?"

"You know, I think you might be on to something. Kleio, we're going parallel. We need to crunch some numbers."

"I am at your service, Philosophus."

Philo crossed his arms and closed his eyes. A minute passed before his eyes shot open and his mouth formed an O.

"Something wrong?" Raibert asked.

"Uhh..." Philo clapped his jaw shut and didn't make eye contact. "It's nothing. Just an interesting wrinkle in the data."

"Are you sure? Because, you just made a face."

"It's not important now. I'll flag it for later analysis." Philo visibly collected himself before continuing. "It looks like you're definitely onto something, but the biggest problem with what you said is quantum variation between the two timelines. The more variation, the weaker the connection. However, if we start looking at cases with fewer atoms, we can cut down on the variation considerably and improve our chances of finding someone with strong resonance."

"So we look for someone who was a child when the Knot formed?"

"No, even further back than that. A child already has a developed connectome. Even if there was any resonance, I think the existing connectome would just step all over it. *You* certainly didn't have dual memories. We want as blank a slate as possible with as few atoms as possible when the resonance is established. I'm thinking what we're looking for is someone who was just a pair of gametes in his or her parents *before* the Knot and was then conceived *after* the Knot." He let out a long, slow exhale. "This is going to be a problem."

"How so?"

"Do you know how many sperm get fired off during inter-course?"

"Umm...no."

"About a hundred million. Factor in all sorts of tiny varia-tions, and the chances of pregnancies being the same across both timestreams becomes vanishingly small. And the pregnancies *have* to be the same. Otherwise, there's nothing to resonate with."

"But our chances aren't zero."

"No, definitely not zero. We're just looking at a very small subset of pregnancies."

"*How* small?"

"Around two per billion."

"Hmm." Raibert slouched, feeling deflated. "That is small."

"But not zero," Philo repeated. "This can still work. We have the resonance pattern recorded off your old body. We know what we need to search for. We just need the parents to exist before the Knot. That increases the number of pregnancies in the set that could be duplicates and improves our odds of finding one that is."

"How close do we have to be to detect the resonance?" Raib-ert asked.

"We're going to have to be in phase and very close. I'd say within a kilometer for our array to pick up a clear signal."

"Then we need to narrow down our search further. We can't hunt aimlessly with the Admin on the prowl."

"Agreed."

"Any thoughts?"

"The resonance might cause mental problems if the dual memories take hold. We could look for that."

"All right, then." Raibert shifted the graphical timeline over into the twenty-first century. "Since Shigeki's looking for us in the twentieth century, I say we start in the twenty-first. We can drop in here, at 2060, and take a look around. We don't have to pass through the storm to reach it, and whatever global infosys-tem exists in this timestream should be robust enough by then. All we do is drop in, link up, and peruse their medical records at our leisure."

"Sounds like a plan to me."

"Kleio, how's the shroud doing?"

"It is fully operational, Professor. I should be able to remain undetected by period surveillance systems."

"Good," Raibert said. "Then that's where we head."

"So this is the storm that will destroy the universe," Shigeki said. *Pathfinder-Prime* lurched, but the seat harness held him firmly in place. The churning, writhing seizure in time filled his virtual vision, and eleven chronoports held their distance at plus two hours while *Pathfinder-12* flew ahead.

"We're entering the storm now, Director," Hinnerkopf sent from *Pathfinder-12*. The ship's telegraph possessed only limited bandwidth for data transmission, so Hinnerkopf's response came through as text that was then converted into synthesized speech. The voice lacked the inflection and subtlety of speaking to her in person, but it beat having to read out every response.

"How are you doing?"

"Let me put it this way. I'm glad I ate a light lunch."

"I can imagine." Shigeki chuckled, but then the humor washed away as *Pathfinder-Prime* shook again.

"Traversing the storm is rough but manageable. However, we should cross it slowly. I recommend nothing above a kilofactor. Anything higher and we might damage our impellers."

"Understood. Are you getting everything else you need?"

"Yes, Director. Data collection is proceeding smoothly, though I'll need some time to study it afterward. However, one thing is immediately obvious. This massively powerful chronometric phenomenon is closing on the True Present."

"And that means what exactly?" Kloss sent from *Pathfinder-2*.

"It means Professor Kaminski is right. The universe is going to end in about thirteen hundred years."

"And perhaps a lot sooner for us," Shigeki murmured.

"Precisely, Director. Everything we find corroborates his story. It only makes sense that his existential threat to our timeline is also true."

"And that's why we're not going to let it happen. *First* we deal with him; *then* we deal with untying this damned 'knot' of his."

"*Pathfinder-12* now clear of the storm, Director. We're moving on to our next objective."

"Good. Report your findings when ready."

"Yes, Director. Phasing in now."

Shigeki waited while *Pathfinder-12* made a series of quick microjumps through 2049. It took no more than a few minutes of absolute time.

"Test complete, Director," Hinnerkopf sent.

"And?"

"I wouldn't have believed it if I hadn't seen it with my own eyes, but it's true. Changes to the timeline within the storm do propagate downstream. This section of history is, for whatever reason, in a highly malleable state."

"What's your takeaway from this?"

"Again, it matches everything else we learned from the professor. Beyond that, I honestly can't say what the risks are. This phenomenon is too far outside our experiences for anything beyond guesswork. I need more time."

"In that case, we'll play it safe," Shigeki said. "Once we pass the storm, all chronoports are to remain non-congruent unless you spot the TTV or receive authorization from *Pathfinder-Prime*. For now, we proceed as planned and establish the picket. Captain Durantt, take us through the storm."

"Yes, Director. Pathfinder Squadron: ahead one kilofactor."

Raibert poked at the sizzling filet mignon. The blue cheese crumble melted over the top, and the meat underneath was so tender he could cut it with his fork. He jabbed it a few more times and gave it a gloomy eye.

"Philo?"

"Yeah?" The Viking appeared on the other side of the command table. Something seemed off about the avatar's mood, but Raibert ignored it.

"I'm not hungry," he moaned.

"Then don't eat."

"But I haven't eaten all day. I should be hungry."

"Then eat."

"But there's no reason for me to eat this succulent, mouth-watering, perfectly cooked steak, is there?"

"Please don't say it like that. Now you're starting to make me hungry."

"Sorry."

"But to answer your question, no, there's no reason for you

to eat it. Admin synthoids do need some maintenance, but the occasional microbot injections will take care of that for you."

"I want to want to eat it, but I don't want to eat it. Does that make sense?"

"Perfectly. It's called PSS."

Raibert tossed the fork onto his plate and crossed his arms.

"Look, I'm just being honest here," Philo said.

"I know you are, buddy."

"You doing okay?"

"Yeah, I guess so." Raibert pushed his plate aside.

"You've been getting better. All things considered, I'd say you're doing quite well."

"Pfft!"

"No, I'm serious," Philo said. "I know it's been tough, but I'm actually surprised by how fast you've adjusted to your new body. For one, I thought the size difference would give you more trouble."

"Oh, that?" Raibert's expression brightened and he gestured across his broad chest. "I actually figured out a good trick for that. I've just been pretending I'm Terry again."

"Aha!" Philo snapped his fingers.

Raibert winked at him.

Terisobok-Kazanyari the Burninator (or "Terry" to his friends) was Raibert's level 12 lawful-neutral character from *Solar Descent*. The massive lizardman grenadier might not have been *exactly* the same size as his STAND synthoid, but spending more hours than he cared to admit inside the science-fantasy abstraction had made getting used to the *physical* aspects of his new body almost an afterthought.

Philo had introduced him to the game years ago, and it had quickly become a favorite of theirs, which pleased the AC to no end. Philo had been regularly playing the game since before Raibert was born and sometimes joined in with one of his pantheon of max-level characters. But more often than not the AC took on the role of game master for Raibert and their close circle of friends, where he used his expertise to arrange results both hilarious and cruel. It still cracked Raibert up when he thought back to their epic rescue of Lola the teenage star seer. They'd battled their way through waves of reassembling necro-drones, nearly became puppets of a cruel cyber-lich, and even vanquished a lesser avatar of the abyssal god Singularity before finally rescuing the seer...only to hear the petite girl give them their next quest in Philo's gruff voice.

"Didn't think of that," the Viking admitted. "That's pretty clever."

"See? I have some good ideas on occasion. Though I will say..." He glanced over a shoulder, "the lack of a tail is throwing me off a bit."

"We could always ask Kleio to add one, if you think it'll help."

"Oh, hell no!" He spun to face Philo and pointed a stern finger, but the effect was ruined by a grin that slipped out. "Don't you dare give her any bright ideas!"

Philo chuckled. "I'm kidding, of course."

"So, have we found anything yet?" Raibert brought up the TTV's external view. The ship hovered over the North American eastern seaboard and was now lazily floating south past Norfolk, Virginia, with the metamaterial shroud wrapped around the hull.

Each *Aion*-class TTV came equipped with a deployable stealth shroud capable of concealing the entire craft from most photon-based detection systems. However, the vessel was limited to subsonic speeds when shrouded due to the low error tolerances of the metamaterial's light-bending configuration. When in high-speed or temporal flight, the shroud would be retracted and stowed in shallow blisters that dotted the hull.

Preservation TTVs on smash-and-grab missions rarely required such subterfuge, though stealthier approaches had become more common after the Alexandria Raid. Observation TTVs, on the other hand, very often needed to preserve the sanctity of the timeline, and the shroud's ability to fool anything from the human eye to advanced radar systems proved essential when concealing a flying time machine as large as a twenty-first-century naval destroyer.

"Nothing I'd call a solid lead," Philo said. "Some maybes I'm filing for later if we don't turn up anything better."

Two dozen green dots on the map showed the location of the *Kleio*'s stealthed remotes as they connected to the Internet or infiltrated various medical and government institutions by physically attaching to their server farms.

"I've been downloading a lot of eBooks, though," Philo said.

"Oh yeah? What for?"

"Been stocking up on twentieth-century history writings. That way, we at least have better information on what the current timeline is all about."

"Good idea. Well, keep at it."

Raibert picked up his knife and fork, then cut another piece off his half-finished filet mignon. He was about to plop it into his mouth when he noticed Philo's forlorn expression.

"Some light reading has also helped take my mind off..."

"Off of what?" Raibert set his utensils down and walked over to the avatar.

"Well, it came up when Kleio and I were analyzing the resonance."

"Yeah? What about it?"

"We found something I didn't tell you about right away."

Raibert raised an eyebrow at him.

"Not that I was keeping anything secret, mind you!" Philo held up both palms. "It's just you had enough crap to deal with. And now, since we seem to have some downtime, I thought you might want to know."

"Know...what?"

"You're not going to like it," the avatar admitted. "And you don't *technically* have to hear about this. It doesn't *directly* relate to the Knot."

"I don't know why you're pussyfooting around. I've had a lot of practice recently with absorbing bad news. How bad could it be?"

Philo cringed.

"Is it worse than my body getting tossed into a blender?" Raibert asked pointedly.

"Probably?" Philo offered.

"Okay, but there's no way it's worse than the Knot."

"Umm. Maybe?"

"*Maybe?*" Raibert blurted. "It's *maybe* worse than the destruction of sixteen universes?"

"Depends on your point of view."

"My point of view? And you don't think I have to hear this?"

"Not if you don't want to."

"Well, it's a little late for that, Philo! You brought it up, so just get this over with and hit me with the bad news already!"

"All right." The avatar cleared his virtual throat before continuing. "You know those sixteen universes that are all tangled together?"

"*Yes,*" Raibert said suspiciously.

"Where did they come from?"

"I..." He stopped and thought. "Okay, I have no idea. I guess I just assumed they were always there or something. You know, part of the grand multiverse or whatever you want to call it."

Philo shook his head.

"They're not?" Raibert asked.

"No. Some of them formed recently, relative to the Edge of Existence."

"Then where did they come from?"

"Raibert," Philo sighed, "I think we've been wrong all along."

"Which 'we' are you referring to here?"

"ART. The Ministry. SysGov. Take your pick. I think we've been very wrong for a very long time."

"Well, we've known that about *ART* for quite a while, buddy!"

"No, Raibert. This is worse. Way worse."

Raibert swallowed audibly and waited for the AC to continue.

"Imagine a possibility, if you will." Philo put both his hands together as if praying. "We now know for a fact that time can be changed. What if, just for the sake of argument, the timeline was *always* being changed?"

"But that's impossible. We have mountains of evidence that it wasn't."

"Do we?" Philo formed a V with his hands. "What if instead of the changes fading away on their own, each intrusion caused the timeline to branch"—he spread his hands apart—"and spawn a new universe?"

"But that..."

"Would mean that everything we've done and everything ART has done is real. Not in our universe, but still very real in one next door."

"But that would mean that there's a universe where I helped Julius Caesar." Raibert's eyes widened. "That would mean there's a version of Earth where a bunch of demons showed up, ransacked the Great Library of Alexandria, and killed *hundreds* of people! That instead of time travel having no consequences, it's the *complete opposite!*"

"Yeah."

"Are you sure about this?"

"Not a hundred percent," the avatar admitted. "But close. It became clear when Kleio and I took another look at your resonance.

Searching for a connection to a previous state of this universe was the key. Raibert, *three* of the other universes share the same core characteristics. They're *each* subtle variants that must have branched off a common source, and at least two formed *after* SysGov started experimenting with time travel."

"Oh, God, Philo! We used to plunder the past and gun down anyone who stood in our way! They were completely helpless to stop us! And this means it was real! It was all real!"

"Yeah," Philo sighed.

"We were nothing but a band of time-traveling mass murderers!"

"Not all of us."

"But this is horrible! This is...this is *beyond* horrible!"

"Try to calm down."

"*Calm?* How could I possibly be calm right now? My entire life's work is a terrible mistake! I thought we were *helping* when we forced ART to reform, but it turns out we're still part of the problem. Every trip back—Preservation *and* Observation—rewrites history? *We're* the reason the universe is going to die!"

"And that just means it's our responsibility to put it right. All of it."

Raibert gulped and looked at his companion. Somehow the calmness and clarity in the Viking's eyes steadied his own nerves.

"Don't forget," Philo continued. "I've actually been on Preservation missions before. I've participated in their abuses, which means I just discovered I have real blood on my hands. Not as much as most of them, but...it's there, and that's something that I'll have to come to terms with."

"You seem to be taking it well."

"No, I'm not," the AC admitted. "I'm just keeping most of my drama from showing up on my avatar."

Raibert chuckled sadly. "A lot of swearing going on inside your connectome?"

"You better believe it."

"Any of it directed at you-know-who?"

"Every last word."

"Figured as much." Raibert smiled sadly. "I didn't mean to belittle what you're going through. Sorry, buddy."

"It's all right. This is a lot for both of us to take it. But you know what?"

"What?"

"I know exactly how I'm going to deal with it. Not by sitting around and feeling guilty for myself, but by taking action and *doing* something about it. We're not going to stop at unraveling the Knot. We need to do that, of course. Who knows how exactly, but we'll get it done. And after that, after SysGov is back, we take this to the Ministry and we shut the whole thing down. We can't undo what's already been done, but we can all atone by doing everything in our power to make it right."

Raibert sighed. "You're right of course. But..."

"Yeah?"

"But how about we take this one step at a time?"

"Oh, what's this?" Philo exclaimed suddenly.

"Hmm?" Raibert murmured, opening his eyes but not bothering to straighten from where he'd rested his head on the command table when he drifted off.

"Raibert! Raibert! Raibert!" The Viking hurried around the table and bent down so that their heads were next to each other. "Raibert!"

"Yes? I can tell you're excited about something," he muttered with his face squished against the table. "Well, what is it?"

"I found something that's *guaranteed* to raise our spirits!"

"I find that claim highly dubious right now."

"Well, prepare to be amazed, because you are *not* going to believe what I just found!"

"All right then." Raibert sat up and wiped the drool from his lips. "Let's have it."

"Check this out!" Philo shoved the local map aside, and a dossier appeared in its place. The middle-aged man in the picture was tall and broad shouldered with dark hair combed to the side and piercing gray eyes. Not as big as Raibert's new body, but still an impressively stout individual.

"Meet Doctor Benjamin Schröder," Philo began. "Former *chairman* of the *history department* at Castle Rock University."

"A fellow historian?" Raibert remarked, perking up. "Well, that *is* encouraging. Does he show signs of dual memories?"

"Oh, does he ever!" Philo swiped the first several pages aside. "Doctor Schröder experienced a major mental breakdown in 2017. Before that day, there was no history of mental illness in either himself or any member of his immediate family. All of them paragons of health, really."

"Okay. So he went a little crazy. That doesn't prove he had dual memories."

"Ah, but that's where you're wrong," Philo corrected. "It's the nature of his delusions that makes me think we've found what we're looking for. You see, he suddenly started having extremely clear 'fantasies' of an alternate version of himself. And not just of himself, but of a different family with different siblings and even a different world history." The Viking grinned. "That's either one *very* vivid imagination, or his brain is connected to another timeline."

"All right, then." Raibert sat up and nodded. "Let's pay him a visit and verify it. Is he still alive?"

"Not at this point in the timeline. Says here he did quite well after the episode. Got married shortly afterward, no children. Then his wife died in a traffic accident twelve years later. He relapsed—lots of psychotherapy and medication, a few experimental treatments that didn't work. Sounds like he slowly became unable to separate the two realities. Depression. And finally a suicide in 2038. Drug overdose."

"Sheesh!" Raibert grimaced. "Poor guy! And I thought I had it rough. Go ahead and suck out my connectome and puree my body any day of the week over *that*. Can we verify the resonance off his corpse? I'd like to prove this out while we're phased in if we can. Less chance of Shigeki's goons spotting us that way."

"They're probably well past the storm front by now, but I agree. Best to not take unnecessary risks. And on that note, I've already turned us toward his grave site. We'll be there in less than an hour. If I'm right, there should still be some faint resonance on the body."

"Perfect! And this also narrows our search, right?"

"That's right. As long as the resonance is there, we can eliminate anything after he was conceived. That shaves fifteen years off the search window."

"Then we're making progress." Raibert rubbed his hands together. "So, if this is our guy, when do you think we should say hello?"

"I'd say shortly after his first round of psychotherapy. From the record, that seems to be the period where he's most stable, and it's still quite a ways from where the Admin will be looking for us. So, call it early 2018?"

CHAPTER TWENTY

Denton, North Carolina
2018 CE

THREE HEAVY KNOCKS REVERBERATED THROUGH THE HOUSE.

Benjamin lowered his hand from the alarm console and turned back to the front door. Couldn't people read the "No Solicitation" sign? He shook his head and was about to set the alarm when another three deep, insistent knocks came from the door.

"Fine." He checked his phone. Still plenty of time. "All right! I'm coming! And if you're selling something, I can recommend a great optometrist!"

He headed back into the living room, wondering who it could be. Anyone he cared to see would have had the politeness to call ahead of time, and he did have the sign up, so they were either being ignorant or they really needed to talk to him.

A familiar lump of anxiety built in the pit of his stomach as his mind started calling up worst-case scenarios, like the police coming to report Elzbietá had been in a fatal car accident. That a drunk had killed her the same way one had killed Miriam. That he'd have to deal with—

He shook the dark thoughts away as he'd done many times since The Day. No, it wasn't going to happen. The universe wasn't really hellbent on crushing anyone he ever let himself love. That was just stupid emotions talking, yammering away in the back of his brain because he was so nervous.

He took a calming breath, and checked the peephole.

A big, blond-haired man in a black pinstripe suit and wide-brimmed hat stood a few paces from the door. He wasn't holding any pamphlets and he didn't have a police badge, so Benjamin wasn't sure what to expect. He removed the chain lock, slid the bolt aside, and opened the door.

"Doctor Benjamin Schröder, I presume?" the big guy asked with an accent Benjamin couldn't quite place. Maybe Chinese? For what little sense that made, given his obvious ethnicity.

"That's right." His anxiety built at the mention of his name. This was no random solicitor. "What do you want?"

"I'm sorry. Have I come at a bad time? If you like, I can return later. It's literally no trouble at all."

"No, that's fine. You're here now. Just tell me what this is about."

"Of course, Doctor."

The man took off his hat and held it before him in both hands. For some reason, his posture gave Benjamin the impression of a small man trapped in a huge body.

"Doctor Schröder, my name is Raibert Kaminski. Professor Kaminski, actually. I'm a historian, like you, and I need your help."

"Are you serious?" Benjamin snapped.

"I'm sorry?"

"If what you say is true, then you should know I've taken a leave of absence. Doctor Chalmers is the acting department chair. Go talk to her if you need something. Don't show up at my house uninvited. Now, if you'll excuse me, *Professor*, I don't have time for whatever game you're playing."

Benjamin pushed the door closed, but Raibert bolted forward, and the door rebounded off his foot. For such a big guy, he moved *fast*.

"What are you doing?" Benjamin growled. "Get your foot out of the way!"

"Please, Doctor! I really do need your help! There's no easy way for me to tell you what you need to hear. Just please hear me out."

Benjamin saw genuine fear in the big man's eyes. Whatever Raibert was talking about, he at least believed it to be a matter of great importance.

"All right." Benjamin eased the door back. "Let's hear it, then."

"Thank you, Doctor." Raibert stepped back. "As I said, there's no good way to start talking about this, so I'll get right into it. The reason why you—and *only* you—can help me is because of the episode you had eight months ago."

"What do you know about that?" Benjamin demanded sharply.

"A lot more than your psychologist does. You see, I know why it happened."

"You're lying."

"Doctor, I'm not…" Raibert's eyes grew distant for a moment, almost as if he were listening to someone. "Sorry. Maybe I've been going about this the wrong way. Doctor, I understand a lot of this is going to be difficult for you to hear, and I don't expect you to believe me without proof—which I can provide, by the way—but it may make more sense if you'd please be patient and consider what I have to say as a whole."

"Fine." Benjamin didn't know what this Raibert, if that was even his real name, was after, but maybe he could deal with the man better once all the cards were on the table. "Out with it, then."

"Thank you, Doctor. First, I wasn't *completely* honest when I introduced myself."

"Why am I not surprised?"

"Not a lie, you understand. Just an omission. My name *is* Raibert and I *am* a historian. In fact, I specialize in ancient Greek and Roman history. It's just that I'm a historian from the thirtieth century."

"You don't say?" Benjamin smirked. "Oh, this ought to be good. Please don't let me stop you now."

"Thank you, Doctor. To answer your next question, yes, I have a time machine."

"Well, of course. Why wouldn't you have one? Have you found yourself marooned in 2018 for some reason?"

"No. It's fully functional."

"*Sure* it is."

"The reason I find myself in 2018 is because of you. Or rather, the connection you have with another version of the timeline."

The humor drained from Benjamin's face.

"You see, the timeline is…" Raibert started, then frowned before continuing. "The timeline *appeared* to be immutable, which is why people like me could hop into our time machines and explore the past at our leisure without fear of any consequences.

"However, the timeline *has* changed, and that's...not good. I won't bore you with the technical details, but if the timeline isn't restored, then this entire universe and fifteen of its neighbors will be destroyed."

Benjamin's face was stone as Raibert continued.

"That's why I need your help. The change took place somewhere in the twentieth century, before you were born. I don't have detailed records on this period, and my knowledge of ancient societies is, as you can imagine, next to useless here. I need someone with firsthand knowledge of what the twentieth century *should* be. The trait I've searched for is a pregnancy that occurred after the timeline diverged. A pregnancy that occurred in *both* timelines, which happens a lot less than you might think. Those rare people would then be able to resonate with the timeline's previous state, and their minds could then develop a connection to their alternate selves."

Benjamin's frozen-helium glare should have flash-frozen his visitor where he stood.

"You, Doctor Schröder, are one of those people. Your 'mental breakdown' was nothing of the sort. All of those memories are real; they're simply from another version of the timestream. One that *must* be restored. The timeline *must* be set to right, and I need your help to do it."

Benjamin exhaled deeply as powerful emotions crashed and echoed deep inside him.

"Doctor Schröder, I'm sure this is a lot to take—"

He slammed the door in Raibert's face, locked the bolt, and turned away.

"Umm, Doctor?" Raibert knocked again. "I'm not finished yet."

"Yes, you are! Go away! Go the hell away!"

Those memories were real? Impossible! Absolutely impossible! They were delusions brought on by an overactive imagination, nothing more. He'd come too far and fought through too much to succumb and lose himself in that dark chasm of alien memories now.

"Doctor, could you please open the door?" Raibert jangled the knob. "I know this comes as a shock, but I'm more than willing to help talk you through it."

"If you're really from the future, why don't you just vaporize the door with your laser pistol?" he spat.

"I don't have one. Besides, they don't work like that."

"Forget it! I'm done talking to you! Just go away!"

Wood splintered behind him, and he turned to find the door open with Raibert frowning down at a lock ripped free of the wall but still attached to the door.

"Sorry," the big man said bashfully. "I honestly didn't mean to do that."

"Get out of my house!"

"Doctor, please calm down." He stepped in and suddenly smiled. "Hey, consider the bright side of the situation. You're not crazy! There's a perfectly reasonable and wholly scientific explanation for everything that's happened to you."

"You think what you just said is 'reasonable'?"

"Well, yes," Raibert said. "Doctor, perhaps I didn't stress this enough. The universe will be destroyed if the timestream isn't repaired."

"But that doesn't even make any sense! How does changing the past destroy the universe?"

"Well, put simply, there's a lot of energy pouring into our universe from the fifteen neighbors we're entangled with. When that energy hits what we call the Edge of Existence in about thirteen hundred years—a measurement made from an absolute reference, mind you—the entire universe will explode in a cataclysm that will make the Big Bang look like cheap fireworks."

"Thirteen hundred years? Thirteen *hundred* years?" Benjamin laughed sadly. "How is any of that my problem?"

"Technically, it's everyone's problem. Besides, you have the knowledge I need to prevent it."

"Do you have *any* concept of what's different?"

"No..." Raibert said carefully, "but I'd love to hear all about it."

"Death!" Benjamin shouted, backing into the kitchen. "That's what's *different*! Try these numbers on for size! Thirty million in the Chinese Revolution! Fifty million in Stalin's Soviet Union. *Eighty* million in World War II! Oh, and let's not forget the industrialized genocide of the Jews!"

"Okay, yeah." Raibert followed him into the kitchen. "I'll grant you, those are some big numbers. But we're talking about saving an entire *universe* here! I hate to break morality down to mathematics, but a couple million is like a drop in the ocean compared to the apocalypse I'm trying to stop."

"No! That's not it at all! You're asking me to help you murder millions of people by changing the past! And not just them, but their children and their children's children all the way up to *your* thirtieth century! How many lives is that? How much blood are you trying to coat my hands with?"

"Did I mention that another fifteen universes blow up along with ours? I may have missed that detail. So, it's actually a drop in a whole row of vast oceans."

"A thousand years from now! So I say, who the fuck cares?"

"Well, I care. And you should, too."

"Either you're lying, in which case you're crazier than me! Or you're telling the truth, which means I'd be crazy to help you!"

"But think of the lives you'll be *saving.*"

"No way! No fucking way!" Tears trailed down Benjamin's cheeks. His breathing was jagged, shallow, and the icy tendrils of an anxiety attack's prelude tightened the muscles in his chest. He'd come too far to go to pieces now. This madman was lying. He had to be. None of those memories were real. It was all in his head. It had to be!

"Doctor, please." The big man spoke in a soft, pitying tone. "If you would just calm down and seriously think about what you're saying."

"You don't understand! He *cannot* be allowed to live!"

"*He?*" Raibert keyed in on the word. "Which 'he' would that be?"

"I told you to get out!" Benjamin grabbed the cleaver from the wooden stand on the counter and brandished it at Raibert.

"Yeah, umm, how to be polite about this?" He pointed at the blade. "I know you're trying to threaten me, but that really doesn't do the trick anymore."

"Get out! Get out! Get out!"

Raibert frowned down at the advancing cleaver.

"All right. I'll leave." He put his hat back on. "But please take some time and give what I said some serious thought. Also . . ."

"*What?*" Benjamin fumed.

"I truly am sorry about the door."

He left. The door swung shut, and the broken lock crunched against splintered wood.

"Well, that could have gone better," Philo said through an audio-only connection.

"Yeah, tell me about it," Raibert replied without speaking aloud. He put his hands in his pockets and started down the sidewalk. "What's he doing now?"

"Pushing furniture around to barricade the door."

"Looks like I hit a nerve. Did you catch what he said near the end?"

"About someone not being allowed to live?"

"That's the one. Doctor Schröder knows where the timeline diverged."

"Or at least thinks he does. He didn't seem quite right in the head."

"He's got two lifetimes bouncing around in there. Of *course* he's not right in the head." Raibert sighed, shaking own his head. "The guy's got it rough, and we just made it a hell of a lot rougher."

"Should we try to find someone else?"

"Are you kidding? He may have his problems, but he's been able to sort through all that mental noise and figure out where the two realities split. That couldn't have been easy, but he somehow soldiered through it and held himself together. Anybody who can do that has got to have one *hell* of a robust personality, whatever finally happened to him in this timeline. *And* he's a historian. What are the odds we'll find someone better than him?"

"Pretty close to zero."

"Then he's our man."

Raibert couldn't help feeling sorry for Benjamin. The guy had just been living his own life when the universe decided to explode in his brain. He hadn't asked for any of this, hadn't done anything wrong to bring this misfortune down on his head. And on top of that, he'd managed to sort through his own scrambled mind and would live, at least for a few years, a normal life.

And then I came by, Raibert thought with remorse. *And told him oh, by the way, all those delusions you just got finished sorting out? Yeah, they're all real. Sorry to be the bearer of bad news.*

"There wasn't much ambiguity in his refusal," Philo pointed out.

"I know," Raibert sighed. "That's a problem."

"What are we going to do about it?"

"Is there anything in his psych profile we could use?"

"No, unfortunately. Almost all of it is about his 'pretend' family, especially the death of his father in a terrorist attack and the brother that was never born. There's very little information about the differences in the history, and what's there is too contemporary for us to use."

"Thought so." He glanced back at Benjamin's house. A sleek black roadster pulled out of the garage and sped down the road in the opposite direction. Twin red lights glared in the distance, then vanished around a bend. "Oh well."

"So what are we going to do?"

"I'm going to try talking to him one more time."

"Just once?"

"Yeah." Raibert resumed walking down the street to where the TTV was parked overhead. "Just once."

"And if that fails?" Philo asked. "Then what? We just leave and try to find someone else?"

"No. If I can't convince him, then we grab him and take him with us."

"Seriously, Raibert? We're going to kidnap the poor guy?"

"What other choice do we have? A whole chunk of the multiverse is at stake, and he has the information we need to fix it. We can't afford to be squeamish when so much is riding on us. If we fail, then all that's left are Shigeki's goons blundering around, and you said yourself we can't rely on them. Even *if* they somehow find another way, a way that we with all our technological advantages can't see, it *still* means everything and everyone we know and love back in SysGov will never have been. We can't let that happen, and especially not when we're the only ones who know the past *can* be changed. Sooner or later, the Admin is going to run into something just like this all its own. You were right; we have to see this crisis through ourselves. *Sixteen universes* have a death sentence, and it's up to us to save them, because no one else will."

"All right, Raibert. I'm just..."

"What?"

"I know it's not the same, but this is the sort of thing I would help you-know-who do."

"This is different. You and I aren't like him, and you know it."

"You're right. It's just... it hits a little close to home, you know? I did a lot of things I'm not proud of back then."

"Like I said, we don't have a choice. And look at it this way. At least you're not the one who has to do the dirty work."

"Somehow, that doesn't make me feel any better."

"Me neither, buddy," Raibert admitted. "Kleio?"

"Go ahead, Professor."

"Print out some prog-armor I can wear under my clothes."

"Would a standard pattern SysPol bodysuit with retractable helmet meet your requirements?"

"Yeah, that sounds about right. Also, I'll need a weapon."

"Could you be more specific?"

"Something small enough to conceal on my person but with enough punch to blow holes in twenty-first-century tanks."

"I will see what I have in the pattern catalog. Do you expect to need that level of lethality, Professor?"

"Well, I don't *know*, Kleio, but my days haven't gone well recently. Do you know what will happen if I try to nab Benjamin?"

"No, Professor."

"Can you guarantee I won't have problems with the indigenes?"

"No, Professor."

"Then be a helpful ship and print me out the goddamned gun."

"Yes, Professor. I believe I have a pattern that will meet your requirements. Would a Popular Arsenals PA5 Neutralizer anti-synthoid hand cannon suffice?"

"That sounds lovely. I'll take it."

The TTV's outline showed up in Raibert's virtual sight. At least his synthoid body included a rudimentary connection that allowed for virtual sight and sound, even if it didn't extend to tactile sensations, and the *Kleio* had extended a small antenna through the shroud to allow for two-way traffic. Now the TTV hovered over the tree line just after the next intersection, and he shook his head and continued down the street.

A part of him agreed with Philo.

Wait, no. That wasn't quite right.

All the parts of him agreed with Philo. The very idea of kidnapping someone was so outside of anything he'd ever normally consider that it almost made him sick. Or at least as close to sick as a synthoid could become. He'd spent decades of his life just being a simple guy with a passion for history, and now he was arming up on the likely chance that he'd have to kidnap an innocent man.

I'm just a historian, he thought sullenly. *I didn't even want to be in the time-travel program. Why did it have to be me in this mess?*

And then he remembered.

In a strange way, this was all Philo's fault.

Raibert Kaminski, newly hired professor of history, left the luxury shuttle and followed dozens of other guests through the umbilical's moving walkway. He transferred from the shuttle's gravity field to the ACCI station's with barely a bump, stepped off the walkway, and followed the golden virtual line deeper into the giant space station.

"You've been awfully quiet this whole trip," Raibert noted. "What are you up to?"

"Me?" Philo chortled in his virtual ear. "Up to something? *Pfft!* Perish the thought."

"Uh-huh," Raibert replied skeptically.

The Alpha Centauri Colonization Initiative had finished *Grand Sending* station more than a century ago, and the twenty-kilometer-long cylindrical edifice remained the most accurate, most powerful connectome transmission laser ever built, but it had never actually been used except for short-range tests.

Until now.

After all, the biggest connectome transmitter ever built needed something to transmit *to*. It had taken the ACCI's colony ships and their abstract crews decades to reach the neighboring star system, though, Raibert supposed, the word "ship" was probably too grandiose a word for what the ACCI had actually sent. More like a small flotilla of graviton thrusters, each with an infosystem and a small microbot reservoir strapped to the front.

But that had been enough.

Once the abstract crews reached their destination, they'd established a small industrial base out of their ships' resources. In the two centuries since, that base had grown exponentially to allow the construction of the five-hundred-kilometer-wide receiver array necessary to accept additional colonists. With both *Grand Sending* and *Grand Receiving* now operational, ACCI was ready to transmit the first wave of volunteers that would supplement humanity's vanguard in Alpha Centauri.

Theoretically.

"Do you think this'll work?" Raibert asked.

"It should," Philo reassured. "Though I guess we'll only know for sure when we hear back from *Grand Receiving*."

"Do you think Dad cares that it hasn't been proven out yet?"

"Not in the least."

"Yeah," Raibert grimaced. "I thought you'd say that."

"There's only one thing Tavish fears."

"And what's that?"

"Being second best at anything."

"Ha!"

The colonization of Alpha Centauri might not have been the largest SysGov initiative currently in progress—that distinction easily went to the Dyson Realization Project, whose first step was to convert Mercury into an energy collecting megastructure around the sun—but it did have the advantage of *not* being stalled in the courts by the Mercury Historical Preservation Society.

Raibert followed the golden light to the reception hall where physical and abstract guests mingled with the ACCI colonists. A physical model of *Grand Sending* hovered over several tables at one end of the hall and a massive—if not quite built to the same scale—depiction of *Grand Receiving* took up much of the opposite wall. A brilliant laser connected the two, its red light shimmering through foggy atmospheric effects near the ceiling.

Additional dioramas depicted the original colony ships, the industrial cluster the colonists had built, as well as a few replicas of their first rudimentary synthoids. There was even a "live" view from inside the colony, though Raibert wasn't sure how anyone could call the four-year-old signal "live." Finally, a large virtual timer at the far end of the hall counted down the remaining hours to the first extrasolar connectome transmission.

"Son!" Tavish exclaimed, materializing next to Raibert. "You made it!"

"Hey, Dad. You know I wouldn't miss this for anything."

"Congratulations on getting hired by the university, by the way."

"Thanks. I'm excited to start. I think it's going to work out really well."

Tavish only grinned smugly.

"What's with that face, Dad?"

"Oh, nothing. Nothing."

"Except it's very much *not* nothing."

"Well, yes," Tavish admitted, still smiling.

"Does this have something to do with why Philo's been so quiet?"

"He's got us there," the AC said, appearing in his virtual sight.

"It's not hard to tell," Raibert said. "You should know the firewall gets real quiet when you're up to something. It's very conspicuous."

Philo shrugged. "I'll try harder next time."

"Don't blame him for this," Tavish said. "He just wanted it to come as a surprise. We both did."

"And that surprise would be what exactly?"

"Remember when I told you to take a physics minor?"

"Yeah. It was interesting enough, I guess, but I still think it was a waste of time."

Both Philo and Tavish chuckled.

"'Waste of time,'" Philo parroted.

Raibert rolled his eyes at the allusion to tired ART jokes.

"Son, how would you like to join ART?"

"Seriously?" Raibert crossed his arms. "That's the big surprise?"

Both ACs nodded.

"Come on, Dad. You know how I feel about ART. And Philo, you're in on this, too?"

"Oh, don't be like that," Tavish dismissed. "Besides, this is different."

"Just hear us out," Philo said. "I think you're going to like it."

"All right," Raibert said. "I will. But this had better be good."

"As you know," Tavish began, "the Ministry of Education has nearly doubled ART's budget since I left, and most of that is being poured into new TTVs. I've recently had some discussions with my old colleagues about how to best apply these resources, and, in short, ART's mission is being expanded."

"Actually split," Philo clarified. "Into two branches."

"That's right," Tavish said. "The Preservation branch will handle what you could think of as the classic missions of preserving tangible relics from history, while the new Observation branch will be more focused, as you might imagine from the name, on studying history with little to no disruption."

Raibert's face lit up.

"And since you're now a professor of history *with* a chrono-metrics minor," Tavish continued, "and both Philo and I happen to be ex-ART, well, a few strings have been pulled to get your university assigned a TTV of its own. *And* to make sure you're on the top of the list to pilot it."

Raibert's grin could barely fit on his face.

"See, I told you he'd like it," Philo said.

"Dad, I don't know what to say. Thank you! Thank you so much!"

"Ah, ah. Don't thank me," Tavish corrected. "This was Philo's idea. I just helped set things in motion."

"It was?" Raibert faced the AC.

"Well, you know..." Philo shrugged bashfully.

"You," Raibert said, pointing a finger at the AC, "are awesome."

"I do what I can."

"That's a fine companion you have there, son," Tavish said. "And it makes me very happy to see the two of you together."

"Philo?" Raibert asked as he finished buttoning his dress shirt over the prog-steel bodysuit.

"Yeah?"

"I want you to know this is all your fault."

"Okay? Where did that come from?"

"I was just thinking about how I got roped into time travel in the first place."

"As I recall, you didn't need much in the way of encouragement."

"True enough." He chuckled, then took the hand cannon off the table and fitted it into his shoulder harness. "But you know something else? There's no one I'd rather be stuck with in this mess than you."

"Hey, right back at you, buddy."

"Now, I wish we could just microjump and try the original scenario all over again, but that's not an option anymore. What do you say we give Doctor Schröder some time to cool off? Maybe jump ahead three days? You think we're safe to do that?"

"I don't see why not," Philo said. "We're twenty-three years from the window you gave Shigeki. Not even SysGov arrays are that good."

"In that case, let's jump and try this again."

"And if he still says no?"

"Then I'll have no choice but to completely ruin his day."

"Sounds like a plan to me."

CHAPTER TWENTY-ONE

DTI Chronoport *Pathfinder-12*
non-congruent

THE CHRONOPORT EXISTED SLIGHTLY OUT OF PHASE WITH THE normal flow of time, but the *absolute* flow of time marched on within its hull and in sync with the True Present. Because of that, Katja Hinnerkopf did what she could to stay busy and stave off the boredom of watching 2005 and its surrounding years.

She floated in the cramped space that now served as her office, surrounded by virtual charts while her PIN tensed and relaxed muscle groups as part of her daily exercise regimen. She pushed one chart aside and pulled the next one in front of her before the PIN finished her abdominal sets and moved up to her arms. The raw chronometric data would have been indecipherable to most, just a jumble of terrifyingly high numbers, but she saw the patterns emerging from the chaos.

Everything Kaminski had said was true. This universe was doomed if they did nothing. But was the only solution what he had suggested? Was there another way to untangle the Knot and halt the deluge of foreign chronotons flooding into their universe? Was there a path that canceled the death sentence *and* preserved the Admin?

She didn't know if she'd be the one to find that solution, but she *would* start the search. After all, the Admin had over a thousand years to find a way. If it existed, then she or her successors would discover it.

She truly believed that. Or at least wanted to believe it. And she *would* have believed...except for one small detail.

Time was becoming scarred.

The scarring manifested only behind the storm front, but she couldn't deny it. Something was happening to the underlying chronometric structure of the universe. Within the boundaries of the storm, the timestream could be changed, and that malleability equated to weakness. Indeed, if her interpretation of the numbers was accurate, it couldn't *not* be changed by an extratemporal interaction. Kaminski had already made some changes in 1986, and she could see the damage in the data she'd requested from *Pathfinder-8* as well as the analysis of her own intrusion into 2049.

How much more abuse could time take? Was there an upper threshold where this part of the timeline could no longer be altered without permanent consequences? What would happen when they exceeded that threshold? Would the Knot then be impossible to unravel? Would something worse happen?

She didn't have the answers, but she knew where to find them. The universe guarded its secrets well, but data was the gateway to truth, and so she pored over the numbers with almost religious reverence.

"Wait a second," she muttered and zoomed in on a ripple in the chronoport's dish replay. The anomaly was almost assuredly noise given its amplitude and the level of accuracy she could expect from the equipment, but something about it looked familiar. Why was that? Had she seen the same pattern before? If so, then where?

She frowned, shifted the chart aside, and thought for a moment. If this truly was nothing, then a quick check of the auxiliary array should clear it up. She opened a second chart, fast forwarded to the same absolute timestamp, and zoomed in.

There it was again. The same ripple.

"Ah. That's why it looked familiar." She'd already seen it once when she'd reviewed the auxiliary array's data. At the time, she'd discounted it as noise, but two independent systems had detected the *same* noise.

"How could I be so careless?" she chided herself as she overlaid the two sets of data and filtered out any differences between the two.

The ripple became more pronounced while neighboring data settled down to background chatter.

"What could this…oh, no. How did I miss this?"

Hinnerkopf pinned the virtual charts to her person, kicked off the wall, and floated past the opening door. She grabbed a handrail and climbed through the chronoport's central corridor to reach the bridge.

"Telegraph, take the following dictation!" She adjusted the cross-referenced chart and zoomed in again. "Possible TTV phase-in detected at 2018, thirty-five north latitude, negative seventy-eight west longitude. *Pathfinder-12* requests permission to break from picket and investigate. Send that message immediately to the attention of *Pathfinder-Prime*."

"Director?" Captain Kofo Okunnu unstrapped himself and folded out of his seat. The tall, lanky man's head almost brushed the ceiling before he pushed off it.

Like most of Shigeki's inner circle of loyalists, Okunnu had been with the DTI since its formative years, when he'd distinguished himself as one of the first chronoport pilots, and even before that, as a brash and rather handsome physics student assisting then-Professor Hinnerkopf with her experiments.

"Are you sure?" Okunnu asked. "We've been watching the scope, and nothing's come up. Besides, our dish doesn't have the range to monitor that far into the future."

"I know what I'm seeing in the data." She waved the chart in the air. "And you have your orders, Captain."

"Very well, Director. In that case, yes I do." Okunnu faced his crew. "Telegraph, send the message as dictated."

"Yes, sir. Spooled…and sending."

Her message pulsed through time as peaks and valleys of chronometric energy that equated to ones and zeros. The signal reached *Pathfinder-10*, which then relayed the message to *Pathfinder-8*, which then relayed it further down the picket until her messaged reached *Pathfinder-Prime*, holding position non-congruent at 1945.

They didn't have to wait long for the response.

"Sir, message reads: 'Permission granted. Good hunting, *Pathfinder-12*.'"

"Very good." Okunnu turned to face Hinnerkopf. "Your orders, Director?"

"Proceed to 2018, but quietly."

"Understood." Okunnu floated behind his navigators as they

pulled up a map of Earth. "There," he pointed. "Plot us a course roughly one hundred kilometers southeast of the target location. We can set down in the Atlantic Ocean and deploy our Scarabs and the Cutlass from there."

"Yes, sir." The realspace and temporal navigators worked their virtual consoles with practiced ease.

Hinnerkopf's heartbeat quickened as she realized what she'd just set in motion, and she rubbed her moist hands together. She'd seen the damage the TTV had done to the suppression towers, and while *Pathfinder-12*'s weapons greatly outclassed the enemy's, the risk to her life wasn't zero. She didn't think it was cowardice that ate at her now, but she had to admit she'd been relieved when Shigeki assigned her chronoport to the far end of the picket. Surely Kaminski would focus his attention somewhere near the middle of the twentieth century while she sat safely in the early twenty-first century and pored over her data.

But that wasn't to be.

What are you up to, Professor? she wondered. *What's in 2018 that we don't know about?*

"Course plotted and ready, sir."

"Pilot, extend all baffles around the impeller and lock for a stealth approach."

"Yes, sir. Baffles extending...and locked."

"Take us out. Seventy-two kilofactors."

As much as she wanted to stay out of the action, she had a job to do. She straightened her back as the power pulsed into the impeller and they sped into the future. Nox wouldn't hesitate in a moment like this, and neither would she.

Hinnerkopf opened her hand and called up the artwork she'd commissioned years ago. A sturdy gray pillar rose from her palm, and a vine with purple flowers wrapped itself around it. She'd never shown her beloved "pillar of strength" the engagement sigil, and perhaps she never would.

But she wanted to. Oh, did she want to. And she wanted what it stood for even more. More than anything else she'd ever longed for. And when she did finally gather the courage to present him with the sigil, she wanted the "yes" to pass easily from his lips because he saw the same strength and resolve within her that she saw in him.

She released the image and clenched a fist.

The professor had to be stopped. And if the task fell to her, then so be it.

She would not fail.

Irwin's Steak & Seafood was not the sort of restaurant one walked into without a reservation, and Benjamin had reserved the small candlelit table over a month ago.

"Happy Valentine's Day, Ben!" Elzbietá declared, raising a glass of white wine with her good hand.

"And here's to many, many more," Benjamin replied, clinking her glass and taking a sip. He wore a freshly pressed dark red shirt with white bowtie and suspenders, and Elzbietá had chosen a black dress with a V-front that dipped in very flattering ways.

"Ahh..." she sighed contently and set her glass down as she leaned back. "This is nice."

"Yeah, it is."

She turned and stared out the window. Irwin's was built on a shallow hill with the parking lot in the back, so she had an unobstructed view down to the four-lane street that curved around its base. Headlights and taillights shone against damp asphalt as dusk transitioned to night.

"You doing okay?" she asked, glancing back at him.

"Mostly," he admitted. "I'm still a little shook up from Sunday."

"Yeah, I can tell. So what was with that guy?"

"I wish I knew." Benjamin gazed down at his drink and swirled it gently. He hadn't told her everything Raibert had said because he no longer fully trusted his own memory. And, honestly, what was he supposed to tell her? The experience had been so surreal that he wondered if he'd hallucinated the whole thing. There was the door Raibert had broken, of course, but what if Raibert didn't actually exist? What if the sanity he'd carefully clung to was starting to slip away? What if *he'd* busted the door and his subconscious had conjured this Raibert fellow as the explanation?

The thought made him shiver.

Was he really sane anymore? And if not, did he have the right to drag this remarkable woman into his fractured life? She would say yes. He knew with all his heart she would.

But should he even ask?

The lacquered box felt suddenly heavy in his pocket.

"Have you seen or heard from him since?"

"No." Benjamin shook his head. "No knocks. No calls. I tried looking him up on the Internet, but I didn't find any college faculty anywhere in the country that matched or came close."

"Probably not his real name, then."

"Yeah, probably."

"You think he might be one of Braxton's other patients? Maybe some nutcase's idea of a prank? I mean, seriously, what kind of professor goes to someone's house unannounced, asks for help, and then busts down the door when you say you're on leave?"

"A crazy one."

"All I'm saying is this guy better think twice before he shows up again. God help him if he breaks in when *I'm* home because even with one eye and one hand, I will *still* hit my mark at that range."

"Well," Benjamin chuckled, "hopefully it won't come to that."

The waiter came around and dropped off two salad wedges with house vinaigrette dressing, blue cheese crumbles, baby tomato halves, and minced bacon.

"I had another echo yesterday," he confessed, slouching a little. "It was a pretty bad one."

"Hey, now. Don't be like that." She took his hand into hers.

"I just wanted you to know."

"Ben, you don't have to be afraid around me." She squeezed his hand. "I don't claim to know exactly what you're going through, but I've been through something similar. And that means I can help."

"It's just"—he took a ragged breath—"sometimes I feel like I should be making better progress, and that I'm letting you and everyone else down when I have these episodes."

"But don't you see? It doesn't matter to me if you show the occasional moment of weakness, because that's going to happen. Sometimes fighting through trauma like this is two steps forward, then one step back. But as long as you keep pushing forward, you're going to make it."

"Yeah. You're right." He held her hand tightly in his.

"You know I am, buster."

They chuckled and he let go.

"Thanks, Ella."

"Anytime."

"Let's talk about something else, if you don't mind. This is our night. We should be enjoying it."

"I couldn't agree with you more." She raised her glass and brought it to her lips.

"I guess I just wanted to make sure"—Benjamin took a deep breath—"that what I'm about to ask for is the right thing."

Elzbietá paused mid-sip, then carefully set her glass down.

"And what might that be?" she asked delicately.

"How about I show you?"

He placed the lacquered box between them and opened it.

Elzbietá gasped as the ring's diamonds transformed flickering candlelight into dazzling fire.

"Oh my God, Ben!" She placed a hand over her mouth. "It's beautiful!"

"This ring is an heirloom of my family, passed down through three hundred years of Schröders. My grandfather presented it to both of his wives when he asked for their hands in marriage... and now I present it to you."

He took the ring out of the box and knelt before her.

"Ella, you are an extraordinary woman. But more than that, you're the rock that's supported me through the darkest days of my life. Everything seems clearer and brighter when I'm beside you, and there is no one I would rather spend the rest of my days with. Will you, Elzbietá Abramowski, join me in this crazy adventure we call life?"

He lifted her real hand and held the ring before her finger.

"Will you marry me?"

At first she only nodded with eyes moist with joy. Then she licked her lips and spoke a soft, almost inaudible:

"Yes..."

Benjamin slid the ring onto her finger. She wrapped her hand around his suspenders and tugged. He rose, and she released the suspenders and moved her hand to the nape of his neck and pulled him close before planting a long, passionate kiss upon his lips.

The kiss seemed to last forever, but when it finally ended, all was right with the world.

He sat down, a giddy grin on his face.

Elzbietá held her splayed hand out and admired the ring.

"It fits *perfectly*, too," she said.

"Whew!" he sighed. "That went even better than I'd hoped."

"Were you nervous?"

"Very."

"Why? Did you think I'd say no?"

"No, it's not that. I just didn't know if I was good enough for you."

"Well, cast aside all doubt, because you'd better believe you are!"

He smiled at that.

The waiter came around again, and Benjamin looked up at him. "She said yes!" he declared triumphantly.

"Oh? Well, congratulations, sir. And to you, ma'am."

The waiter set a bottle of expensive scotch on the table, followed by a triple-decker slice of chocolate cake, a cheesecake slice with a chocolate sail stuck on top, a slice of apple pie with a scoop of vanilla ice cream on top, and a hot fudge sundae with nut sprinkles and three cherries.

"I'm sorry. What is all of this?" Benjamin asked as he took in the unexpected invasion of their table. "Our order must have gotten mixed up."

"Compliments of the gentleman at the bar. Also, your bill for tonight has already been paid."

An icy finger traced down Benjamin's spine and he slowly turned toward the bar.

Raibert Kaminski sat atop a barstool and stared straight at him. He wore a pleasant smile as he dipped his hat, then stood up and walked over.

Pathfinder-12 settled into the Atlantic Ocean off the coast of North Carolina, and Hinnerkopf steadied herself with a hand on the wall as contact with the water jostled them. The chronoport slipped into the ocean, and its variskin adjusted both its reflectivity and dynamic emissions to match their surroundings across most of the electromagnetic spectrum.

The chronoport became an unremarkable part of the background as it sank deeper into the water. Variskin countered most photon-based detection methods, including radar and infrared, but the human eye could still catch flaws in the disguise.

The human eye, Hinnerkopf thought, *or an AI using the surveillance drones I know the TTV has.*

She stepped up to the map alongside Captain Okunnu and watched forty-one icons spread across North Carolina. The largest icon represented the chronoport's only Cutlass transport and its cargo of one STAND in her combat frame, eleven special operators, eight Wolverine drones, and eight Raptor drones. The other forty were Scarab reconnaissance drones that supplied live feeds back to *Pathfinder-12* or supplemented their own capabilities by tapping into indigenous surveillance systems.

Variskin coated every operator, craft, and drone, but that didn't make them invisible, and the TTV undoubtedly had advanced detection systems at its disposal. Still, the variskin should at least dampen their effectiveness.

"Hmm?" Okunnu murmured as he expanded the feed from Scarab-27. "Got a match."

"What? Already?"

"See for yourself, Director."

Okunnu shifted to the side and expanded Scarab-27's feed until it filled the whole wall with a familiar synthoid sitting at a bar.

"I don't believe it! He didn't bother to change his face!" She turned to Okunnu. "Captain, your orders are to draw out the TTV and destroy it. I leave the details in your capable hands."

"Very good, Director." He restored the map and zoomed in on the restaurant. "Open a link to the Cutlass."

"Open, sir."

"Agent Cantrell, land the Cutlass two kilometers south of these coordinates, then send all drones forward to the target area."

"Confirmed, Captain. Should I deploy as well?"

"Negative. You're too much for one synthoid historian to handle, I think. I want Kaminski scared and hurt enough that he calls in the TTV."

"Pissing his pants, but not dead. Got it, Captain. Anything else?"

"Whatever happens, you and all operators are to stay clear of both Kaminski and the TTV."

"Why's that?"

"Because we're going to hit the entire area with a missile barrage."

"Understood. We'll stay clear. Drones only in the engagement zone. Anything else?"

"No, Agent."

"Then all mission parameters are clear. Ready to execute."

"Engage the target at your discretion. Good luck, Agent. *Pathfinder-12* out." Okunnu pulled up the chronoport's external armaments. "Weapons: stand by for a sixteen-missile volley. Set

Kaminski as the preliminary target and lay in a low-altitude flight path. Launch as soon as the TTV is spotted."

"Yes, sir."

"Director, do you believe that level of firepower will be sufficient to destroy the TTV?"

"Probably, but we can't be sure." Hinnerkopf closed her eyes and rubbed her chin. "The TTV's armor proved surprisingly resilient to our cannon fire, plus it demonstrated that its Gatling guns are an effective defense against incoming projectiles."

"In that case, we'll err on the side of caution. Weapons: prep for a *thirty-two*-missile volley."

"Yes, sir!"

CHAPTER TWENTY-TWO

Irwin's Steak & Seafood restaurant
2018 CE

"IS THAT HIM?" ELZBIETÁ WHISPERED.

"Yeah. That's him," Benjamin said as anxiety tightened his chest. The evening had gone so perfectly, but now it was falling to pieces before his very eyes. At least Elzbietá could see this Raibert fellow. That meant he *was* real, unless *all* of this was a hallucination, and he'd tumbled even deeper into a self-concocted dementia.

He shivered at the thought as the big man grabbed a chair from the next table and brought it over.

"Hello again, Doctor Schröder." He waved a hand across the desserts. "Please accept this and the rest of your meal as a small token of my regret. I'm very sorry for how our last conversation went and would like to make amends."

"Excuse me!" Elzbietá stormed. "I don't know who you think you are, but we're having a private meal here!"

"My apologies, Mrs. Schröder," Raibert said, sitting down. "I'm sorry for intruding, but I have a very important matter to discuss with your husband."

"My *husband*?"

Raibert blinked and his eyes focused on something past them.

"Oh. My mistake." He tapped his forehead. "I'm not used to going into situations like this without a mental connection to my abstract companion. It seems I missed a small detail. The two of you get married *next* year."

"That's rather presumptuous of you! He just proposed!"

"And the date will be..." Raibert paused and looked past them again. "Sunday, June 16, 2019. Ah! The same as your birthday. I can see why you'll choose it. Or at least you would have if I weren't here upsetting the timeline."

"I don't know what kind of con you're trying to pull," Elzbietá leaned in, "but I've had quite enough of it!"

"No cons here. Just a simple time traveler trying to set things right."

"What the hell are you talking about?"

"I take it he didn't mention I'm a historian from the thirtieth century?"

"I told her you were crazy," Benjamin quickly interjected. "Which you clearly are."

"It might actually be better if that were true. Then at least it'd only be me with the problem and not the whole universe."

Elzbietá grabbed her purse off the floor and unzipped it.

"Ma'am, I appreciate what you think you're doing, but I know about the"—Raibert paused as if someone were speaking to him—"V10 Ultra Compact or whatever you call that peashooter in your purse."

Elzbietá visibly tensed.

"Anyway, it's not going to be enough to take me down."

"You wearing body armor under that suit?"

"In a manner of speaking."

"In that case, you step out of line, and I'll shoot you in the head."

"Ah, but my head isn't where my mind is stored."

Benjamin and Elzbietá exchanged a quick look, and she mouthed the word "crazy."

"Raibert, what the hell do you want?" Benjamin asked.

"To talk." He clasped his gloved hands together on the table.

"That's all?" Benjamin asked, noticing a matte gray material between Raibert's black leather gloves and his cuffs. Was this loon wearing a jumpsuit under his clothes that he thought was some sort of futuristic armor?

"That's all," Raibert echoed. "Just an honest and open talk with you. Really, that's all I'm after."

"And then you'll leave?" Benjamin asked.

"Sure," Raibert said, looking away. "Then I'll leave."

"You're lying," Elzbietá stated. "I'm blind in one eye, mister, not both, and I know a liar when I see one." She reached into her purse and released the safety on the locked and loaded automatic.

"Honestly, there's no need for violence," Raibert stressed. "We're all civilized people here. This can all be resolved peacefully, so I recommend we just talk this through and see where it leads us. How's that sound?"

"Just talk?" Benjamin asked.

"Just talk."

"All right, then." Elzbietá clicked the safety back in place but kept her hand in the purse. "Talk. But I warn you, you do anything to threaten me or my fiancé, and I swear to God I will paint the walls with your brains."

"Ah, if only that were still possible," Raibert spoke with a sad smile. "Anyway, I'm not here to bore you with my problems, of which there are many. Instead, let's discuss the one very important task I need your help with."

"The one involving the end of the universe?" Benjamin asked.

"That would be it. This timestream's been altered and it needs to be set back to the way it was. If we do nothing, then this universe is doomed. And guess what, Benjamin? You're the only person who can help me put it back on track."

"You're a total nutcase!" Elzbietá declared.

"No, ma'am. I'm not. The doctor's condition isn't some strange mental illness. The 'fictitious' reality in his head is one that actually existed, and one that needs to exist again. I require the information he has to repair the timeline and prevent this universe from going boom. Though, to be frank, 'boom' is an understatement for what's in store for us. More like a Big Bang that obliterates every part of this universe simultaneously."

Benjamin tried to ignore Raibert's words, but the muscles in his chest still tightened.

"An event somewhere in the twentieth century has gone wrong. I don't have access to records from before the change, and while I'm a historian, I'm an expert on the wrong period to solve this problem. I can't fix this without his help. He needs to identify the Event and what was changed with enough precision for me to go back in time and correct it."

Anxiety built within Benjamin, sweat glistened on his brow, and he concentrated on taking smooth, deep breaths.

"I know what you must be thinking, but I can offer proof of everything I've said, if you would only give me the chance. I do, after all, have a time machine, and I'd be more than happy to let both of you inspect it."

Benjamin put a hand over his heart as the tightness became painful. It wasn't real. It wasn't real! IT WAS NOT REAL!

"Look, I've heard enough of this bullshit!" Elzbietá snapped. "Can't you see what you're doing to him? This sick game of yours has gone too far. You said your piece, and our answer is no. Now get the hell out of here!"

He wiped the sweat from his brow and nodded in agreement.

"Please don't be hasty," Raibert urged. "Perhaps if I were to call in my time machine so you could see it for yourself? I'm sure you'd find it quite impressive."

"No! I'm through listening to this insane drivel you've been spouting!" She pointed her artificial hand at the door. "You lift your butt out of that seat, and you take it straight out that door!"

"Then maybe some form of remuneration might smooth this over? I'm sure my ship could—"

"Enough! Not another word out of you!"

"I see." Raibert's eyes darkened. "In that case I...wait... what was that, Philo?"

"Who the hell are you talking to?"

"You think you spotted *what* heading this way?"

"You're completely bonkers!"

"Oh, no!" Raibert's eyes bugged out. "Get down!"

He grabbed Benjamin by the shirt and yanked him away from the window.

Elzbietá pulled the gun from her purse.

The window burst into a shower of glinting glass, and the table exploded in a spray of dessert, wine, and splinters. Something hit Raibert in the arm and blew his sleeve clean off, but the gray jumpsuit underneath remained intact. His collar tore open, and thick strands wrapped around his head until it was completely cocooned in the material.

Raibert shoved Benjamin down, and he hit the floor on his back. The impact forced the air from his lungs, and he struggled for breath as Raibert loomed over him and reached into his coat. He retrieved a heavy, long-barreled pistol from a shoulder harness and swung it around.

An unclear shape leaped through the window, pieces of glass tinkling with its passage.

Raibert fired.

The weapon's discharge stunned Benjamin's ears and rattled his teeth. Part of the ceiling exploded upward, and the shape that had vaulted over them crashed onto an unoccupied table, collapsing it. He turned his head to the side and saw what looked like a mechanical dog with a gaping hole in its abdomen and a narrow snout that might have been a gun. Oily fluid leaked from the wound.

"See?" Raibert shouted, rising. "Not quite the same when I can fight back!"

Rapid gunfire shattered more windows, shredding booth cushions and their occupants alike. Their waiter's head burst like a balloon, and screaming filled the restaurant.

"Ella!" Benjamin cried. He rolled onto his hands and knees and crawled toward her. "Ella!"

"That's it, Philo! Keep painting them for me!" The hand cannon cracked twice.

Another indistinct shape smashed through a window to the right of the carnage, and gunfire chattered against Raibert's back. The attack shredded his coat and threw him forward, but he twisted around and fired again before dropping to the floor. The shape flew back, slid across a table, and collapsed to the floor in a heap of twitching, now-visible limbs.

"Sneaky bastards!" Raibert blasted three quick holes in the wall. A flying shape spiraled out of control and thudded into the ground.

"Ella, no!" Benjamin screamed. She lay on the carpet with her head to the side as a wet stain spread from her abdomen.

"Philo, bring the TTV over here now! We're getting out of here!"

"No-no-no!" Benjamin crawled through his fiancée's blood and pressed his hands against her stomach. Blood. So much blood, and it continued to spurt through his fingers.

"Time to go, Doc!" Raibert rose to a crouch and grabbed Benjamin by the shirt collar.

"No!" Benjamin screamed as Raibert dragged him away. He reached out and seized Elzbietá's ankle with both hands. "I'm not leaving her!"

"Fine then!" Raibert dropped him and flipped over a long rectangular table. "Head out to the parking lot! I'll get her out of here!"

"I'm not about to trust you with her life!"

"Go!" He shoved Benjamin away. "A table is *not* suitable cover for what they're packing!"

"But—"

Wood chips flew into the air, and gunfire perforated the half of the table Raibert crouched behind. The shots shredded what remained of his coat, and he fell back onto his butt.

"Damn it!" His hand cannon blew the table in half, and a flying shape outside the restaurant exploded into burning pieces that pattered down on the front lawn. "I said I've got her! Now go!"

Raibert lifted Elzbietá onto his shoulder, and her blood quickly stained his back.

"Are you deaf?" he shouted, and fired twice. "Out the back! Help is on the way!"

Raibert shoved Benjamin toward the restaurant's parking lot entrance, and Benjamin stumbled for a moment before regaining his balance. He gritted his teeth, turned and ran. The two sets of double doors were closed, but their glass had already been shattered. Benjamin hurried straight through, and Raibert followed.

A four-legged shape that blended into the grass skittered around the corner.

"To the left!" Benjamin shouted.

"I see it!" Raibert swung his hand cannon around and fired through the wall. An explosion blew out one side of the creature, and scrap metal tumbled down the hill.

Shapes buzzed over the restaurant roof. Raibert snapped off two shots, and the shapes crashed and tore grooves in the shingles. Another three faint outlines popped over the building, but then a loud, continuous roar assaulted Benjamin's ears, like the voice of some chainsaw forged in hell, and a line of fire and metal tore across them.

"About time, Philo!"

Benjamin looked up to see a huge elliptical craft descending upon their position. At first he wasn't sure how large it really was because he didn't have a solid frame of reference to judge its size, but then it kept coming closer and closer, and he finally realized it had to be larger than any aircraft he'd ever seen.

"What the hell *is* that?" he exclaimed.

"That, Doctor Schröder, is my time machine!"

✧   ✧   ✧

"And there it is," Okunnu announced. "TTV sighted moving toward the engagement zone."

"Target locked. Missiles away."

The chronoport's four missile pods each launched one missile per second for eight seconds. The long, conical projectiles engaged solid-propellant boosters and rocketed out of the ocean in sprays of water and steam.

The thirty-two missiles skimmed the ocean surface and accelerated at twenty gees, splitting the air as they broke the sound barrier in less than two seconds.

"So much for the professor," Hinnerkopf said.

"They fired *what*?" Raibert blurted. "Then what are you waiting for? Hurry up and get down here!"

"Behind you!" Benjamin shouted.

Raibert spun around, but the aerial drone fired first. One shot pierced his gray jumpsuit at the elbow and blew his forearm off in a cloud of viscous fluid and snapping, flexible bands. The second pounded into Raibert's back and left a divot in his jumpsuit, and the third punched through Elzbietá's spine in a fountain of blood and bone.

"NO!" Benjamin screamed.

Raibert staggered to his knees and fired. His shot caught one of the machine's propellers, and it twirled through the air before crashing nose first into the pavement. Two more ground-based shapes crested the hill, and the huge aircraft cut loose with twin guns that blasted topsoil into the air and set the ground ablaze.

"Hurry it up, Philo!" Raibert shouted, pushing himself up with a shattered, inhuman arm and steadying Elzbietá with his good one.

The craft dropped sharply. Its exterior appeared seamless, but then an opening formed and a ramp extended. The craft's descent settled, but its ramp still crushed a red sports car and set off its shrill alarm.

"Come on, Doc! We're leaving!" Raibert shouted and ran up the ramp.

Rage, anguish, and stunned disbelief swirled in Benjamin's mind, but all he could focus on was the man taking Elzbietá's broken, bleeding body away from him. He snarled and charged up the ramp after him.

"This is all your fault!"

"Probably!" Raibert snapped back. "Kleio, get us out of here!"

The ramp closed and sealed them in a tall, well-lit space with a roof three stories high that might have been the vessel's cargo bay.

"Well, yes!" Raibert growled. "I'd be *happy* to come to the bridge!"

"She's dead!" Benjamin cried. "She's dead because of you!"

"And we will be, too, if we don't get out of here!" He ran to the back of the cargo bay, and Benjamin followed as fast as he could, then stopped as Raibert floated up a shaft without any visible support.

Benjamin's brain started to catch up with his body, and he began to process all he'd just seen. Invisible robots. Raibert's fake arm. His unusual weapon. And now a giant aircraft where gravity was optional on the inside.

Could all of Raibert's rantings be true?

Or am I slipping further away? Benjamin looked down at the blood on his hands—Elzbietá's blood—and wondered if it was real. Could she really be dead?

Is this what's it's like to go crazy? How can any of this be real?

He shook the dark notions away and steeled himself until all he could see was Elzbietá's corpse in his mind's eye. He hurried onto the circular platform Raibert had used.

"What the hell do I have to lose at this—whoa!" He suddenly felt as if he were falling, but instead of falling down, he fell *up* through the shaft Raibert had disappeared into. The shaft opened at the top into a corridor, and he spotted Raibert racing down it.

"Kleio, engage the impeller!" Raibert shouted. "Get us out of here!"

"*Raibert!*" Benjamin charged after him.

"Not now, Doc! We need to—"

The ship rocked from a sudden impact, and Benjamin stumbled forward. A great tearing noise echoed through the ship, it turned onto its side, and he slipped and cracked his head against the wall that now served as a floor.

The room spun around him. Stars filled his vision. Sound deafened his ears. Another great shudder ripped through him. Through the ship. Through the world.

"Ella!" he gasped as everything went dark. "No!"

CHAPTER TWENTY-THREE

Transtemporal Vehicle *Kleio*
non-congruent

"KLEIO, ARE YOU TRYING TO BE OBSTINATE ON PURPOSE?"

The voice fought its way through layers of mental fog.

"Just do as I tell you and everything will be fine."

Benjamin cracked his eyes open, then squinted at the harsh overhead lighting.

"No, I don't care if you found old injuries. Fix everything, you hear me? *Everything.*"

He blinked and a sterile white room slowly came into focus.

"Yes, yes, the hand and eye too. That'll be a pleasant surprise, and it'll make for a nice show of our good will."

Where was he? Who was talking? What had happened?

He rubbed his face with clean hands, and when he opened his eyes again, the silhouette of a man blocked the light. His eyes adjusted, and the man came into focus.

"Ah. You're looking better."

Who was that again? Wait, yes. Raibert was his name. Raibert. Raibert.

Raibert the crazy.

Raibert the liar.

"How do you feel, Doc?"

Raibert. The man responsible for Elzbietá's death.

Benjamin's eyes snapped open as visions of blood and bone and his fiancée's slack corpse filled his mind. His hands shot outward and his fingers locked around Raibert's thick neck like a vise.

"She's dead because of you!" he screamed, and pushed his thumbs into the man's throat. "Those things were after *you*! She'd be alive if it weren't for you!"

"Well," Raibert remarked, clearly unimpressed. "Not the greeting I'd hoped for, but I guess it'll do."

Benjamin gritted his teeth and squeezed with all his might.

"I know how shocking all this must be." Raibert gestured around them with one arm. "But could you please give me a chance to fill you in?"

Benjamin sat up, put his back against the wall for more leverage, and pressed in from both sides.

"Or I can just wait until you finish," Raibert said with a grimace.

The big man's outer flesh gave, but underneath Benjamin encountered something far more solid and not where bones should be. Visions of Raibert's broken arm flashed through his addled mind, and he remembered oily lubricant and bands that might have been artificial muscles dangling from the end.

He slowly let go of the man's throat and looked him over. Yes, there was the missing arm, except he'd capped the end with a dark cast.

"There, that's better," Raibert said. "Try taking some deep breaths. Maybe that'll help calm you down."

"You're not human, are you?"

"Kid, that is such a twenty-first-century thing to say." He placed his only hand across his chest. "I'll admit I'm a little offended."

"What are you?" Benjamin asked, letting his legs hang off the side of the bed.

"Exactly what I said. I'm Raibert Kaminski, at your service." He stepped back and bowed theatrically. "Professor of history, specializing in ancient Greek and Roman cultures, with a minor in chronometric physics for the aforementioned time traveling. And also, due to an unfortunate—*ahem*—misunderstanding, currently the inhabitant of one stolen synthetic body."

"So you're a thief, too?"

"In all fairness, the people we stole it from turned my old body into fertilizer."

"*We?*" Benjamin noted. "There are more of you?"

"Yes, though you can't see him. His name is Philosophus, and he's my abstract companion. You'd call him an artificial

intelligence, though again, that's a really dated way to put it."
He paused as if listening, sighed, and rolled his eyes. "And yes,
I guess there's the ship too. The *Kleio* is run by a nonsentient
attendant program. Care to meet them?"

"Do I really have a choice?"

"Well, given that we're passing 2026 right now, I'd say it'd be
best if you did. We're running away from the twentieth century
for now. Figured it'd be safer to put some distance between us
and Shigeki's goons until we have a better idea what to do."

"Look, that's all very interesting." Benjamin rubbed eyes that
threatened to tear up as his memories became increasingly clear.
"But can I see Ella? I just . . . I just want to see her."

"Of course you can. Sorry, I got a little distracted. I meant to
show her to you as soon as you came to. She's right over here."

Raibert backed away and gestured to one of two glass caskets
in the room, both with machinery and thick piping running up
from the floor into their raised bases.

Benjamin swallowed and stood. He crept up to the casket and
gazed inside to find a flurry of activity around Elzbieta's body.
Her clothes had been removed, her skin cleaned, and dozens of
tiny arms zipped in and out of her wounds.

"What are you doing to her?" Benjamin demanded, turning
to Raibert.

"Repairing all her wounds." He knocked on the equipment
and smiled. "She should be up and about in, oh, six hours I'd
say. Give or take a little."

"You mean she'll . . ." Benjamin looked back down at her, and
now that he really looked, he could see her chest rising and falling,
and the color had returned to her skin. The injuries still looked
horrible, but there, just on the edge, he could see the gunshot
wound to her stomach contracting. He drew a deep, shuddering
breath and wiped under his eyes. Could it be true? Would she
really be all right?

"Don't worry, Doc. Your fiancée is going to be fine. Kleio didn't
detect any signs of brain damage, so all her injuries are fixable.
In fact, we may have a little surprise for you along those lines."

"Don't mess with me. I'm not in the mood and I don't like
surprises."

"Just bear with me on this one. Trust me, you'll like it."
Raibert leaned against the wall and crossed his arms. Or at least

tried to. The gesture didn't quite work with half an arm gone, and he frowned at his own missing appendage.

"So this stuff is really from the future?" Benjamin brushed his fingers across the casket's glass.

"The True Present, actually. Technically, you're the one from the past."

"If you say so. The important part is this thing will save her life."

"Yup. Nothing to it, really."

"All right." Benjamin nodded and faced the big man. "It seems I'm stuck on your ship with nowhere to go. Now what?"

"First things first."

Two misshapen beads and a pair of glasses made from a hideous swirl of purple and pink descended from the ceiling on gossamer strands until they came level with Benjamin's head.

"What's this?" he asked.

"The ship's infosystem is designed to interface with thirtieth century wetware, which you don't have. I had Kleio print out some kiddie glasses and earbuds for you."

Benjamin plucked the glasses from the tiny threads they hung by.

"You expect me to wear this abomination?" he asked.

"Sorry, but that was the most conservative design in the library. Go on. Try them out. You'll see and hear the difference."

Benjamin grimaced as he put them on, and the sterile room burst alive with color and information. He swung his view about to find displays around his body, around Raibert's damaged arm, and a flood of information over Elzbietá's casket.

"Wow."

"The virtual displays are being autotranslated for you, so you're welcome."

He shifted his view and took in how alive and even beautiful the ship's interior had become.

"It would be easier to use spray on lenses and earbuds, but I'm guessing you're probably not comfortable with tiny robots building the lenses right on your eyes."

"People actually do that?"

"I did it for years before I got my implants. It's perfectly safe, by the way."

"I'll stick with the glasses for now." Benjamin gazed out the open door. "Uh, Raibert? Someone's idea of a Viking is staring at me."

"That's just Philo. Philosophus, remember? He's the *Kleio*'s abstract pilot."

"He's an AI?"

"Sure, if that's the term you prefer."

"Does he know that Vikings didn't actually have horns on their helmets?"

Philo flashed a toothy grin and his lips flapped silently.

"Good show, Doc. He already likes you." Raibert patted him on the shoulder. "Put the earbuds in and you'll be able to hear him and Kleio."

"Okay, then." Benjamin snatched the two earbuds out of the air and fitted them in.

"Welcome aboard, Doctor Schröder," the Viking said. "We honestly wish you'd come here under better circumstances."

"Yeah. Better circumstances." He glanced back at Elzbietá.

"Now to show you where we stand." Raibert pointed his thumb out the door. "This way."

He led Benjamin to a circular room with a round table at its center. Like the medical bay, this room was suffused with colorful displays, and the most prominent ones resided over the table itself.

"Take a look." Raibert gestured to what appeared to be a graphical representation of the ship. A representation with *a lot* of red. "As you can see, the *Kleio* is in pretty bad shape right now. Kleio, would you give us the rundown?"

"Yes, Professor," a soothing feminine voice replied. "The Admin's missile attack breached my hull in three places, and I have suffered heavy surface and moderate internal damage. The port defense gun was destroyed, graviton thrusters one and two are heavily damaged, the metamaterial shroud is nonfunctional across thirty percent of the surface, two nodes on the chronometric array are damaged and require realignment, the shell around the hot singularity is cracked, though I have contained the radiation leak, and one of four heat exchangers has been destroyed. Please note that the prog-steel armor is compromised and will provide only minimal protection until I can reinforce it."

"That doesn't sound good," Benjamin said.

"It's not," Raibert agreed. "We just got our butts kicked by a single chronoport, and there are twelve of them out there hunting us."

"Fortunately," Kleio added, "the Admin failed to damage my impeller, and all printers are still operational. My ability to remedy the damage remains unhindered, and my internal stock of raw materials is sufficient for the tasks at hand."

"The Admin?" Benjamin asked.

"They're the jerks who are after me," Raibert said.

"The same ones who shot Ella?"

"The same."

"And why, might I ask, are they after you?"

"Well, just the small detail that if I fix the timeline and save the universe, their version of the thirtieth century, which I might add *shouldn't* be there in the first place, goes away. So, yeah. They have a pretty good motive to come after me."

"Why do I get the feeling there's something you're not telling me?"

"Ha!" Raibert exclaimed. "Trust me, there's a *ton* of stuff I'm not telling you, but that's just because I can only talk so fast. Besides, I figured we'd wait until the love of your life wakes up so I don't have to keep repeating myself."

"Okay. I guess that'll do for now," Benjamin admitted.

"Hey, Kleio?"

"Yes, Professor?"

"What about my arm? You forgot to mention my arm."

"I have not forgotten your arm, Professor. It is merely a lower priority than the other damage I mentioned. I have an appropriate pattern queued for the printers, and the microbot cast is busy expanding and prepping the outer layer. It should match the performance of your original arm very closely."

"I would certainly hope so."

"I am doing my best with the resources available to me, Professor."

"Wait a second," Benjamin said suddenly. "If your ship is this banged up, and it was right over the restaurant when the Admin attacked. What happened to everyone else?"

"Given what hit us..." Raibert pulled up a virtual chart. "Yep. That would be a really big crater."

Benjamin narrowed his eyes at Raibert.

"Don't give me that look. It wasn't me who fired those missiles."

"But you were the target."

"Okay, granted, that much is true. But look at it this way. They didn't hit us with nukes or antimatter or heavy stuff like that, so your town is still *ninety-nine* percent there."

"It should *all* still be there."

"Look, I'm sorry if I sound callous, Doc, but in case you forgot, the universe explodes if we don't fix this problem. There's just a teeny tiny bit of pressure on me right now."

"Get one thing straight, Raibert. I'm glad you're healing her wounds, but I never said I'd help you change the past."

"Uh!" Raibert slouched over the table. "Fine! How about we put this discussion on hold until Elzeba wakes up? Maybe you'll be more reasonable then."

"Elzbietá," Benjamin corrected.

"Whatever. Philo?"

"Yes?" The Viking appeared at his side.

"Make sure our guest doesn't do anything stupid. I'll be in my room. It's been a *day*."

"Sure thing."

Raibert left the bridge without another word, and Benjamin walked up to the image of the Viking, who then flashed a toothy, if uncertain, grin at him.

"So you're an AI."

"Yes, though we prefer to be called abstract citizens."

"Fully self-aware?"

"As much as you are."

"And what do you think of all of this?"

"Well, Doctor Schröder," the Viking began as he took on a look of great contemplation. "If you'd like my advice, I suggest you look on the bright side of this situation. You may be on a busted up time machine heading into a future you know nothing about with a guy you don't trust, but at least you know you're not going crazy. That's got to count for something, don't you think?"

"You're one of those glass-half-full people, aren't you?"

"At this point, Doctor, it's basically a requirement for people on this ship."

The recovery casket opened, and Benjamin draped a white gown over Elzbietá as she stirred and stretched.

"Hey," he whispered.

Elzbietá licked her lips and held a hand over her face.

"What..." she murmured. "Where am I?"

"Take it slow."

She blinked and her eyes adjusted to the light. Both of them.

"What's going on?" She closed one eye, then the other, then alternated back and forth rapidly.

"Uh, Raibert?" Benjamin asked.

"Yeah?"

"She has two eyes."

"So do most people. So what?"

"*So what?* She only had one eye when she went in. How does she have two eyes now?"

"Uh, hello?" Raibert put his only hand over his chest. "Time traveler from the thirtieth century standing right behind you. This was the surprise, Doc. Besides, would it be too much to ask for a little gratitude around here?"

Benjamin caressed her cheek with the tips of his fingers. All signs of reconstructive surgery had vanished, and he couldn't help but marvel at the radiant beauty those scars had obscured. Her skin was warm and soft to his touch, and he smiled down at her.

"Hey, beautiful."

"I can feel that," she said and raised her right hand to touch her own face. "I can *feel* that! The dead spots are gone!"

"I thought I'd lost you," he whispered back and ran the backs of his fingers down her cheek.

"Yeah, what happened? I remember the window shattering, and noise and screaming, and then...a cold, dark place." She sat up, and Benjamin adjusted the gown over her. "Wait, what?" She looked down and stared at her left hand splayed on the recovery casket.

"Yep, that's fixed, too," Raibert said.

She raised her left hand unsteadily, held it open before her eyes, then slowly opened and closed it.

"You're welcome, by the way."

"How is this possible?" She looked up at Benjamin and Raibert.

"Allow me to officially welcome you to the Transtemporal Vehicle *Kleio*," Raibert said.

"You mean you were telling us the truth?"

"The correct thing to say at a time like this is 'thank you for saving my life,' but at this point I'll settle for both of you not trying, in your own cute little ways, to kill me."

"Thank you," she muttered halfheartedly, and sat up a little straighter, slipping her arms into the gown when Benjamin held it out to her.

"Well, that didn't sound genuine at all," Raibert groused.

"What is all of this stuff?" She looked around.

"What stuff?" Benjamin asked.

"These glowing things." Elzbietá snatched at the air as if she were trying to catch an unseen butterfly. Then she did it again at another spot. "What are they?"

"What things?" Benjamin asked. "What are you talking about?"

"There are shapes and symbols all around me. Don't you see them?"

She grabbed an unseen object in front of her and pulled it close.

"Raibert, what is she doing?" Benjamin asked urgently. "Is she okay?"

"Huh."

"What is '*huh*' supposed to mean, damn it?"

"Just that I didn't expect this."

Elzbietá stared at an invisible object in the palm of her hand, then turned it as if scrutinizing the object from multiple angles.

"It's got numbers and letters and diagrams, but I can't make sense of it." She extended empty hands toward Benjamin. "Don't you see it?"

"Raibert, what's going on? What's wrong with her?"

"Oh, calm down. Nothing's wrong with her. Far from it, in fact."

"But she's seeing things, and that can't be good."

"Quit worrying and put your glasses back on."

"What? Oh." Benjamin reached into his pocket and unfolded the interface glasses. He didn't put them fully on, but instead held them in front of his face and peered through their lenses. He immediately saw a medical diagram from the recovery casket in Elzbietá's hands. "You can see that stuff?"

"Yeah. Can't you?"

"Put your earbuds back in, Doc. I think we both want to hear this explanation."

"Sure." Benjamin did as requested.

"Hey, Kleio!"

"Yes, Professor."

"Can you explain why the patient has SysGov wetware now?"

"I merely followed your instructions to fix everything, Professor."

"Don't give me that crap. I never told you to give her wetware."

"If you will recall, I did attempt to clarify the situation, but you were adamant that I fix all injuries to the patient. Since Elzbietá's wetware appeared to be defunct, I replaced it with a fresh implanting."

Raibert smacked his face.

"Who's talking?" Elzbietá asked, looking around. "I can't tell where the sound is coming from. It's like the voice is in my head."

"That's because it is." Raibert shrugged his one and a half arms. "Oh well. Looks like you're wetwared up to thirtieth-century standards now. Bonus surprise, I guess."

"Is that dangerous?" Benjamin asked.

"Not in the least. All physical adults have them from where I come from. I suppose we could take them out, but they're not meant to be removable. We're talking invasive neural surgery."

"In that case, no," Benjamin stated firmly.

"Hey, Kleio? Patch her wetware with the same autotranslation Doc is using."

"Yes, Professor."

"Whoa!" Elzbietá jerked back. "Everything just changed and... and now I can read these displays!"

"Still waiting for a sincere thank you over here."

"Thanks, Raibert." She swept her gaze all around her, then stopped and stared at the door. "Umm, is that a Viking standing outside the room?"

"Yes and no," Raibert said. "If you'll come this way, I'll explain everything."

"And that's our story," Raibert finished an hour later.

"I'll be honest here," Benjamin said. "Every time you say 'chronometric,' I think a part of my brain commits suicide. Can you be a little clearer about what's really going on with the timeline?"

"Sure. Maybe an analogy might help." Raibert thought for a moment. "Ah! This one ought to do the trick. Are you familiar with the Gordian Knot?"

"Sure I am," Benjamin said.

"Great. I thought you would be. See? We have so much in common. It's like we were meant to work together."

"Just keep telling yourself that, Raibert."

"Alexander the Great, right?" Elzbietá said and gave Benjamin a wry half smile. "Sorry, Ben. I'm afraid I was more interested in physics when I was in high school and an undergrad. I think I've got the basics, but it's not really my period."

"Not a problem." Benjamin smiled back at her, astonished by

how light that smile had made his heart. He reached across the table to squeeze her hand, then looked back at Raibert.

"The Gordian Knot refers to a myth associated with Alexander of Macedon," Benjamin began. "As the story goes, he marched his army into the city of Gordium, capital of Phrygian, in 333 BC. Inside the city he found an old ox wagon with an impossibly complex knot tied about the yoke, the ends of which were well hidden. According to Phrygian tradition, the wagon, which was then kept in a temple dedicated to Zeus, had belonged to Gordius, father of King Midas. An oracle had once proclaimed that any man who could unravel the knot would become the ruler of all Asia, and this had piqued Alexander's interest.

"He confronted the ancient puzzle, and, after struggling with it for some time, he *supposedly* drew his sword and severed the knot with one mighty stroke. That night, a great thunderstorm raged over the city, and Alexander's prophet Aristander interpreted this as a sign that Zeus was well pleased and that he would grant Alexander many victories."

"Not supposedly," Raibert corrected. "It pretty much played out exactly like you described."

"There's some dispute on the matter," Benjamin continued, giving Raibert a doubtful look. "Modern scholars question whether he actually cut the knot or if he used another solution such as pulling the pin out of the pole the yoke was tied to."

"Oh, come on," Raibert protested. "Time traveler, remember? I actually inserted myself as one of Aristander's assistants and even recorded Alexander cutting the knot. Interesting fellow, as far as twenty-three-year-old world conquerors go."

"Fine," Benjamin conceded. "I guess I can't top that. Go ahead and take all the mystery out of it."

"The important part," Raibert said to Elzbietá, "is a Gordian knot is a seemingly impossible problem that can be solved only in an unconventional way. And that's precisely what we have here. Forget all the 'chronometric' whatevers I mentioned. All you need to know is that sixteen universes, including this one, have become knotted. To any casual observer, the Knot appears impossible to unravel, which is why I need a sword to cut it. A sword represented, in this case, by the Event that has to be put back the way it was. A sword that currently resides in *your* head." He pointed a finger at Benjamin.

"Well, you can't have it."

"Oh, come on! Seriously?"

"Why not?" Elzbietá asked. "You heard what he said. *Sixteen* universes including our own are at risk. Everything else he's told us has panned out to be true, so I don't see any reason we should doubt him or his sincerity."

"At last!" Raibert gestured to her with an open palm. "Someone is *finally* willing to take me at my word and not throw me in prison or shoot me or try to strangle me. Thank you, ma'am! Thank you!"

"It also makes sense now why not-Benjamin's memories are so complex," Elzbietá continued. "They really are a second set of memories from another reality. He and you are simply two versions of the same person. Ben, everything we've seen fits."

"I know, and I agree with what you're saying."

"Then why don't you want to help him?" She came up to him and placed her hands at his sides. Her movements were still weak and unsure, but she had the strength to stand on her own.

"It's because neither of you understand what you're asking me to do. What you're asking me to give up."

"Then make us understand." She placed a hand on his cheek. "Please."

"Is it because of all the extra people that will die in the twentieth century after the change?" Raibert asked.

"No, it's not that. Or rather, that's not all of it."

"Then what is it?" She cocked her head and smiled at him. "Please tell us."

"Ella . . ." He struggled to articulate the pain in his heart, for what had once been a delusional fantasy was now a reality. A reality that once was and could be again. "Ella, if those other memories are true, you don't exist in the world Raibert wants to re-create."

Her mouth hung open, and he looked down at the floor.

"I can't know for certain," he continued, "but your grandparents would almost certainly have been killed in the Nazi concentration camps. You would never have been born."

She closed her eyes and tears leaked from them.

"That's why I can't help this man, more than any other reason. I'm sorry, but I can't lose you." He pulled her close and hugged her.

"Ahh," Raibert mocked. "That's so sweet."

"Shut up. It's not like *you* have anything to lose when the timeline gets restored!"

"Oh, you think so? Well, let me tell you something, Doc. I'm currently stuck in a synthetic body that is native to *this* version of the thirtieth century, and there's no way I can be pulled out of it. So, I honestly have no idea what's going to happen to me if or when we unravel the Knot. You think I'm doing this for myself? I'm probably not going to exist when we're done! In fact, the one person here with the *least* at stake is you!"

"That's where you're wrong," he said, stroking Elzbietá's hair.

"No, I'm not! We know with one hundred percent certainty that you exist in both timelines. You're *guaranteed* to survive! The rest of us? Who the hell knows?"

Elzbietá pushed him back and wiped away the tears.

"Are you okay?" Benjamin asked.

She shook her head.

"It's all right. Don't worry, I've made up my mind. I'm not going to help."

"No, Ben." She wiped under her nose and sniffled. "You have to."

"But..." His voice trailed off as his heart sank.

"I'm not going to place my own life ahead of everyone else, and I don't want you to do that either." She inhaled deeply and composed herself. "This is bigger than us."

Benjamin couldn't find the words. He simply gazed into her clear blue eyes. He saw the terror, the fear not simply of death but of never even having *existed*, yet behind that terror—stronger than any fear—was a steely resolve that had taken her through the Mato Grasso air strike, through the long, agonizing recovery, through her own PTSD and *his*. The strength that *would* not be broken.

By anything.

"I've always told myself that it would have been okay if I'd died that day," she said as if she'd read his mind. "Sixty-two people died to destroy that missile complex, and I was almost one of them, but we saved *hundreds* of *thousands* of lives. Their sacrifice was worth it, and if I'd died that day, mine would have been worth it, too."

"Ella..."

"And now that I'm confronted with the same choice, only with an uncountable number of lives on the line, do you really expect me to put my life ahead of everyone else's? This isn't just millions, or billions, or even *trillions* of lives, Ben. This is sixteen entire *universes*. Sixteen solar systems. Sixteen Milky Ways. Sixteen Magellanic Clouds and sixteen Andromedas. The human mind can't even begin to *conceive* how many planets and stars and species we're talking about here! And you think I could put *my* life ahead of all of *that*?"

"No," he admitted sadly. "I don't."

"Then this is something you need to do. If you love me and you're truly the man I know you are, you'll do this. I know it'll hurt, and I'm scared, too, but this is something you have to do. Our lives are too small and the price to save them is too high. I *refuse* to pay it."

Benjamin lowered his head.

"So please do as I ask." She took his hands into her own and squeezed. "Please help him."

Benjamin clenched his eyes shut.

"Please?" she whispered.

"All right." He opened his eyes and raised his head. "Raibert?"

"Still here. Just being patient while you two sort things out."

"The sword you're looking for is a train traveling from Cologne to Berlin. It was attacked near the city of Stendal as it crossed the Elbe River. Everyone on board was killed."

"See? That wasn't so hard. What's the date?"

"May 16, 1940," Benjamin said. "The day Adolf Hitler was assassinated."

"There, Director." Captain Okunnu highlighted the icon on the chronometric chart. "Contact reestablished with the TTV at plus three months. Signal is solid on our scope."

"Are we at risk of losing sight of them?" Hinnerkopf asked.

"Doubtful. They almost gave us the slip when we passed through the storm, but now that we've reacquired their impeller signature, I think the chances of us losing the trail are quite low."

"And do you believe they know we're behind them?"

"I don't pretend to be able to read minds, but the TTV's given no indication it's aware of our presence. We're safely within the center of its wake, and our baffles are fully extended. They may have the technological advantage, but our chronometric signature is significantly lower at our present speed. They may not be able to detect us at all."

"Their advantages may not be as great as we initially thought," Hinnerkopf observed.

"How so, Director?"

"At no point have we witnessed the TTV exceed seventy kilofactors. Perhaps that's the design limit of its impeller."

"But didn't your report say its impeller design was one we're incapable of replicating with current technology?"

"I did, but that doesn't *necessarily* make it better. It only means it's harder to make." Hinnerkopf pursed her lips and tapped a finger against them. Was her design the superior one after all? It was a flattering notion, but she couldn't afford to underestimate her quarry.

"In that case, should we attempt to overtake them?" Okunnu asked. "Our baffles remain effective up to seventy-two kilofactors. And even if we're spotted, our maximum speed easily outstrips theirs."

"No." Hinnerkopf's voice was firm. "Continue to match their speed and course. If they slow down, we slow down."

"Understood, Director," Okunnu said after a moment's hesitation.

"You don't approve, Captain?"

"It's not that."

"But it is . . . what?" she pressed.

"As you say, Director," he responded neutrally. "It's not my place to judge."

"There are a number of reasons we're going to play the waiting game." *And none of them are because you're scared. Right, Katja?* "First, we've already expended half our long-range munitions. We hurt them, but how badly? If our next attack doesn't finish them off, we're left with only the Switchblades: a weapon that's already proven largely ineffective against their armor. Furthermore, we'd have to phase-lock with them in order to launch our missiles."

"We *can* hit the TTV with them while non-congruent," Okunnu replied a bit stiffly.

"But only if we get dangerously close," Hinnerkopf countered, and the captain was forced to nod.

Without impellers of their own, chronometric drag would

begin shifting the missiles out of phase the instant they left their launchers. Worse, the phase gradient would climb quickly...which made "dangerously close" a pretty drastic understatement, actually.

"That's a valid point," he acknowledged with manifest unwillingness.

"Yes, it is. But there's an even more important reason we should wait and see."

"What's that, Director?"

"Once this current threat is eliminated, it will fall to the Admin to unravel the Knot in a way that preserves our existence. What does the professor know that we don't? Why was he in 2018? Why did he take on passengers there? Why is he moving away from the Knot now? Is there some complexity to this phenomenon hidden between the twentieth and thirtieth centuries? Is there a secret he didn't share with us? Too many unanswered questions, Captain. Too many of them for my liking."

"I see your point."

"And so we'll wait and see where he phases in."

"What if we find nothing unusual at the phase-in point?"

"Well, Captain," Hinnerkopf said with a thin smile. "Then at that point, I say the professor has nothing more of value to show us."

CHAPTER TWENTY-FOUR

Transtemporal Vehicle *Kleio*
non-congruent

BENJAMIN SQUINTED AT THE CLOUDY FLUID IN THE EYEDROPPER as he sat in what had become his study. Virtual readouts of eBooks filled the space around him, but he couldn't see them since he'd taken off those ghastly interface glasses. He'd taken out his contacts, too, which had reduced the room to a blurry mess.

"You sure this'll work?" he asked.

"Quite sure," Philo said through the one earbud he still wore.

"The little robots aren't going to eat my eyeballs or something?"

"Good grief! Why would you even think that?"

"I don't know," he grumbled and picked up the eyedropper.

"Just one drop in each eye and ear."

"Right, I remember." He took the earbud out, peeled open his right eye, and tapped the button on top of the dropper, which released a pre-sized droplet.

The fluid wasn't anything like a saline solution. It was syrupy, white, and opaque, and when he tried to blink it away, the fluid flowed back under his eyelid as if it had a mind of its own. Which it probably did.

He administered a drop each to his left eye and both ears. The fluid crawled deep into his ear canals, and he shivered from the intrusion.

"Unpleasant," he complained, blinking rapidly.

The door split open, and he turned and squinted to see who

it was. The cloudiness over his eyes quickly faded, and the world started coming back into focus, but he still couldn't identify the person who'd stepped inside.

"Hey, Ben! Hey, Philo!" the newcomer said.

"Oh. Hey, Ella." He blinked some more and the space around him came into sharp focus.

"Good morning, ma'am," Philo said, his voice coming through clearly.

"What are you working on, Ben?" she asked.

"Just trying out these magic eye drops. You?"

"Getting used to my implants. Check this out!" Elzbietá spread her arms, and virtual displays spawned above her hands, then twirled around at high speeds before collecting in a neat pile in front of her. She clapped her hands together and they vanished.

"How did you do that?"

"I don't know," she shrugged. "I just can. It's as natural as breathing."

"That's by design," Philo stated.

"Do the implants make you feel any different?" Benjamin asked.

"Not that I'm aware of. Have I been acting differently?"

"No. You've been perfectly normal." He glanced around and grimaced. "For whatever counts as normal in this place."

"You've taken quite well to them," Philo said. "In fact, I think you'll soon be better at interacting with the *Kleio* than Raibert is."

"Because he's in an Admin synthoid now?"

"That's right."

"How about you?" She sat next to Benjamin and rubbed his thigh. "How are you holding up?"

"Surprisingly well, actually. It's strange. I've been fighting these dual memories for months, but it's actually much easier to simply lie back and accept them."

"Well, it's not like you had any reason to accept them before now."

"True, but now I know my memories of David and my father's death and all the other stuff is as much a part of me as my memories of you. Coming to that realization's helped center me in some way. I don't feel normal—not like I did before The Day—but I think I can honestly say I've never felt this close to normal since."

"Hey, that's great!" She patted his thigh. "I'm really proud of you, Ben."

"Thanks. I genuinely do feel like I've turned the corner here. I'm not going crazy. I haven't been hallucinating. It's all real. It's all a part of me, and the secret to living with myself is accepting *all* of who I am."

"That's just wonderful to hear." She leaned in and gave him a quick peck on the cheek. "So, have you made any progress on the Event?"

"Sort of. I've been having some difficulty getting used to all these intangible displays floating around the place. That's one of the reasons I put in the eye drops. I need to be able to search through the material Philo saved more effectively."

"We could print it all out," Philo offered, "but we currently don't have enough raw material to print that many paper books. We probably could if we phased in and let the microbots eat a few trees. Or maybe print them with plastic pages."

"It's not worth the hassle," Benjamin said. "I'll get used to it. Kleio has more important things to worry about than printing out a library for my sake. Besides, that's not the biggest problem."

"What is?" Elzbietá asked.

"The chronoton storm," Benjamin said. "Or rather the 'malleability of time upstream of the storm.'"

Elzbietá looked blank, and Benjamin sighed.

"Philo can explain the details," he said, "but the short of it is we get one shot at correcting the Event. If we screw it up, that's it. No redos."

"Why?" Elzbietá asked. "We have a time machine. We have infinite redos."

"Unfortunately, that's not true," Philo stated. "We now know that time is malleable, at least in the sense that any interference with it can create distinct, parallel universes going forward. But we're trapped within the boundaries established by the chronoton storm, and if our interpretation of the numbers is correct, nothing we do can break outside the existing, intertwined universes. The energy which *should* have created another universe had to go somewhere, so it only pours even more energy into the moving storm front, and *we're* stuck with every change—and its consequences—we make. There are no 'redos' on this one.

"*Any* changes we make to the events of May 16, 1940, in this universe will ripple down the timestream to the storm front. Of course, that's exactly what we *want*...but only if those changes closely follow the original version of that day. I don't believe we need to *precisely* match the original sequence of events, but key features *must* align for the Knot to unravel. Otherwise, the phenomenon will only worsen. Our interferences will become a permanent part of the Event, the timeline will diverge even farther from its original form, and the storm front will be only stronger. I estimate that would make the Event almost impossible to repair, as any subsequent visits would only introduce more variables."

"Like he said, no redos," Benjamin summarized.

"Oh, I see," Elzbietá said. "So, basically, us going into May 16 is like cutting open a patient, and when we're done there'll be a scar. If we fail and try to go in again, not only do we have to fix the original problem, but we have to fix the scar, too."

"Huh." Philo raised his eyebrows. "That's actually a very good way to put it. Yes, it *is* as if time is being scarred by our interactions."

"See? This stuff isn't so hard to understand," Elzbietá beamed.

"Uh-huh," Benjamin grumped. "Anyway, the problem is that while I do know the time and place of the Event, we also need to restore it to something as close to the original as possible. And on that note, I should really get back to it. I've got a lot of reading ahead of me." He turned back to his desk and pulled the next eBook interface over.

"Well, you keep right at it." She stood up and hugged him from behind. "You'll figure it out."

"I'm going to do my absolute best. You have my word."

"Oh!" Philo started, and the others turned to him. "Raibert just called. He'd like both of you to join him on the bridge. It sounds important."

"Good important or bad important?" Benjamin asked.

"He didn't say."

"Nope, this just isn't going to cut it." Raibert shook his head and crossed two whole arms. "We need something bigger, Kleio."

"That is the largest weapon pattern in my database."

"Well, it's not big enough. Not nearly big enough."

"If you are concerned about size only, perhaps I could come up with a trebuchet design that is larger than this."

Raibert narrowed his eyes. "Kleio?"

"Yes, Professor?"

"No one likes a smartass."

"Professor, it is impossible for me to be a smartass because I am not sentient."

He put both hands on the command table and hung his head as Benjamin and Elzbietá entered the bridge.

"Ah, good. Come on over, you two." He beckoned them closer.

"Problem?" Benjamin asked.

"Yeah. We need bigger guns."

"What is that thing?" Elzbietá pointed at the weapon diagram hanging over the table.

"That, young lady, is a 45mm defensive Gatling gun."

"That's a *defensive* weapon?" Benjamin exclaimed.

"Yep. Beautiful, isn't she? Seven barrels, each nine meters long. Cyclic rail capacitors capable of accelerating three thousand rounds per minute. And to top it all off, each round hits with over six hundred kilojoules of kinetic energy, plus a variety of internal payloads that include high-explosive, incendiary, and antipersonnel dispersal types."

Elzbietá whistled.

"What are you defending against?" Benjamin demanded. "The apocalypse?"

"Admin chronoports, Doc. There are a dozen of them out there searching for us, and we need to be ready for them. This vessel originally came with two 12mm Gatling guns, one of which got blown off, and even if we still had both, they're not exactly the sort of weapons I want to charge a militarized time machine with. We can print a replacement, but I think we need to do more. Fortunately, we also have patterns for larger weapon systems like this. Unfortunately, it's not *quite* big enough for what I have in mind."

"Which is?"

"Popping Shigeki's chronoports like they're big metal piñatas."

"Not that I'm opposed to more firepower, but you're a historian," Benjamin said. "What could this ship possibly need a gun that big for?"

"Generally speaking, the *Kleio* wouldn't ever need a monstrosity like this." Raibert gestured through the "defensive" weapon. "But she has the same pattern library that ART Preservation TTVs get."

"Art preservation requires Gatling guns?" Benjamin looked at Elzbietá, and she shrugged at him.

"It does if you're going to show up in the past and take whatever you want, which ART, the Antiquities Rescue Trust, regularly did. Or does. Or will do. Or ..." Raibert waved a hand aimlessly through the air. "Philo, which verb tense should I use here?"

"Don't look at me. Old English wasn't built for multiverse time-travel scenarios. Just go with whatever feels right."

"What happened when the people from the past didn't feel like giving up their property?" Benjamin asked.

"Well, you see ..." Raibert grinned fiendishly. "That's where the aforementioned 'defensive' guns come in."

"That's horrible!" Benjamin blurted.

"Hey, don't look at me. Philo and I managed to stop the worst of ART's rampages long before we knew how much of a mess time travel was actually making. And now that we *do* know, we're going to put a stop to them for good ... assuming we actually make the transition back to that reality." Raibert suddenly lowered his head. "Ah, damn it. Now I'm starting to depress myself."

"It's okay, buddy," Philo said. "If I make it through this and you don't, I'll be sure to spread the good word."

Raibert smiled bravely at the avatar.

"Hm?" Benjamin took half a step back, and his face scrunched up as if he were reappraising Raibert.

"What?" the synthoid asked. "Something on my face?"

"Sounds like you regularly butt heads with your superiors."

"Yeah, sure. I guess you could say that." Raibert shrugged indifferently. "ART's pretty powerful in the Ministry of Education. Philo and I *did* give them one hell of a black eye and also managed to stick them with a whole host of restrictions, but stop them?" He shook his head. "Wasn't going to happen."

"I thought so." He flashed a crooked smile at the big man. "You know, that's actually not too different from my own situation. I've been fighting against the collegiate establishment for some time. My parents too, in fact."

"What are you talking about?" Elzbietá chuckled. "You're the *chairman* of the history *department*. You're like the poster boy for the establishment."

"In this universe, sure," he said, and the humor drained from her face. "But the other Benjamin—who I must now accept as a part of me—has had a very different experience. His college is infected with a noxious form of groupthink that tries to silence voices of dissent rather than engage in honest debate. Raibert, as strange and surprising as this is to admit, I can honestly see some similarities between us. We're both outsiders who have fought against entrenched ideas we believe are wrong. I... almost feel a sense of kinship with you right now."

"Almost?" Raibert asked, raising an eyebrow.

"Let's just say you've given me something to think about. In a good way."

"Oh. Well, you're welcome." He scratched the back of his head. "I guess that's a start."

"Now, you were saying something about popping chronoports before I interrupted you."

"Yes. So, the problem is we need bigger guns. I want something that's going to split those chronoports right down the middle. Just blow the fuckers right in half."

"My database does not contain a weapon system that meets those requirements," Kleio stated.

"And that's why we need to look elsewhere," Raibert said.

"You mean else-*when*," Elzbietá corrected.

"Oh, look at you!" Raibert grinned. "Now you're thinking like a time traveler. You're exactly right. And that's why we're still moving down the timestream. We need to get closer to the thirtieth century. The closer we are, the more effective any goodies we pick up will be."

"But where can we stop?" Philo asked. "The Edge of Existence is guarded by Admin time machines."

"I said closer, Philo, not right on top of it. We need to be smart about where we stop."

"*When* we stop," Elzbietá corrected again.

"Yeah, what you said," Raibert dismissed.

"Obviously, I don't know a whole lot about the thirtieth century," Benjamin began, "but is the Admin currently at war with anyone?"

"No, Doctor," Philo said. "They're the dominant solar power in this version of the timestream. Most of their problems come from within their sphere of influence. Secessionists, terrorists, protech radicals, that sort of thing."

"Protech radicals?" Benjamin asked.

"The Admin was originally formed to enforce a group of

laws called the Yanluo Restrictions. They're basically regulations that forbid or heavily regulate technologies. Protech radicals are one of the countergroups that support the roll back or even the repeal of the Restrictions."

"Both the Admin and SysGov spawned from similar formative events," Raibert said. "The Admin had a weaponized AI called Yanluo and its self-replicating swarm go out of control. We, on the other hand, had the Near Miss: an industrial accident that turned a large strip of China into pinballs."

"I'm sorry, did I hear you right?" Benjamin chuckled. "China gets turned into *pinballs* in your timeline?"

"The Near Miss is no laughing matter, Doc. That disaster killed millions and pointed out the need for a global governing and regulatory body. In fact, it's what motivated the nations of Earth to form SysGov. It's as important to me as the formative... something-or-other is to your country."

"The American Revolutionary War?" Benjamin offered.

"Right. Exactly. That thing. Just as important."

"You really don't know a whole lot about my time period or what led up to it, do you?"

"Hey, there's a *lot* of history out there. I can only keep track of so much."

"But *pinballs*?" Benjamin pressed.

"The Chinese were experimenting with industrial biotech and microtech self-replicating systems," Philo said. "They were designed to mass produce simple objects quickly and cheaply, but an outbreak during beta testing led to a ragged strip of Asia a thousand kilometers long and as wide as seventy-five kilometers at some points being 'processed.' The construction pattern loaded into the initial swarm was for a basic pinball with very loose requirements for base materials, since it was meant to test the swarm's capabilities with a simplistic goal.

"The swarm took that pattern and ran with it, converting most of the landscape, as well as the entire development team and anyone else unlucky enough to be in the swarm's path, into giant piles of pinballs fabricated from whatever materials were present at the time, including people's bones."

"*Bone* pinballs?" Benjamin asked.

"Yeah. Bone pinballs," Raibert said. "Philo, do you still have that video with the dog?"

"Yes, it's in my personal cache," he answered cautiously, "but are you sure you want me to show it to them?"

"Damn right I want you to show it. I'm sensing a lack of cultural sensitivity from our twenty-first-century friends here, and we're going to show them the dog."

"What?" Benjamin asked. "Is this like one of those funny Internet videos?"

"You'll see. Play it, Philo."

"All right, then." The avatar shuddered. "Here goes."

The weapon diagram vanished, and a 2D video feed showing an abandoned city street replaced it. The angle of the view indicated it was coming from a surveillance camera, perhaps one mounted on a streetlight.

Black sludge crept into view, oozing out of windows, seeping from the sewage drain, and sluicing across the sidewalk.

A small off-white orb popped out of the sludge and pattered down the street.

Then another.

And another.

"Was that ...?" Benjamin asked quietly.

"You'll see," Raibert said.

The camera angle shifted to the side and revealed a whole city block buried in moving tar. A building collapsed in the distance, and tiny orbs popped out of the sludge and rolled away.

The goo advanced and pushed pieces of debris with it.

But not just debris. Bicycles, trash cans, cars, buses. Even a helicopter with busted blades.

And bodies. Lots of bodies.

The camera zoomed.

Sludge pushed along an elderly man's corpse half submerged in the ick. His arm caught on a piece of rebar, the sludge rolled him over, and the camera revealed that only half of him remained.

A dog floated in the muck next to him, a Maltese puppy with its legs submerged in the filth.

Or, more correctly, with its legs already eaten away.

Black ooze crept over its back, and it howled and whimpered as tiny bone beads plinked out of its body.

"That's ... just horrible," Elzbietá breathed.

"Yeah, it is." Raibert swiped the video aside. The weapon design reappeared. "I like to show that when people tell me we shouldn't regulate self-replicators so much. And the death toll from the Yanluo disaster was a hell of a lot worse, even if the tech was way different. *We* lost millions; they lost *billions*. I'm no fan of the Admin, but they have some good reasons behind their Restrictions. You need to place bounds on tech like this."

"If that's the case, the thirtieth century may not be the best place to search," Benjamin noted.

"What are you thinking?" Raibert asked.

"Well, sounds to me like their tech base is artificially stagnant. If that's true, then we can expand our search to include a wider selection of earlier time periods. Restrictions or not, wars are a strong impetus to develop and innovate. What if we focus our efforts on the time periods after major conflicts the Admin fought?"

"Now that's what I'm talking about," Raibert said. "Good thinking, Doc. If we phase in right after a war finished, there might be some surplus hardware lying around."

"And since the war is over, people will be less diligent about guarding it," Benjamin added. "Possibly."

"Worth a shot. Philo?"

"Searching...and, got one."

"Damn," Elzbietá said. "I could have really used you when I was writing my dissertation."

Philo dipped his horned helmet to her.

"What do you have for us?" Raibert asked.

"In 2773, a cold war between the Admin and NEDA, the Non-Earth Defense Alliance, went hot, and it didn't end well for NEDA. The Admin's superior numbers and resources stomped all opposition into the ground, and the war ended in 2775 with Mars and the rest of the NEDA members being absorbed into the Admin. That's actually where a lot of its present day problems come from. The interesting thing, though, is why the war started in the first place. In the years preceding the war, NEDA actively developed forbidden tech in flagrant violation of the Yanluo Restrictions."

"Including weapon systems?" Elzbietá asked.

"Oh yeah. You better believe it. They call it the Violations War for some very good reasons. I grabbed everything I could when I infiltrated the Admin's infosystems, but the records I got don't have a lot of detail about past wars. There's enough to tell me that at least some of NEDA's weapons should meet our piñata-popping requirements, though."

"Nice!" Raibert exclaimed. "Sounds like we have a winner. Now we just have to narrow it down further. We need to figure out which year and geographic location we'll phase into. If our assumptions are correct and the Admin's tech has been fairly static, then their twenty-eighth-century military will be just as nasty as thirtieth-century Peacekeepers."

"Maybe even more so because of the proximity to a war," Benjamin said. "Their military forces will be battle hardened."

"Nothing ventured, nothing gained," Raibert countered. "Philo, any thoughts?"

"None that I like. I've got the locations of the largest Peacekeeper bases, but those might be too risky for us."

"Yeah, not unless we have a solid plan. Phasing in at a *military* base and blundering around at random is a surefire way to get more of the *Kleio* blown off."

"What about a museum?" Benjamin suggested.

The other occupants faced him.

"A museum?" Raibert asked pointedly.

"What? Lots of museums have weapons from past wars in them."

"Oh, right," Elzbietá said. "And even if they're not perfectly functional, the *Kleio* should be able to restore them to working order. Or just use them as patterns for new build versions."

"Hmm," Raibert murmured. "I guess it's a thought. Not one that I had, but it's a thought. Philo, anything?"

"Yes, actually."

"Seriously?"

"Seriously," Philo echoed. "A lot of the combat between the Admin and NEDA was fought in space. Mars contributed the bulk of the NEDA space fleet, and their ships were the most advanced, so they're the ones we're interested in. At the end of the war, Mars was required to surrender all of its surviving ships before signing the Articles of Cooperation and becoming an Admin member state. Most of the ships had their forbidden tech stripped and were refitted for use by the Peacekeepers, but one was converted into a museum commemorating the Admin's victory."

"Well, then!" Raibert rubbed his hands together. "That sounds *very* promising. Sorry I doubted you, Doc. No offense."

"None taken."

"The ship is a supercarrier called the FPNS *Lion of Aurorae Sinus*," Philo continued, "and as chance would have it, the gunboats it carried are almost the same size as the *Kleio*. It was handed over to the Admin in early 2776 at an L4 shipyard, and it's still there in 2979 in museum form."

"Then we know exactly where to find it," Benjamin said. "We just need to pick the year."

"Let's go with 2777," Raibert said. "Give things some time to cool down after the war, but hopefully not enough time for them to strip the *Lion* of all its dangerous goodies."

"That should work," Philo said.

"Kleio, adjust course for the L4 Lagrange point, 2777 CE."

"Yes, Professor. Adjusting course."

"All right, everyone," Raibert said. "I say we phase in, grab the most dangerous guns we can find, and phase out before anyone realizes we were there."

"Sounds like a plan to me," Benjamin said.

CHAPTER TWENTY-FIVE

Transtemporal Vehicle *Kleio*
non-congruent

"NOW THAT'S JUST BEAUTIFUL," RAIBERT SAID AS STRANDS OF microbots lifted the last components of the massive weapon out of the printers and maneuvered them into place.

"It looked smaller on the diagram," Benjamin remarked, gazing up at the suspended weapon.

"They always do." Raibert folded his arms and smirked. "Can't wait to try this baby out."

"Just how much better is this compared to a twenty-first-century gun?" Benjamin asked.

"To put things into perspective," Elzbietá began, "the 25mm cannon on my F-21 had a comparable rate of fire, but put out one sixth the kinetic energy into each shot. And I have to assume the payload in each round is superior as well."

"Significantly so," Raibert said. "And not just because of the increased caliber."

"I have finished expanding the weapon blister," Kleio reported. "The new weapon can be moved there as soon as assembly is complete."

"What about the rest of the repairs?" Raibert asked.

"Repairs to the hull and the shroud are nearly complete. The crack on the reactor has been reinforced, and I have not detected any radiation leakage since. Graviton thruster one is fully functional. Thruster two still requires some realignment of its exotic matter, and I should have that resolved within the hour. The chronometric array presents some problems because of how precisely the exotic matter must be recalibrated, but I expect to have it fully restored in one to two days."

"Good. Now start making another big gun."

"Yes, Professor."

"You're building more of these things?" Benjamin asked.

"Why settle for one when you can have a thousand?"

"Professor, damage control and weapon production is placing a considerable drain on my raw material reserves. I have enough stock on board for three, perhaps four additional weapon systems of this size and configuration, but after that my bulk printers will begin running out of crucial raw materials in several categories."

"Three or four?" Raibert frowned. "Are those all the guns I'm getting?"

"Yes, Professor, though if you require more I could begin to cannibalize sections of the prog-steel hull. That would free up some of the materials necessary for additional weaponry. I would also have to recycle some of my noncritical systems."

"What, and make us easier to shoot down?" Raibert exclaimed. "No! Hell no!"

"Then I am afraid I am limited in what I can produce without additional supplies."

"Well, do the best you can, but *don't* strip our armor to make it happen."

"Understood, Professor."

Microbots locked the components in place and flowed over the surface as pearly white droplets that collected along breaks between segments. The printers below whirred to life again, and Raibert gestured for them to follow him out.

"There's another small problem we have to contend with," Raibert said as they left the printing bay, then took a counter-grav tube up to the bridge. "The *Kleio*'s thrusters are a bit oversized for what she normally does; there's plenty of spare capacity for hauling heavy artifacts built right into her design. That's great for me because we can move fast when we need to, and I'm in a synthoid. The g-forces aren't going to affect me all that much, but you two are regular squishy humans. We need to make sure you're safe if we have to push this ship to its limits."

"How many gees?" Elzbietá asked.

"Five. Sustained indefinitely."

"No problem. Give me a g-suit and good place to sit, and I can handle that."

"In any direction?" he asked. "Including down?"

"Ouch. Okay, never mind."

"Why's that?" Benjamin asked. "What's the difference?"

"The human body has very low tolerances for negative g-forces," Elzbietá said. "The blood pools in your head and you pass out in a matter of seconds. Doesn't matter how good your g-suit is or how much training you've had."

"Hence, we have these nice compensation bunks on the bridge in case of emergencies." He rapped his knuckles on a section of the rounded wall, and the prog-steel parted to reveal a row of five upright glass caskets.

"So we just climb into these things if we fall under attack?" Benjamin asked.

"That's right. The microbot soup they get filled with isn't pleasant, but it'll keep you conscious and intact."

"Don't you have some sort of device that cancels out g-forces?"

"Nope," Raibert replied bluntly. "We can create new gravity fields, and we can counteract existing ones, but if you're under acceleration, you're feeling the gees. Period."

"Ah!" Elzbietá's face lit up and she snapped her fingers. "Because of Einstein's Principle of Equivalence?"

Raibert nodded.

"What?" Benjamin asked.

"Acceleration and gravity are essentially the same thing," Elzbietá explained. "That's why they can't counteract the g-forces. The only way to not feel the gees is to not accelerate."

"You knew that off the top of your head?" Benjamin asked.

"Oh, come on. You've seen my reading pile. Some of the crazier things in physics are like candy for my brain."

"I'll take your word for it." He grimaced. "But if I'm not mistaken, Einstein would have had a few strong words to share regarding this time machine."

"True," Raibert said, "but you'd be surprised what he said when shown our Theory Of Everything."

"What do you mean *when* he was shown?"

"Oh, there *may* have been someone in ART who went back and interviewed Einstein to see what he thought of our society's definitive science equation. Spoilers, he had a lot of nice things to say. Really just an all-round heartwarming interview. Very touching."

"You did that?" Benjamin asked.

"Nah. My Dad."

"So your father was in ART? That had to be rough on you."

"Actually, he abstracted and his connectome was transmitted to Alpha Centauri before I got involved with ART."

"What?" Benjamin looked to Elzbietá for help.

"They e-mailed his brain to another star system," she translated.

"Again, what?"

"In truth, ART didn't start their big downhill slide until Lucius took over," Raibert added.

"Who?"

"Here's an idea, Doc." Raibert urged them out. "How about the two of you grab a bite to eat—it's almost lunchtime anyway—and I'll join you and share the story of the biggest time-traveling ass cave there ever was."

Lucius Gwon strode into Archiving Hall Five and immediately became the center of attention. Every AC in the grand cubical chamber noted the ART chairman's unexpected appearance and quickly informed their physical counterparts. Those archeologists looked up or down from their work and began to murmur amongst themselves.

Discreetly. Lest they come off as rude around the boss.

Walkways cut across the archiving hall at various heights with counter-grav tubes joining them to form a scaffold around some of ART's larger recent acquisitions: the Statue of Liberty from nineteenth-century New York City, Christ the Redeemer from twentieth-century Rio de Janeiro, and the Colossus of Rhodes from 280 BCE. Several smaller monuments occupied the hall, but those weren't grand enough to warrant physical exhibition and would probably be reclaimed once the archeologists finished their work.

Lucius slowed his pace along a catwalk halfway between the ceiling and floor, then stopped above the Colossus of Rhodes. The monument of Helios stood over fifty meters tall when its octagonal base was included. Bronze skin blazed from spotlights hung under the catwalk, and Lucius took hold of the railing and gazed down with an unreadable face.

His slicked-back hair matched the black of his suit, and two bold red sashes crossed his chest while twin streamers fluttered actively behind him. The sashes and streamers retained a fixed color and pattern, in contrast to prevailing fashions, but fitting in was never good enough for Lucius Gwon. He wanted to stand out from the crowd, and his evocative style made that clear to everyone around him.

"What's the chairman doing here?" Raibert wondered aloud from a counter-grav platform hovering behind the left knee of the Colossus. "Philo, did you hear anything about this?"

"Gotta go!" the AC announced.

"Wait, what?"

Raibert reached out across the firewall, but the AC was already gone.

"Well, that's odd." He turned to Teodorà. "You or Fran hear he was coming today?"

"If we had, you would have been the first to know." She winked at him.

"Yeah, you're right." He smiled back. "Silly of me to ask, though it does look like he's interested in the Colossus."

"Maybe he wants to feature it in an exhibition," Teodorà offered. "It *is* quite striking when the sun hits all this bronze. For the technology of the time, the ancients really pulled off the look of a sun god."

"It's big and it's flashy," Raibert acknowledged with a grimace. "*Perfect* for an ART exhibition."

"Oh, don't you start that again."

"Sorry." He flashed her a lopsided smile. "Old habits die hard."

Dating Doctor Teodorà Beckett certainly came with a lot of perks, like how ancient Greek and Roman history fascinated both of them. She could hold her own on just about any topic he cared to debate, and it didn't hurt that her dark hair, olive skin, and almost elfin physique were easy on the eyes. Or that she'd proven surprisingly adventurous in bed. A little *too* adventurous in some cases, but he'd dealt with that by setting *very clear* boundaries in their relationship.

No, the *real* problem was how he had to watch his tongue when it came to ART's wrecking ball approach to archeology. Teodorà not only worked in the Preservation branch but had rapidly advanced to more prominent mission roles, whereas Raibert could care less about ART's internal politics. He was perfectly happy embarking on one Observation mission after another despite Teodorà's warnings that he needed to be more career focused.

Sure, it impressed sponsors when ART scooped up whole monuments like the Colossus of Rhodes, and it certainly made his job easier when he could study the artifact in a climate-controlled environment with modern technology at his fingertips, but stunts like this kept missing the point.

Raibert didn't want to answer only *how* the Colossus was built; he wanted to know *why*, as well. Why spend twelve years constructing a towering bronze monument to Helios? Why were certain engineering techniques used over others? Why did it look the way it did? What was the thought process behind its design? What compromises were made between art and engineering? What problems were encountered during those twelve years that altered the original plans?

So many questions remained unanswered, but Lucius and the rest of ART's management thought that yanking the Colossus out of time and plopping it down in front of ignorant sponsors was somehow equivalent to understanding the ancient humans who'd built it.

It wasn't.

And, ultimately, he was okay with that because he planned to dig into those mysteries himself. History wasn't stone and metal and sand and architecture. It was love and hate and joy and grief and blood. *So* much blood. Understanding history didn't come from pointing at an artifact and saying "Hey, look at what people without counter-grav were able to do! Isn't that fascinating?"

No. To understand history, one had to understand the people *in* history, and the best way to do that was for someone to go back in time and live among them.

Which was why Raibert had spent every available minute scrutinizing the Colossus and the engineering techniques used to erect it. He needed to be completely comfortable with all manner of technical topics before he inserted himself into the company of Chares of Lindos, the sculptor behind its design. Did the man live to see the project completed, or did he really commit suicide as some accounts seemed to indicate? If he'd committed suicide, what drove him to that tragic end?

"Aren't those more interesting questions than 'How'd they

put the head on this thing without counter-grav?'" he murmured to himself.

"Raibert!" Teodorà hissed.

"Hmm?"

"Hey, Raibert!" She poked his shoulder.

"What?"

He turned around and looked up at Lucius Gwon. The man's strong jaw, high cheekbones, and chiseled body hinted at the lavish genetic licensing his parents had paid for, but his face remained uncomfortably stone-like, giving Raibert the impression of a carefully cultured mask to be worn in public. His integrated companion remained equally unreadable; the AC, which had integrated itself so tightly with Lucius over the years that it no longer used an independent name, portrayed itself as moving star fields within the man's own shadow.

"Ch-chairman!" Raibert straightened, his voice squeaking slightly. "What can I do for you?"

Lucius stepped across the platform and rubbed a hand over the bronze back of the giant knee.

"Would you mind telling me a little bit about what you're working on?" he asked.

"Of course, sir. I'm studying the engineering techniques used in the construction of the Colossus. It's part of my pre-insertion prep."

"You're going back to Rhodes?" Lucius tapped his knuckles against the bronze.

"Yes, that's right."

"And what's your plan?"

"I'm going to get a job working for Chares of Lindos. He's the sculptor behind the Colossus."

"I see. A fairly standard Observation mission, then?"

"That's right. Not too much risk and plenty of interesting questions to answer."

Lucius nodded, then picked at a rivet with his fingernail.

"I hope to leave next week," Raibert added.

"And after that?"

"Well, I haven't really thought about it. I'm going to be back there for a few months at least, so I suppose I'll check out what's available when I return to the thirtieth century."

"Any interest in Preservation missions?" Lucius asked, glancing his way.

"Not really," Raibert said, and Teodorà tensed behind him. "I'm quite happy with the assignments that have come my way."

"What he means to say"—Teodorà placed a hand on his shoulder—"is that he's in a serious rut right now and would *love* to branch out to other assignments."

"No, thank you." Raibert flashed a sour look her way.

"Come on, Raibert," Teodorà replied. "You could be—and *should* be—doing so much more in ART."

"I'm fine right where I am, thank you very much."

"Actually, I have to agree with her." Lucius turned around, and the streamers fluttered elegantly. "I took a look at your file before coming down here, and I couldn't help but notice how... safe it seems."

"I like safe. Safe is comfortable."

"Tavish would have been bored to tears with missions like these."

"I'm not my father," Raibert said, perhaps a little too forcefully. But if Lucius was offended, he didn't show it.

"Raibert, no one expects you to be some sort of reincarnation of your father. But at the same time you can't ignore the legacy he left behind. We know the kind of raw talent you have because we've all seen it in action. Which is why I find your selection of missions a little disheartening."

"Sorry to disappoint, I guess," he said with a shrug.

"How is Tavish doing these days, by the way?"

"He finally got transferred to a more lifelike synthoid, so he almost looks like his old self again. I got some mail from him last month, and it's actually exciting to see how the colony's taking shape. You could probably find something similar in the solar system a few centuries ago."

"That's very good to hear." The smallest glimmer of joy in the form of a thin smile leaked through Lucius's cool exterior. Raibert knew Tavish and Lucius had worked closely together during ART's early days, so maybe that's where this sudden attention was coming from. Maybe Lucius just missed his old buddy and saw helping the son along as a sort of replacement.

Not that I need the help, Raibert thought.

"Well, I can tell you're quite dedicated to the Observation branch. Of course, I have to admit that while it isn't the most exciting part of what we do, it's still very important work."

"Thank you, sir. That means a lot coming from you."

"Still, there's nothing wrong with shaking things up a little."

Raibert frowned at this.

"Tell you what." Lucius rubbed his jaw thoughtfully. "A mission I'm personally supervising is slated to leave for the battle of Marathon in a few days. I want you on the Observation team that goes in first."

"*Me?*" Raibert blurted. "But I haven't prepped for Marathon!"

"Consider it a challenge," Lucius stated. "One I'm confident you'll rise to meet."

"But why me? Can't someone else do it?"

"Of course, but it's you I want to work with. Besides, I have a few special assignments I think you'll find...interesting."

"I don't know about this."

"Did I just hear you say yes?" Lucius asked as if Raibert's response didn't matter.

"I—"

Teodorà jabbed him in the ribs before he could get another syllable out.

"Ouch." He rubbed his side. "Sure. Why not? I'm in."

"Splendid. I'll forward you the details of your special assignment when we're close to the appropriate year."

"I don't find out what I'm doing ahead of time?"

"What would the fun in that be?" Lucius quirked a smile. "A challenge, remember?" He nodded to both of them, then took the counter-grav tube up.

Raibert deflated with a long sigh after he was gone. "What the hell was that all about?"

"This is great!" Teodorà slapped him on the back. "How does someone like *you* get noticed by *Chairman Gwon*?"

"Just lucky, I guess."

"Well, you'd better use that luck for all it's worth and impress the hell out of him."

"Sure. I'll get right on that," he replied sardonically. "Do you have any idea what he's going to have me do?"

"Not a clue, though Fran has heard about him handing out special assignments like this in the past. He might be sizing you up to see if he wants to work with you more in the future."

"Well, that's just great," Raibert grouched. "Why did you have to tell him I'm in a rut? I could have done without that part, you know."

"Come on." She kissed his cheek. "We've talked about this before. It's good for you and good for your career to take some more risks. Preservation work isn't nearly as bad as you think."

"Really?" Raibert raised a skeptical eyebrow. "Then why does ART seal the recordings from Preservation missions and make everyone involved sign nondisclosure contracts?"

"Look, all the Ministry and our sponsors want are the artifacts. They don't care how we get them. They don't *want* to know, and it works fine that way. Besides, it's not like we ever do any *permanent* harm when we go back."

"Is he gone?" Philo asked, materializing in their shared virtual vision.

"Yes, and where the *hell* have you been?" Raibert snapped. "The ART chairman shows up and you scamper off to who knows where?"

"Something came up."

"Uh-huh. I bet."

"It was really important."

"Fine. What was it, then?"

"Can't say. It's personal."

Raibert sighed and rubbed his forehead.

"So, what happened?" Philo asked.

"Here." Raibert opened the firewall around his short term memory. Philo dipped into it, and his eyes widened into saucers.

"Something wrong?" Raibert asked.

"I don't think you should go," Philo said softly.

"What are you talking about?" Teodorà crossed her arms. "Of course he's going."

"It's a . . ." Philo seemed to struggle with his words. "The whole thing seems shady. You should turn him down."

"I already said yes."

"Then call him up and tell him no."

"And kill his career in the process?" Teodorà warned. "No way! He'll be stuck in dead-end Observation missions for the rest of his life!"

"Doesn't sound so bad to me," Philo countered. "That's where you like it, anyway."

"But what if he changes his mind in a decade or two? Do you really want to burn that bridge and forever lose the chance of taking on more exciting missions?"

"Look, I appreciate the concern, Philo, but Teodorà's right. The chairman just came down here and *personally* asked me to help him out with a special assignment. How do I say no to that? Besides, even if it is a little shady, how bad could it be?"

"So how bad was it?" Benjamin asked before taking another bite of his tuna salad sandwich.

"Pretty fucking terrible," Raibert replied. "The day before the *Kleio* reached 490 BCE, I received a telegraph from Lucius with my instructions. The *Kleio* was to enter a separate instance of the battle from the other Observation TTVs, and my job was to research the Marathon runner, whether he really existed or not, whether he ran to Sparta before the battle or Athens after the battle or both, and most importantly, Lucius wanted to know the man's real name, assuming he existed in the first place, of course."

"That doesn't sound bad at all." Elzbietá stabbed a fork into her creamy Caesar salad.

"I thought the same thing at the time," Raibert said. "It seemed like Teodorà was right, that Lucius wanted to challenge me with an assignment I hadn't prepared for to see if I really was like my father. I also learned that Lucius's own TTV, the *Aion*, would phase-lock onto the same instance of the battle and watch my progress."

"Okay, now that's a little creepy," Elzbietá said. "No one likes the boss looking over their shoulder."

"My task started well enough," Raibert continued. "The *Kleio* phased in above the Plain of Marathon just south of the city, and we watched the battle through our remotes. Phalanxes of Athenian hoplites advanced under a hail of arrows. But they were undaunted by the Persian horde's greater numbers. They charged in, and when they finally smashed into the Persian ranks, the sound was almost indescribable. Metal and wood crashed against flesh and bone. Spears skewered flesh. Iron clinked off bronze armor. Men screamed. Bones broke. The Athenians rolled forward in an unstoppable mass of spears, shields, and men that crushed the wounded Persians underfoot.

"Late into the battle, Philo and I spotted a runner heading south from the plain. I left the ship to make contact with the man, still thinking this was some test."

"And was it?" Benjamin asked.

"No." Raibert shook his head and leaned forward with one elbow on the table. "It wasn't anything of the sort."

The runner sprinted through a grassy plain dotted with trees and bordered by foothills to his right. His chest heaved with each stride, and sweat glistened on his brow. The sun beat down on him. His muscles ached, but the message of victory that he bore filled him with vigor, and he refused to let his legs falter.

He continued across the field and rounded a hill when he spotted a man sitting atop a wooden barrel. He slowed to a jog, wary of this new fellow after nearly being killed by Persian archers earlier that day, but the man bore no weapons he could see. In fact, he seemed dressed like a common farmer, and the runner relaxed a little.

"Good day to you!" the farmer greeted him with a wave of what looked like a canteen, then raised the container to his mouth. Water gushed out, and the farmer gulped most of it down while the excess dribbled down his chin and soaked into his tunic.

The runner licked his parched lips, suddenly conscious of how thirsty he was. The farmer continued to chug the water down for several long, delicious seconds, and the runner found himself slowing to a halt next to him.

"Ahh!" the farmer exclaimed and wiped the spilled water from his lips and chin. "Hot today, isn't it?"

The runner worked up a bit of spit and moistened his cracked lips.

"It is," he agreed, his eyes fixed on the canteen. He wanted to ask for a taste, but a sense of wrongness stayed his speech. Was this man really a farmer? He was dressed like one—that much was clear—but his skin hadn't been baked by days in the sun, and though he had commented on the heat, his clothes were unstained by sweat.

What was he doing out here? And where did that barrel come from? Had he rolled it all the way here by himself? With those scrawny arms? Perhaps someone else brought it out here for him. Was he an aristocrat, then? If so, then why dress in such a humble manner? And for that matter, where were his servants?

None of this made sense.

The farmer brought the canteen up to his lips again, and the runner swallowed spit down a dry throat.

The farmer stopped, glanced toward the runner, then lowered his canteen.

"Ah, pardon my rudeness. You're probably thirsty."

"I am," the runner managed.

"Here, let me fill it up for you."

The farmer stood off the barrel and crouched next to it. He turned a valve at the bottom, and water gurgled into the canteen. What luck was this? The whole barrel was full of water?

"That should do it." The farmer closed the valve and held out the canteen. "Help yourself to as much as you want."

The runner took the canteen, and his fingers brushed against the other man's palm. Aha! He may have looked like a farmer, but his hands were too soft to have seen much labor. Still, water sloshed within the canteen, and the runner brought it gingerly up to his lips.

How cool and clean it tasted! Like water from a mountain stream! His body rejoiced with each gulp, and not just because of the heat and his exhaustion. He had never tasted water so pure, so delicious, and he began to wonder if this out-of-place man and the perfect water in the barrel had a supernatural origin.

Was this farmer a divine being masquerading as a man? The runner pondered this as he emptied the canteen.

"You can have more if you like," the farmer said. "I imagine you have quite the run ahead of you."

"That's right. And thank you."

"Oh, don't mention it. Help yourself to more."

"Again, thank you."

"But first..." the farmer began, and the runner felt his muscles tense at the change in tone.

"Yes?" he asked.

"Would you mind if I ask you a few questions?"

"Questions?" the runner echoed.

The farmer nodded. "Just a few. I promise they'll be easy."

"Well, friend," the runner replied, relaxing. "If that is the payment you request, then I'll gladly pay it."

"Wonderful. Now, for the record, would you please state your name?"

"My name?" the runner asked.

"It's Pheidippides, isn't it?"

"Pheidippides?" The runner shook his head. "No."

"Really?" the farmer frowned. "I could have sworn that was it. It must be the other one, then. Philippides, am I right?"

"Philippides?" What sort of strange questions were these?

"You're not Philippides?"

"No, I'm not."

"Huh." The farmer slouched. "Well, then. I'm out of guesses. Shows what less than twenty-four hours of mission prep will do. So what *is* your name?"

"Well, good sir, my name—"

His head suddenly exploded.

Raibert recoiled as the headless corpse collapsed to the ground, gore spurting from the ruined stump of his neck. Blood splattered Raibert's face and tunic, and a piece of spongy brain slid down his cheek like a misshapen slug before finally dropping off.

"What..." he muttered, his mind struggling to push through the image of an earnest face bursting like overripe fruit. He shook his head and tried to wipe the blood off his face, but only succeeded in smearing it.

He stood up and turned in a circle, looking for the source of the carnage.

"What just happened?" he demanded. *"Philo?"*

No answer came. He reached across the firewall, but couldn't find the connection.

"Anybody?"

Nothing.

And then laughter, over his virtual hearing.

"Oh, you should have seen your face. Here, let me show it to you."

A window opened in his virtual sight, and the runner's head exploded again in slow motion. Raibert watched the replay of himself flinching back before his face finally settled into a fishlike O.

"Lucius?"

A figure in a metamaterial suit rose from the grassy plain and rested a sniper rifle on his shoulder. He walked casually up to Raibert and peeled back his hood.

"You killed him!" Raibert snarled.

"Oh, please! Don't be so dramatic." Lucius prodded the runner's corpse with a boot. "I couldn't kill this man if I tried. He died thousands of years ago, and the way he died is impossible to change. Even with all of ART at my command, there's nothing I could do to change his life." He smiled and snorted. "Or death."

"But that's still no reason to brain him!"

"Why does there have to be?"

"Because it's pointless and wrong!" Raibert spat. "And why can't I reach Philo?"

"I put a block on the connection to your TTV," Lucius said. "Chairman privileges, you know. That killjoy doesn't need to be a part of this. I take it he never told you he used to be my companion."

"What?"

"Still keeping secrets, I see." He pointed a thumb over his shoulder at a shadow swirling with starlight. "My current companion is such an improvement. We share everything. No mental boundaries; no secrets. That's the way it should be. So much healthier than what Philosophus and I had, though he went by a different name back then. Honestly, his old moniker was better. Philosophus makes him sound too self-important."

"But you told me to learn the runner's name! Why kill him?"

"To have some fun, of course," Lucius chuckled. "But also to make a point for you. All of this"—he stretched out his arms and turned in a circle—"is our playground. We can do whatever we want, take anything we see, satisfy any desire we have, and all of it without any consequences. We're more powerful than any deity these indigenes could ever conceive. All of history is here, perfectly preserved for our taking. So why not take? Why be squeamish about it? Your father never hesitated."

"I am *not* my father!"

"Look, I know I won unfairly this time. How about this? Let's jump out and start over. This time, *you* try to keep me from learning his name." He offered the weapon. "You want to use the rifle?"

"No!" Raibert pushed it back. "I'm not playing your stupid game!"

"Why not?"

"Because I have someone's *brains* on my face! This is wrong, Lucius!"

"Wrong? But that's exactly what I'm trying to show you. None of this is wrong. Everything is ours for the taking. Want to bed Cleopatra or Helen of Troy? Just hop in a time machine and do it! Who's going to stop you?" He put a hand to his chest. "I sure won't. In fact, I'll even help cover your tracks."

"I will *not* use my time machine to have sex with famous people!"

"Well, that's probably for the best," Lucius dismissed. "A lot of them are letdowns." He leaned in and whispered conspiratorially. "If you ask me, Helen is *really* overrated. Still haven't tried Cleopatra, but she's on the list. I'll get to her eventually."

Raibert recoiled. "You mean you actually—"

"And why shouldn't I? For that matter, why shouldn't you?"

"Because I'm here to study *history!*"

"So am I, but why not have a little fun while we're at it?" He chuckled and shook his head with a bemused expression. "This one time I dropped a fifty-ton mech armed with lasers and microwaves into the middle of the Battle of the Bulge. It was *hilarious*! Everyone was scurrying around like ants trying to dent the thing, while it's flash-vaporizing the water in their bodies and popping them like zits, one after another after another." He started laughing so hard he had to catch his breath. "Oh, wow. Whew! You really should have seen them. So funny."

"That's monstrous! How could you do something like that?"

"Come on, Raibert. Don't be like that." He looked him square in the eyes. "Your father's the one who got me started on this."

Hot rage flared inside Raibert, and he punched Lucius in the jaw with all his might.

It barely fazed the man.

"I see he never shared that little secret with you." Lucius rubbed his cheek. "Oh well. This mistake is on me, thinking the cloned son would be just like the father."

"Well, I'm glad I'm such a disappoint—!"

Lucius smashed the rifle butt against Raibert's skull, and the world went dark.

"What an asshole," Benjamin remarked.

"Yeah, tell me about it," Raibert said.

"So, did your father really abuse his power as a time traveler like that?" Elzbietá asked.

"I don't know. I never asked him."

"Why not?"

"Well, for one, even if he had abused his authority, he'd clearly moved on with his life. Two, Lucius was right, none of that was *technically* illegal. Just completely immoral. And three, can you imagine having to wait *eight years* for the response to a question like that? I wasn't just afraid of the answer, but the waiting itself.

And what if his answer only raised more questions? I'd have to wait *another* eight years to hear back on those." Raibert sighed and shook his head. "No, it just wasn't worth it. He was busy building a new world for humanity, and he didn't need me dragging up the past. So instead, Philo and I did our best to expose Lucius's abuses."

"How'd that go?" Benjamin asked.

"Not very well." Philo materialized in a virtual chair at the table. "At least initially."

"Good of you to finally join us," Raibert said.

Philo shrugged. "It's not a topic I'm particularly fond of. The Gwon family is *not* to be trifled with."

"That's an understatement. They used the Ministry to block us at every turn, and Lucius made it clear that if we stepped too far out of line we'd never see the inside of a time machine again." Raibert chuckled sadly. "Which is kind of funny when you think about it, because then we wouldn't be in this mess."

"We still tried, though," Philo added.

"And failed spectacularly," Raibert continued. "At least until the Alexandria Expedition. Before that, I approached Teodorà to get her on our side, and that didn't end well. She got fed up with my 'anti-ART activism' and the harm it was doing to her career. And then she broke up with me! Though on the bright side, at least we didn't have to put up with her pressuring us into having foursomes anymore. Am I right, Philo?"

"Yeah." He shuddered. "Good riddance to *that* idea."

"Anyway, Lucius stripped all of my ART seniority, which meant everyone else got to select from the open mission docket first, and we had to choose from what was left."

"It could have been worse," Philo pointed out. "Most of them weren't interested in the missions we liked anyway."

"I'm sorry. I know the rest of that was important." Elzbietá eyed Raibert, then Philo, then Raibert again. "But . . . foursomes?"

Raibert glanced over to Philo, but the AC held up both hands.

"Hey, don't look at me. *You're* the one who brought it up. *You* explain it."

"Fine, whatever," Raibert huffed.

"You don't have to if this is a sensitive topic," Elzbietá offered. "I didn't mean to pry."

"No, it's not like that." Raibert grimaced as he rubbed his temples. "Look, just let your imagination wander for a moment. We're from a society where *every* physical adult has access to full sensory overlay. What do you think some of them are going to use it for?"

"I can make a pretty good guess," Elzbietá admitted.

"Right. Only it's a bit more complicated than that because most of us have integrated companions. Now in polite society, when two physical citizens wish to"—he waggled his hands in a vague and decidedly nonexplicit manner—"you know, engage in consensual activities, a bunch of mental firewalls go up and their ACs go do something else for a while."

"In *polite* society," Philo emphasized.

"I just said that."

"I know, but I thought it deserved repeating."

"Look, am I explaining this or are you?"

"Oh, please." Philo raised both hands again. "Don't let me stop you."

Benjamin rested his cheek on a fist. "Is this conversation really necessary?"

"It is now." Raibert glared at Philo before continuing. "Anyway, what some physical citizens do is get their ACs in on the . . . festivities, shall we say? Basically, you have two people going at it like they would in any century, but their mental firewalls open up and their integrated companions do what they can to"—his expression soured—"enhance the mood."

"Enhance the mood?" Elzbietá echoed. "How so?"

"Mostly just sensory overlays," Philo explained. "Visual imperfections get smoothed over and the scene is augmented with virtual lighting, sound effects, textures, aromas, music, that sort of thing."

"I thought I was explaining this."

"I decided to help."

"That doesn't sound too out there," Elzbietá said.

"Maybe to someone with a glandular system and a reproductive drive," Philo began, "but I don't have either. Can you imagine how *awkward* that makes it for me?"

"Which is why the physical and abstract halves of normal society give each other a little privacy sometimes," Raibert continued, "and edgy stuff like foursomes is frowned upon."

"Let me guess." Benjamin leaned back crossed his arms. "The asshole was into that sort of thing."

"Yup." Raibert glanced at his companion. "And we have a firsthand witness to prove it."

"It was so humiliating!" Philo shuddered with disgust. "I had to edit and record *everything*!"

"That's terrible!" Elzbietá said.

"Yeah, but I'll grant Lucius this one pardon." Raibert wagged a finger. "Of all his perversions, the sexual escapades were probably his most harmless."

"You wouldn't say that if—" Philo began, but then stopped and took on a look of great contemplation.

Raibert raised his eyebrows.

"Okay, yeah, I'll give him that one," Philo admitted finally. "Everything else was worse."

"At least it's all behind you." Raibert reached over to comfort Philo with a firm pat on the shoulder, but then stopped. He withdrew his hand and grimaced down at it. "Fucking Admin garbage synthoid body," he breathed.

"I'd give you a hug right now," Philo said, "but I can't."

"I *know*! And that's the problem!"

"I guess there are worse time travelers we could have gotten stuck with," Benjamin said.

"Was that supposed to be a compliment?"

"Maybe it was."

Raibert looked up to find a thin but warm smile on Benjamin's face, and he realized that another piece of the barrier between them had just been knocked over.

"Report!" Hinnerkopf demanded, floating into the bridge.

"TTV phase-in confirmed." Okunnu unstrapped from his seat and glided over to meet her. "They're within the L4 Lagrange point, 2777 CE."

"So he wasn't trying to get back to the thirtieth century after all. But there's nothing unique about this part of the timeline. Why here? Why so far from the storm front?"

"I couldn't even begin to guess, Director."

"What's our status?"

"We stopped as soon as we spotted the TTV decelerating." He gestured to the virtual displays at the front of the bridge. "Current position is negative three months from the TTV, non-congruent."

"Why did he stop here?" she muttered. "Why this year, and why the Lagrange point?"

"Your orders, Director?"

"It doesn't make sense," Hinnerkopf stated aloud. "This year and place are too far from the Knot *and* the storm front to have any relevance."

"Then perhaps the professor has nothing left to show us."

"Perhaps..." Hinnerkopf stared at the clutter of military space stations, industrial asteroids, and cylindrical habitats scattered around the L4 Lagrange point. Several of those icons glowed bright Admin blue, and she nodded as a clear course of action came to her.

"Take us in," she said firmly.

"Yes, Director."

"Quietly," she stressed.

"Understood." Okunnu spun toward the bridge crew. "Pilot, move us in at ten kilofactors, maximum stealth approach. Phase-lock with the TTV and bring us in one hundred kilometers off the target's estimated position."

"Yes, sir. Accelerating now. ETA is thirteen minutes."

"Variskin online and loaded with standard spaceborne stealth profile."

"Shall we ready a missile volley?" Okunnu asked Hinnerkopf.

"Thank you, but that won't be necessary."

"We're not taking him out?" His brow furrowed.

"You misunderstand me, Captain," Hinnerkopf smirked. "We're going to use every resource at our disposal to prevent the TTV from ever making it out of this century."

"Then, I'm afraid I'm not following you."

"Take a good look at when we are, Captain. The professor has blundered into the years following the Violations War."

Okunnu faced the display, but still seemed to be playing mental catch-up with her.

"There are *so many* Admin warships and Peacekeepers just sitting around with no enemy to fight," she continued. "And we have every authentication code ever used by this era."

"Ah. I see what you mean now."

"Oh, Professor." She smiled cruelly as the chronoport sped forward through time. "There were so many simpler ways for you to commit suicide."

CHAPTER TWENTY-SIX

L4 Lagrange point
2777 CE

"NOW THAT'S ONE BIG SHIP," BENJAMIN SAID AS THE IMAGE OVER the command table resolved in his interface lenses.

"The FPNS *Lion of Aurorae Sinus.*" Raibert leaned forward and placed both hands on the table. "Nearly two kilometers from bow to stern and with enough launch bays for a hundred twenty gunboats our size. Not much in the way of external weaponry, but with that many little helpers, who's counting?"

"Its name comes from a creature out of this timeline's Martian folklore," Philo commented. "A lion with a pure white pelt who comes to the aid of those with hearts untainted by evil."

Benjamin snorted out a laugh.

"What? Was it something I said?"

"Sorry. I just find it amusing that Mars has been colonized long enough to have its own folklore."

"We're a long way from home, all right." Elzbietá rubbed Benjamin's shoulder. "The size of that thing is unreal, but some of those other ships are almost as big."

To Benjamin, the Admin shipyard resembled a coarse blue comb, several times as long as the enormous carrier, with ships resting between its few thick teeth. The *Lion* was clearly the largest and rested at one end of the shipyard, but fourteen smaller ships occupied scattered slots, some nothing more than skeletal structures, while others looked nearly complete. A white stripe ran up the main shaft of the shipyard, and a silver shield adorned the center.

Lighting banks illuminated the work of men and women in what had to be spacesuits while a few small industrial craft maneuvered heavier components into place. The space around the *Lion* was dark and deserted by comparison, and the shipyard showed little activity within half a kilometer of the Freep supercarrier.

"External weapons are still in place," Philo observed. "But that appears to have been a cosmetic choice. From what I can tell, they've been disabled, either by emptying the ammunition stores or removing critical components. Its conversion into a museum is definitely underway."

"But it also doesn't appear to be a high priority," Benjamin said. "Otherwise we'd see more activity around it."

"Maybe it's something the Admin works on when they don't have anything better to do," Elzbietá commented.

"Forget the outside weapons." Raibert shooed the notion aside. "The gunboats are what we're here for. How do those look?"

"Some of the launch bays are open," Philo said. "And those that are have been emptied. Most are still closed."

"Probably part of the decommissioning process," Benjamin said. "If you look at which have been opened, it's like they're working their way through the ship from front to back. We could park the *Kleio* in one that's next to the closed bays and try to get inside from there."

"Sounds like a good place to start," Raibert said. "Kleio, take us in."

"Yes, Professor."

The *Lion*'s launch bays were stacked three high and twenty across on each side of the massive ship. The *Kleio* eased closer, its hull obscured by the metamaterial shroud, and it slid invisibly into one of the bays. The shroud constricted a little more tightly for clearance around the weapons blisters, and the *Kleio* came to rest with its entire hull inside the bay.

Raibert and Elzbietá activated the helmets on their prog-steel suits, while Benjamin opened a virtual interface over his wrist and triggered his manually. Metallic tendrils enveloped his head, prompting a flash of claustrophobia before his interface lenses shone the external view straight into his eyes.

"You still okay with me coming along?" he asked once all of them were sealed inside their armor.

"The faster we get this done, the safer we all are," Raibert said through Benjamin's earbuds. "Besides, we're in this together. Just be careful what you touch."

Two fat-barreled, snubnosed pistols descended from the ceiling on microbot strands. Benjamin grabbed one while Elzbietá took the other.

"Uhh, Kleio?"

"Yes, Professor?"

"What are those supposed to be?" He pointed to the weapons.

"They are Popular Arsenals PA13 Watchman burst pistols."

"Okay, fair enough. Next question. *Why* are you handing out modern weapons?"

"Because Doctor Schröder asked me to print out a pair."

"And who approved the order?"

Philo raised a hand.

"Really, Philo?"

"They're part of the team now, right?"

"Well, yeah, but..." He trailed off and shrugged his shoulders.

"I looked through your ship's catalog and thought they might prove useful," Benjamin said. "You don't sound happy."

"I just like to know when we're handing out weapons to the time-traveling newbies. When's the last time you used a gun, anyway?"

"About twenty years ago," Benjamin answered, which was more or less the truth.

Raibert gave him a doubtful look. "Well, be careful with that thing."

"Afraid I'll shoot one of us by accident?"

"Nah," Raibert dismissed. "The software on those things wouldn't let that happen unless you bypassed the safeties, which you'd better not even *think* about doing. Just remember it's not a toy. That gun will pulp an unarmored human."

Benjamin inspected the weapon and the displays that spawned around it, peered down its virtual sights with the barrel pointed to the floor, double-checked the safety, then adhered it to his hip. He grabbed a half dozen extra magazines the microbots dropped and stuck then to the opposite side of his hip.

"Hmm." Raibert nodded slowly. "All right. That makes me feel a little better."

"We're wasting time," Elzbietá said, grabbing her own spare ammo. "Lead the way, Raibert."

"Right."

Benjamin and Elzbietá followed the synthoid down the tube to the cargo bay. The tube exit contracted shut behind them. Each of them strapped on a backpack filled with a microbot reservoir.

"Equalizing pressure," Philo said. "Deactivating gravity."

Benjamin had to suppress a moment of terror as his body screamed out that he was falling. The boots of his prog-steel armor stuck to the deck as unseen mechanisms sucked the air away. He inhaled and exhaled deeply as he came to terms with the falling sensation. Each breath seemed louder than before, and he thought that was because it was one of the few noises he could still hear.

"Open it up," Raibert said.

The *Kleio*'s bow split open and a ramp extruded to the launch bay. Benjamin found the first few steps to be less awkward than he'd imagined. The suit actively increased or decreased the adhesion of each sole, allowing him to maintain an almost normal stepping motion.

He left the *Kleio* and looked around the launch bay, which was six times as deep as it was wide and tall. The back wall formed a dark square covered with white orthogonal outlines and white text that might have indicated openings in the otherwise flat, featureless surface. All of the markings were turned on their side and used the wall to his right as the "floor," which he supposed made sense. If the ship had to operate while accelerating, then its interior would be laid out like a two-kilometer-tall tower. That way, it could function both in free fall and under acceleration.

Benjamin walked to his right, placed one boot on the "wall," then stepped fully onto it and stood up. The markings were all oriented correctly, and visual edits from his interface lenses allowed him to read the weird combination of Spanish and English this timeline used.

He turned around and gazed out into the cold depths of space. A few lights shone in the distance and moved majestically across the star field.

Something tapped his shoulder, and he turned to find Elzbietá standing on the "wall" with him. The interface lenses allowed him to see her face even though the prog-steel weave completely obscured her head.

"You take me to the nicest places." She tilted her head and winked at him.

"It's because you deserve only the best."

"Come on. Over here, you two." Raibert ran his hand down one of the white outlines.

"Is that supposed to open?" Benjamin asked, walking over.

"Yeah, but the malmetal doesn't have any power."

"Maybe there's a manual bypass," Elzbietá suggested.

"Sure. I've got your bypass right here." A prog-steel blade extruded from his wrist, its edges faint from what might have been high-speed oscillation. He stabbed it into one corner of the outline, then stroked it down to the floor. The blade vanished back into his suit, and he shoved his fingers into the cut and tore the malmetal sheet aside.

"There. Bypassed," he announced.

"Not exactly the most elegant solution," Benjamin observed.

"I do what I can." Raibert stepped through the opening and entered a hallway that eventually turned left. "Philo, start mapping the interior."

"On it."

Six remotes from the *Kleio* zipped past them and hurried deeper into the ship. Raibert led the way, and Benjamin took up the rear. They proceeded cautiously into the dark, followed the hall to a junction, and took another left that led to a white outline.

Raibert cut another hole to reveal one of the neighboring bays. The bay door was closed, and a boxy vessel almost as large as the *Kleio* sat clamped to the floor.

"Philo, what do you make of this one?" Raibert asked.

"Looks like a troop transport of some kind. Tough armor, but minimal weaponry."

"Not what we're looking for, then."

"Should we move on?" Benjamin asked.

"Hold it, Doc." Raibert raised a hand. "There's an opening on the side. I'm going to take a peek at the interior first."

He kicked off the floor and floated along the craft's side, slapped a hand against the hull, then pulled himself in until his feet stuck to the side. He crawled forward on his hands and knees and looked through an oval gap in the outer hull.

"Hmm."

Raibert reached inside, stuck his hand to an unseen surface, and swung himself in.

"Raibert?" Benjamin asked.

"This won't take long. In fact...aha! Well, well, well! What have we here?"

"You tell me. I can't see what you're doing from down here."

"Be *very* careful with that!" Philo warned.

"Find something we can use?" Elzbietá asked.

"Maybe. Check this out!"

Raibert popped his upper body through the hatch and held out a device resembling a rocket launcher.

"It's...smaller than I was expecting," Benjamin admitted.

"True, but this thing can take out a whole *continent* with the right tweaks."

"It can?"

"Yeah. It'd take a while, but sure. This thing could do it."

"How exactly?"

"Please stop waving it around like that!" Philo pleaded.

"Don't worry. It probably has built-in safeguards that terminate the growth after a few generations."

"Until they mutate unexpectedly!" Philo added.

"Yeah, that would be the downside."

"What are you two talking about?" Elzbietá asked.

Raibert patted the launcher's barrel, and Philo squeaked out the audible equivalent of a wince.

"This thing fires canisters of weaponized self-replicators. Microbots that will reproduce like mad and eat anything they splash against. Ships, buildings, people, whatever. Doesn't matter. It'll turn them all into goo that makes more goo."

"Without end?" Benjamin asked.

"Looks like the number of generations they'll spawn can be set, so the operator can adjust the yield." Raibert shook his head. "Can you believe these Martian idiots gave *self-replicators* to their *infantry*? No wonder the Admin fought a war to end this madness."

"You still want to take some, don't you?" Philo asked.

"You better believe I do!" Raibert declared. "The Admin's playing for keeps, and so am I. Think the remotes can haul some of these back to the *Kleio*?"

"That shouldn't be too difficult," Philo replied. "I'll send a few your way and have them—*carefully*—transport any launchers back."

"That'll do." Raibert let the rocket launcher float away, planted his feet on the transport's side, and kicked off. He spun around and landed next to Benjamin.

"Can't Kleio print out weapons like that already?" he asked, indicating the microbots in his backpack.

"Nope," Raibert answered. "Too many limiters built into her software and the printers. Weaponized replicators aren't just dangerous as hell, they're also illegal in *my* timeline, which is why I'm not surprised the Admin fought a war to end stupidity like this." He pointed for them to leave. "Come on. Let's check out the next bay."

They returned to the hallway and followed it farther away from the *Kleio* until Raibert opened another entrance to another launch bay.

"And that would be the second troop transport," Philo reported.

"No good, then," Benjamin said.

"Well, those are the two closest bays," Raibert said. "We have two options now. We can head down toward the engines until we hit the next level of bays, or we can head across to the bays on the other side of the ship."

"It would make sense for them to cluster similar craft together," Benjamin said. "I say we head to the far side."

"We'll check both," Elzbietá suggested. "I'll take care of the bays below us. You two scope out the other side."

"You sure?" Benjamin asked. "What if there are more unpowered doors?"

She made a fist. A prog-steel cutter snapped out of her wrist and oscillated to life.

"I think I can handle that." She opened her hand, and the cutter morphed back into her armor.

"Maybe I should check the bays below. You can stick with Raibert." He opened a virtual menu and began scrolling through his suit options. "Just give me a moment to figure out how to do that."

"Don't worry about it," she said. "*You* stick with Raibert. The faster we find a gunboat the better."

"Works for me." Raibert placed a hand on his shoulder. "Come on, Doc. Let's get moving."

"Right..." he replied hesitantly.

Elzbietá knelt down next to a white circle in the floor and began cutting it open. Benjamin grimaced as he turned away and followed Raibert deeper into the ship.

"Tough fiancée you've got there."

"You don't know the half of it."

A long, narrow corridor opened at the end to reveal the *Lion*'s central, hollow spine, where a network of heavy conveyors lined the inner walls and branched off to either side of the ship. Most of the conveyor sections were empty, but a few had square containers clamped in place.

"Those conveyor lines look like they connect back to our bay," Benjamin noted. "We might be able to use them to transport the weapons back to the *Kleio*."

"Maybe. We need to find some first."

They reached an observational balcony at the end of the walkway and gazed down the ship's spine into a black, bottomless chasm. Benjamin gripped the railing tightly with both hands without thinking.

It's not bottomless, he corrected. *Surely it ends a kilometer or so below us at the engines.*

The thought provided little comfort.

"We could go around," Benjamin suggested.

"Or we could jump across."

Without another word, Raibert kicked off the walkway and floated across the chasm.

Benjamin stared down at the abyss again, steeled himself with a few deep breaths, then kicked off the ground to follow Raibert. His inner ear told him he was falling as he floated over an endless chasm. His breaths shortened and he tried focusing on the walls instead.

"Is it stupid to be afraid of falling in zero gravity?" Benjamin asked urgently.

"Doc, I'm in a body that makes me almost immortal and *I'm* afraid of the fall. It's not stupid."

"That..." He took a few breaths, slower and deeper this time. "That actually makes me feel a little better."

"Glad to help."

Raibert landed on the other side, then reached out, grabbed Benjamin's arm, and pulled him in. Sweet relief filled him once his boots were firmly planted on the opposite walkway.

"You okay?" Raibert patted the side of Benjamin's helmet.

"Yeah." He gulped down another breath. "I'm good."

They proceeded further through the ship, now in corridors that mirrored those they'd come from. They'd almost reached the closest bay when Elzbietá called in.

"Hey, guys."

"What is it, Ella?" Benjamin asked.

"I've checked all three bays on this level. We're oh for five right now. More troop transports, same as the first two."

"Great," Raibert grumbled.

"Should I head down further?"

"Hold position," Raibert said, extending a cutter. "We're almost to our first bay. Let's see what we find first."

He cut through the malmetal portal, peeled it aside, and peeked in.

"Well, would you look at that?"

Benjamin joined him at the opening. The craft inside possessed an air of dark, sleek deadliness, as if it had been built to contain only what it needed—and what it needed were engines and weapons. Its hull formed a long cylinder that tapered down to a wide hole on the side he could see.

"That's doesn't look like a troop transport to me," Benjamin remarked.

"Me neither."

"Is that hole for the engine exhaust?"

"Don't think so," Raibert said. "Looks like the barrel of a mass driver."

"*That's* the barrel?" Benjamin exclaimed. "Look at the *bore* on that thing! It might be a snug fit for you or me, but I bet Ella could crawl right into that thing. What's a gun that big meant to take out?"

"Warships like the *Lion*, I'd wager." Raibert unstrapped his backpack and headed inside. "Come on. Let's get started."

"Ella, did you hear that?" Benjamin asked.

"Loud and clear. Even the part about me being slim and sexy."

"Start making your way toward us. Looks like we found what we came for."

"On my way."

Benjamin removed his backpack and mirrored Raibert's actions by sticking it on one side of the barrel. The backpack dissolved into a white liquid that thinned out over the gunboat and flowed into the barrel before vanishing.

"First step is to build a rough schematic of the gunboat," Raibert said. "After that, we can direct the swarm to cut the mass driver free without accidentally damaging it."

"Sounds like it should work."

"Probably."

"Probably?"

Raibert shrugged. "When's the last time you did this?"

"Never."

"Well, same here, Doc."

"Everyone," Philo called in. "We've got a problem."

Raibert let out a tired sigh. "New problem or old problem? You know you have to be specific at this point."

"I just lost one of the remotes below your position. I don't know what happened to it."

CHAPTER TWENTY-SEVEN

FPNS *Lion of Aurorae Sinus*
2777 CE

"WHAT DO YOU MEAN YOU LOST IT?" RAIBERT PRESSED URGENTLY.

"The transmission ended without warning. Cause unknown."

"Indigenous Admin?"

"Could be. In fact, I think that's fairly likely."

"Damn," Raibert hissed, and pulled out his hand cannon. "Time to go."

"Ella, change of plan." Benjamin retrieved his burst pistol and switched off the safety. "Get back inside the *Kleio* as fast as you can."

"But what about you two?"

"We're getting the hell out of here, that's what!" Raibert announced. "Everyone back on board! We'll phase out and try again!"

"Where'd the remote go silent?" Benjamin asked.

"Two levels below your position."

"Can you show me?"

A marker pulsed in his interface lenses and faint gridlines of the unseen levels enhanced his spatial awareness. He hurried over to the bay exit, pistol raised in both hands, and was about to glance through the opening when Raibert grabbed his arm and yanked him back. He put a splayed hand against Benjamin's chest and pressed him against the wall.

"Stay behind me," the synthoid warned. "If one of us is going to get shot, let it be me."

"I can take care of myself."

"*Sure* you can. But a headshot won't kill me." He eased off and raised his own weapon. "You ready for this?"

"No." Benjamin licked his lips, and his heart pounded furiously in his chest.

"Same here." Raibert glanced down the hallway. "Clear. Let's go!"

They darted into the passage, moving in a fast walk that required them to always keep one foot on a surface. The path ahead branched to either side, leading toward nearby launch bays, and white circles indicated closed shafts leading up and down.

"Hold," Raibert ordered.

Benjamin hung back and knelt to press a hand against the floor.

"Vibrations," he whispered. "Hard to tell how close."

"We're not alone." Raibert leaned out and checked both directions.

Gunfire from the left ricocheted off his shoulder, and he staggered back, barely sticking to the floor.

"Wolverines!" he shouted. "Or something close to them!"

Outlines of four-legged robots lit up Benjamin's lenses. They scuttled across the walls and ceiling, almost insect-like, and Raibert discharged his hand cannon twice. Soundless detonations blasted one of them to scrap, but more poured into view. Gunfire sparked against the walls, casting the environment into brief stark relief, and Raibert fired again.

"That's two!" he announced.

Benjamin couldn't shoot past Raibert with the man taking up the whole corner. Or rather, he couldn't in a normal environment. Floor and ceiling didn't mean much in this place, and he climbed the wall, planted his boots on the "ceiling" and positioned himself upside down, directly above Raibert.

"Careful, Doc!"

"Careful isn't going to get us out of this!" he spat, and swung out of cover. Drones scurried into view, and he cracked off three quick shots. The first armor-piercing round punched through the head of a Wolverine. Once past the outer armor, software detonated its payload and released a spray of shrapnel that gutted the robot's sensitive internals.

His second shot pierced through a Wolverine's belly and blew its head off. A third shot nearly grazed the shoulder of his last target. The shell's onboard software determined this was as close as it was going to get and exploded, showering the robot with shrapnel and crippling its neck joint and a leg.

Benjamin ducked back into cover.

"*Damn*, Doc!" Raibert swung out and finished off the wounded drone. "You said it's been twenty years since you fired a gun!"

"In *this* universe!"

"Aha!"

Two more Wolverines scurried into view, and Benjamin and Raibert swung out. They fired in almost perfect unison, and the drones flew back from direct hits, then crashed against the back wall. Their limbs twitched erratically, then fell inert.

"Is that all of them?" Benjamin asked. Broken pieces of robotic dogs floated about the now cluttered hallway.

"I've spotted another group moving toward your position," Philo reported. "Mix of drones and Peacekeepers."

"You need to get back to the ship!" Elzbietá urged.

"We're working on it!" Raibert replied. "Come on, Doc! Let's go!"

"Right behind you!"

Hinnerkopf frowned at the datafeed from the indigenous shipyard.

"I was expecting better from our predecessors."

"They had to find the professor first," Okunnu stated. "We're fairly certain the TTV is somewhere near the shipyard and it looks like we were right that he was on the *Lion*, but that still leaves a huge amount of ground to cover. Now that the local Admin has him spotted, their next attack should prove more effective."

"If you want something done right..." she muttered.

"Director?" Okunnu turned to her.

"Or we could just finish him off ourselves now that we know where he is." She adjusted the collar of the pressure suit Okunnu had insisted she put on and looked up at him. "Missiles?"

"He's in the belly of a warship. Even with its defenses offline and bay doors opened, it can still absorb an incredible amount of punishment. Our missiles will be ineffective unless he's near the surface, and the last sighting had him moving deeper into the interior."

"Then what do you suggest?"

"Direct engagement of the enemy inside the ship." Okunnu gave her a confident nod. "Agent Cantrell is standing by in her combat frame, and all special operators and drones are onboard the Cutlass. I'd like to send both Switchblades out as well, to provide fire support and, if the professor gets too close to the ship's surface, to try and snipe him with a railgun shot."

"Do it."

"Why don't we take off and help them?" Elzbietá demanded as she hurried onto the bridge. The ship's gravity was on again, and she stopped herself next to Philo's avatar at the command table. "The guns on this thing could tear any of those drones to shreds. Why don't we swing to the other side and pick them up at the bay they're closest to?"

"Because we've got another problem," the AC stated calmly. "Look here."

He indicated a cluster of icons seventy kilometers from the shipyard and closing.

"What are those?" she asked.

"It's hard to tell, but I think they're Admin attack drones. Two or three of them. They might even be Switchblades or something similar. Those are fairly ubiquitous Admin drones armed with 115mm railguns."

"Are they a threat to the *Kleio*?"

"In numbers, yes." Philo highlighted the path the drones were taking. "They're trying to make a stealthy approach, but the *Kleio* has a direct line-of-sight to them out the launch bay, so we're sporadically picking them up."

"Then let's get out there. We'll take them out, then go pick up our boys."

"It's not the drones I'm worried about, but the ship they came from. Look at the direction they're coming from."

Elzbietá did so. "There's nothing out there."

"Exactly."

"So? That just means their carrier's hidden."

"But we're in a *post-war* time period," Philo emphasized. "Why is a stealthed vessel hiding this close to the heart of the Admin's power? And why would they send their drones in so timidly?"

"Could they have spotted the *Kleio*?" Elzbietá suggested uncertainly.

"I don't know. I don't even know how they found Raibert and Benjamin so fast. It's almost as if they started searching the *Lion* as soon as we got here, which doesn't make sense unless..."

"Unless what?"

"Oh, no," Philo breathed, then opened the channel. "Raibert, come in!"

"Little busy right now!" A few seconds passed and then he added, "What is it?"

"I think there's a chronoport somewhere outside the *Lion*."

"Well, that's just *great*!"

"It might even be the one that hit us in 2018," Philo added.

"How'd it track us this far?"

"No idea."

"Well, stay put! We're making our way toward you! We can't risk the TTV in combat until we're ready!"

"Understood."

Philo muted the channel.

"So you're just going to *sit* here?" Elzbietá asked.

"You heard him."

"We need to get out there and help them!" She swiped a hand through his avatar and was surprised when he flinched back from her simulated touch. For a moment there, she actually felt the texture of his tunic and mail armor against her palm.

"Look, I appreciate the sentiment," Philo said, recovering. "But if I'm right, there's a militarized time machine out there, and it nearly killed us once. Kleio's no good in a fight, and I'm a historian. Most of the action I've seen is from ancient Greece. I don't know the first thing about flying a ship like this in actual combat! In fact, I barely got us out of the thirtieth century, and half of that was dumb luck!"

Elzbietá put both hands on her hips, tilted her head to one side, and fixed him with a glare that could melt prog-steel.

"What? Why are you staring at me like that?"

She widened her eyes and leaned uncomfortably close to his face.

"What?" he asked. "Seriously, what?"

"Five hundred meters to target."

"Switchblades hold here," Agent Cantrell ordered.

"Four hundred meters. Switchblades breaking."

"All operators, stand by," Cantrell said. "Move into the *Lion* on my order only."

Red lights illuminated the cramped interior of the Cutlass

troop transport, their dull light revealing twin rows of heavily armed and armored special operators, light combat drones, and a lone STAND crouched in her combat frame. A tense air hung wordlessly over them, and she waited for the inevitable release of combat.

She wasn't human. Not right now, anyway. Her body, or at least the one that most resembled Susan Cantrell when she'd possessed flesh and blood, had been left on board *Pathfinder-12*. In its place was a cold, mechanical shell that existed for only one purpose:

Killing any enemy of the Admin that crossed her path.

She was a machine, and this was her purpose.

But that was fine with her. She'd come to terms with her own inhumanity long ago, and her mind floated comfortably within a sea of senses many would find alien. The combat frame possessed no sense of touch, but its audio and visual inputs revealed the world in ways no natural body could.

"Three hundred meters."

She wasn't human anymore, but one didn't have to be human to serve with purpose and honor.

"Two hundred meters. Braking."

The Cutlass spun around. Squirts of thrust slowed the craft, and it eased toward the open launch bay.

She rose from her crouch, not as an eternally young woman, but as a black skeletal machine with weapons and boosters strapped to its limbs and back.

"I'll take point," she declared.

No one objected. The human operators checked their weapons behind her, but she didn't need to. Her whole body was a weapon, and if it had possessed a pulse, it would have quickened at the promise of action.

"One hundred—"

The side of the Cutlass blew inward, and operators exploded in showers of gore.

Cantrell sprang into action without thinking. Her shoulder boosters flattened her against the floor as continuous fire raked across the interior and tore clear through the other side. A rain of heavy shells blew every operator to bits, then pulverized the tumbling pieces of their bodies to a crimson spray, slickening the walls with guts and blood and bits of broken hardware.

She felt nothing. Didn't have time to. She had to act quickly if she was to survive. That was all that mattered now.

The doomed Cutlass yawed, and the cannon fire cut through at a different angle.

She fired her leg boosters, slid along the floor to a mangled hole in the side, and shot through. The dark outline of the *Lion* loomed ahead, and she angled her flight path toward the safety of the nearest launch bay.

She'd almost reached it when the weapons still chewing the Cutlass to pieces suddenly slewed toward her. Impacts blasted off two of her limbs, sent her spiraling out of control, and another explosion tore open her chest.

A long list of malfunctions flashed through her virtual vision, and she spun away into the cold dark of space.

"What just happened?" Hinnerkopf demanded as the Cutlass and both Switchblades disintegrated under a sleet of metal.

"New contact near the launch bays!"

"Is it the TTV?" Okunnu asked.

"Unknown. Signal is weak and intermittent. I...I've lost it!"

"Find it again!"

"Working on it, sir!"

Okunnu faced her. "Strap in, Director, and get your helmet on!" He pushed off the ceiling and landed in his seat. The harness deployed around him and tightened.

Hinnerkopf quickly did the same.

"Stand by all missiles!" Okunnu ordered. "All hands, prepare for combat maneuvers!"

Hinnerkopf put a hand to her chest. The cold touch of anxiety tightened the muscles around her ribcage, and she tried to regain her composure. Yes, the TTV had spotted their drones and the transports, but it had no way of knowing where the chronoport was. They just had to stay quiet, keep their drives and impeller off, and wait for the right moment to strike.

That's what she kept telling herself, at least. She tried not to look at the status display for the operators, but finally glanced quickly at them. Every silhouette was filled with a baleful red, and she swallowed as icy fear gripped her mind.

"Where's my target?" Okunnu growled.

"Still searching, sir, but the signal vanished shortly after it finished firing."

"I want a targeting solution on the TTV as soon as we spot it. We're not letting it get away again."

"Yes, sir."

Hinnerkopf put her helmet on and sealed the pressure suit. Cool, dry air tickled past her face, and she tried to slow her panicked breathing.

"Where *are* they?" Okunnu asked.

"Sh-shouldn't we back off?" Hinnerkopf asked.

"No, that's about the worst thing we could do," Okunnu stated, forceful and in control. "They spotted our drones when they got close, but they can't have any idea where we are. Backing away now might reveal our position, and I'd rather—"

"Sir, new contact! Seventy-seven kilometers off the *Lion*!"

"Show me!"

"It's coming right for us!"

A visual of the craft appeared on Hinnerkopf's virtual display. Stars shimmered around an unseen rounded shape, then began to bunch up. Tears opened in space itself, revealing seams of rich, metallic gray that at first formed a circular grid, then expanded to fill in the whole shape.

The metamaterial shroud retracted into blisters on the TTV's hull, gun ports snapped open, and it charged forward.

"Full power to the thrusters!" Okunnu shouted. "Evasive maneuvers!"

The TTV opened fire with a 45mm Gatling gun that showered *Pathfinder-12* with over fifty rounds per second. Armor piercing heads quaked against the malmetal hull, and high-explosive payloads shuddered through the ship. Hinnerkopf screamed as shells began punching through their armor and systems winked out one by one.

The TTV closed aggressively, and its fire grew more accurate as it added its surviving 12mm Gatling to the mix. The whole chronoport convulsed from an unending stream of impacts, almost as if it were a wild beast trying to shake her from her seat. The harness straps bit painfully into her shoulders, and hot, glowing pieces of shrapnel shot through the walls and ricocheted around the bridge.

Crewmembers cried out. A severed head floated up from the

seats. Blood spurted out to collect in wobbly globules, then funneled into a breach in the ceiling that suddenly burst wider. An explosion rocked her from behind, and debris scythed through the back of Okunnu's seat.

The seatback—and the top half of the captain—floated up and away and tumbled through the breach.

The pilot fired the chronoport's thrusters, and acceleration pinned Hinnerkopf in place. Blood or some other fluid splashed against her visor, but the terrible, ceaseless pounding had ended.

"Orders, Captain?" the pilot shouted.

Hinnerkopf touched the blood obscuring her vision with quivering fingers and slowly drew four ragged lines through it. Didn't they know he was dead?

"Orders, sir!" the pilot repeated.

Hinnerkopf smeared the blood aside and stared at the lower half of Okunnu. She suddenly remembered the bright and eager young man whom she'd taken on as a research assistant all those years ago. Something hot and vengeful ignited within her, and its fury pushed aside the fear and anguish that clouded her mind.

"Fire the missiles," she ordered in a clear and strong voice.

"Director?" the pilot turned around in his seat, then gasped when he saw what was left of Okunnu.

"Fire them, damn you!" Hinnerkopf roared, rage overtaking everything. *"Fire all of them!"*

"Oh, they didn't like that!" Elzbietá worked the virtual controls Philo had spawned for her and looped the TTV around behind the chronoport.

"How did I ever let you talk me into this?" the avatar moaned.

"Because you know I'm right, that's how!"

"We hurt them, but they're not down yet."

"Then let's swing around and finish them off!"

The TTV accelerated hard at her command, but her body didn't feel any g-forces. Or rather, her *abstract* body didn't feel it. She wasn't entirely certain what Philo had done once she'd sealed herself in the compensation bunk, but this virtual version of the bridge looked and felt real.

Only it wasn't.

She glanced over her shoulder and saw her own body suspended in a glass casket filled with microbot-infused goo.

Talk about an out-of-body experience.

"They're firing missiles at us!" Philo exclaimed. "Count is thirty-two!"

She took in the distances, vectors, and acceleration factors before her, and a cruel smile slipped over her lips.

"Perfect," she declared and adjusted course away from the chronoport. The TTV's omni-directional graviton thrusters responded instantly.

"How exactly is this *perfect*?"

"Watch and learn. You handle the guns. *I'll* make sure none of them get close."

The Admin missiles accelerated at twenty gees, and that seemed impressive next to the TTV's five, but whoever was in charge of the chronoport must have fired them in panic, because they'd launched them in the wrong direction. That meant the missiles and the TTV were accelerating *away* from each other at twenty-five gees, and those missiles, while fast, couldn't switch their boosters off once lit.

The missiles swung around, imparting lateral velocity that *also* had to be corrected for. Elzbietá flew perpendicular to her original path, turning against them, and managed to delay their approach even further.

"Are these controls the best you have?" she asked as she worked to keep the distance open. "They're a bit clunkier than I was expecting."

"Sorry!" Philo protested. "It's the best I could come up with under pressure!"

"You going to fire at them?"

"I was about to!" He targeted the nearest projectiles and showered them with cannon fire. One by one, they flickered off the display. Another group of missiles came into effective range, and he hosed them down as well. He whittled through the entire volley that way until none were left.

"See?" she said. "Nothing to it. It's just positioning and momentum. Not too different from dogfighting in my F-21."

"Are you actually having fun right now?"

"I might be." She quirked a smile at him. "How many missiles do you think they have left?"

"A chronoport's weapons are modular, so there's no way for me to know."

"Then they might be empty?"

"*Maybe*," he warned.

"In that case"—she worked the controls and powered toward the chronoport—"let's find out!"

Hinnerkopf watched in horror as each and every missile vanished from their scope. The TTV danced away from them and zipped about with insane agility, almost as if it was laughing at their efforts to destroy it.

"Thruster Two isn't responding well. I can't maintain full power."

Hinnerkopf shook her head in dismay, the rage that had buoyed her minutes ago drowned in the reality of the broken, bleeding, weaponless chronoport she now commanded.

The TTV turned once more and accelerated straight for them. She watched it come in and knew it intended to finish them off. Her heart sank, but she wasn't beaten yet.

"Director?" the pilot asked urgently.

"Spin up the impeller!" she ordered. "Get us out of here! *Get us out of here!*"

But it was already too late.

The TTV strafed past her battered chronoport. A rain of 45mm shells bashed one of the wings off and cracked Thruster Two's plasma containment. A stream of plasma hotter than the sun cut through the ship, and she turned to see a blinding light that charred her eyes to ash.

She wailed as the torrent stripped flesh from bone.

Then ate the bone as well.

Plasma leaks shredded the chronoport, and its impeller burst into a sprinkle of glittering, phasing fragments.

"Take that!" Elzbietá pumped the air triumphantly.

"Okay, I'll admit it," Philo said. "You're *really* good at this."

"See? Told you so."

"Hey, what the hell is this?" Raibert demanded. "We're at the bay but there's no fucking time machine!"

"Sorry." She adjusted their heading back to the *Lion*. "Change of plans."

"Well, can you unchange those plans and come pick us up?" Raibert asked. "These Peacekeepers are getting *really* insistent, and I'm running low on ammo!"

"Sure thing. We're heading back now. Is Ben okay?"

"I'm fine," he said, and Elzbietá smiled at the sound of his voice. "Got hit a few times, but the suit did its job. It's pretty amazing how fast it repairs itself. I'm going to have a few bruises after this, though."

"Let's make it quick," Philo said. "Some of the really big, really mean-looking ships have started heading our way."

"What about that chronoport?" Raibert asked.

"I shot it down," Elzbietá said succinctly.

"Oh..." Stunned silence filled the channel for several seconds. *"Really?"*

"Yes, really."

"Wow." Raibert seemed to struggle to find the words. "Uhh, good job. That's ... yeah, good job, there."

"You're welcome."

"Philo, how the hell did she ..." He trailed off again. "And didn't I tell you not to ..."

"We're coming in to pick you up," Elzbietá announced. "Stand clear."

"We're in the hallway," Benjamin said. "Come on in."

Elzbietá eased the *Kleio* into the same launch bay they'd started in.

"What about the weapon?" she asked as the cargo bay opened and the internal gravity switched off, which didn't affect the version of herself on the abstract bridge.

"We'll grab it after we microjump." Raibert hurried up the ramp. "That way we won't have the indigenous Admin breathing down our necks."

"I'm not sure what you mean by that, but okay."

"Kleio, get ready for a negative one-second microjump. I'm coming up to the bridge."

"Yes, Professor."

CHAPTER TWENTY-EIGHT

DTI Chronoport *Pathfinder-Prime*
non-congruent

"TRANSFER THE DATA, CAPTAIN." CSABA SHIGEKI UNSTRAPPED himself and kicked off to the front of *Pathfinder-Prime*'s bridge. He wore a stern face as he girded himself for the bad news.

"Yes, Director." Durantt pulled out the data case loaded with *Pathfinder-10*'s findings and slotted it into Vassal's access port with all the delicacy of a punch to the face. The presence of the AI clearly unnerved him, which was why Shigeki had given the man control over what data the AI could access and what interface restrictions were lifted.

Durantt placed a hand on the PIN interface. The UNBOXED warning glowed red and the green STASIS indicator switched off.

"This is Admin-sanctioned AI Vassal. I stand ready to receive your orders."

"Vassal," Shigeki said, "*Pathfinder-10* has returned to the picket after searching 2018 and the surrounding years for *Pathfinder-12*. We have provided you with their complete records. Analyze their findings."

"Yes, Director. A few moments please."

Durantt pushed away from the AI and joined Shigeki, as if the added distance somehow protected him.

"Preliminary analysis complete."

"Begin your report," Shigeki ordered.

"Temporal disruptions in 2018 caused by the TTV and *Pathfinder-12* have once again altered the timeline. These changes, both from their insertion into 2018 and subsequent combat, have propagated downstream into an altered timeline that ends at a current point of temporal discontinuity in 2051. No changes have propagated beyond the storm front, and I surmise this phenomenon is responsible for preserving the thirtieth-century Admin as we know it."

"What about *Pathfinder-12*?" Shigeki asked, even as he dreaded the answer. "Why haven't we heard back from them?"

"I calculate the odds of *Pathfinder-12*'s survival at seventeen percent."

"There's no way it could be that low," Nox protested from *Pathfinder-6*. The text from the telegraph had been rendered into deadpan vocals, but Shigeki doubted the original had been so calm.

"I believe I have accurately accounted for all known variables," Vassal stated. "The TTV was damaged by *Pathfinder-12*'s missile attack, phased out, and fled down the timeline. *Pathfinder-12* pursued it and, very likely, was destroyed."

"But you just said the odds aren't zero," Nox sent. "Director, we should dispatch one of our chronoports to search the timeline downstream."

"And increase the chances of Kaminski slipping past us here in the twentieth century?" Kloss sent from *Pathfinder-2*. "No, we need to face the facts. We would have heard from them by now if they were still alive."

"I concur with that assessment," Vassal stated. "It is highly likely we would have been contacted by now if *Pathfinder-12* were still functional."

"But what about the damage the TTV suffered in 2018?" Jonas sent from *Pathfinder-6*.

"Yes, the TTV was hit by *Pathfinder-12*'s missiles," Vassal acknowledged. "However, I have taken into account the TTV's actions in the thirtieth century as well as the apparent lack of damage in 2018. This gives me a minimum baseline for system performance and self-repair abilities. I have also factored in the prohibited technologies at its disposal, which allow it to self-modify and increase its overall lethality."

"We're still underestimating him." Shigeki shook his head.

This was his fault. He'd thought a lone chronoport could take down the TTV, and now he'd lost not only a ship, but also a member of his team, not just an assistant, but a companion who'd worked by his side for *decades* to help him to build the DTI into what it was today. She was dead because he kept underestimating Kaminski, and all he could do now was not repeat the mistake.

"There is a small probability that both craft were destroyed in whatever subsequent conflict took place," Vassal added.

"I'm not about to bet the future of our *entire* reality on wishful thinking," Shigeki growled.

"Do we have any idea why Kaminski was in 2018?" Kloss sent from *Pathfinder-2*. "We thought he was targeting 1905 to 1995."

"But he doesn't know where to start," Shigeki pointed out. "The people he picked up must be a part of this. Vassal, analyze the historical records in your possession. Search for known family members, workplace colleagues, anything of that sort. Look for significant interactions with historical events, either directly or by people they would know."

"Yes, Director. I already performed this analysis in anticipation of your question and have identified one significant match."

"Let's hear it."

"The man is Doctor Benjamin Schröder, chairman of the history department at Castle Rock University in 2018."

"Then that explains Kaminski's interest," Jonas sent. "What about the woman?"

"I have identified her as Elzbietá Abramowski. However, I do not believe she is a person of significance. Judging from Professor Kaminski's actions in the restaurant, her acquisition was not a priority. I believe circumstances forced him to save her because of her romantic involvement with Doctor Schröder."

"I see." Shigeki nodded at this. "He protected her in order to ensure the historian's cooperation."

"That is the most likely explanation," Vassal concurred.

"Makes sense," Jonas sent. "This version of the timeline is alien to him, and he's trying to learn more about it."

"Partially," Vassal stated. "I believe there is more to Doctor Schröder's selection than his historical expertise."

"What else do you have?" Shigeki asked.

"Doctor Schröder is the grandson of Graf Klaus-Wilhelm von Schröder, a prominent military and political figure from the twentieth century who served in both World War II and the Great Eastern War, and subsequently served as the provisional governor of Ukraine until its induction into the United Nations."

"So not only is the guy a historian," Jonas sent, "but he's also related to a major player in this part of the timeline? That can't be a coincidence."

"Sounds like a solid lead to me, Boss," Kloss sent.

"Agreed." Shigeki could hardly contain his elation. Yes, Katja might be dead, but *finally* they had something that shed light on the professor's intentions.

"So what do we do about it, boss?" Kloss sent.

"We tighten the noose, that's what. Vassal, let's assume the Graf is important to the Event. Within what range of years does he have the strongest impact on the course of history?"

"I believe 1926 to 1958 is the best period upon which to focus our attention. The beginning of his military service to the end of his governorship."

"Then let's shift the picket to cover that period and a little more." Shigeki pulled up a linear representation of the timeline. "Say, 1920 to 1960. We can cover the entire range with two chronoports staged at each ten-year increment. Also, since the TTV is probably downstream from us right now, we'll send *Pathfinder-10* back to 2018, both to act as a forward scout and to stand watch in case the professor returns there."

"Good thinking, boss," Kloss sent. "We cut his last visit short with a missile barrage, so he might have unfinished business in that year or one nearby."

"We can shift the existing picket assignments over easily enough," Durantt noted.

"Why not deploy single chronoports in five-year increments?" Jonas sent. "We'll have a better chance of detecting the TTV that way."

"Because of what almost certainly happened to Hinnerkopf," Shigeki stated firmly. "I don't want to lose anyone else, you hear me? We double up and hit the TTV hard wherever it shows itself. No chronoport is to engage the TTV on its own unless it has no other choice. If *Pathfinder-10* spots something, it comes back for help. Understood?"

"Perfectly clear, boss," Kloss sent.

"Yeah, understood," Jonas sent.

Captains from the other chronoports called in and acknowledged his instructions.

"Good," Shigeki stated. "All chronoports will pair up and

reform the picket. We'll resume telegraph silence once everyone is in position. Captains, you have your orders. Make it happen."

"Oh, would you just look at this thing!" Raibert gazed up from the cargo bay floor to behold their newly acquired Freep "Thunderbolt 5" anticapital mass driver. "Beautiful! Just beautiful!"

"Do you and the big gun need some time alone?" Elzbietá asked.

"Nah, I'm fine." Raibert planted his fists triumphantly on his hips. "Just enjoying the view."

The mass driver rested in a microbot-erected scaffold, and the full length of the 375mm weapon extended from the back wall all the way out the front of the *Kleio*. Ammunition handlers, quick-discharge capacitors, heat sinks, alignment gimbals, shock absorbers, and other support systems branched out around the gun and filled the middle story of the bay's three-story height. Superconductor lines, data cables, and high-pressure coolant pipes drooped off the device and followed a tightly packed utility trench that lead out the back wall to the ship's rear.

"It definitely *looks* impressive," Elzbietá teased. "But looks can be deceiving."

"Not in this case," Raibert assured. "Right, Kleio? How are we doing?"

"The mass driver is fully integrated with my systems. I have completed all requested diagnostics and can find no fault in the weapon's operation. It is ready to use on demand."

"*Stellar* work."

"I aim to please, Professor."

"What sort of performance can we expect out of it?" Elzbietá asked.

"Kleio?"

"Each shot accelerates a one-ton projectile to a velocity of four kilometers per second. Upon impact, a stationary target will suffer sixteen million kilojoules of focused kinetic energy. The payload will then detonate, adding another seven million kilojoules as an area effect that scatters two hundred kilograms of weaponized microbots in the process."

Elzbietá whistled. "Damn!"

"I know, right?"

"Alternatively, the payload can also be detonated early to produce a shotgun effect that improves to-hit probabilities for distant or fast moving targets at the expense of raw destructive force. The self-replicators are currently set to expire after ten generations, though that number can be adjusted if you feel a larger or smaller area of effect is desirable."

"What's the rate of fire?" she asked.

"One point two shots per minute," Kleio reported. "The weapon's capacitors take fifty seconds to charge after firing."

"Any way to improve that?"

"Let's avoid anything that might cause complications," Raibert warned. "Yes, we could probably improve the rate of fire because of how much better our tech is, but we might also muck something up in the process. This thing comes from a foreign tech base, so I don't want to risk it."

"I see your point," Elzbietá admitted. "How many rounds do we have?"

"Fifty-six," Philosophus replied. "All they had left in the gunboat magazine."

"Good!" Raibert nodded sharply. "Too bad the built-in restrictions against weaponized self-replicators won't let *Kleio* make more of 'em. On the other hand, if we need more than fifty-six rounds for this baby, we're too screwed to worry about it. We'll focus our remaining efforts on the Gatling guns as secondary weapons, instead. And speaking of which"—he rubbed his hands together—"how are my other lovelies coming along?"

"I have finished installing the second 45mm defensive Gatling gun," Kleio said. "The third should be completed tomorrow and fully installed the following day."

"Nice! So, am I getting a fourth?"

"I am afraid that three is the limit I can recommend mounting," Kleio replied. "I have replaced the destroyed 12mm Gatling in its original module, but producing additional larger weapons would cut dangerously into my printers' bulk reserves in several categories. To date, we have been engaged only by single Admin vessels. My projections suggest that we are increasingly likely to be engaged against multiple adversaries simultaneously, however, and our experience of their weapons suggests, in turn, that we are likely to sustain significant damage if we are. I cannot produce still more weapons—and the ammunition for them—without depleting my bulk reserves to a level which is likely to preclude my ability to repair combat damage as it occurs. If you wish me to produce additional Gatlings, I believe it will be necessary for me to begin cannibalizing internal systems to provide the needed materials, instead. Shall I proceed?"

"Well, damn." Raibert visibly deflated. "No, Kleio. No, you're right about how bad we're likely to get hurt, and the last thing we need is to compromise your damage control ability. I guess this is as deadly as we can make you. I hope it's enough."

"As do I, Professor."

"What about the power drain of all this hardware?" Elzbietá indicated the utility trench. "Is using the mass driver in combat going to affect the ship's performance?"

"Umm..." Raibert blinked. "I don't...think so?"

"Didn't consider that, did you?"

"My dear." He put a hand to his chest. "Historian, remember? Not an engineer."

"Kleio, how about it?" she asked. "Is the power drain going to be a problem for you?"

"I do not anticipate any issues. My hot singularity reactor has sufficient spare capacity, so it should be possible to fire the mass driver, Gatling guns, and run all other systems simultaneously without complications."

"Well, then," Raibert smiled, "that answers that. Good to know, either way."

"Combat isn't all about firepower. You need to make sure you don't compromise our maneuverability. Hitting hard is fine, but never getting hit in return is better."

"Your expertise on the matter is *duly* noted."

"So what's a hot singularity reactor?"

Raibert raised an eyebrow. "Why do you ask?"

"Just curious."

"Philo, you want to take this one?"

"Sure." The Viking materialized in their shared vision. "It's basically a collector for black hole radiation."

"The time machine's powered by a black hole?" Elzbietá exclaimed with wide-eyed wonder. "Wicked!"

"A *tiny* artificial one," Philo emphasized. "Only a thousand tons. The mass is important because a black hole's rate of evaporation is inversely proportional to its mass."

"Is it safe going into combat with something like that in the ship?"

"The reactor's already been cracked open once," Raibert commented, then shrugged. "So yeah. Seems safe."

"But couldn't it suck all of us inside if the reactor was blown open?"

"That's not possible," Philo assured her. "First, the singularity is surrounded by a shell of exotic matter that regulates the rate of evaporation and also shields us from harm, even if the ship loses all power. We actually dump our excess thermal energy into it. It's quite sturdy, as the previous attack demonstrated. Second, even in the case of the reactor's catastrophic failure, the negative mass in the shell is designed to cancel out the black hole, preventing an explosive release of energy. Third, even though it *is* a black hole, its mass is still only a thousand tons. Gravitational pull is basically nonexistent."

"Ah. I see. So it won't suck us in."

"Nope. No sucking."

"Good thing Doc isn't here," Raibert chuckled. "I bet this conversation would have burst one of his blood vessels. Where is he now, anyway?"

"In his quarters," Philo stated. "Studying the Event."

"He making any progress?"

"I'm not sure. He seemed a bit...frustrated the last time I checked in on him."

"Best to leave him alone and let him concentrate," Elzbietá said.

"You heard the lady." Raibert paced over to the counter-grav tube. "The three of us will take care of the ship, and then Doc will tell us how we fix this busted timeline."

"Professor?" Kleio asked.

"Fine. *Four* of us. Whatever." He took the tube up and vanished from sight.

"You know." Elzbietá turned to Philo. "I think that's the happiest I've seen him."

"I'm not surprised now that we finally have an option for dealing with the Admin other than running away. You weren't there when they ripped out his mind and threw his body down a recycling chute."

"Yeah. I can't even imagine what that must have been like."

"I think he's looking forward to finally taking the fight to them. Plus putting you in control of the *Kleio* was an unexpected bonus. You made taking down that chronoport look easy."

"You weren't too bad out there, yourself." She nudged the avatar in the arm. His virtual body shifted slightly, and she once again felt the sensation of chain mail against her elbow.

"I mostly focused on making sure we didn't die," Philo chuckled. "By the way, Raibert and I set up your pilot profile today, so the two of us can authorize time travel now instead of just Raibert and me."

"I think we made a good team back there. We should keep it up. Me at the flight controls. You on the guns."

"You think so?" He stroked his beard thoughtfully.

"Yeah, I do. What do you say?"

"Well, sure! I'm more than happy to help you out when you're flying the ship."

"Also, is there anything we can do about those controls?"

Philo scrunched his brow. "What wrong with them?"

"They *clearly* weren't designed by a fighter pilot. There wasn't any feedback through them, so I had no idea when I was reaching output limits, and it took way too many complicated hand motions to do what should be simple course changes." She snapped her fingers. "Say, if I told you what to build, do you think you could set up the controls to match what I'm used to in my F-21?"

"*Build?*" He let out a long raspberry. "As in something physical? I can do *way* better than that!"

Elzbietá opened her eyes within the abstraction and turned on her heels. She stood on an endless stretch of clouded glass with a cobalt sky hanging overhead. Shooting stars streaked past the horizon, and she walked over to a sturdy chair, the only object in sight. She noted the throttle floating over the left armrest and the joystick floating over the right.

"I thought this might be something closer to what you're used to."

She looked over her shoulder to find Philo standing behind her.

"Definitely." She sank into the seat and took hold of both controls. Virtual displays sprang to life around her, and the clouded glass vanished for a clear view in every direction.

"Some of the literature we picked up in the twenty-first century had pictures of cockpits, so I started from those." Philo walked across nothing and knelt by her side. "Is this a little more to your liking?"

"We'll have to make some adjustment for the omnidirectional thrusters, but this is a great start." She wiggled her fingers around the controls and settled the tips over familiar tactile buttons. "Can I give it a try?"

"Sure. This isn't patched into the *Kleio* yet, so we're in a pure simulation. Do whatever you want."

Elzbietá reached out to adjust a virtual display Philo's head was blocking when her fingernails scraped across his helmet.

"I can touch you!" she marveled, then rested a hand firmly on his shoulder. "*Really* touch you. It's not just a simulated sensation without weight."

"We're both abstract right now, so I'm as real as you are here."

"And my body is still on the bridge? In the compensation bunk, right?"

"Exactly. Same as the first time." He rested a large, calloused hand atop hers. "Back then, I brought you into an abstract copy of the bridge, but I can bring you into any environment you want, equipped with any sort of interface you desire."

"This is really something!" She grinned as she looked around, then stopped and said, "Hang on."

"What?"

Something tickled her nose, and she sniffed.

"What's that smell?" she asked. "Smells like a combination of sweat and horse."

She brought up the hand she'd touched Philo with and inhaled deeply.

"Sorry," Philo said. "I'll turn off that part of my avatar."

The odor vanished.

"Where are you going to sit?" she asked.

"Wherever you want me to. Tandem, side by side, or even outside this VR. We can set it up however you want."

"If we're working together, I think it'll help if I can see you. Set yourself up to my left."

A seat appeared there, and Philo rounded her and sank into it. Virtual controls for the *Kleio*'s guns and armor lit up in front of him, and he cracked his knuckles.

"Good." She adjusted the position and angle of each virtual display, then eased forward on the throttle. A simulated fraction of the g-forces pressed her into the seat, providing feedback without being uncomfortable or distracting.

"Let's start by working on the throttle." She dropped the thrust to zero. "That okay with you?"

"Sure. Just guide me through how you want it to work."

"First, set it up so I can pull the throttle in any direction. Have the thrust applied on a matching vector."

"Easy enough."

"Next, it needs to provide more resistance the closer it gets to maximum. And finally, it should center itself if I let up."

"Got it, and done."

"All right." She flexed her fingers and gripped the controls again. She was about to pull the throttle to the side, but stopped and faced Philo. "Hey, another question?"

"Go right ahead."

"Can I make stuff in this simulation, too?" She glanced quickly at his helmet.

"Sure you can," Philo replied, sounding a little baffled by the question. "I just figured I would take care of that since you're new to working in an abstraction."

"I'd like to give it a try."

"In that case, be my guest." He leaned back and gestured across the emptiness before them. "What do you want to make?"

"It's a surprise." She smiled as she opened a new set of menus. "But given your tastes, I think you'll like it."

"You mean . . ."

"Yeah, it's for you. You're doing all of this for me, so I want to make something for you. We're going to be partners in this, so why not?"

"Umm . . ." he shrugged. "Okay, sure. Why not?"

"This is allowed, right? I'm not inadvertently offending you or something?"

"No, certainly not!" Philo reassured quickly. "I just didn't expect this. In fact, I've *never* had a physical citizen make me an abstraction before, and I'm older than I look."

"First time for everything, huh?"

"Guess so."

"Can you forward me those eBooks with the cockpit pictures? I think I know where to find what I'm looking for."

CHAPTER TWENTY-NINE

Transstemporal Vehicle *Kleio*
non-congruent

"SO HERE'S THE BAD NEWS." BENJAMIN SAID ONCE RAIBERT AND Elzbietá had joined him on the bridge.

"Did you really have to start off like that?" Raibert leaned against the wall and crossed his arms. "I was having a really good day until now."

"Stop it, Raibert," Elzbietá warned. "Let him speak."

He held up his hands apologetically.

"This needs to be said, and said clearly," Benjamin began. "I'm still confident I've accurately identified the Event, but my knowledge of 1940 is sketchy at best compared to other periods. I know Hitler wasn't supposed to die on his way to Berlin on May sixteenth. But aside from the fact that his death led to the restoration of the monarchy, it really didn't have much effect on the subsequent wars and political events, and the literature Philo picked up has conflicting reports of the attack. That means I don't know for certain how the Admin version of the timeline played out. Not to the detail we need to plan our alterations. There's a lot of historical confusion surrounding his death, so what actually happened is one of the minor mysteries of World War II."

"Okay," Raibert sighed. "That's bad."

"Even worse," Benjamin continued, "I don't know what *actually* happened in the SysGov timeline. May 16, 1940, is a day of no historical significance, at least as far as my other self, who *also* isn't a World War II expert, is concerned. I hate to admit this, but my memories can't help us beyond identifying the day and place."

"Then wouldn't the original Event have been fairly routine?" Elzbietá suggested.

"*Maybe,*" Benjamin stressed. "But that leaves a lot of questions. Was there an attack in the original timeline? If so, how was it thwarted? If not, what caused it to be aborted? What security procedures were in place? How did those procedures succeed in one timeline and fail in another? What military assets were on hand in one version and not the other? Why was there a discrepancy? Was the attack partially successful? If so, who should live and who should die on that train? I don't *know.*"

Raibert let out a frustrated growl and raked a hand through his hair.

"So that's the bad news," Benjamin concluded.

"Look, we don't need to change the Event back *perfectly,*" Raibert said. "If we had to do that, there's no way we could ever succeed. Fortunately for us, time is straining to return to its original form. It should snap back if we get the Event close enough to the original."

"*Should?*" Benjamin asked pointedly.

"That's what we see in the Knot," Raibert shot back. He pushed off the wall and walked up to the command table. "The change in this timeline is what's entangled all those other universes. Each one is tugging on the whole, trying to return to normal, but they can't because of the Event. If we fix it, or even *partially* fix it, it might be enough for the whole mess to break free and return to its original state."

"But if we fail in our first attempt, then all we've done is made it worse. Time becomes even more scarred, and we've failed."

"I'm not going to sit back and let Shigeki and his goons win," Raibert growled at Benjamin and leaned forward. "At some point, we're going in with the information we have."

"I actually agree with you completely on that."

"You do?" The big man blinked and backed off.

"That's right. And the good news is I know exactly where to get the expertise we need."

"Oh." The fire drained from Raibert's voice. "Well, why didn't you say so?"

"We need someone with firsthand knowledge of World War II and, most importantly, German military organizations and procedures. I believe that will give us the advantage we need to get the Event as close as possible to the original."

"So you want me to pick up another hitchhiker?" Raibert asked.

"That's right."

"Hmm, I don't know . . ."

"What's wrong?" Elzbietá asked.

"Well, it's just I have such *fond* memories of meeting the two of you. You reacted *so* well at first. You know, besides brandishing a knife, threatening to blow my brains out, and trying to strangle me."

"This is different," Benjamin insisted. "I've met the individual, and he's also family. I know I can get him to listen. Even to a story as crazy as ours."

"All right." Raibert gave him an indifferent wave. "Who is this guy?"

"Graf Klaus-Wilhelm von Schröder."

"Wow. Now that's a name and a half. So he served in the German military?"

"He joined the Reichswehr in 1926, following our long-standing family tradition. Von Schröders had served Germany—and Prussia before that, and Brandenburg before *that*—since well before 1600 when the Barony of Schröder was created. He was raised with the understanding that military service was both his destiny and his highest calling, and he grew to adulthood seeing the weakness of the Weimar Republic and the bloody street fighting between Bolsheviks and the freikorps."

"I thought you said you weren't an expert on World War II?"

"Neither version of me is," Benjamin said, and for a moment he wondered how he'd ever come to utter a sentence that strange. "But I'm quite familiar with the family history part of it."

"Ah. Well, I guess that makes sense. So this guy is pretty well known inside your family?"

"You could say that," Benjamin flashed a grin and continued. "In 1940, at the time Hitler was assassinated, my grandfather was in France commanding a battalion of motorized infantry attached to Erwin Rommel's 7th Panzer Division. In the timeline we're trying to restore, he was seriously wounded in the fighting and, when he returned to active duty, he was transferred to intelligence duties. Eventually, he ended up serving under a fellow named Reihard Gehlen in *Fremde Heere Ost*, the organization inside the General Staff responsible for analysis and counter-intelligence against the Soviet Union. He and Gehlen were both active in an unsuccessful plot to assassinate Hitler in 1944 but managed to escape detection. After the war, he continued in the Gehlen Organization—an intelligence service set up by Gehlen and the US mostly to keep an eye on Stalin and the USSR. That eventually morphed into the *Bundesnachrichtendienst*, the federal intelligence service of West Germany, in 1956, and he served as one of its senior officers until he retired in 1960.

"But things went a little differently in the Admin timeline. In a lot of ways.

"First, there was a *huge* succession fight inside Germany following Hitler's assassination, and it did enormous damage to the Nazi party. While the army and the SS divisions were moving into France, what amounted to a civil war broke out in Germany behind them. The Prussian police, the Luftwaffe, and about half the Gestapo supported Herman Goering, who was openly allied with Rudolph Hess; most of the SS, the rest of the Gestapo, and some of the SA backed Heinrich Himmler; and the rest of the SA and some of the SS backed Joseph Goebbels. At the moment all this began, the Army—my grandfather included—was too busy invading France to take sides back home.

"But that changed when Himmler made the serious mistake of arresting—and *shooting*—*Generalfeldmarschall* von Brauchitsch 'on suspicion of complicity in the Fuhrer's murder' and issuing orders for the arrest of all three Army group commanders in France. He apparently hoped to decapitate the Army's leadership before any organized resistance to himself or the Nazi Party could form. Unfortunately for him, while he managed to execute Brauchitsch, his attempt to arrest the Army group commanders failed miserably, which led to the open fighting in France between SS formations and regular Army formations shortly after the British surrender at Dunkirk. The fighting didn't end well for the SS, and Erwin Rommel and—under his command—Klaus-Wilhelm von Schröder, played a prominent role in suppressing the Nazi-loyal SS divisions. They were fast, they were ruthless, and it was bloody as hell."

"Fast and bloody suppression, huh?" Raibert mused. "*And* he has a history of killing Nazis? I'm liking this guy already."

"With Brauchitsch dead and Himmler blamed for his death, the Army swung its support largely to Goering and Hess. They formed what might be considered the 'conservative' wing of the

German power struggle, and they enjoyed the backing of many German industrialists and the upper class, as well as support from the Army, Luftwaffe, and Navy.

"Back home in Germany, Army units, Luftwaffe units, Gestapo, and even regular uniformed police came into conflict in several cities. The actual armed combat went on for no more than a couple of weeks, with Himmler—handicapped by having so much of the SS's manpower neutralized in France—quickly losing ground. Goebbels made the mistake of throwing in with Himmler immediately after Hitler's assassination because of his personal rivalry with Goering, and the two of them, plus a fellow named Reinhard Heidrick, were rounded up and shot somewhere in Zwikau in August 1940.

"Most everyone in Germany breathed a sigh of relief following the executions. But that still left Hess and Goering, and if this part of history is any indicator, Nazis are very good at eating their own.

"Hess was assassinated in October of 1940, ostensibly by a diehard SS officer loyal to Himmler. In fact, that's probably what happened, but the general belief in Germany was that Goering had decided to eliminate his last true rival. Neither the Army nor the Navy were at all happy with the situation, and the tinderbox ignited when a local Luftwaffe commander attempted to forcibly disarm an Army battalion whose commander, he *erroneously* believed, was prepared to attempt a coup against Goering. That battalion commander was *Oberstleutnant* Graf von Schröder, and the result was an unmitigated disaster for the Luftwaffe CO."

"Your grandfather doesn't take crap from anyone, does he?" Raibert chuckled.

"You could certainly say that," Benjamin agreed, returning the smile. "In fairness to the Luftwaffe guy, Grandad had decided he *really* hated the Nazis—in both universes—even before the war broke out. Something called *Kristallnacht* in 1938 had a lot to do with that. The Luftwaffe guy was a member of the party and apparently pretty damned arrogant about it, and that *had* to've rubbed Grandad the wrong way even before the idiot screwed the pooch by trying to disarm his men.

"Anyway, Grandad's reaction—and what happened to the Luftwaffe—was the spark that set off open fighting *again* in November, and this time, the conflict went on for several months as the *regular* armed forces started fighting each other, and my grandfather led his troops to victory in some of the worst urban battles of the conflict."

"Yep." Raibert nodded. "Liking this guy more and more."

"Then in February 1941, *Goering* was killed by a roadside bomb in Berlin, which created fresh chaos and an enormous void at the top of the political structure. Admiral Wilhelm Canaris of the Abwher, Admiral Eric Raeder from the Navy, and *Feldmarschall* Gerd von Rundstet from the Army stepped in to fill that void.

"The Luftwaffe and the remnant of the SS were pretty much crushed by June 1941, and, to the astonishment of non-German observers, the Triumvirate formed by Canaris, Raeder, and von Rundstet invited *Kronprinz* Louis Ferdinand to assume the old imperial crown. No one outside Germany saw it coming, but the national mourning when Louis Ferdinand's older brother Wilhelm was killed in France suggested that the House of Hohenzolleran retained a lot more public support than those non-Germans—or the Nazis, for that matter—had suspected. I don't know if the Triumvirate *did* suspect that or if they simply saw him as a last, desperate alternative to the now thoroughly discredited Nazis. Whatever they may have *thought*, though, it worked.

"Louis Ferdinand agreed to a new constitution which was roughly based on the pre-World War I imperial constitution but with clearer limitations on the Crown's powers, and he assumed the throne officially on January 1, 1942."

"That's all very fascinating," Raibert acknowledged, "but can we get back to your granddad? I want to hear more about him."

"I'm getting there," Benjamin said. "I have to set the stage first. Anyway, Germany contacted Great Britain and basically said 'Look, those lunatic Nazis, who our soon-to-be monarch bitterly opposed—and that actually seems to have been true, by the way—got us into this stupid war with the wrong people. At the moment, as you're undoubtedly aware, we're still significantly stronger militarily than you are, except at sea. However, we have no wish to continue fighting, so we propose turning the cease-fire into a permanent peace treaty.' This along with the return of a significant portion of the territories the Nazi regime had seized—and the repatriation of the entire British Expeditionary Force, after its surrender at Dunkirk—eventually led to the Treaty of Berlin—the peace treaty between Germany, France,

Great Britain, Holland, Belgium, and Poland—which was signed in Berlin in March 1942."

"Still waiting for the granddad to show up again," Raibert complained.

"*Getting* there," Benjamin replied. "When the treaty was signed, Joseph Stalin became deeply alarmed by the growing rapprochement between Imperial Germany and its erstwhile enemies in France and the British Empire. Unlike Germany, he refused to relinquish his share of the Polish conquests, partly out of sheer greed but also because he'd become more convinced than ever that he needed a defensive frontier as far west as he could get one. He saw a restored Germany which was possibly even more dangerously anti-Bolshevik than the Nazis had been, and therefore a threat to him and the Soviet Union.

"Overall, the various European communist parties were steadily losing power and members. Stalin saw the Soviet Union becoming even more of a pariah nation than ever, cut off by and isolated from Western Europe. And *then* Louis Ferdinand and his Foreign Ministry released the Nazis' secret pre-war treaties with Russia, which made it pretty *damned* clear what Stalin had been planning before Hitler's assassination.

"By December 1944, an increasingly paranoid Stalin had largely completed his own rearmament program and the reform of the Red Army, and there were 'spontaneous' pro-Communist uprisings in Hungary and Romania. The Red Army mobilized and moved in, summoned by its 'fraternal socialist brothers,' at which point the Kaiser demanded Stalin withdraw his troops. Stalin ignored all diplomatic efforts. Germany mobilized as part of the Western Alliance, and the Great Eastern War began in April 1945.

"By then, Klaus-Wilhelm had been promoted to *generalmajor*— the equivalent of a brigadier general—and placed in command of an armored brigade in Army Group South. He served with distinction as the panzer commander who spearheaded the advance through the Balkans and into Ukraine, and by the end of the war, he was a *generaloberst*—or a four-star general—in command of an entire Panzer army of several corps. He's the man most recognized for the liberation of the Ukraine in the war that finally overthrew Joseph Stalin in August 1951. In fact, he was so beloved by the people of the Ukraine, that they asked Louis Ferdinand to name him as their provisional governor, and he served in that post from 1952 until 1958, when the Republic of Ukraine became a full member of the United Nations."

"All right! All right!" Raibert held up his hands. "The guy has impressive credentials. I *get* it. You realize you sold me at swift and bloody suppression, right? So where and when do we make contact?"

Click.

"I think 1958, at the tail end of his governorship, is our best bet," Benjamin said. "Almost all of the partisan attacks by diehard Communists had ended by then, so it should be easier to approach him. He'd be fifty-two years old at that point, but according to my dad, he was still a dauntingly fit veteran who'd survived over a quarter century of active military service, including some of the most intense combat in human history. He was certainly still a tough guy by the time *I* knew him!"

Click.

"He's a leader and a survivor," Raibert observed, nodding. "I *like* him."

Click-click.

Raibert scrunched his brow and half turned at the noise.

"And even if I can't convince him to join us," Benjamin added, "he's a living, interactive encyclopedia for the information we need."

Click. Click-click.

"Plus 1958 puts a good amount of distance between us and the Event," Elzbietá noted. "If one of those chronoports spots us, they'll still be in the dark about our final destination."

Click-click. Click-click.

"Good point there." Raibert rubbed his temples. "Philo?"

Click. Click-click. Click.

"Philo!" Raibert whirled around. "What the *hell* are you doing?"

The three of them turned to see Philo frozen with his hand against a small tab on the top of his helmet. Instead of his usual faux-Viking headwear, this one looked like it belonged to a twenty-first-century fighter pilot . . . except for the two horns sticking out the sides.

"What?" He slid the tab down the front of the helmet, and a reflective visor extended to cover his face.

Click.

"Would you *please* stop that?" Raibert asked. "We're trying to concentrate here."

"Sorry." He shoved the tab up again, and the visor clicked into the retracted position.

"What is that thing, anyway?" Raibert asked.

"It's my new helmet." Philo pointed to Elzbietá. "She gave it to me."

"He's going to act as my weapon systems officer, so I thought I'd help him look the part."

"It looks weird on you," Raibert stated.

"Well, I like it. See, she even put horns on it for me."

Click.

"Fine. Whatever," Raibert fumed. "Are we all in agreement finally? Do we want to pick up your granddad when he's a governor?"

Benjamin and Elzbietá nodded, and Philo gave him a thumbs up with his free hand.

Click.

"All right, then," Raibert declared. "Kleio, take us to Ukraine, 1958!"

Elzbietá stepped into Benjamin's quarters to find him in the midst of a dizzying array of flat and 3D virtual images. World War II Nazi uniforms, coats, boots, gloves, hats, helmets, gas masks, and an equally extensive selection of period civilian clothing were mixed with pistols, rifles, machine guns, grenades, and even Panzerfaust and Panzerschreck rocket launchers.

Benjamin stood with his back to the door and stared at a physical bullet in his palm.

"You wanted to see me?" She parted the forest of images with a gesture and came to his side.

"Yes, I did." He held up the bullet, which she now recognized as a 9x19mm Parabellum. "I had Philo print this out for me. How easy do you think it would be for us to hide something a little more lethal in it?"

"Pretty easy, I would think. SysGov high explosives pack a hell of a punch, so it wouldn't take much. Why do you ask?"

"I had an idea." He tossed the bullet into the air, then caught it. "When we go into 1940, we need to minimize disruptions to the timeline, and that means we dress the part."

"Hence all of this?" She gestured to the virtual displays around them.

"Right. I figured my time would be better spent working on this while we're on our way to 1958, but I realized I'm going to need some help."

"Not sure I'm the right person to help you make the costumes more historically accurate."

"True, but that's not what I'm thinking." He pocketed the bullet and pulled a virtual MP40 machine pistol over. "Take this for instance. Sure, it'll work against the assassins, but if the Admin shows up while we're trying to set the timeline right, we're in for a heap of trouble."

"So you're thinking thirtieth-century tech hidden in a twentieth-century façade." She grinned slyly.

"Exactly."

"Now *that* I can help you with."

"I thought you might like this. You've taken to their technology a lot better than I have, so I'd appreciate the assist."

"We could start by putting a prog-steel weave in the uniforms." She pulled a virtual trench coat over and spread it out in front of them, then summoned abstract components from a catalog. Metallic gray tendrils worked their way across the lining until they covered the entire inside of the coat. "It won't be as good as the armor we were wearing on the *Lion*, but it's definitely better than plain cloth."

"I can't believe you did that so fast." Benjamin chuckled and shook his head.

"Something wrong?"

"Nothing." He scratched the back of his neck. "Just reminded of how much I don't deserve you."

"That's where you're wrong, buster. If you didn't deserve me"—she grinned hungrily and took hold of his suspenders—"you wouldn't have me."

She pulled him close and let him know just how much he deserved her.

CHAPTER THIRTY

Transtemporal Vehicle *Kleio*
non-congruent

"SO THIS IS WHERE YOU TWO HAVE BEEN."

"Hey, Raibert," Elzbietá said without turning. The *Kleio*'s six cubical bulk printers each stood nearly two stories tall and sat back to back to form a row under a high, rounded ceiling. Twelve smaller atomic printers stuck out of their sides, and Benjamin and Elzbietá had busied themselves at a table near one of the smaller output slots of Bulk Printer One. Every printer hummed with activity. Benjamin pulled a black trench coat from Bulk Printer One's open slot while microbots flowed over the third 45mm Gatling gun suspended over other printers further down the chamber.

"What is all this stuff?" Raibert asked as he surveyed the haphazard stacks of clothing and military paraphernalia.

"Costumes for 1940." Benjamin set the trench coat on the table, splayed it open and ran his hand across the interior. Both sides of the collar had what might have been two lightning bolts or two stylized letter S's, and the left sleeve had a red armband marked by a white circle and a black cross with ends bent at right angles.

"Costumes with *kick*," Elzbietá corrected.

"What sort of kick?" Raibert asked.

"The thirtieth-century kind." She placed a helmet and gas mask next to the trench coat, then adjusted the straps on the mask and pulled it over her head. She turned her head from side to side, up and down, and picked up a helmet with the same two lightning runes and fitted it in place.

"How's that version?" Benjamin asked.

"Still could use some work." She repeated the exercise, her voice muffled by the mask. "The screen fixes the visibility problem, but I'm still not happy with the lack of prog-steel coverage around the neck. Mind if I try a slight deviation from history?"

"Go ahead," Benjamin responded. "We may have to make compromises in a few places to ensure the equipment's effective. We'll look it over when you print out the next one."

"You put a physical screen in the gas mask?" Raibert asked.

"We need this equipment to work for anyone, including my grandfather, who doesn't have wetware and may not be keen on us dousing his eyes with tiny robots."

"Hmm, okay. Good point."

"We're making sure it's as simple to use as possible because of that," Elzbietá added. She took off the helmet and mask, set them aside, then summoned a virtual version between her hands. The straps on the mask widened until they merged and formed a hood.

"You need my help with...I don't know, any of this?" he asked.

"We're fine for now," Elzbietá said. She still hadn't looked his way.

"Okay, but is this going to slow down my next gun?" He knew the question was silly when he asked it.

"No, Professor," Kleio reported. "The third 45mm Defensive Gatling gun will be completed well before we arrive in 1958. Their requests are having minimal impact on my printing capacity. I have allotted two percent for their use, and they have yet to take advantage of half of that."

"Okay..." Raibert frowned at the bustling activity that he was, regrettably, not a part of. "Keep it up, I guess. As you were."

He was about to leave when Benjamin looked up.

"Hey, Raibert?"

"Yeah, Doc?" He turned around, perhaps a little too eagerly.

"Whatever happened to the ass cave?"

"Oh." He frowned again. "You mean Lucius?"

"Yeah, that guy. Did he really get away with abusing time travel?"

"I suppose we can tell you about that. Hey, Philo?" The Viking aviator flashed into existence next to him as he pointed a thumb at Benjamin. "He wants to know what we finally ended up doing to Lucius."

Philo's grin almost reached his ears. Literally, since it was impossible for anyone else in the room to grin that big.

"You ready for this, buddy?" Raibert asked as he stood before the vaulted entrance to the newly opened Alexandria Exhibition on the top floor of the Ministry of Education. Lucius Gwon had personally organized the mission to preserve the entire contents of the Great Library of Alexandria, and soon he and his chief archeologists would begin their presentation.

Hundreds of honored guests filtered past him from the shuttles parked around the top of the Ministry, and since he was still—officially at least—a member of ART, he possessed a standing invitation to the opening ceremony for every new exhibit. He could walk right on in, and no one would think anything was out of the ordinary.

It was a perk he'd never taken advantage of.

Until today.

"More than ready," Philo replied through audio only. "I've been waiting a long time for this day."

"Well, the wait is over. For both of us. Let's do this."

"Right with you, buddy."

Raibert tossed his scarf over a shoulder, adjusted his white wide-brimmed hat, straightened his pristine suit, and strode into the exhibition. Half a million books and scrolls took up an impressive amount of space, and the Ministry had combined several reception halls to accommodate the rows upon rows of carefully laid out relics.

Physical patrons walked back and forth down the curving aisles while ACs darted through the infostructure and occasionally revealed their avatars when they found an interesting artifact and wished to converse about it.

The rows curved inward and the distance between them shrank to lead patrons toward an elevated center stage where Lucius and several of his archeologists waited to begin their presentation.

Raibert made his way slowly past the outer displays, lingered here and there for the sake of appearances, and even stopped to read about a collection of scrolls upon which Teodorà Beckett had provided analysis.

"She's still at it," he said with a pang of regret.

"Miss her?" Philo asked.

"Not so much anymore." He gazed over the gathering crowd and spotted her next to Lucius. "I can't believe she chose *him* over me."

"Well, look on the bright side," Philo added with relish. "She's *really* not going to like this."

"That's an understatement," Raibert chuckled.

"I'm heading off to do my thing."

"All right. See you up on the stage."

"See you." The AC vanished into the surrounding infostructure.

Raibert followed the curving, contracting rows of books and scrolls to an open space around the center stage and quietly slid up to the back of the crowd. He didn't have long to wait before the show began.

"Ladies and gentlemen and abstracts!" Lucius Gwon announced, his voice carrying across their shared senses as a close-up of his face opened in front of Raibert. "Welcome to the Alexandria Exhibition! Every book opened before you, every scroll unrolled in this hall, all of it was once lost to humanity! But now, thanks to the tireless work of the Antiquities Rescue Trust, this lost heritage has been returned to us!"

A cheer rose from the crowd, and Lucius basked in their admiration, while Teodorà and the others waved.

Raibert swiped the pop-up window closed and began picking his way through the crowd. He gently urged a few people aside and made his way to the edge of the stage.

"Ready?" he asked without speaking.

"Ready," Philo announced. "These jokers really should improve their security."

The cheering died away, and Teodorà looked down at him with a start. She recovered, glowered at him, then sent a text that appeared in his virtual vision.

What the hell are YOU doing here? it read.

He merely dipped his hat to her.

She shook her head and looked away.

"Tonight, we have many wondrous artifacts and stories to share!" Lucius held out his arms. "But first, let us take you on a journey back to 30 BCE! Back to the Great Library of Alexandria at the pinnacle of its glory!"

The floor vanished, replaced with a sweeping flyby of cottony clouds that parted to reveal the city of Alexandria on the banks of the Mediterranean Sea. The view dipped down to sea level, shooting across glistening waters, past the Pharos lighthouse, over the harbor, and then into the city itself. The camera angle darted through empty streets, down back alleys and wide roads alike, zigzagging back and forth through ancient architecture until it returned to Great Library near the harbor's edge.

The view dashed into a huge, colonnaded hall with racks upon racks upon racks of books and scrolls, all flashing by at high speed.

"Interrupting the simulation..." Philo said in Raibert's brain. *"Now!"*

The view froze, then turned around and retreated out the way it came. It gained a little altitude, flew over rooftops, and then settled into a wide shot of Alexandria.

Lucius frowned and turned to his shadow. The star field flickered in what might have been a shrug.

Raibert grabbed the edge of the stage, hooked a leg over the side, and hauled himself onto it with a groan.

"What are you doing?" Teodorà hissed at him.

He stood up and dipped his hat as he walked past her.

"A lovely presentation, Lucius." He clapped his hands, voice booming across same the shared audio Lucius used. "It's a shame I had to interrupt it."

"I'm sorry, everyone," Lucius said, barely acknowledging Raibert's presence. "We seem to have an uninvited guest on the stage. Please give us a moment. We appreciate your patience."

Then and only then did Lucius turn to fix him with a glare that announced his intention. He would destroy Raibert utterly and completely, tear him down and humiliate him in front of the whole world, and take from him everything he cherished.

Raibert laughed at him, even as his heartbeat quickened.

"You've made a grave mistake," Lucius sent without his lips moving. "I was content to let you enjoy your humble role in all of this. A small role for a small man. But no more. You're finished, Raibert. You hear me? Finished!"

"I've made a lot of mistakes over the years," Raibert admitted aloud. "Which is why I can't in good conscience let this presentation continue without showing your adoring fans all the hard work ART did to retrieve these artifacts."

Teodorà grabbed his shoulder, but he shook off her grip.

"What are you talking about?" Lucius demanded aloud.

"Come on. You led this mission yourself! Your guests deserve to know how tough this assignment was for ART's Preservation teams."

Lucius glared at him, but something else finally appeared in his eyes. It was the glimmer of sweet, delicious fear, and Raibert savored it. The star field within his shadow vanished, and he knew Philo would have to handle it and the security ACs on his own.

"Now, Lucius," he continued, his voice low and menacing. "I'm going to show them exactly what ART does when it plunders the past. All of it." He snapped his fingers.

The viewpoint switched to the nose camera of a TTV—one of ten flying in formation across the harbor. The view slowed, then stopped over the Library campus before four TTVs descended while six smaller craft formed a ring-shaped overwatch. Scholars and gardeners on the surface scattered as massive ovoid bulks splintered trees, and crushed statues and living, breathing people with equal disregard.

Some people in the exhibit audience gasped, and Raibert grinned cruelly. He had *much* worse to show them than this.

"Ladies and gentlemen and abstracts!" he announced. "I give you our dirty little secret: the hard working men and women of ART Preservation!"

Blood drained out of flattened bodies, glistening from the swaying light of oil lamps as it followed grooves in the intricate stone paths. The TTV forward ramps lowered with a crash, and ART security synthoids stormed out. Indigenes screamed, weapons barked, and hyper-velocity darts designed to punch through prog-steel body armor pulped flesh and bone. Precise gunfire silenced the cries in the gardens, and the synthoids fanned out.

Murmurs rose from the exhibit audience.

"Everyone, please disregard what you are seeing!" Lucius pleaded. "We are experiencing technical difficulties! Nothing more!"

"Why do you look so worried, Lucius?" Raibert laughed. "All those non-disclosure contracts can't save you now!"

The view jumped to the Library interior where several scrolls had been unrolled on a long wooden table within a columned hall, its walls lined with rack upon rack of paper scrolls. A balding elderly man flung his arms wide in an attempt to scoop up the scrolls on the table when four synthoids charged into the hall and fired through his back. Viscera and bits of paper scattered into the air, and the old man collapsed over the table.

A dozen scholars ran for it, but a young librarian raced across the hall in the opposite direction, for some reason intent on reaching a particular rack of scrolls. A synthoid tagged him with a triple burst as the other three synthoids dropped the fleeing scholars.

The young librarian collapsed to the ground, but he wasn't dead yet, and he clawed his way forward on his belly, intestines unwinding out of his abdomen. He reached up with trembling fingers toward the nearest rack of scrolls, tears streaming down his cheeks until he coughed up blood and dropped into a puddle of his own fluids.

One of the synthoids knocked the other on the shoulder with a fist. Floating text marked them as ZHENG and ROSSI.

"Hey, man!" Rossi shouted at his comrade. "Watch where you're shooting. You're going to piss off the geeks with all the blood splats."

"So?" Zheng dismissed.

"So? It means more work for us. You know they're going to make us microjump back here and collect anything we damage."

"And why's that a bad thing?" Zheng pointed his gun down the hall. "Means we get to play through this shooting gallery all over again." He chuckled, and soon Rossi joined in.

"Oh yeah. Didn't think of that."

"And that isn't the half of it. This your first mission?"

"First one this size, yeah."

"Then just watch and learn." Zheng clapped Rossi on his armored shoulder. "You'll see. We make a few choice mistakes, slow down the doctors, and then we get to have *all* sorts of fun on these missions."

Three of the synthoids laughed heartily, and soon Rossi joined in. As a team, they raised their weapons and hurried into the next room.

"Turn off this fabrication!" Lucius shouted.

"Oh, this is no fabrication!" Raibert faced the crowd. "Honored guests, I have to wonder, should we as a society consider this a *moral* use of our time machines? Would anyone like to comment on this fascinating philosophical question?" He turned to Teodorà and the other archeologists on the stage. "Anyone? Anyone at all?"

The view changed again, this time showing one of the escort TTVs targeting a detachment of royal guards marching toward the Library as men, women, and children fled in the opposite direction. A 12mm Gatling gun spewed a continuous stream of fire—and erased the guard detachment from existence.

Night switched to day, and a tiny remote swept its scopes across the same street. Everyone in the audience felt the heat of summer, heard the buzzing of flies in the streets of Alexandria, and smelled the stench of decomposing corpses. A guest near the dais vomited.

"Turn it off!" Lucius stormed. "Turn it off right now!"

Raibert flashed a grin. "No."

"I told you to turn it off!" Lucius grabbed him by the collar. Raibert's hat fell off, but the grin never left his face.

The crowd grew louder, both from the onslaught of graphic violence filling their shared sight and also from the security synthoids shoving their way toward the stage.

Lucius clutched two fistfuls of Raibert's scarf and pulled him so close their noses almost touched.

"Tell that piece of trash AC of yours to turn it off," he breathed, "or I swear I will choke you to death right here on this stage."

"Do it if you think you have the guts," Raibert said, then spat in his face.

Lucius recoiled, then decked Raibert with a hook that sent him sprawling. The chairman turned in a circle, took stock of the horrified eyes, the shocked stares, the words of shame not only whispered but spoken and even shouted, and then he faced the hell he and his organization had turned Alexandria into.

"This isn't over," he growled at Raibert's prone form before he fled the stage and shoved aside anyone who got in his way.

The vignettes of violence from Alexandria continued to play, and Raibert picked himself off the floor and rubbed his aching jaw.

"Gather around, everyone!" he shouted, laughing and holding out his arms in a parody of Lucius's earlier gesture. "Gather around and see what you are sponsoring!"

Security synthoids vaulted onto the stage and swarmed over him.

"Can you believe we call ourselves *ART?*" he laughed as they hauled him away.

"So what became of Lucius and the rest of ART?" Benjamin asked.

"He resigned," Raibert said.

"That's it?"

"Well, officially. Unofficially, most of the major ART sponsors were so disgusted by the truth that they forced him out along with his strongest supporters. There was a *huge* SysPol investigation into time-travel uses and abuses. SysPol being the police in my time. A bunch more people lost their jobs, new management got put in place, and so on. Some new laws were written too. For one, ART teams were restricted to nonlethal technology except in the case of self-defense, and any time one of their teams *did* use lethal means, they had to justify that use to SysPol or lose their time-travel privileges. SysPol also put a few undercover ACs to work in ART, and that led to several arrests after the new laws were on the books."

"I bet a lot of people didn't like that," Benjamin said.

"Now that's an understatement!" Raibert exclaimed, smiling. "Most of my old colleagues were *pissed.* They felt the decision to outlaw lethal force was totally unjustified because, as far as we knew back then, no one was really dying, and the restrictions only served to put our Preservation teams at greater risk. The first time a team got pincushioned by Zulu spears, ART mounted a pushback campaign against the restrictions. Almost got them overturned."

"So people died because of the new laws?" Elzbietá asked.

"Very rarely. You've seen what our medical science can do."

"Right. How can I forget?" She smiled and blinked both eyes.

"Deaths were pretty rare," Raibert added, "but there were a lot of injuries, especially early on as everyone got used to the new restrictions. Teodorà got hurt pretty bad. Some random Persian ran his sword through her stomach at Thermopylae. She ended up switching to a synthoid body after that and makes it a point to send me regular hate mail."

"And you?" Elzbietá asked.

"They let me and Philo stay right where we were. Our status

as whistleblowers helped shield us from the Gwon family and the other parties that weren't happy about how the status quo had changed. In the end, we got to keep doing the Observation missions we love."

"Sounds like you really shook things up," Benjamin said.

"Eh." Raibert shrugged as if it were nothing. "It was—"

"Everyone, get to the bridge now!" Philo screamed across their virtual hearing. "There's a chronoport out there!"

"Shit!" Raibert dashed through the doorway with powerful synthoid strides. A Nazi helmet clattered to the ground, and Benjamin and Elzbietá hurried after him. They took a counter-grav tube up a level and raced onto the bridge.

"How far?" Raibert asked.

"Negative ten months and closing."

"And there's just the one?"

"Just the one. It's in 2016, moving down the timestream."

"Are you *sure* it's alone?"

"As sure as I can be."

"Have they detected us?" Elzbietá asked.

"Doubtful," Philo said. "It's moving at ninety-five kilofactors. The Admin's chronoports seem to be half-blind when moving that fast. It's heading somewhere, not looking for us. Now at negative nine months."

"Then this is our chance." Elzbietá turned to Raibert. "We have the drop on them and we have our new weapons. I say we phase-lock with that time machine and blow it straight to hell."

"I appreciate your gusto," Raibert cautioned, "but there are at least eleven of those things out there. Somewhere, somewhen. We don't know where they are and we can't take them all on. Fighting is still a last resort for us, even with our new weapons."

"Chronoport at negative eight months," Philo warned. "Make up your minds fast, people."

"We can take them, Raibert," Elzbietá urged. "You know we can."

"Sorry, but no. Kleio, phase us in. We'll hunker down and wait for the chronoport to pass."

Elzbietá huffed out a frustrated breath and shook her head.

"Yes, Professor. Three...two...one...phase in."

Benjamin's eyes bugged out. He clutched his skull and collapsed to his knees.

"Doc, are you okay?"

"Ben?" Elzbietá asked.

He let out a long, plaintive wail that escalated into an ear-splitting scream that tapered off only when his lungs emptied. He sucked in a breath and cried out again as he crumpled to the floor.

"What's wrong with him?" Raibert asked.

"How should I know?" Elzbietá snapped as she hurried to Benjamin's side and crouched down next to him. "Ben, what's wrong? What is it?"

"David!" Benjamin wailed as he raked harsh fingers down his cheeks.

"David?" Elzbietá uttered. "But that's your..."

"He's dead!" Benjamin wailed, fingers clawing at his face as if he could tear the invading memories from his mind.

"How is this happening?" Elzbietá grabbed his hands and pulled them away. Benjamin's cheeks were already bleeding. "It's exactly the same."

"What's the same?" Raibert asked urgently. "What are you talking about?"

Benjamin yanked his arms back, curled up in a fetal ball, and wept bitterly.

"It's just like the day he gained his other memories! He's even saying the same things! I know! I was there!"

"But that's..." Raibert and Philo exchanged looks, and Philo shook his head in bafflement.

"Oh, no," Elzbietá muttered as sudden realization hit her. "Maybe it's *all* the same. Quick, what's the date?"

"September 1, 2017," Philo reported.

"It *is* the day! We're back at the *exact* same point in time when he gained those memories!"

"He's dead..." Benjamin whimpered. "Dead..."

"Philo?" Raibert asked. "Could that be it?"

"Maybe, uhh," Philo began. "Maybe his resonance with the old timeline is getting amplified because there are two of him here now."

"But that doesn't make sense! That's an asynchronous temporal effect!"

"Then explain this." Philo pointed at their twenty-first-century historian curled up in a gibbering ball.

"We need to leave!" Elzbietá demanded.

"We *can't* leave!" Raibert replied. "There's a chronoport out there, and we need to wait for it to pass!"

"Chronoport at negative five months," Philo reported.

"Oh, hang in there, Ben." Elzbietá cradled his head against her chest as tears streamed down his cheeks, and he moaned the same name over and over again. Minutes dragged by, and she was once again the rock he clung to in a private sea of chaos.

"Negative three months."

He wrapped his arms around her and squeezed her painfully tight as his entire body shuddered around a string of loud, coughing sobs. She stroked his hair and bent down to kiss his forehead.

"Negative one month."

He shuddered and whimpered wordlessly. She rocked him back and forth and waited as the minutes ticked by.

"Chronoport has passed," Philo reported. "We're in its wake."

"Kleio, phase us out!" Raibert ordered. "Take us to non-congruence. No destination."

"Yes, Professor. Three . . . two . . . one . . . phase out."

The tension in Benjamin's body melted away almost immediately. He rubbed a shaky hand over his face and looked up at her.

"Hey," she whispered and smiled down at him.

He returned the smile, weakly, and brushed trembling fingers across her cheek.

"Thank you," he whispered.

She brushed his hair aside and kissed his forehead again.

CHAPTER THIRTY-ONE

DTI Chronoport *Pathfinder-6*
non-congruent

JONAS SHIGEKI WATCHED THE TTV'S IMPELLER SIGNATURE CLOSE in on 1960, where *Pathfinder-8* and his own *Pathfinder-6* held non-congruent positions to form the downstream end of the picket. The two chronoports hovered side by side, laser linked to allow communication without the use of chronometric telegraphs.

"Any thoughts on how they slipped past *Pathfinder-10*?" he asked as the red blip moved backward through 1961 at seventy kilofactors.

"Impossible to tell," James Noxon said. His face was the same blank mask it had been for days and his flat voice was devoid of all emotions. "*Pathfinder-10* is out of telegraph range, so we couldn't contact them if we tried."

"And even if they were close enough, sending out the telegraph would alert Kaminski to our presence."

"That's very likely, sir."

Jonas hugged his shoulders and watched the distance drop. Even though the TTV would pass right by his two chronoports in a *temporal* sense, they were still separated by a *physical* distance of over five thousand kilometers, so he wasn't concerned about Kaminski suddenly phase-locking on his position and attacking.

"Either the TTV slipped past them or they were destroyed." The gray-skinned synthoid faced him, and Jonas shivered, both at the possibility of losing *another* chronoport and at how robotic Nox had become after Katja's death.

"Either way, we should proceed with caution," Jonas replied.

"Agreed, sir."

Jonas waited for something more in the way of a response, but none came. He found it difficult to meet the synthoid's blank gaze, and he turned away to expand the TTV's physical position until a map of the Earth filled the bridge.

"Look here." He tapped the nation on the map, and a white border highlighted it. "The TTV is already physically in the Ukraine. Vassal was right. Kaminski's going to make contact with Schröder's grandfather."

"So it would seem, Director."

"What years was he the Ukrainian governor again?"

Nox pulled up Vassal's report. "1952 to 1958, and he was fighting in the country as early as 1948."

"Perfect." Jonas swung the view over to *Pathfinder-2* and *Pathfinder-4* waiting non-congruent in 1950. "With a little luck, Kaminski will phase in near the next part of our picket, and we'll be able to hit the TTV with four chronoports at once."

"Destroying his time machine may not be enough anymore," Nox stated.

"How so?"

"We can't discount the possibility that the professor has isolated the Event precisely enough to correct it. I won't consider this over until both the TTV is destroyed and the professor is dead."

I assume Katja's death has nothing to do with that assessment. Right, Nox? he thought, but he also could see the man's logic. Kaminski had slipped out of their grasp too often, made too much progress as they sat and waited for him to make his move. It was time to end this with overwhelming force.

"TTV now passing into 1960."

"Let them reach negative two months, then lay in a pursuit course," Jonas ordered. "Maximum stealth."

"Yes, Director."

"Baffles fully extended. Plotting course now."

"*Pathfinder-6* to *Pathfinder-8*. Stand by to move out. Orders are to pursue the TTV once it reaches negative two months. Maximum stealth. Hold formation and maintain telegraph silence."

"Confirmed, *Pathfinder-6*. We'll follow your lead."

"*Six* to *Eight*," Jonas said. "We don't know where Kaminski will phase in. We may get lucky and be able to call in *Two* and

Four for assistance, but we may not have that luxury. Make sure you're ready for anything."

"Understood, *Pathfinder-6*. We'll be ready."

"With your permission, Director"—Nox grabbed a handhold on the ceiling and turned himself around—"I'll make sure the operators are briefed and that my combat frame is ready for deployment."

Jonas blinked at the slight change in Nox's tone. Was that eagerness he heard? Or was he just imagining things?

"Go ahead, Nox. You don't need my permission for that."

"Yes, sir." The big synthoid grabbed a second handhold and launched himself toward the exit. He floated to it and steadied himself with a hand on either side of the opening.

"Nox," Jonas suddenly called out and faced him.

"Yes, Director?" He rotated around, and Jonas was once again unsettled by what he saw. There was nothing in the synthoid's yellow eyes. No hate. No grief. No rage. No pain. Just a deep, unsettling, inhuman void.

He licked his lips before speaking.

"He's going to pay for what he did."

Nox cracked his mouth open ever so slightly, almost as if he intended to say something, and for a moment Jonas saw a flicker of emotions behind those eyes. A flash of bottled-up sorrow and rage that threatened to finally be unleashed.

But then it vanished as quickly as it had appeared. The synthoid, once again fully a machine, turned away and left without saying a word.

"I am *not* going down there unarmed," Raibert proclaimed, left hand on hip.

"Is that supposed to be a joke?" Benjamin asked, eyeing the stump where Raibert's right arm used to be attached.

"No, I'm being very serious here."

Elzbietá grabbed a set of freshly printed period clothes, each with prog-steel weaves, and set them on the table for Raibert and Benjamin to change into.

"Just because I'm going in packing heat doesn't mean I need to *look* the part," Raibert continued. "Kleio's putting my gun in the forearm."

"I see." Benjamin stripped down to his undershirt, underwear, and socks, and grabbed a pair of discreetly armored pants.

"Yeah, I'm going to be firing mag darts out of my palm," Raibert said as he struggled to don his own pants onehanded. "Should be awesome."

"Wow," Elzbietá smirked. "That could lead to some horrible mishaps. Are you a righty or a lefty when you...you know?"

Benjamin shuddered.

"Admit it," Raibert proclaimed. "You're just jealous because *you* don't get an arm that can blow holes through tanks."

"No, I'm not," Elzbietá laughed.

"Don't discharge that thing around my grandfather, please."

"Just so long as I don't have to."

"You expecting an unfriendly welcome?" Benjamin asked as he grabbed a shirt off the table.

"You shouldn't underestimate how hard this is going to be," Raibert warned with one leg successfully in his trousers. "You may *think* you know your granddad, but people change over the years. Take it from the guy with the time machine who can hop forward a decade or two at will. The man you knew is not the man we're going to see."

"I realize he's not the same man I knew when I was a kid. He'll be close enough."

"Okay, but on top of that he's the governor of an entire *nation*. I normally spend months preparing for an insertion that involves high-ranking government officials or royalty, and we're basically going to jump into this cold. We may not get past the front gate."

"We will." Benjamin finished buttoning up the shirt. "I know exactly how we'll get his attention. He'll want to see us. I guarantee it."

"And when we do see him?"

"Just let me do the talking. I've got this."

"You sure you're okay? Because yesterday, you were a little—"

"I'm *fine*," Benjamin interrupted. "The episode passed and I'm back to my normal self. Or what's passing for normal these days."

"All right," Raibert shrugged his shoulders. "Don't get me wrong, I agree leaving this to you is our best shot. Just don't underestimate the problem and don't screw this up."

"I won't."

"So what kind of family magic will you use to get us in there?"

"Actually…" Benjamin looked over hesitantly. "Ella, I'm going to need your help for this."

"Me?" She placed a hand to her chest.

"Yeah…I uhh…" He rubbed his hands together and walked up to her. "I need to ask you for something."

"Sure. Anything."

"I need something back from you. Something I just gave you that I'm very sorry I have to ask for."

"Oh," Elzbietá sighed as realization dawned on her face, and she lowered her head, crestfallen.

"What?" Raibert asked, turning from Benjamin to Elzbietá and back. "What are you two talking about? What's wrong here?"

Elzbietá looked down at the backs of her fingers—and at the glittering ring she wore on one of them.

"I understand," she whispered.

"I knew you would. And I'm sorry."

"No, no. It's okay." She pulled the ring off her ringer and held it in her palm.

Raibert hurried over to them and looked at the ring. "Is that what this is about?"

"Don't intrude," Benjamin warned, then lifted Elzbietá's chin. "I'll bring it back. I promise."

"I'll understand if you can't. I mean, it's just a thing, after all. It can be replaced."

"But it's the one I want you to have."

"That little thing?" Raibert pointed at the ring. "That's what you two are worked up about?"

"It's an heirloom of my family, and it's also her engagement ring. So yes, it's important to us."

"Pfft!" Raibert snatched the ring out of Elzbietá's hand and stomped over to the nearest printer.

"Hey!" Benjamin shouted.

Raibert flicked the ring into the analysis port.

"What are you doing?" Benjamin demanded.

"Solving your problem." He stuck a hand on his hip and looked up at the printer. "Kleio!"

"Yes, Professor."

"You see the ring in Bulk Printer One?"

"Yes, Professor."

"Make an exact copy."

"Right away, Professor."

"There." Raibert turned triumphantly to the others. "Problem solved."

Benjamin frowned as he walked over and stared into the analysis port. The ring floated in a gravimetric field as lasers, cameras, and spectrometers spun around it.

"Didn't think of that," he finally said.

"That's right, you didn't." Raibert slapped him on the back. "Good thing you have me here, huh?"

"Yes, Raibert." Elzbietá crossed her arms. "We're all *very* glad to have you along."

"I'm detecting a slight hint of sarcasm there."

"Slight?" Benjamin asked, and all three of them laughed.

Raibert and Benjamin walked along the paved street that led up a gentle slope through dense woodland. A chill wind whistled through the trees, and Benjamin buttoned his coat and turned up the collar to shield his neck. Flakes of snow fell from a gray overcast sky as afternoon transitioned into evening, and their boots crunched on a light dusting of snow.

"Not much traffic on this road," Raibert observed.

"This street leads directly to the mansion and nothing else." Benjamin shivered and took out a wool cap. He pulled it over his ears. "Button up your coat."

"What?"

"Button it up. At least try to look cold."

"Oh. Right." Raibert put on his own cap and drew his coat tighter.

They trudged up the slope and came to the edge of a wide clearing.

"There it is," Benjamin said, smiling at the baroque two-story mansion built in the middle of the clearing. Tall, rectangular windows were set evenly spaced across the second story's pale blue exterior, while smaller windows looked out through the white marble of the first story. A parapet adorned the roof, and smoke billowed from several white smokestacks.

The building sprawled out with expansive wings to the east, west, and north, and a tall, wrought-iron fence sectioned off the carefully manicured inner grounds and a parking lot with a mix of expensive-looking American, German, and Ukrainian vehicles.

"I've seen bigger," Raibert dismissed.

"Well *of course* you have." Benjamin shook his head and trudged onward.

"Still, it's nice. A bit fancier than I was expecting."

"This is the Provisional Residence. When Klaus-Wilhelm accepted the position of provisional governor, he was offered the Mezhyhirya Residence, which is a luxury estate on the banks of the Dnieper River. He refused, however, because he said it would be improper for him to live in such opulence, since he was merely a *provisional* authority. He declared that the Mezhyhirya Residence should be held in trust for future presidents once Ukraine became a permanent member of the United Nations."

"Then where did this place come from?"

"The Ukrainians built it for him. It's modeled after Mariyinsky Palace, which was unfortunately destroyed during the Great Eastern War. Because of that, it's sometimes called Little Mariyinsky or Second Mariyinsky."

"He refuses to live in a luxurious house on the river, so instead, the people of Ukraine build a palace for him?"

"And his family, too. He took a Ukrainian wife in 1953. Gräfin Yulia von Schröder—my grandmother. I think you'll like her . . . if she doesn't decide to shoot you out of hand. She and their three children are probably in there right now."

"They must have really loved him."

"He spearheaded the campaign that freed this country from the Soviet Union. So yeah, you could say he earned it."

"Sounds to me like your family used to be a big deal."

"What do you mean 'used to be'?" Benjamin gave him a sour look.

"Oh, don't be like that, Doc." The synthoid glanced over his shoulder. "I'm a time traveler. *Everything* is past tense to me."

"I suppose I have to give you that." Benjamin glanced back as well. An outline on his interface lenses illustrated the shrouded TTV's location. "Ella, how are we looking?"

"There's a sniper on the roof watching you."

"Can you mark his position for us?"

"Sure."

A virtual arrow indicated the sniper's position, but Benjamin made an effort not to look directly at it.

"The residence has a lot of security," Elzbietá continued. "I'd say about fifty soldiers in and around the grounds. Most of them have MP44 machine pistols backed up by squad automatic weapons of some sort. Not just MG42s, either. I know what those are when I see them, and this isn't them. Looks more like a German version of the BAR."

"*Fallschirmjägergewehr* 42s, probably," Benjamin said. "The MP44 was technically a machine pistol, but it was really the ancestor of all assault rifles, with a special 'short' cartridge to reduce recoil on full auto. The FG42 was something the Luftwaffe's paratroopers came up with in competition. Fires a full-sized seven-point-two rifle round that gives it more reach and more terminal energy than the MP44, and it's magazine fed, so there's no ammo belt to worry about. But no one could control it on full auto as well as the MP44, so they adopted *both* of them, with the FG42 in the support role because of its greater range."

"You do have the damnedest tidbits tucked away. Guess it comes from having a German general for a grandfather!" Despite the tension, there was more than a trace of laughter in her voice, and Benjamin could picture her smile as she shook her head.

"In addition to that, though," she went on, "I see a lot of Panzerfaust 200s, the postwar variant. Mostly US M1911s for sidearms, for some reason, and I even see a few M20 super bazookas—guess that's crossover from the Western Alliance? Your grandfather had...eclectic tastes in weaponry, didn't he, Ben?"

"You might say that." Benjamin smiled. "He always told me the nine-millimeter was good for pissing people off. If you really wanted to *kill* them, you went with a .45."

"I'm sure all that meant a lot more to the two of you than it did to me," Raibert groused. "To summarize, they have a lot of scary period guns."

"Yeah, that about sums it up. A dozen dogs, too. Mostly German Shepherds."

"They sound *so* friendly," Raibert commented.

"It's to be expected," Benjamin said as the road met the iron fence. Baroque flourishes crowned it, and they followed it toward the main gate and security kiosk. "There are still occasional partisan attacks from people trying to rekindle the Soviet flame. Not as many as there were immediately after the war, but Residence security still needs to be ready for it."

"Is that sniper aiming at us?" Raibert asked.

"At you, actually."

"Great. He targeting my head?"

"As a matter of fact, he is," Elzbietá replied.

"Well, at least he won't shoot off anything important."

They walked along the fence to a gate wide enough for two lanes of traffic with a marble security kiosk to one side.

"Six soldiers in the kiosk," Elzbietá reported. "One FG42, five MP44s, plus grenades and pistols. One more walking from the residence to the kiosk, maybe in response to your arrival. And a dog, in case that's a problem."

"I don't know." Benjamin turned to Raibert. "How *do* dogs react to Admin synthoids?"

"I guess we're going to find out. You ready for this?"

"Just leave it to me. I'll get us in."

Benjamin fingered the ring in his pocket, then thought better of it and pulled his hands out despite the chill. He let them dangle where the men with the guns could see them.

"Raibert, take your hands out of your coat. You're going to make them nervous."

"But I thought I was supposed to act cold."

"Just shut up and do it."

Major Anton Silchenko hated this part of his job.

Sure, the war—a war *some* called the Great Eastern War, but one he simply thought of as the liberation of his homeland—had been a brutal crucible. It had tested his will to endure pain and hardship, but at least those Bolshevik dogs had the common decency to wear *uniforms* most of the time.

There was a simplicity to that life, however cruel, where everyone wore their affiliation on the outside. He'd served under the governor for most of that conflict and he'd come out the far side with scars both physical and mental, but in a strange sort of way, he preferred that reality to one where plainclothes civilians could be partisan agents who attacked without warning.

Anton didn't think the two men were partisans yearning stupidly for the Soviet Union. They were *far* too conspicuous for that. No, they were something else; he just didn't know what yet, and that made him uncomfortable.

He stood back and watched as the two men continued to argue with *Landser* Roderich Garlesch.

"I'm sorry, sir," the ginger-haired Bavarian repeated, "but the governor is away on business."

"No, he's not," the one calling himself Benjamin said with complete certainty, and Anton understood why. It was a rather obvious lie, though it worked more often than one might think. The governor attracted all sorts of uninvited visitors. Not all of them had anything... untoward in mind, but some of them certainly did. And most of the others were nuisances, at best. His security detail was his first line of defense, and simply denying he was home was usually sufficient to discourage all but the most persistent. And when it wasn't, well...

Anton shook his head. He didn't know what kind of game these two were playing, but they'd come to the wrong place. The security at the mansion, which Anton commanded, was composed almost entirely of veterans from Klaus-Wilhelm's days as one of the Western Alliance's hardest-driving and most-charismatic panzer commanders.

Good luck, fellas, he thought. *You're not getting past* us *without an invitation.*

"I'm sorry, sir, but the governor *is* away," Garlesch repeated once again with deliberate, pigheaded stubbornness. He sometimes thought the kid liked to see whose will would break first when obstinate visitors came knocking.

"Would you please stop lying to me?" the smaller of the two asked. "This is completely unnecessary."

The man calling himself Benjamin had only given his first name. He sounded like an American, though something was a little off about his accent. Then again, the United States was a big country, and Anton hadn't worked with *that* many Americans over the years.

The other man, a big guy with a German look about him, hadn't spoken yet. Anton didn't know what to make of him other than the fact that their dog, Balthasar, hadn't taken his eyes off the newcomer since he walked up. But despite all the attention the fellow was getting from Balthasar, the animal hadn't growled at him or shown any sign of hostility, almost as if he were confused by something rather than sensed a hidden threat.

The big man noticed the dog watching and waved at the animal. Balthasar tilted his head to one side and let out a soft, questioning whine.

"Sir, if you would like to petition the governor for an audience upon his return, I can assist you by providing the necessary paperwork."

"No, I would *not* like to fill out any forms."

"Then, I am sorry. But there seems to be nothing I can do to help you."

"Look, it's *very* clear you have no interest in helping me."

"I'm sorry you feel that way, sir."

The big man stirred and took a step forward.

"No, I'll handle this," Benjamin snapped, then turned back to Garlesch. "I demand to speak to your superior."

"I'm sorry, but my superior is away on business."

Anton almost blurted out a laugh, but he quickly coughed into his fist.

"Am I really expected to believe that?" Benjamin asked.

"The governor and his staff are very busy people. I'm not sure what you were expecting, sir."

"He may be busy, but he's sitting in his office right now!"

"And how do you know that?" Anton asked, speaking for the first time since the two men arrived. He walked forward, and Garlesch stepped aside to let him pass.

"I assume you're the person in charge here," Benjamin said.

"You assume correctly."

"In that case, I have a very important message for you to deliver to the Governor."

"And why would I bother him with what you have to say?"

"Because after you deliver it to him, he'll order you to bring us inside."

Anton stared at the man's cool gray eyes, but all he found there was absolute certainty, and he began to doubt if this was a game at all.

"Search them," he ordered, and the soldiers at the kiosk sprang into action. Rifles snapped up, and Garlesch and two others moved in and began patting down the two men. Benjamin held up his hands, never taking his eyes off Anton, while the big man behind him raised his arms with a bored expression on his face.

The search didn't take long because the two men had almost nothing on them.

"No papers," Anton remarked. "No money. No identification. Now don't you think that's a little odd?"

Benjamin said nothing.

"In fact, the only thing you were carrying is this." Anton held up a ring. The diamonds on its five interlocking circles glittered fiercely even in the dull evening light. "Now why would this be the only thing you two are carrying?"

"Because that"—Benjamin smiled—"is my message."

CHAPTER THIRTY-TWO

Provisional Residence, Ukraine
1958 CE

GOVERNOR KLAUS-WILIIELM VON SCHRÖDER LEANED BACK IN THE generously padded leather armchair and took a sip of his customary evening beer. He savored the gentle bitterness of the imported Erdinger weissbier, then lit his customary evening cigarette, drew in a deep breath, and exhaled a puffy cloud.

Flecks of snow stuck then melted against the tall windows of his office in the east wing. The sky darkened, and hints of city lights from Kiev could be seen in the distance, splashing against more intense snow beyond the treetops.

He tapped the ash off his cigarette into the tray on his wide wooden desk and took another measured sip. The ubiquitous beverage from his birthplace in Brandenburg remained to this day one of his few indulgences. He enjoyed one—and only one—in the evening when he sat down for the mindless administrative work that concluded most of his days.

The governor cast a jaundiced eye at the stack in his inbox. Always more papers to sign. Always more petitions that *urgently* needed responses. Always more problems to solve. A part of him was happy he'd soon be done with all this, but the other half knew he'd miss it. To have a hand in the rebuilding of a whole nation was an opportunity few could lay claim to, and he'd attacked the problem with the relentlessness that was at his very core. He had some regrets and wished he could undo some of his decisions, but overall, he felt content with how this chapter of his life was coming to a close.

Life wasn't only about work. Perhaps it was finally time to set duty and honor aside and focus on family.

A knock came from the door.

"Enter."

The door opened and Anton Silchenko stepped in. Klaus-Wilhelm didn't like the look on his face at all.

"Sir, sorry to disturb you at this hour."

"It's all right." He stubbed out his cigarette and sat up behind his desk. "What seems to be the problem?"

"We have two unexpected visitors at the main gate. Americans as far as I can tell. Normally I wouldn't bother you with something like this, but they're not the usual sort we get."

"Are they looking to cause trouble?"

"I don't think so, sir. One of them had a message for you and said you'd want to see him once you received it."

"Very well. Let's hear it."

"The message is actually an object, sir." Anton reached into his pocket, retrieved a gold and diamond ring, and set it down on the desk blotter.

Klaus-Wilhelm frowned at the instantly familiar object, then picked it up and turned it round between his fingers.

"Interesting."

"You recognize it, sir?"

"Indeed I do, but this has to be a forgery. I know exactly where the real one is."

"In that case, shall I have them dismissed?"

"No." Klaus-Wilhelm set the ring back on the blotter and knitted his fingers together. "Have they been searched?"

"Yes, sir." He pointed to the ring. "That was all they had on them."

"Nothing else? No papers or passports?"

"No, sir."

"That seems unusual."

"My thoughts as well, sir."

"Search them again, just to be sure, then bring them to the foyer. I'll call when I'm ready to receive them. Keep them under armed guard at all times."

"Yes, sir."

"But before that, check in with the Gräfin. If she's free, I'd like her to come to my office. If not, I'll deal with this on my own."

"Understood, sir. I'll make sure I'm not intruding."

Klaus-Wilhelm nodded, and Anton left and closed the door. He picked up the ring again.

"What are you two doing with a forged von Schröder heirloom?" he wondered aloud. He honestly didn't know what they expected to gain out of this, but they were right that he would want to see them. The heirloom's history within the von Schröder family wasn't common knowledge, so it would take a von Schröder or someone very close to the family to understand the ring's significance.

Were one or both of these men such people? If so, who could they be?

The ring had once been worn by his first wife, Elfriede, and he felt his mind being drawn back to her as he turned the ring over and over in his fingers. She'd passed away over fourteen years ago, but somehow seeing the ring off his second wife's hand brought back long-forgotten echoes of grief and pain.

The door opened without a knock this time, and Yulia Obolenskaya von Schröder swept inside, looking as beautiful as the day he'd met her in May of 1946, although it was a little difficult to see that tough-as-nails young Ukrainian Insurgent Army major in the elegant German noblewoman of today.

His spearhead had been driving north out of Romania, only a few kilometers into Ukraine, still almost five hundred kilometers from Kiev, and the Ivans had started recovering. They'd been dug in hard, there seemed to be no end to their damned T34 and KV tanks, and the not-too-distant rumble of their artillery had told him it was about to get still uglier, when Майор Obolenskaya turned up at his HQ and insisted on speaking to him. To him—personally. He'd been amused by her demand, at first... but only until he'd actually set eyes on her. She'd been all of nineteen years old and she should have been home worrying about boyfriends. That had been his first thought. Of course, he hadn't known—then—that she'd been fighting Stalin's Communists since she was fifteen, but he remembered thinking that not even the baggy uniform could conceal the absurdly young major's graceful—and shapely—carriage. Yet the fact that she was a beautiful young woman had been the farthest thing possible from *her* mind. Her hair had been short, the fingernails cut short and square, the strong fingers calloused, the high cheekbones and rich mouth devoid of even a trace of cosmetics, and the only thing *she'd* been interested in that day had been trading her partisan unit's ancient Mosin-Nagant rifles for something better.

His staff had tried to shoo her away. The commander of an entire armored corps cutting its way into enemy territory had far too many important things to do than to waste time talking to a single, brash, *teenaged* female major from a so-called army made up of lunatic Ukrainian nationalists! But something about her had caught him. God only knew what, yet he'd held up a restraining hand at his chief of staff, beckoned her closer, and as he'd found himself listening gravely to her impassioned plea, he'd realized this was no ordinary young woman. He would never forget the way her eyes had glowed as if he'd just crowned her *kaiserin* when he'd ordered his *quartermeister* to issue her unit three hundred Gewehr 43 semiautomatic rifles. Or the way those long, calloused fingers had fieldstripped one of them in seconds...or the way she'd zeroed the sights as quickly as any of his own veterans could have done it. She'd been half his age, anything less like his beloved Elfriede would have been impossible to imagine, and yet...and yet...

She'd come into his life at a time when he'd been half a man, a creature of pure duty who'd lost his wife and pushed his only son away to keep him safe. He hadn't thought himself unhappy...until she'd filled the empty husk of his life with warmth and light and he relearned through her what it meant to be a complete person once more. And now, as she stepped into his office, he marveled yet again at the way the brunette hair flowed down either side of her strong, oval face. At the proud lift of her head, the sky-blue eyes under the birdwing eyebrows that produced a regal air that belied her youth. She might be two decades his junior, but she possessed a strength of will equal in every way to his own...and he had no idea how his own heart leapt into his eyes whenever she entered a room.

He rose from his seat and smiled warmly, holding out his hand to her.

"You wanted to see me, *kohanij*?" she said, squeezing his hand as he kissed her cheek.

"Yes, *Liebling*." He gave her fingers a quick answering squeeze—feeling their softness, remembering those warrior's callouses—and then released her hand and held out the ring. "Would you take a look at this?"

Yulia tilted her head to one side, then took it and held it next to the ring on her finger.

"Where did you get this?" she asked. "It's the same as mine. Are there two of them?"

"No. Only one was ever made. *This* must be a forgery."

"If so, it's a very good one. I can hardly tell the difference."

She held both up for him to compare under the light, and he too had trouble finding any fault in the forgery. The diamonds in the new ring shone even more brilliantly than the real one, but that might have been a result of the gems being cleaned recently. He did notice *very* subtle differences in the smoothness of the setting. The forgery possessed a few wear marks Yulia's ring didn't have and had been adjusted for a different-sized finger, but other than those few discrepancies, they were identical.

"Someone showed up at the gate with this," Klaus-Wilhelm said. "I'm having them brought in to see what this is about. Are the girls in the north wing?"

"They should be."

"Go get them. Take them to the safe room."

Those brilliant blue eyes narrowed suddenly, and *Майор* Obolenskaya looked out of them at him.

"Are you expecting trouble?" she asked quietly.

"I'm not sure, and I'm not about to take chances. Go get them. And tell Misha I said no one gets near any of you until I tell him differently."

"All right." She leaned up and kissed him on the cheek. "I'll see to it."

"Thank you."

She left, and Klaus-Wilhelm opened the right-hand drawer in his desk. He took out the gunbelt, buckled it around his waist, drew the engraved, presentation Smith & Wesson Model 29, and loaded six .44 Magnum cartridges. Then he reholstered it and shrugged, settling his unbuttoned jacket around its undeniable bulk. The weapon had been introduced by the American gunmaker only two years earlier, and this one had been a gift from General Ernest Harmon. He and the American had become firm friends at the 1949 Berlin Conference where the Western Alliance and its new transpacific allies had met to coordinate Operation

Oz with the brutal campaign on the Eastern Front, and they'd remained close since. Some of his fellow Germans would no doubt pooh-pooh the huge revolver with its five-inch barrel as typical American overcompensation, but it fit Klaus-Wilhelm's hand perfectly.

And whatever he hit with that gun was going to *die* . . . which was just the way he liked it.

He picked up the phone and dialed the foyer.

"Yes, sir?" Anton answered.

"Bring them up here."

"Both the professor and Doctor Schröder are inside," James Noxon stated, watching the feed from the lone Scarab reconnaissance drone. They'd deployed only one drone, both to reduce the chances of detection and because they'd been almost certain where Kaminski was heading.

And they'd been right.

"Recommendations?" Jonas asked, standing near the front of the bridge with Earth's gravity pulling them down for a change.

"I'll lead our operator team in an assault on the residence," Nox said. "We'll take both men out before anyone knows we're there."

"Or we could just charge in with two chronoports and level the place," Jonas countered.

"The chronoports aren't expendable."

And I swore to your father you'd come back from this alive, Nox thought. *I'm not about to fail again.*

"*You're* not expendable, either," Jonas countered.

"We don't know where the TTV is. It's too risky."

"Forget it. I'm not sending you and the operators in unsupported. I've seen firsthand what that ship's weapons do to people. It'll tear you to ribbons and then mulch the ribbons for good measure."

"It won't get me."

"I said *forget it*," Jonas said, almost shouting now.

"As you say, Director," Nox replied with deadpan calm.

Jonas sighed. He closed his eyes and rubbed his temples.

"We're three hundred kilometers back from the residence. It'll take too much time for us to reach you if it falls into the crapper and the TTV attacks."

"Then what are your orders?"

"We'll send a Cutlass in first like you suggested." Jonas looked up, pondered the map for a moment, then drew a line north of the residence. "But the chronoports will sweep in behind to *here*. We go in low and quiet. We should be far enough back to avoid being noticed but close enough if you and the operators need assistance."

Nox nodded. The staging point looked far enough away from the action to him.

"In that case, I'd like your permission to transfer into my combat frame."

"Granted. Load up, Nox."

"Sir." He turned away and walked to the bridge exit.

"And Nox?" Jonas asked, never turning from the map.

"Yes?" He looked back at the son he'd been placed on this ship to protect.

"Don't do anything stupid out there."

He couldn't think of anything worth saying to that, so he turned again and strode to the back of the ship, then took a ladder down to where eleven special operators were gearing up for combat with variskin armor, rail-rifles, and guided grenades. Two of them ran final diagnostics on the combat drones.

They stopped what they were doing and waited for him to speak.

He walked past them to a black endoskeleton cocooned against the wall by malmetal bands and festooned with weapons: right-arm heavy rail-rifle; left-arm incinerator; shoulder-mounted grenade launcher; dynamic malmetal armor; full variskin coverage; maneuvering boosters in the legs, shoulders, and hands; and a full suite of active and passive scopes. The operators had already loaded *Pathfinder-6*'s backup chronoton telegraph into the frame, which was standard procedure for DTI ground missions.

He looked upon the smooth, eyeless head. The combat frame represented the pinnacle of Admin ground combat for something the size of a human. He'd been one of the first volunteers to inhabit these killing machines, and he had *hundreds* of successful sorties to his credit.

"Put me in," he ordered, and took off his jacket.

The operators cut through a thin seam in his artificial skin shaped like a U halfway down his back and peeled it up to reveal the access slot to his case. He sent the release code, and they pulled the unlocked case from his spine.

The world vanished, replaced with simple shifting patterns of color and almost musical background sounds designed to prevent sensory deprivation should his connectome be kept in this state too long.

The loading VR vanished after only a few seconds, and he didn't have to open his eyes.

He didn't have any.

The room, the eleven operators, and the vacant shell of his synthoid body formed around him as intricate constructs of visual light, infrared, ultraviolet, sonar, and radar. He wasn't human anymore, but an amalgamation of weapons, armor, and technology. He didn't look human, didn't feel human.

And he had no desire to *be* human.

Not anymore.

Anton Silchenko led Benjamin and Raibert across a gold-accented foyer lit by crystal chandeliers hanging from a high, vaulted ceiling, then up a grand flight of red-carpeted stairs to a second-story balcony that branched off toward the three wings. The second story of the Provisional Residence was over twice as tall as the first story, allowing for truly expansive interiors designed to impress visitors with their scope and grandeur, while rooms in the lower floor served more mundane functions.

Two men from the security detail followed them with machine pistols at the ready.

Benjamin wondered if his father was somewhere in the residence that very moment. He did some quick math in his head and figured Klaus Schröder would be about seventeen in this part of the timeline. Klaus had visited Klaus-Wilhelm in the Ukraine toward the latter part of his governorship, after the worst of the partisan attacks had died down, but he'd spent most of his time in the US, so Benjamin didn't think he was likely to run into him.

Which suited him just fine, because he had enough to deal with right now without throwing a teenage version of his own father into the mix.

"More guns," Raibert muttered under his breath. "Why does everyone we meet want to point a gun at me?"

"Calm down," Benjamin whispered back. "This is what we wanted."

"I am calm. Just frustrated, is all."

They took a right into the east wing where cooler colors replaced the warm reds and golds of the foyer. Swirls of light and dark blues climbed the walls and rich purples spiraled across the floor.

"Well, we're getting that audience," the synthoid whispered. "What's your next move?"

"Just leave it to me. I've got this under control."

Raibert glanced back at the soldiers. While not *technically* holding them at gunpoint, they were still holding guns.

"Sure, you do."

"You trust me, don't you?"

"Yeah, I guess."

Anton led them down a hallway taller than it was wide with walls covered in paintings of wild animals and scenic vistas. The seasons changed as they walked by, ending in desolate paintings of Ukrainian winter directly outside a thick oak door.

Anton knocked.

"Enter," came a muffled voice.

"The governor will see you now." Anton opened the door and beckoned them to come in.

Benjamin walked into a rectangular office, small but expensively furnished, and met his grandfather's eyes. He was tall and broad shouldered like most Schröder men, with a buzz of blonde hair and gray eyes that he would someday use to skewer grandchildren when they lied.

But this was no withering patriarch of the family with sunken cheeks and failing vision. His back was strong, his muscles firm, and his gaze unwavering. Deep inside, Benjamin had still expected the loving grandfather who would regale him with stories of familial pride, but instead he found a towering figure with ten times the presence.

Klaus-Wilhelm grimaced ever so slightly at Benjamin.

He sees the family resemblance, Benjamin thought. *Well, of course he does. He's tough and smart. I'd expect nothing less.*

Klaus-Wilhelm held up the ring. "Which one of you brought this?" he asked in English.

"I did, sir," Benjamin said, almost instinctively standing a little straighter.

"You have some explaining to do."

"Yes, sir. I do."

Klaus-Wilhelm nodded at the direct, respectful tone. It had worked well for Benjamin when he'd been a kid currying favor, and it was working right now.

"Well, then. Let's hear it."

"Sir. First let me say that while you don't know me, I do know you."

"A lot of people can lay claim to that."

"Not the way I can," Benjamin continued. "I know you on a personal level for reasons you may already suspect."

Klaus-Wilhelm's jaw tightened at the remark.

"I also know that you are a man who does not tolerate obfuscation. You respect truth and directness, and so that's exactly what I'm going to give you."

He took one step forward and spoke in a clear voice.

"My name is Benjamin Schröder. I am your grandson from the year 2018 and I have traveled back in time because I need your help to save the universe."

Raibert palmed his face with a loud smack.

The two chronoports hovered over the Dnieper River to the north of Kiev and the Provisional Residence, their hulls obscured by variskin illusions. Jonas and the rest of *Pathfinder-6*'s bridge crew sat strapped to their seats, ready for combat, and the entire craft was tensely quiet as a single icon slid southward across the map of Ukraine, then came to rest.

"We've touched down," Nox reported from *Pathfinder-6*'s Cutlass transport. "No indication we've been spotted. Proceeding to target."

Icons representing eleven special operators, eight Wolverine light ground-support drones, eight Raptor light air-support drones, two Condor sniper drones, and one STAND combat frame disembarked from the Cutlass and advanced south through the forest.

"Director, we have a possible scope echo from near the residence. Could be the TTV."

"Let's see it."

A window opened in Jonas's virtual vision, and he zoomed in on the cloudbanks over Kiev. The replay began and, for a brief moment, a section beneath the billowing clouds flashed with higher than normal thermal activity. It could have been that their analytic programs were trying too hard to find abnormalities in something as naturally irregular as the weather.

Or it might be from a large vessel with advanced stealth systems hiding in the clouds.

"Move us in closer," Jonas ordered, "but keep it quiet. Weapons, program a missile barrage for maximum area of effect. We're going to flush them out of that cloud."

Fusion thrusters powered up, and two chronoports slid forward over the rippling water.

CHAPTER THIRTY-THREE

Ukraine
1958 CE

"OUCH!" ELZBIETÁ WINCED AS SHE WATCHED THE MEETING THROUGH Raibert's eyes. "Was that really such a good idea?"

"It was certainly *direct*," Philo observed with a worried grimace. "As far as it being direct in a *good* way?" He shrugged.

"I take it you and Raibert never tried this approach."

"Uh-uh." The avatar shook his head.

"Well, good luck, Ben. You're going to need it."

She peered through Raibert's senses again to find Klaus-Wilhelm having none of this nonsense. At first she thought he'd dismiss the two out of hand, but he didn't, and instead he and Benjamin began a long, drawn out duel of claims and questions, arguments and stories.

Klaus-Wilhelm's made it abundantly clear that everything Benjamin said was ludicrous, but the two were still talking, still probing at each other. Benjamin knew far too much about his grandfather and the von Schröder family for Klaus-Wilhelm to not at least suspect *something* was going on, even if he didn't know what. He was listening, paying rapt attention to everything Benjamin said. He clearly didn't *believe* it. Not yet at least, and certainly not in total, but perhaps he already saw a glimmer of truth hidden in Benjamin's fantastical story.

Was Ben's brutally blunt approach actually working? Had he read his grandfather correctly after all? If Klaus-Wilhelm was a

401

man as steeped in honor and duty as Benjamin said he was, then perhaps giving him the complete and unrestrained truth was the best way to earn his trust.

No matter how difficult delivering that truth might prove initially.

"You've got this, Ben," she whispered.

"Hmm?" Philo murmured.

"What's up?"

"Not sure." He opened a map of the Dnieper River before it narrowed and flowed through Kiev. "Take a look at this."

Elzbietá closed the virtual feed from the residence and put her hands on the command table railing. A string of intermittent signals traced a ragged path south down the middle of the Dnieper.

"Chronoport?" she asked in a hushed tone.

"Could be."

"Do we have a remote nearby?"

"I've got one stationed in Kiev moving that way now." He highlighted a pip on the map. "It should cross the path of whatever's out there in two minutes."

"I should get ready."

"Good idea."

Elzbietá hurried over to the open compensation bunk and stepped in. The glass front closed and the interior flooded with milky fluid. She interfaced her wetware with the fluidized microbot swarm, closed her eyes, and opened the cockpit abstraction. Her wetware took over her real body's functions before she had to deal with the unpleasantness of breathing down that goop, and the abstraction unfolded around her.

She stood on an invisible floor next to the side-by-side cockpit she and Philo had designed. A panoramic view surrounded her with low, gray clouds that parted to provide brief glimpses of snow-kissed evergreen forests and sparse buildings on the outskirts of Kiev.

She jumped into her seat, and Philo materialized to her left. Virtual displays activated, and she reached for the joystick and omnidirectional throttle.

"Positive sighting," Philo reported. "*Two* chronoports moving south over the Dnieper, heading in our general direction."

Two large icons appeared on her displays.

"Damn," she breathed and opened an audio link. "Hey, Raibert. We've got a problem."

"Why wouldn't we?" he sent without vocalizing. "What is it now?"

"Two chronoports moving south along the river."

"Well that's just *fantastic*. Can you deal with them?"

"Leave it to us. We'll take them out."

Elzbietá closed the channel and eased the TTV around until its nose pointed north.

"They're coming in low and slow," Philo reported. "Looks like they're trying to make a stealthy approach."

"For all the good that'll do them." Elzbietá switched the throttle to its lowest sensitivity setting and inched it to the side. A trickle of power energized the graviton thrusters, and the TTV maneuvered sideways out of the clouds. She spawned a line on the map that passed through both the TTV and the chronoports, then checked to make sure the residence wasn't anywhere near the line of fire.

"Mass driver charged and ready," Philo reported.

"Boy, are they in for a surprise." Elzbietá bit her lower lip and flexed her fingers over the controls. She checked her position relative to the governor's office. "Hey, Raibert?"

"Yeah?"

"Tell Klaus-Wilhelm to look out the window. We're about to put on quite a show."

"Setting self-replicators to fourteen generations," Philo said. "That should be just enough to liquefy an entire chronoport."

"How's your field of fire look?"

"Give me a little more altitude."

Elzbietá raised the omni-throttle, and the TTV levitated underneath the cloud cover.

"There. That's good." Philo reached for his controls, then glanced at her. "You know, we never covered this."

"Covered what?"

"Do you give the order to fire or do I just do it?"

"We're partners, Philo. You're in control of the weapons, which means the honor is all yours."

"All right!" He grinned inhumanly. "Adjusting precision gimbals. Opening hole in the shroud. And . . . fire!"

The one-ton projectile blasted out of the mass driver with

a boom that shook snow from trees and rattled every window pane within miles. It streaked through the air like a lambent line of fire and pierced a long, diagonal groove into the heart of the chronoport.

Variskin flickered and failed, and the payload detonated, releasing a deadly spray of weaponized microbots even as the head of the projectile punched out the other side, and water geysered up from the river.

The chronoport listed. A wing dipped down into the river, and water sprayed up behind it. One of the fusion thrusters sputtered, and the time machine spun on its vertical axis, slid across the water almost sideways, then crashed into the river bank in a fountain of soil, rocks, and twisted malmetal.

"*Hell* yeah!" Elzbietá cheered.

"Second shot loaded. Capacitors charging."

The unharmed chronoport banked hard, and its dual fusion thrusters lit under full power.

"Looks like someone doesn't like the odds anymore," Elzbietá noted.

"I'm detecting survivors making their way out of the crash."

"Not for long." She retracted the shroud, switched her throttle to the highest setting, and shoved it forward. Gravitons surged through the TTV's thrusters and it rocketed forward. "Strafe the crash site. We don't want anything getting close to the residence."

"Got it." Philo activated their trio of 45mm Gatling guns. The weapon pods moved dynamically across the prog-steel armor, clustered at the bottom of the craft, and snapped open.

Jonas Shigeki shoved a warped panel aside with a shout of pain and staggered out from under the wreckage. Blood drained from a wide gash across his forehead, and he limped through the gutted, roofless remains of the bridge and over mangled pieces of his crew.

He had no idea what just happened. A part of him knew he should have been horrified by the contorted bodies, parts of them still strapped into their seats, but there was no room for terror in his mind. Only stunned disbelief.

The attack had come with precious little warning. First a shout from the realspace navigator of a sudden scope echo near the clouds. And then the world became noise and light and a ship careening out of control.

A biting wind blew across his skin, and he rested a hand against the shattered front of the bridge. He leaned forward to catch his breath and lowered his head.

Someone called out from behind him, and he turned to see two distant silhouettes freeing themselves from the wreckage.

Survivors. There were other survivors.

Good.

And then he realized his hand felt unusually warm despite the chill.

He glanced down and gasped. A plague of rust-tinged drop-lets flowed over his skin. The warmth they provided became an itch that escalated into fierce burning as his skin melted off. The fluid spread rapidly.

He tried to smear the liquid across a jutting piece of debris, but then cried out. All he did was strip chunks off his own flesh that then expanded in spidery radial patterns. The fluid stripped flesh from bone and flowed up his arm, consuming more of his body by the second.

Jonas screamed and stumbled back until he splashed into a puddle, and his legs warmed uncomfortably. He looked down to find his boots submerged in rusty syrup up to the ankles. The outer layer of his boots dissolved, and then the meat around his bones floated off into the puddle.

His ankles gave out, and he collapsed, knees and hands sink-ing into the puddle. The all-encompassing burning climbed his arms and legs and then poured into his bloodstream. Ravenous microbots flowed through his body and proceeded to eat him alive from the inside out.

He wailed in terror and agony.

And then he fell silent, just a frozen man-shaped parody of oozing flesh that sank slowly into the deathly puddle. Life had completely left him before the first high-explosive rounds blew what was left of his body to pink mist.

An alarm whooped, and fifty-four German and Ukrainian veterans from Klaus-Wilhelm's security detail raced to their posi-tions without question and braced for attack.

Klaus-Wilhelm's gun had leapt into his hand the instant that solid beam of lightning streaked across the sky. The windows rattled, pens rolled off his desk, and picture frames fell outside his office. The beam had appeared to come from nowhere, but then a *massive* ship materialized in the sky where the attack had originated.

At first Klaus-Wilhelm thought it might be a dirigible because of its elongated shape and how it hovered in the air. He didn't know how he'd missed it initially, and he didn't get much time to ponder the question, because the craft darted across his view with a startling burst of speed and then vanished from sight.

Too much speed *far* too quickly for something that size.

"No aircraft can do that," he breathed.

"Not yet," Raibert corrected.

Klaus-Wilhelm spun around sharply, the gun still in his hand.

"Please don't." Raibert raised his hands. "I've honestly had it with people pointing guns at me."

"Ella, how are you doing?" Benjamin asked, holding a finger to one ear. He nodded, then said, "Understood, don't let it get away. We'll take care of things down here."

Did he have a whole radio set in his ear? That seemed impossible. But then, it wouldn't be the first impossible thing Klaus-Wilhelm had witnessed today.

"Mind explaining what I just saw?" he demanded.

"Of course, sir." Benjamin lowered his hand. "Our time machine, the *Kleio*, detected two enemy time machines approaching from the north. It shot one of them down. The second one fled, and the *Kleio* is now in pursuit."

"That massive thing"—Klaus-Wilhelm pointed out the window—"is your time machine?"

"Yeah." Raibert grinned. "Isn't she a beauty?"

"Kill the noise but keep everyone on guard," Klaus-Wilhelm ordered.

Anton nodded, picked up the phone, and dialed.

"Alarm off," he said, and the whooping stopped shortly afterward. "Yes, that's right. Don't send the stand-down order yet. And get me a radio in here—*now!*" He set the phone back on its receiver.

Klaus-Wilhelm nodded his approval, then turned back to his visitors with a grimace.

"You realize that even with that...*thing* of yours out there, you have to be insane, don't you? You *truly* expect me to believe any of this?"

"Yes, sir," Benjamin said. "I do."

"You claim to be my grandson from the future."

"Because it's true. I'm Klaus Schröder's firstborn."

"And you claim *this* is real." Klaus-Wilhelm held up the ring.

"It's the same one your wife is wearing right now, only a few decades older."

"Then how did you come to have it?"

"My father gave it to me so that I could propose to the woman of my dreams."

"She say no?"

"She's piloting the time machine."

"Of course she is." Klaus-Wilhelm said ironically. Then he stopped and nodded, remembering the inner strength of another woman who wore a ring just like the one in his hand. He glanced at the big man next to his supposed grandson. "So what's your story?"

"I'm a historian from the thirtieth century who specializes in ancient Greek and Roman civilizations and who currently inhabits a synthetic body from an alternative version of the thirtieth century because my real body was recycled. Oh, I'm also the one who recruited your grandson to help me save the universe from total annihilation by correcting a knot in time centered on an assassination in 1940."

"I see it was my mistake for asking," Klaus-Wilhelm grumbled.

"I'm surprised you actually told him all that," Benjamin flashed a crooked smile at Raibert.

"Well, I figured what the hell. You're going the super-honest route, so why not go all in?"

"Enough!" Klaus-Wilhelm barked, and the two men immediately shut up. He glanced out the window again at where the impossibly large and fast aircraft had appeared out of thin air to fire a weapon he'd never seen before. Then he looked down at the perfect "forgery" in his palm, and finally turned to and studied the man claiming to be his grandson.

There was more to Benjamin's assertion than just words. The man *did* bear a striking resemblance to his seventeen-year-old son, and Benjamin knew stories Klaus-Wilhelm had never told anyone. How could those be explained away?

How could *any* of it be explained away?

Klaus-Wilhelm stepped forward, stood directly in front of

Benjamin, and stared into his eyes. The same gray penetrating eyes his son Klaus had. He saw no doubt or deception in them, only a cool certainty from the man that he would eventually get his point across.

Satisfied, Klaus-Wilhelm nodded slowly, then held out the ring.

"I assume she'll want this back." He proffered the ring, and Benjamin took it and put it back in his pocket.

"Thank you, sir."

"So you need my help to save the universe?" he asked, taking a step back.

"That's right."

"Well, I'll give you one thing." He holstered his weapon. "You have the balls to be a Schröder."

"Thank you, sir." Benjamin smiled. "That means a lot coming from you. More than you may realize."

"All right, then." Klaus-Wilhelm crossed his arms as one of the security force jogged into the room and handed Silchenko a hand-held radio. "Why don't you start at the beginning? And this time, I think I'll stay quiet and let you finish."

Yulia von Schröder turned the basket on its side and spilled colored wooden blocks across the rag carpet.

"But why doesn't Daddy want to see us?" Veronika pouted from the couch as she clutched her favorite doll.

"Daddy *does* want to see you," Yulia answered with practiced patience, going down on one knee to start separating the blocks. "But he has to work late tonight."

"Again?"

Yulia glanced over her shoulder at the fair-haired, broad-shouldered man standing in the doorway behind her. Mikhail Lukovich Hrytosenki—onetime *Staršiná* Hrytosenki of the Ukrainian Insurgent Army and presently Uncle Misha to the von Schröder children—looked back at her and she smiled faintly. Then she turned back to her daughter.

"Yes, again, I'm afraid, *doroga*."

"Want Daddy!" Xristina half gurgled from her crib, then stuck a thumb in her mouth.

Yulia finished separating the blocks for her middle daughter, Diana, and stood. None of her daughters had paid much attention to the sweater she'd put on before leading the way to the safe room in the residence's basement. Despite the cheerful rag rugs, comfortable couches, and indirect lighting, the armored, windowless room had more in common with a bunker than a nursery, and for a very good reason. Now she reached behind her, touching the hard, angular shape at the small of her back, concealed by the loose sweater, and smiled at her daughters.

"Sometimes I wish he didn't have to work so much, too," she said warmly.

"Well, what if I told him to *stop* working so much?" Veronika asked.

"I don't think that would go over very well, *doroga*."

Yulia watched Diana begin selecting blocks and stacking them carefully. Her expression was intent and she stuck out just the tip of her tongue as she worked. Yulia shook her head, smile broadening, then glanced back at "Uncle Misha." He arched an eyebrow, and she nodded at the corridor behind him. He nodded back, stepped back out of the safe room, and swung the door shut behind him.

It made a very solid sound as it closed.

"Mommy?" Veronika said.

"Yes, *doroga*?"

"Does Daddy love us?"

Yulia frowned, then sat down on the couch next to Veronika.

"Now why would you ask a question like that?"

"Because he *clearly* loves working more than us," she proclaimed.

"Oh, but that's where you're wrong! The reason he works so hard is *because* he loves you."

Veronika frowned and beat her doll against the arm of the couch, looking thoroughly unconvinced by this argument.

Yulia put a gentle hand on her head and was about to continue when she stiffened and her eyes narrowed. The sudden, strident whoop was faint through the safe room's thick, armored walls, but she knew exactly what she was hearing.

CHAPTER THIRTY-FOUR

Ukraine
1958 CE

"WHAT DO WE DO, SIR?"

Nox hunkered down at the edge of the tree line north of the Provisional Residence and took stock of the situation. The half-liquefied remains of *Pathfinder-6* glared in his virtual vision like the hellspawn of Yanluo, and markers denoted each fallen comrade. None survived.

I failed, he thought and turned away from it. His mind existed within the mechanized shell of the combat frame, and he possessed no tears to shed for the fallen. But somehow that made the sting of his failure even worse.

How could he ever face Shigeki again? How could he ever face *himself* after this?

"Agent Nox?" one of the special operators asked.

"*Pathfinder-8* has drawn the TTV away," he heard himself say in a cool, even voice that flowed easily from the combat frame's hardware. "And we still have a job to do. So we do it."

"What are your orders, sir?"

"*Pathfinder-8* may not survive its engagement." Cold. So cold. Why were his words this cold? "We must take that into account and act accordingly."

"Meaning, sir?"

"We cannot know what the professor's objective inside is, and so we must be as thorough as possible. Anything and anyone in there could be important to his cause. Therefore, all of them must be eliminated."

There was an uncomfortable pause, and then someone said, "There are women and children in there."

"We take no chances. The residence will be swept clean."

No one else responded.

He passed his enhanced gaze across the surroundings. The two-story building sprawled out in three wings with the central, north-facing wing closest to his position. An iron fence surrounded the entire perimeter, and the alarm from earlier had sparked fresh activity in the form of guards and guard dogs patrolling from inside the fence.

"Take up these positions." He marked locations around the perimeter of the residence. "Wait for my orders."

The operators and drones spread out in both directions, sticking to the forest as they formed a loose circle around the building.

He checked *Pathfinder-8*'s position. The chronoport had successfully led the TTV hundreds of kilometers away to the east, but then damage indicators from the chronoport scrolled down his vision, and he knew his time was short. His troops wouldn't last long without the time machines backing them up.

The operators and drones all reached their containment positions. The sturdy stone construction of the mansion would provide a reasonable level of protection against their weapons, but anyone who tried to flee would be gunned down.

No one was getting away from this fight.

He activated his weapons, powered up his boosters, and faced the residence once more.

Landser Roderich Garlesch watched the road from the gate kiosk as he crouched on the concrete floor with his MP44 leveled across the stone counter. The floor made his knees ache, and he wished he had a blanket or a pillow to throw under them. He didn't know what that strange crack of lightning had been earlier—or that weird dirigible, for that matter!—but he assumed they were part of why there'd been no stand-down order.

Balthasar's ears perked up. Then they flattened, and the dog stood on his haunches. His lips curled back to reveal long rows of yellow teeth, and he threw an angry bark toward the darkening woods.

"What is it, boy?" Garlesch asked as he swung his machine pistol in the same direction. He squinted but didn't see anything besides dirt, snow, and trees beyond the road.

Balthasar barked again, then rumbled a long, throaty growl.

"You hear something?"

A shadow shimmered in the distant gloom, and Garlesch brought his machine pistol around to face it. He lined up his iron sights and rested a finger on the trigger. *Something* had Balthasar spooked, and he was almost certain he'd seen movement in the trees.

A strange noise caught his attention.

"Hold it." He sat up a little and strained his hearing. "Do you hear that?" he asked the other guards.

Balthasar started barking like mad, which made it hard to concentrate on anything else, but Garlesch could have sworn he'd heard something faint. Sort of like a small desk fan, he thought.

And then he heard it again. Only clearer and growing louder.

The guided grenade flew through the open window of the gate kiosk on tiny malmetal wings, propelled by a small malmetal propeller and shrouded in variskin. It dispersed a thick aerosol that filled the kiosk and poured out the open windows. When its reserves registered empty, the grenade exploded.

The incendiary aerosol ignited in a violent blue flame that cooked flesh and blackened rock. Roderich Garlesch died instantly, and Balthasar's charred, flaming corpse flew out the window and bounced limply down the road.

Flames whooshed out of windows across both floors of the residence. Screams and shouts pierced the air, and the alarm rose once more.

"Deploy Condors," Nox commanded.

The closest operator to his right took the bulky launcher off his back, stabilized it atop his shoulder, and then aimed it straight up. He fired the first Condor skyward, loaded the second rocket-shaped drone into the launcher, and sent it up after the first.

The Condors soared into the air, higher and higher until they reached the operator-programmed altitude. Then their aerodynamic outer shells split and unfurled to form trios of malmetal blades that lengthened and spun up to hold the altitude. Sniping rail-rifles actuated from the bottom of each drone and took aim on targets far, far below.

"Condors in position, sir."

"Provide me with targeting authority."

"Transferred." The permissives lit up in his virtual vision.

Nox unfolded from his crouch and stood straight and tall at the edge of the woods. Admin ground forces followed a two-tier philosophy of direct and indirect combat. Special operators tended to perform their duties indirectly, either by controlling drones or engaging their targets at long range, because, even with their armor and weaponry, they were still squishy, vulnerable humans. Drones and, more importantly, STANDs formed the direct-combat side of that same coin.

Nox locked his weaponry onto two men and their German Shepherd racing back toward the residence across a half-empty parking area.

He lit his shoulder and leg boosters, cleared the distance to the fence in four booster-assisted strides, and vaulted over it. The dog bolted straight for him teeth bared, and the two guards turned and brought their rifles up.

He tagged both men, and the Condors fired in perfect unison. Magnetically accelerated darts pierced the tops of their heads and didn't stop until they shot out their groins. The men flopped to the ground, and the dog leapt for him with flecks of drool flying from its jaws.

Nox snatched the dog out of the air by its face, rammed a long finger into one of its eye sockets, and crushed its skull. Bits of brain oozed out between his spindly, mechanical fingers, and he tossed the dead animal aside.

"Wolverines and Raptors forward. Operators suppress."

Sixteen drones charged out of the tree line, and the hypersonic cracks of rail-rifles ripped the air. More screams and shouts came from the residence, and primitive, sporadic fire chattered in response. A sniper rifle barked from the rooftop, and a Wolverine went down. One of the Condors swiveled its own weapon and punched a hole through the sniper's head.

Nox boosted across the parking area, smashed through a first-story window in a shower of glittering glass, and tackled a man cowering on the other side. The man wore all white with a white cap and a white apron, and they both hit the tiled floor of a room lined with metal ovens and refrigerators. Heavy pots and pans hung from the ceiling, clattering against each other, and half a dozen men and women in white fled to either side.

Nox jammed the barrel of his heavy rail-rifle down the man's throat and blew his brains out, then swung his other arm in a wide circle and swept the room with the incinerator. Pure blue flame shot out in a radiant arc that stripped flesh from bone, and the men and women collapsed screaming.

He boosted across the flame-spackled room, smashed shoulder first through the door—breaking it off its hinges—and found himself in a hallway lined with doors, some opened. A woman screamed at the sight of him, and he shot her through the heart. Gunfire rattled somewhere deeper inside the building. It might have been primitive, but there was a lot of it.

His sonic and infrared scopes identified which rooms were occupied. He kicked the doors down systematically and doused each room with flame that left charred corpses in his wake, not all of them adults. Smoke clouded the corridor when he finished, and he boosted deeper into the residence.

Rifles cracked from the left, and bullets zinged off his armor. Four men had toppled a heavy wooden table to form a makeshift barricade and fired steadily from behind it. He swiveled his boosters and retreated back into the hallway.

Even with the building ablaze and people dying left and right, these soldiers didn't panic, didn't run. Nox had expected the indigenes to break and flee from the residence, where his operators would gun them down in the open, but that didn't seem to be happening.

A quick status check showed half the drones had been taken out. Troubling. Dozens of indigenes had been killed already, civilian staff members fled before his approach, but the soldiers among them were working in teams, communicating effectively, responding quickly to each disaster.

This wasn't some motley security force. No, these men had seen combat and death before, and they stood their ground and fought against weapons and horrors they couldn't possibly understand. What could inspire them to fight and die against thirtieth-century weaponry?

He pushed the question aside, because in the end, it didn't matter.

He fired two grenades, and the projectiles flew around the bend. They detonated above the four soldiers and flayed them with twin showers of deadly shrapnel. He boosted into the junction.

If they'd formed a barricade *here*, then that meant there was something worth protecting behind it.

Or someone.

Good. I'm on the right track.

An alert popped up in his virtual vision, and he saw that *Pathfinder-8* had been lost with all hands.

Damn.

The TTV would be back in minutes, and when it arrived...

He felt the seconds trickling through his metallic fingers and boosted ahead with reckless speed. Someone had closed the door at the end of the passage, and he smashed through it and flew out into a huge foyer. Wide, curving stairs led up to a second-level balcony, and crystal chandeliers swayed under a high, vaulted ceiling.

Two waiting security troopers staged on the balcony with *Maschinengewehr* 42s caught him in a crossfire, and 7.62mm rounds pulverized his back. The individual jacketed slugs weren't that heavy, but between them, the belt-fed MG42s spat out forty every second. He fell forward under the sledgehammer impacts and skidded across the red carpet, damage indicators flashing along his back armor and incinerator. Malmetal flexed quickly to close the gaps and he rolled back upright.

More of the twentieth-century troopers knelt in an arch across the foyer, two of them pouring fire at him. Then the riflemen went prone and a third man, standing behind them, leveled something across his forearm. Nox's eyes would have widened in surprise, if he'd had any at the moment, as his sensors' warning flashed in his virtual vision. Then his combat frame's reflexes hurled him to the side as the Panzerfaust 250's warhead scorched past and a shaped charge capable of penetrating two hundred millimeters of tank armor blew out the foyer's outer wall behind him.

The Panzerfaust gunner dropped back, and the men who'd gone prone to avoid the backblast came back to their knees, pouring fire at their bizarre foe while he reloaded the reusable launcher with frantic speed. More machine-gun fire ripped at Nox, and he engaged his boosters. He flew across the floor toward the arch and the gunners tracked him, blasting a hurricane of divots from the polished marble. Rifle fire hammered him from in front, as well, but he reached the arch. He flew through it, taking out one of the riflemen with a malmetal knee as he passed, and dropped on the man with the Panzerfaust.

The force of the impact crushed his victim's ribs, and Nox ripped his head off. He hurled it at the second rifleman. The indigene was halfway to his feet, already rising, trying to bring his rifle to bear, when the hurled head struck with sufficient force to bowl him over. Nox dropped his rail-rifle's muzzle and shot the prone man, then staggered as still more fire ripped into him from the corridor directly ahead. More soldiers poured into the foyer behind him, and more rifles and *another* machine gun opened fire.

He launched a trio of grenades back into the foyer and engaged his boosters yet again. The men at the end of this corridor wouldn't be standing their ground with such determination if they weren't protecting something vital.

Yulia von Schröder knelt to one side of the safe room's armored door.

Her expression was stone and her blue eyes were frozen, but no colder than her heart as she listened to the thunder sweeping toward her and closed her ears to her daughters' terrified cries. The girls—especially Veronika—had clung to her desperately. For the first time in their lives, she'd screamed at them, actually *slapped* them, to *make* them obey her as she thrust them frantically into the storage cabinet, slammed the door behind them, and then heaved the bookcase against that door to jam it shut.

Now she crouched behind her improvised barricade of furniture, the .45 automatic from the holster under her sweater heavy in her hands, and waited.

Nox expanded part of his malmetal armor into an ablative shield on his forearm, waded into the rifle fire, brought up his rail-rifle, and cut down the three-man fire team with a single, precise burst. The remote sensors he'd deployed in his wake warned him more of the indigenes had charged through the arched passage opening behind him, and he triggered the grenades he'd left to keep the sensors company, killing at least six more of them.

He slammed into the wall at the end of the passage, taking the impact on his shield, reorienting as he saw the stairwell. A tall, fair-haired man opened fire from its foot, and more 7.92mm slugs whined and sparked from his shield. The combat frame's sensors reached out, and Nox snarled mentally as they probed the door behind that single rifleman. It was armored, and the wall into which it was set was reinforced cement sandwiched around a solid slab of armor.

"No!" Klaus-Wilhelm von Schröder cried.

Benjamin and Raibert turned toward him. The governor had the handheld radio to his ear. He'd taken personal command of the security force the instant the attack began, and his voice had been cold, clear, and calm, directing his men, steadying them in the face of the totally unanticipated horror. That voice was the true steely spine of the defense. The men at the other end of that radio *knew* that voice. Most of them had followed it straight into one side of Hell and out the other, and they *trusted* it. It had held them, carried them, and the ferocity of their response had stunned Benjamin. But now—

"No! *Yulia!*"

Silchenko had been crouched just inside the office door, directing the machine gunners on the landing outside it. Now he darted one look over his shoulder at Klaus-Wilhelm. His face went white and he exploded to his feet.

"Follow me!" he screamed to the men on the landing and sprinted down the smoke-choked stairs. The machine gunners and riflemen came to their feet, charging after him.

Klaus-Wilhelm was on the major's heels, but Raibert's hand shot out, locked on his arm, dragged him to a stop.

"Let go!" Klaus-Wilhelm snapped.

"Sir, we need you alive. It's—"

"Let go!" Klaus-Wilhelm jammed the Magnum's muzzle against Raibert's forehead.

"No," Raibert said flatly. "And I don't keep my brain there, anyway!"

"No?" Klaus-Wilhelm's eyes bored into him like twin augers. Then his wrist turned, the muzzle pressed his own temple, and he bared his teeth. "Well I *do*. So if you 'need me alive,' you fucking let go *right now!*"

Raibert's eyes widened, but no one could possibly have misunderstood. He hesitated for one beat of the heart he no longer possessed, then opened his hand.

"All right, but in that case, stay *behind* me," he grated, and charged out the door with Klaus-Wilhelm and his grandson right behind.

Nox's sensors warned him that every surviving indigene within their reach was suddenly charging after him, and triumph glowed deep within. He'd been right. What he was looking for had to be on the other side of that armored door!

The lone rifleman emptied his magazine, slammed in another, and fresh fire pounded the combat frame. None of it missed, but the STAND's shield shrugged it off, and Nox triggered his incinerator. The tsunami of blue flame enveloped the single defender, and his boosters carried him down the stairs.

The safe room door shuddered under the force of some unimaginable blow.

Yulia drew a deep breath and shut out her daughters' cries. Shut out everything except that door and the weapon in her hands.

It shuddered again. And then it slammed open and a nightmare given physical form stormed through it. She'd never seen—never imagined—anything like that skeletal, metal...shape, but she knew Mikhail Hrytosenki was dead. That was the only way Misha would have let something like that past him with her girls behind him.

And it was the only way it was getting past her, as well.

The heavy, familiar weight of the .45 rose in her hands. Her target was barely five feet away, and she squeezed the trigger.

The combat frame's head twitched sideways as the first 230-grain jacketed slug smashed into it at 830 feet per second. Seven more followed. They couldn't penetrate the armored carapace, but two more of Nox's sensor nodes disappeared. He cursed mentally at the fresh damage and turned toward the source of those slugs.

The woman who'd fired them calmly ejected the empty magazine, slapped in another, let the slide slam forward, and raised the pistol in a two-hand grip.

The security force responded to Silchenko's command. Dispersed teams concentrated on the foyer, dashing through the residence's smoke-filled corridors with reckless speed. Two three-man fire teams from the East Wing reached the foyer first and raced into the passage.

✦ ✦ ✦

Nox snarled in fury as he realized he'd been wrong. The stupid indigenes hadn't been protecting the professor after all.

He wheeled, darted back out the broken door, just in time to be greeted by a tornado of rifle fire and the thunder of primitive hand grenades. Some of the rifle slugs evaded his shield and damaged the synthetic muscles in his right leg, and the grenades' blast staggered him, but their fragments bounced uselessly and his rail-rifle swept the stairs above him, slaughtering the three men who'd fired at him. He launched a trio of grenades that flew up, past the top of the stair, bounced down the passage and turned the three-man team still racing toward him into bloody bits and pieces of what had once been human beings.

"Sir, the TTV is back! We're taking fire! We're—"

The roar of the TTV's Gatling guns eclipsed the cacophony around him, and operators and their drones vanished from his virtual vision, icons disappearing with the speed of summer lightning. He would have grimaced if he'd still had a face, but instead he boosted up the stairs and went rocketing back the way he'd come.

Riflemen opened fire as he reemerged into the foyer. Their shots ricocheted from his shield, but another Panzerfaust flew toward him. This one smashed squarely into him, and the explosion blew off his incinerator arm and triggered more alerts in his virtual vision. He tumbled sideways, fired boosters to compensate for his spin, and landed with two feet and his remaining hand on the floor. How many heavy weapons did these people *have*?

Rifle rounds *snicked* through the air, screaming ricochets bounced off marble walls, and he opened fire with his rail-rifle and charged forward.

The wall to his right exploded inward under the TTV's fire, and he dashed into the midst of the defenders, using them for cover against its guns. He ripped one man's arm off, grabbed him by the neck, and held him up as an additional makeshift shield as he tore through the others with his rail-rifle.

More soldiers poured into the foyer, and Nox knew he couldn't kill them all. Not before *they* killed *him*. But he didn't want to. Not anymore. There was only one man he wanted to kill now— only one life that *belonged* to him—and he would claim it before death took him.

He crushed the windpipe of the corpse he held, threw it at the indigenes charging toward him, then boosted toward the foyer staircase. They must have decoyed him into that basement for a reason, and that meant the governor had to be behind them.

And if that was where the governor was, so was *Raibert*.

He fired his boosters at full power, soaring over the defenders still funneling into the foyer, and triumph flared within him as his sensors picked the unmistakable signature of an Admin synthoid out of the knot of men headed down the staircase toward him.

Raibert saw the combat frame's trajectory curve, arcing toward him, and raised his right arm. Anti-synthoid rounds erupted from his splayed palm, Benjamin ripped out short bursts from the MP44 one of the fallen guard force would never need again from two stairs above him, Klaus-Wilhelm's Magnum thundered, and a half dozen of his surviving troopers emptied their MP44s.

Nox staggered under the assault. The anti-synthoid rounds punched holes through his chest armor, ricocheted through internal systems. More fire from behind tore into his weakened rear armor, and more systems blinked abruptly off-line.

His boosters failed. He slammed to the floor, heaved back to his knees, and fired at Raibert. But the rail-rifle's round only dented the woven prog-steel under the synthoid's coat, and still more rifle fire ripped into the combat frame.

He collapsed on his face, juddered as he tried to get back up...then lay still.

Klaus-Wilhelm reloaded his empty revolver.

Nox scrolled through his active systems. There weren't very many of them, but he saw that the chronoton telegraph was still functional.

Good. He could perform one last duty before he died.

He loaded a simple but important text message into the telegraph's spool, keyed the transmit command.

I'm sorry, sir, he thought as the message pulsed outward through time.

One of his remote sensors had somehow survived, still fed his virtual vision. He watched through it, trapped in the inert prison of his combat frame, as Klaus-Wilhelm von Schröder pushed through the circle of troopers around him. The governor's face was like hammered iron. He went to one knee beside the frame, and Nox watched him shove the muzzle of that enormous, archaic, *primitive* revolver into a gash in his armored back.

And then the Provisional Governor of Ukraine squeezed the trigger once...twice...*three* times—

He emptied the cylinder, and somewhere in the process, one of those massive rounds delivered 1,100 foot-pounds of energy to the combat frame's brain case and Special Agent James Nox ceased to exist forever.

She couldn't see.

She moaned deep in her throat as she tried to move. She couldn't. She pushed weakly with her hands, trying to stand— trying at least to crawl—but only her right hand responded and she swallowed a strangled scream as the attempt twisted the shattered vertebrae in her spine.

She tried to call their names, but her voice was too faint for them to hear her over the crackle of flames. She—

"Lie still, *Liebling*," a beloved voice said. She'd never heard it sound that way. Never heard it waver, threaten to crack and fail.

"K-Klaus-Wilhelm?" she managed to whisper.

"I'm here, *meine Geliebte*."

She felt his hands, felt them lifting her head, resting it in his lap. He was sitting on the floor beside her, a corner of her flickering brain realized, and she remembered the summer nights he'd sat on the rattan couch on the residence balcony with her head in his lap while they watched the brilliant stars overhead. His lips brushed her bloody forehead, and *her* lips twitched in a tiny smile. But then she stiffened.

"The...girls, *kohanij*?" she whispered. "Are...are...the girls—"

Her voice failed, and she gasped in anguish as she tried once again to push herself upright.

"Lie still," her husband said again, softly, serenely. The quaver had left his voice, and he stroked her hair. "The girls are fine, *Liebling*. You saved them. They're fine."

"Good..."

The single word ghosted out of her, softer than a sigh, and he kissed her forehead again.

"You can go now," that beloved voice told her gently, lovingly. "You can go now, my love."

"Love...y—" she breathed.

❖   ❖   ❖

Klaus-Wilhelm von Schröder's eyes were dry as he cradled his wife's bloody, broken, mutilated body in his arms. He kissed her forehead one final time, then straightened, still holding her.

"Governor, let me have her!"

He looked up at the man named Raibert—his once fierce eyes stunned and broken—and Raibert leaned closer.

"If I can get her to the *Kleio* in time, we can still save her!" Raibert said urgently. "The . . . the medical facilities in my ship can heal her completely if I can get her there quickly enough!"

Klaus-Wilhelm looked at him, then past him, to the shattered storage cabinet, the scorched, blackened, carbonized flesh that had once been his three daughters, and then back at Raibert.

"And can you save her daughters?"

His voice was flat, level, unshadowed by any emotion, and Raibert's expression quailed before its terrible emptiness.

"No," he said softly. "No, I'm . . . afraid not. Their wounds are . . ."

His voice trailed off.

"Then let her go, too," Klaus-Wilhelm said, and now all the pain in the universe was in his voice. "I won't bring her back to face that. Let her go knowing she saved them. That they're still alive."

Raibert shifted, opened his mouth, but Benjamin put a hand on his shoulder. He looked at the younger Schröder, and Benjamin shook his head ever so slightly. Raibert hesitated for a moment longer, then drew one of the deep breaths a synthoid didn't truly need.

"Yes, sir," he said gently.

A long silence passed, minutes perhaps, and then someone knelt by Klaus-Wilhelm's side. He looked up to find Benjamin next to him, and he knew in that moment they truly were of the same blood. He saw the tears in the man's eyes, the terrible understanding that could come only from someone who *recognized* the four dead people in this room. Who'd *known* them.

He saw the recognition . . . and the grief.

"You really are my grandson, aren't you?" he asked, knowing—and *believing*—the answer he would receive.

"Yes, sir. I am."

"And you need my help."

"Sir, that can wait. Take some time to . . ." he trailed off.

"No." Klaus-Wilhelm looked down. He stroked Yulia's hair one last time, then set her gently aside, stood up, and faced the others. Faced Benjamin, Raibert, Silchenko, and the grief-stricken members of his security force who knew they'd all failed to protect the four most important people in their governor's world.

"The two of you came here to ask for my assistance," he said.

"That's right," Raibert replied.

"And these *monsters* who came here and killed so many of us!" He drew a deep, shuddering breath. "Who *slaughtered* my wife and children with no provocation! Do you stand against them?"

"Yes, sir. We do."

"Then this is not a difficult decision for me to make." His nostrils flared as he laid his palm on the revolver holstered at his side. "Everything I have and everything I am is at your disposal."

He looked to Anton, and the Ukrainian bowed his head ever so slightly.

"Sir, I'm with you, and I'm sure the rest of the men are, too." His voice was hammered iron, and the soldiers behind him nodded in agreement. Klaus-Wilhelm heard the murmur of their voices, recognized the fury and the determination.

"We'll follow you anywhere," Silchenko grated, looking down at the Gräfin's body through tears of his own. "To the gates of Hell, if that's where you lead us."

Klaus-Wilhelm marveled, not for the first time, at how tough his men were. A monstrous mechanical *thing* out of time had just kicked their teeth in. They had every right to collapse, to at least demand time to recover. But they hadn't done that—not *his* men! They only looked back at him, the fury crackling in their eyes, ready to find the ones responsible for this and do some kicking of their own.

"Thank you." Klaus-Wilhelm von Schröder told them softly, reaching out, laying one hand on Silchenko's shoulder and gripping hard. "Thank you all, *meine Kameraden.*"

Then he turned to Benjamin, and his voice was the same unwavering iron as Silchenko's had been.

"What would you have us do?"

CHAPTER THIRTY-FIVE

DTI Chronoport *Pathfinder-Prime*
non-congruent

THE MESSAGE PUNCHED CSABA SHIGEKI IN THE GUT, AND THE beginnings of tears stung his eyes. He struggled to read the whole thing, despite how short it was.

The message from Nox read: TTV engaged in Ukraine, 1958. Pathfinder-6 destroyed. Pathfinder-8 destroyed. TTV combat capabilities HEAVILY upgraded. Ground team eliminated. No extraction required.

Jonas was...dead? And Nox, too?

Shigeki released his harness and floated out of the seat. He squeezed his eyes shut and put a hand to his face.

Was this true? Was his son really dead? But how could that be? How had the TTV taken down *two* chronoports at once? How in Yanluo's burning realms was the professor *doing* this to them?

"Shall we move the picket in response to this?" Durantt asked, then turned and saw the director. "Sorry, sir. I didn't...I can take care of things here if you like."

"No, that won't be necessary, Captain." Shigeki wiped at his eyes, took a deep breath, and shoved his grief down into the deepest pit of his mind. He knew he could only contain it there for a short time, but he locked an iron door closed behind it and pulled himself over to a linear map of the timeline.

"This can wait, sir," Durantt said quietly, urgently.

"No, it can't. We need to stop him. *Nothing* else matters. Vassal?"

"I stand ready to assist you, Director."

"Analyze the situation. Where is he heading next?"

"Assuming Professor Kaminski has made successful contact with Governor von Schröder, his most likely course of action will be to proceed farther up the timeline, possibly to the Event itself. Where precisely, I cannot say."

"Then we must be ready for him." Shigeki selected several icons representing the chronoports and began shifting them. "All chronoports will proceed downstream, but we'll take it slow. The professor might already be on the move, and we need to be able to spot him as we reposition. That goes for all chronoports except the ones in 1920. Have them rendezvous with the center of the picket at maximum speed."

"Are you sure it's wise to leave that part of the timeline unobserved?" Durantt asked.

"I am *through* playing games with this man," Shigeki spat. Then he sucked in air, slamming his control back into place. "The next time we spot the TTV, I mean to *end* this. We are hitting him with *everything* we have, and in order to do that, we start grouping up *now*."

"Understood, sir." Durantt spun to face the bridge crew. "Telegraph, send out the orders."

"Yes, sir. Spooling the first message now."

Shigeki took a few ragged breaths, trying to contain the fire consuming him from within. He needed to remain calm, composed. Giving in to rage wouldn't bring Jonas back, and it might lead to the loss of so much more. He imagined the professor before him as the small, helpless man he'd spoken to in that DTI cell. It would have been so easy back then to wrap his fingers around that scrawny throat and choke the life out of him. And then to condemn his connectome to a one-way abstraction where he would writhe for the rest of eternity in absolute torment.

But that was just fantasy, and Shigeki forced himself to come to terms with the grim reality. Kaminski was pressing ever closer to his goal, and if he succeeded, everything was lost. His son wouldn't simply be dead. He'd have never existed in the first place.

I have to stop you. No matter the price.

But despite what was at risk, this was no longer just about universes. No, this was *personal* now. A personal duel between him and the professor. A battle of wills and wits. He'd made the mistake of showing the man mercy once, but perhaps that private history could be leveraged to his advantage . . .

He wondered.

"Once you've sent out my orders, Captain," he said with a dark, humorless smile, "I have one more telegraph for you."

"To whom, sir?"

"To the TTV."

"Sir?" Durantt's face scrunched up in confusion.

"You're going to have every chronoport blast this message out at maximum power. Wherever and whenever the professor is, I want him to hear it."

"If those are your orders, sir. But we'll have to disable the encryption on the telegraphs. And even then, there's no guarantee the TTV will be able to translate the underlying binary in our transmission."

"That won't be a problem." Shigeki opened part of their twentieth-century archive and held the patterns above his palm. "I know a code they'll recognize."

The TTV sped into the past, and its newly expanded crew prepared for what was to come.

Benjamin had to admit he was impressed by how his grandfather and the twenty-two survivors of the security force took finding themselves on a time machine in stride. Sure, they gawked at their surroundings, marveled at how the medical caskets healed their wounds, and yelled the first time they rode a counter-grav tube, but they quickly settled down and focused on the business at hand. He wondered if *anything* could faze these men for long.

"No," Benjamin said firmly.

"I honestly don't see what the problem is," Raibert countered.

"I'm not telling my grandfather to put those abominations on."

Raibert peered into the bin. "What's wrong with them?"

"They're not appropriate."

"But they can't see the displays without them." He jostled the bin full of pink and purple swirly interface glasses.

"I know, and I thought of that, too." Benjamin pushed the bin back. "Now put those things down somewhere and let me handle this."

"But—"

"I've *got* this." He patted the synthoid on the shoulder. "You can bring the earbuds, but *no* glasses."

Raibert frowned, glanced at the bin full of the interface glasses he'd ordered, then set the bin down next to the period-specific gear Elzbietá was laying out. He grabbed the small bag full of interface earbuds out of the bin. The three of them took a tube up and met Klaus-Wilhelm and Anton on the bridge.

"Sorry about the delay," Benjamin told his grandfather as he unfolded a map of 1940s Germany and laid it out over the command table.

"Seriously?" Raibert complained. "We're using paper now?"

"It works just fine." He smoothed out the map, took out a pencil, and looked across the table at his grandfather. "Now, what can you tell us?"

"This is what I know. During the Battle of Sedan, from May tenth to May fifteenth, Hitler stayed in his field bunker here." Klaus-Wilhelm stabbed a finger against the map. "Felsennest, near the city of Bad Münstereifel. In the early morning of May sixteenth, he took a motorcade from his field bunker into the city, then north to Cologne." Klaus-Wilhelm slid his finger along the route. "There, he boarded his private train for a trip back to Berlin. Teams of SS scouted out the whole route the day before and had nodal detachments spread along it. I don't know their exact locations, but they would have been placed to cover every station and junction, as well as each bridge."

His fingertip slid along the rail line.

"Each detachment consisted of at least one twelve-man squad, but most of the reaction forces were larger, closer to platoon strength. The one that matters, though, is here"—the moving fingertip tapped—"just east of the city of Stendal: a single squad responsible for guarding a bridge over the Elbe River."

"And that's where the assassins blew the bridge," Benjamin noted.

"Correct. Around noon the same day, they blew the supports on the bridge, and the train ran off the rails and into the river. Assassins gunned down every last soul who made it to shore, and not a single person survived. But here's the curious thing. As far as anyone knows, the assassins *never* attacked the SS security detail itself. That security detail was stationed in a farmhouse near the bridge, and every man in it was simply found dead after the fact."

"So they *were* attacked," Raibert said, cocking one eyebrow with a puzzled expression.

"No, they weren't. Or not with any conventional weapons, at least."

"Then what killed them?" Raibert asked. He didn't look any less puzzled.

"It's impossible for me to say for certain," Klaus-Wilhelm admitted. "There was a great deal of honest confusion at the time, and even attempts at secrecy. I've heard just about every conflicting version you can imagine, and the exact nature of what happened was never made public. But there *were* rumors—solid ones, from people I know and trust, who aren't prone to exaggeration—that the security detail was killed by 'unnatural' means."

"Unnatural?" Benjamin asked. "Can you be more specific?"

"Yes, but I honestly never believed it myself until I saw all of this." He indicated the time machine they were flying in. "Even now I'm not too sure, given how bizarre it seemed. But according to my sources, they were *fused* with their surroundings."

"Fused?" Benjamin echoed.

"Corpses halfway imbedded in walls or partially sunk into the ground, their lungs filled solid."

"I never heard any of that before." Benjamin scratched the back of his neck. "How about you?"

Elzbietá shook her head.

"I'm not surprised." Klaus-Wilhelm snorted. "My source said the nature of what happened was suppressed and all evidence destroyed to prevent any sort of 'supernatural' connection to Hitler's fate."

"And you believe this?" Benjamin pressed.

"Why wouldn't I? I'm standing in a time machine talking to a grandson who hasn't been born yet. My capacity to believe the unusual has greatly increased."

"Okay. Fair point."

"But still"—Elzbietá shook her head doubtfully—"people sucked into walls?"

"Huh." Raibert remarked suddenly. He crossed his arms and grimaced at the map.

The rest of them turned and looked at the synthoid.

"Something on your mind?" Benjamin asked.

"Well, it just occurred to me that what he described could have come from a chronoton impeller failure. After all, an impeller allows regular matter to take on a different phase state—namely the weakly interacting properties of chronotons—which allows the time machine to phase through time in the first place. It has the added effect of placing us out of phase with the entire Earth. I mean, we're phasing through regular matter right now, so it's not out of the question that, just for argument's sake, debris from an exploding impeller could have the effect he described."

Benjamin, Klaus-Wilhelm, and Anton exchanged confused looks.

"A damaged time machine might have killed the security detail," Elzbietá translated.

"Then why didn't he say so?" Benjamin asked.

"I *did*," Raibert replied.

"Does it really matter how they died?" Benjamin asked. "It's more important that they *shouldn't* have."

"Agreed," Klaus-Wilhelm stated. "If your goal is to put the timeline back and save this universe, then the security squad has to be in position to prevent the assassination."

"Or a group of substitutes," Elzbietá added, and Anton gave her a curt nod.

"We'll play whatever role you need us to," he said, and Benjamin heard the conviction in his voice. Anton and Klaus-Wilhelm might not have understood *technically* why this particular event in the past needed to be changed, but they didn't need to. Nor did they seem interested in the details. The attack on the Provisional Residence had told them who they stood beside. The crew of the *Kleio* had earned their trust, and they accepted the more esoteric aspects of their new mission with the faith of believers forged in the crucible of battle.

"I think that's going to be necessary," Raibert said. "If there really was a time drive explosion or something like it, then the timeline in that area has been scarred. It might be impossible to save the security team."

"Will merely stopping the assassination be enough?" Benjamin asked. "If we're right, then the security team was supposed to live through this."

"I know," Raibert sighed and leaned over the map. "Look, all we can do is get the Event back as close to the original as we can, and that means saving everyone on that train, including the mass-murdering tyrant. If we're right, that *should* bring the

Event close enough to the original for the Knot to unravel and for the timeline to heal."

"The sword that cuts the knot," Benjamin intoned. "I hope you're right. We're going to be adding a whole new set of variables just by being there."

"I know, but my gut tells me this is it. The information we have is as good as it's going to get, and we've already had too many close calls with Shigeki's goons. It's time for us to end this."

"Professor?"

"Yes, what is it, Kleio?"

"I have received a chronoton telegraph addressed to you."

"You *what*?"

"Is someone else speaking?" Klaus-Wilhelm asked.

"Oh, right." Raibert tossed the bag of earbuds onto the table. "There. Take your pick."

Klaus-Wilhelm peered into the bag, then plucked out a single earbud and scrutinized it.

"You stick them in your ears," Benjamin said. "Just think of them as very small radios."

"All right." Klaus-Wilhelm and Anton inserted the devices.

"Okay, Kleio." Raibert planted fists on hips. "Now what's this about a telegraph for me?"

"It is exactly as I said, Professor. I have received a chronoton telegraph addressed to you. The signal appears to have originated upstream of our current coordinates. Possibly from or around the year 1950. More than that, I cannot say."

"Was it sent from an Admin chronoport?"

"I believe so, Professor."

"Then how did they suddenly learn SysGov telegraph binary?"

"They did not. The message was sent using Morse code."

"Huh." Raibert's eyebrows shot up. "That's actually sort of clever of them. Who sent it?"

"The person sending the telegraph is identified as Director Csaba Shigeki."

"So, Shigeki finally wants to have a chat, huh?" Raibert grinned and rubbed his hands together. "I guess blowing up three of his chronoports got his attention. Well, let's hear what he has to say. Kleio, synthesize the message into voice, and autotranslate it for our guests."

"Playing now."

"Professor Raibert Kaminski of the Consolidated System Government, this is Director Csaba Shigeki of the System Cooperative Administration. I hope you will indulge me for the moment and allow us to set aside those titles, for this is a personal message from one very determined man to another.

"First, I must acknowledge your success in eluding my forces so far. You have frustrated us with your tenacity and ingenuity, and are to be commended for your efforts. But you must also realize that the net we have cast is tightening around you. With each small victory of yours, you shed more light on your intentions, and while you have damaged us, we retain a force of overwhelming power compared to your one, small ship.

"Second, I must also acknowledge why you are fighting us. You truly believe in your cause, and I respect that. You wish to restore your home, your reality, and I could very easily see myself doing the same thing if I were in your position. But I am not. In order for your world to live, mine must die, and that is a result I will not allow.

"Because, Professor, as much as you are fighting to let your SysGov live, I am fighting so that my world, my way of life—indeed, my *family*—will not die. You are the existential threat to everything I hold dear, and you must realize only one of us will survive this war we are waging across time.

"But there is another way, Professor. Let us acknowledge that we have both suffered. You lost your body, and now I have lost my son. But this needn't continue. These grievances can be set aside. I showed you mercy before. I spared you from the punishment our laws demanded, and now I offer you mercy once more. More importantly, I offer you peace.

"Cease your attempts to disrupt the timeline and return to the thirtieth century with me, not as a prisoner but as a partner. Let us stop this madness before either of us loses anything or anyone else. With your technology and my resources, surely we can find another way. Surely there must be some solution to this problem where both our worlds can survive. We have over a thousand years to find it, after all.

"I ask you, sincerely, to give my offer serious consideration. This conflict of ours need not end badly. I await your response."

"Message ends, Professor," Kleio said.

The occupants of the bridge looked around at one another.

"That was unexpected," Elzbietá said quietly.

"Yeah, tell me about it," Raibert replied.

Doubt suddenly gnawed at Benjamin's mind, and he wondered if, just perhaps, there really was another way. If they succeeded, Elzbietá wouldn't exist anymore. He'd thought he'd come to terms with that—win or lose, she wouldn't be there to know it—but Shigeki's words filled him with doubt. What if that didn't have to be?

Even Raibert seemed to be having a similar moment of reflection brought on by the unexpected olive branch. It was a dubious olive branch to be sure, and one that brought with it tremendous risk, but shouldn't they at least consider it? Everyone on the bridge seemed to be thinking the same thing, or at the very least considering it.

Everyone, that was, except for Graf Klaus-Wilhelm von Schröder.

"Was that from the bastard in charge?" asked the man who had just lost his wife and three of his four children.

"Yes, sir," Benjamin said. "That's him."

"Good." He smiled without joy. "Then in that case, I have a few words I'd like to share with him."

"Telegraph incoming from *Pathfinder-2*. They relayed it from a source downstream. Looks like it's a response from the TTV, Director."

"That certainly was quick," Durantt commented.

"Let's have it." Shigeki inhaled deeply and waited.

"Sir . . ." the telegraph operator began. "Uhh, sir? I'm not sure how to read this."

"Then show me."

"Yes, sir."

The message appeared in his virtual vision and read: Fick Dich und das Pferd, auf dem Du her geritten bist.

"What the hell am I looking at?" Shigeki demanded.

"Unknown, sir. It appears to be gibberish."

"Vassal?"

"Director, the message is written in a form of German consistent with the twentieth century."

"Can you translate?"

"Yes, Director."

"Then what does it say?"

"'Fuck you and the horse you rode in on,'" Vassal read with deadpan delivery.

Shigeki sucked in a sharp breath. Captain Durantt and the rest of the bridge crew didn't say a word, though a few of them turned in their seats to catch a glimpse of his reaction.

"Well," he finally said after a long, fuming silence. "Then that's that. Can you trace the signal's origin?"

"I have the raw chronometrics from *Pathfinder-2*, but it appears that a layer of noise has been added to the signal to mask the point of origin. This suggests a very fine level of control of the telegraph's—"

"Yes yes, *thank* you. That will be all."

"Orders, sir?" Durantt asked.

"My orders remain the same, Captain. The next time we spot his ship, we gather our full force and crush him."

"Here's the gear we'll be using." Benjamin gestured across tables laden with trench coats, shirts, trousers, boots, gloves, gas masks, helmets, submachine guns, grenades, magazines, and one Panzerschreck rocket launcher. Everyone had gathered next to the *Kleio*'s printers to arm up for the coming battle.

Klaus-Wilhelm picked up one of the black SS trench coats.

"You know," he said softly. "I've killed a lot of people wearing these. It'll feel strange putting one on."

"I can certainly understand that, sir," Benjamin said.

"It was uncomfortable then, too." He rubbed his thumb over the runic lightning bolts on the collar. "I was a supporter of Hitler's before the war, much to the disappointment of my parents. They never thought much of the 'Austrian corporal.' I always found Nazi populism—and *especially* their anti-Semitism—repugnant, but I also grew up in a humiliated, impotent nation torn apart by civil strife. Hitler's promise to restore domestic peace and rebuild Germany to its rightful place in the world...appealed strongly to me."

"You weren't the only one, sir. And you never hid that from your children or your grandchildren." Klaus-Wilhelm looked at him sharply, and Benjamin looked back steadily. "I know exactly when you recognized how wrong you'd been...and in both of 'my' universes, you took a stand against it. Not only that, you taught your son and your daughters and your *grandson*"—their eyes locked—"to stand for what they believed in. What they knew was right. At the end of the day, that's not so bad a legacy, *Großvater*."

Klaus-Wilhelm looked at him for several seconds, then exhaled.

"Perhaps I wasn't so bad a fellow after all, if I could raise a grandson like you," he said softly, and squeezed Benjamin's shoulder for just a moment. Then he drew a deep breath.

"I take it these aren't like the originals," he said in a brisker tone, holding up the trench coat.

"They're not," Benjamin agreed with a thin smile. "They're camouflaged body armor."

"The uniforms have a prog-steel weave inside," Elzbietá continued. "Think of it like a flak jacket, only much, *much* better. Gloves and boots, too. The helmets have a solid prog-steel layer underneath. Even if you're hit and the armor is damaged, it can adapt and repair itself."

"These gas masks look a little different from the ones I remember," Klaus-Wilhelm observed, setting the coat down. "The front is the same, but the rest doesn't match."

"We made a conscious decision to change that." Elzbietá picked up one of the masks. "Admin drones and special operators have very accurate weapons controlled by sophisticated sensors. We're pretty sure they'll be able to pick up the armor under the uniforms, and if there's a chink in the defenses, they can see it—and *hit* it—at extremely long ranges, so we extended the gas masks to include hoods to protect the back of the head and neck. Every part of it has an armor weave, and yes, as an added bonus, it still serves as a gas mask."

"Remember, if the Admin shows up, gas masks go on," Benjamin said. "There's no point wearing all this armor if your face and head are exposed."

"But we still have to fight back," Anton protested. "I've always had trouble shooting with one of those on."

"Not with my design, you won't." Elzbietá handed him one. "Try it."

Anton frowned at the mask, then fitted the hood over his head and pulled the goggles and respirator into place.

"What? But I can see perfectly out of this!" He waved his hand in front of his face, then around to parts where a traditional gas mask obstructed his field of vision. "I can see right through the mask!"

"We equipped each mask with what you can think of as a camera and color television to allow you to see normally out of them."

"There's a camera *and* a television inside each mask?" Anton peeled it off and turned it around in his hands.

"And radios, too," Elzbietá added.

"But where are they? And how are they so *light*?"

"The future's awesome," Raibert remarked with a casual shrug. "What can I say?"

"They're also linked together via a computer network," Elzbietá continued, "so if one of you can see a target, it will be highlighted for all of you. And they'll also help you see past the camouflage the Admin uses."

"What about the weapons?" Klaus-Wilhelm picked up an MP40 machine pistol.

"They may look the same as the guns you're used to," Benjamin began, "but they're made of better materials and have tighter tolerances. The feed won't jam, even if you pull on the magazine. It's also substantially more accurate."

Klaus-Wilhelm selected a magazine, shoved it in, and yanked on it. It stayed ramrod straight, without even a quiver, and he nodded in satisfaction before he pulled it back out and set it down with the others.

"Half of these have a red stripe down the side. What's that mean?"

"Ah. Right." Benjamin picked up an unmarked magazine. "This is a regular thirty-two-round magazine. Nothing special about it. If the Admin hasn't shown up, this is what we use. It's historically accurate." He set it down and picked up one with a red stripe. "*This* one, on the other hand, can kill a twentieth-century tank, so it should work on just about anything the Admin throws at us. The bullets can also make limited self-correction, so they can turn near misses into hits."

"The bullets seek their targets?" Anton picked up one of the red magazines.

"To a limited degree, yes," Elzbietá said.

"But the straighter your shot, the harder they hit," Raibert warned. "They shed less kinetic energy that way. So remember to aim the way you always have."

Benjamin sidestepped along the table's edge and picked up a grenade.

"Unmarked grenade," he said. "Standard Model 24 potato masher, just like the originals. The only difference is the fuse and casing are better. These won't go off unless you arm the ten-second fuse." He set it down and picked up one with a red stripe. "*This*, however, is basically a guided missile you throw. High yield and very dangerous. There's no need to arm it, and it does come with built-in friend-or-foe detection. Just throw it at high-priority targets like enemy STANDs."

"What's a STAND?" one of the soldiers a few rows back asked.

"The big, scary skeletal things," Raibert replied. "They zip around really fast and carry a lot of guns. Can't miss 'em."

"And the Panzerschreck?" Klaus-Wilhelm asked. "I see it has multiple red stripes."

"Hands off." Raibert strode up to the table and pointed down at the rocket launcher. "This one's mine. No one touch it. It's dangerous."

"What's so special about it?"

"These are canisters of weaponized self-replicators." Raibert tapped a rack with two 88mm rockets, both almost as long as his arm. "They'll eat anything and anyone they hit, and they'll keep making more of themselves and spreading until their generational count runs out. This one weapon, fired at the wrong target with the wrong setting, could end our entire mission. So no. The only person I trust with this thing is me."

"But just in case, we added these small numbered dials." Benjamin indicated the dial near the fins on both rockets. "The number selected determines the yield on an exponential scale."

"Which no one but me should even *think* about touching," Raibert stressed, pointing a stern finger at Benjamin. "Got that?"

"I got it. But if you're"—Benjamin tried to pick a good word to use—"busy for some reason, I can act as the backup grenadier. It's always good to have a fallback plan, right?"

"I guess so," Raibert huffed.

"That body of yours is tough, but not invincible, and the Admin's already blown your arm off once."

"Fine, whatever. Have it your way."

"Question," Anton said. "What's a weaponized self-replicator?"

"The stuff of nightmares." Raibert picked up the stovepipe launcher effortlessly. "Listen, I could literally turn the entire surface of the Earth into pinballs if I toggled this thing to the wrong setting. So, all of you better respect the doomsday weapon on the table, got it?" He set the launcher down.

"Actually, you're the only person who'll be on the ground who could do that," Benjamin corrected. "Ella and I capped the dial so the max manual yield shouldn't eat more than a few acres at most."

"Excuse me?" Anton scratched his head. "Did you say pinballs?"

"Don't make me show you the video with the dog."

"He's serious," Benjamin warned. "It's horrible."

"That won't be necessary." Klaus-Wilhelm ran a hand over the other weapons. "It would seem it's MP40s and grenades for my men."

"One last thing." Elzbietá picked up a tube with milky fluid inside. "Everyone gets a medibot injection. Don't worry about what it is. Just know it'll give you an overall physical boost. Dull your pain, clot your blood faster, help you stay alert. Stuff like that. We'll also have extras for stabilizing more serious wounds during combat."

"Shall we take them now?" Klaus-Wilhelm asked.

"Go right ahead," Raibert said. "It'll stay in your bloodstream for weeks."

"In that case, I'll go first."

Elzbietá administered Klaus-Wilhelm's injection, and then stepped aside as Anton and a few others began distributing gear amongst the troops. Benjamin stepped off to the side and caught Elzbietá's attention with a quick wave. She nodded and came over.

"Can we talk for a moment?" he asked.

"Sure. What's on your mind?"

He nodded to the side and guided her over to one end of the room where they could have some privacy.

"I just wanted to talk to you before we reach the Event." He spoke in hushed, cautious tones. "There are a lot of unknowns, and I don't think any of us can predict what will happen next. To the universe. To me." He paused and looked her in the eyes. "And to you."

"I know. It's been on my mind, too," she admitted. "I know I've been putting on a brave face, but what happens next scares me."

"Me, too."

"But whatever happens, I've made my choice. I'm not turning back."

Benjamin nodded. "I've...had some doubts."

"It was Shigeki's message, wasn't it?"

"Yeah." He glanced away. "I'm wondering if there might be some other way out of this. One where you survive."

"I told you before. I'm not about to place the few short years of my life over so many others. If that's what it takes to set things right again, then I will *gladly* pay that price."

"I know you would. It's just..."

"Ben?"

"Yeah?"

She gently turned his face toward her, brow creased with concern, and ran the backs of her fingers across his cheek. He took her hand in his and squeezed it.

"Ben, whatever happens to me, I want you to always know that I love you."

He smiled sadly at her.

"And if I do...cease to be when the Knot unravels, then the way you honor that love is to live your life to the fullest. No matter what may come next."

"I don't want to lose you." A tear trickled down his cheek.

"Promise me, Ben. Promise me you will."

He swallowed, and she wiped the tear away with her thumb. He sighed and slowly began to nod.

"I will, Ella. I promise."

Dahvid Kloss watched the TTV's signal pass 1950 from *Pathfinder-2*'s non-congruent position.

"And...send it," he ordered.

"Yes, sir. Dispatching telegraph now."

"Follow them, but don't let the distance drop below one month."

Kloss pushed over to his seat and strapped in. The chronoport's impeller spun up faster, and both *Pathfinder-2* and *Pathfinder-4* accelerated into a pursuit course.

"Message coming back from *Pathfinder-Prime*. All chronoports to converge on the TTV's position. We are not to engage until ordered to."

"And here we go," Kloss whispered.

CHAPTER THIRTY-SIX

Stendal, Germany
1940 CE

THE TTV GLIDED THROUGH THE AIR ABOVE THE CITY OF STENDAL. A dense sprawl of reddish-brown roofs transitioned in the distance into a patchwork of farmland and undeveloped woods that ran along the banks of the Elbe River. A noon sun shimmered on clear waters, and a two-track railroad ran out from the city to cross the river on a sturdy truss bridge.

Benjamin stood by his grandfather's side in the *Kleio*'s cargo bay and clutched the MP40 simulacrum in his hands. Twenty-four men and one synthoid in SS trench coats and helmets waited together under the mass driver's looming bulk.

"You ready for this, Doc?" Raibert shifted the thick strap of the Panzerschreck across his back, then rested his own submachine gun in both hands.

"No," Benjamin said honestly but quietly. He didn't want his grandfather to hear.

"Yeah," Raibert sighed. "Me neither. Whole thing scares the hell out of me."

"This is what you wanted, right? We're all here because of you."

"I know. But that doesn't change all the little doubts bouncing around in my head."

"Like if this will actually fix the timeline?"

"More like what will happen to me in this Admin body when we succeed."

Benjamin nodded. "I guess we'll find out."

"Doc, I'm so nervous right now, I think I'd puke if I were in my old body."

"And you're still going through with this?"

"Well, yeah. Of course." He fiddled with the cocking handle on his rifle. "Some things in life are more important than your own...life. Damn, that sentence could have come out better."

"I think I know what you're trying to say," Benjamin whispered and knuckled the big guy in the arm. "We'll get through this."

Raibert flashed him a lopsided grin.

"There should be a two-story farmhouse south of the tracks," Klaus-Wilhelm said.

"Yeah, I see it," Elzbietá replied from the bridge.

"That's where the security force should be."

"Should be and is. I've got eyes on a dozen SS in and around the farmhouse."

"What about Hitler's train?"

"It's fifty-six minutes out."

"Then we should stay clear of them until we know more," Klaus-Wilhelm declared. "Set us down in the wooded area north of the tracks. We'll move through it under cover and keep an eye on the situation from there."

"Roger that."

Benjamin brought up an external view in his lenses as the TTV dipped down and slipped invisibly across the rooftops. The ship slowed over the fields of wheat and corn, then settled next to a dense expanse of beech trees.

The metamaterial shroud parted around the nose, and Benjamin switched off the external view. The cargo bay split open, and a ramp extruded down until it touched against a strip of sun-starved grass on the edge of the woods.

"Go!" Klaus-Wilhelm ordered, and his troops flowed down the ramp and across the grass. Benjamin kept pace with them as they hurried into the woods and then took positions behind trees. Benjamin crouched behind one of his own and held his submachine gun ready.

He glanced over his shoulder. The TTV closed its shroud and lifted away, appearing in his vision as a faint outline.

"Move up," Klaus-Wilhelm called out, and the rough line

of soldiers advanced through the dense forest with practiced, veteran caution.

Sunlight spilled radiant shafts through the thick cover of leaves, splashing the ground with patterns of light and shadow. Leaves rustled and a cool breeze blew across Benjamin's cheeks as he moved up, mimicking what he saw from the professional soldiers.

"Hey, Philo?" Raibert asked.

"Yeah?"

"How's the nearby timestream look?"

"The array is clear, though I'm still worried about that burst of telegraphy we picked up when we passed 1950."

"Any idea what they were saying?"

"No. It's heavily encrypted, and I still haven't been able to crack it."

"We don't need to crack it to know what they said," Benjamin cut in. "The Admin spotted us when we passed 1950, and that means trouble's coming our way."

"Yeah, probably," Raibert admitted with a frown. "Keep an eye on it, Philo."

"I will."

The line swept forward. Boots crunched on twigs and fallen leaves, breeze whispered in the branches, and the dark of the woods eventually gave way to the clearing on the far side.

The troops crouched on the edge of the woods, and Benjamin knelt with his shoulder against a gnarled trunk. A harvested wheat field spanned the distance from the edge of the woods to the railroad tracks and the farmhouse.

"Security detail in sight," Klaus-Wilhelm said.

"And very much not stuck in the architecture." Benjamin turned to the synthoid. "What does that mean?"

"How should I know?" Raibert demanded.

"Well, if you don't know, who among us would?"

"TTV," Klaus-Wilhelm called in, "any sign of the assassins?"

"Negative," Elzbietá responded. "There are quite a few farmers out there. Some of them are clustered together strangely and *might* be the assassins, but it'll be hard to tell until they make their move."

"Let's lie low for now," Raibert suggested. "The security detail's still intact, so we're not in the right part of the timeline yet. We don't want to cause undue interference."

"Hold position, men," Klaus-Wilhelm said.

Benjamin zoomed in on the farmhouse. The building stood two stories tall, but the second story was entirely contained within the heavily slanted roof. Dark horizontal and diagonal timbers broke up the whitewashed exterior. Some of the SS watched from the windows, but a few stood outside and shielded their eyes as they watched the rail line for signs of an approaching train.

Benjamin zoomed in further on the men outside.

"Damn it," he hissed.

"What's wrong?" Raibert asked.

"I got the uniforms wrong."

"You did?" Raibert peered at the farmhouse, then looked Benjamin up and down. "They seem accurate to me."

"The SS markings are different. Their coats don't have the runes on the collar."

"Oh? Is that all?"

"What do you mean 'is that all'? I worked really hard on these."

"Well," Raibert shrugged. "No use worrying about it now."

Benjamin sighed. "Yeah, I guess you're right."

"Guys, problem!" Elzbietá called in.

"Oh, what *now*?" Raibert complained.

"Chronoports incoming! Multiple signals! They're converging on our position!"

"Damn it!" Raibert exclaimed. "How many?"

"A lot! Precise count unknown! They're almost on top of us!"

"Ella, you'll need to draw them away from 1940," Raibert said. "We can't do our job with a horde of chronoports overhead."

"Understood. I'll get their attention. Dropping the shroud and pulling away from your position."

"Masks on," Klaus-Wilhelm ordered crisply. He pulled his mask on, adjusted the hood so it extended beneath his collar, and fitted his helmet back on over it. Benjamin did the same, then removed his MP40's regular magazine and slid in one with a red stripe. Even with their masks on, he could easily tell who was who by the names that hovered over each man's head. Adrenaline surged through his body and his heartbeat quickened.

"They're phasing in to the north!" Philo said. "Count is eight!"

✧   ✧   ✧

Admin chronoports sped across the scattered pockets of farmland and forest in a line abreast.

"TTV spotted, sir. It's pulling away from us."

The large red icon glowed angrily in Shigeki's virtual vision. He and the rest of the bridge crew wore their pressure suits and were strapped in, ready for whatever the enemy threw their way.

"First things first," he said coolly, and marked a rough circle around the TTV. "The professor may already be on the surface somewhere. Deploy all ground forces and have them sweep this entire area clean. I want nothing left to chance."

"Yes, sir," Durantt replied and opened a channel. "*Pathfinder-Prime* to Pathfinder Squadron: release all Cutlasses and deploy in marked area. Kill all threats on sight. No restrictions."

Transports loaded with 88 special operators, 130 drones, and 8 STANDs in combat frames dropped from the chronoports and accelerated ahead of the formation.

"Incoming fire!"

The mass driver slug punched through a fusion thruster underneath *Pathfinder-7*'s wing, and the thruster exploded in a flash of escaping plasma. The chronoport tilted to one side, its underbody seared and blackened, and began shedding altitude. Weapon pods broke off, armor rattled and slipped away, and the second thruster sputtered as its output dropped. Another explosion shredded the rear fuselage, and the impeller warped and began oscillating wildly, its edges losing definition.

"*Pathfinder-7* is going down, sir!"

"Return fire!" Shigeki snapped. "Weapons free!"

"All craft, open fire!"

Railguns split the air, and kinetic slugs battered the TTV's frontal armor. Missiles streaked ahead of the chronoports, and the TTV accelerated erratically to the side, then climbed straight up.

Pathfinder-7 left a wavering, uncertain wake of warped light as pieces broke off its impeller and phased out of existence. The chronoport's wide nose plowed into a two-story farmhouse, and its impeller shattered into wandering fragments of unreality. Sections of the farmhouse, ground, and people in black uniforms phased through each other. The chronoport barely cleared a pair of railroad tracks and smashed into the ground beyond. Topsoil and shorn wheat exploded upward, and the craft bulldozed a long groove through the ground before it came to rest.

Icons lit up around the crash. Most of the crew had survived.

"Secondary priority to the ground teams," Shigeki said. "Secure *Pathfinder-7*'s crash site."

Missiles homed in on the TTV as it shot upward, and weapon blisters snapped open on its flanks. Massive Gatling guns trained out, streams of fire wrecked several missiles, and the TTV reversed course *toward* his forces.

It darted through the gap it had blasted in the missile swarm and surged toward the Cutlasses, weapons thundering, and three transports burst into flames. The damaged craft plunged, trailing black smoke, gouging ragged lines through the forest, and the other Cutlasses quickly went to ground. Troops and drones rushed out and dispersed, frantically seeking cover as the TTV's weapons blazed.

"Again!" Durantt ordered, and more missiles spat from chronoport launchers.

The TTV arced up and away, Gatling guns laying down continuous fire. The missiles had almost reached it when it vanished.

"TTV phase-out confirmed! Now moving downstream!"

"After it!" Shigeki ordered.

The chronoport's impeller burst apart, and the laws of physics lost their grip on reality. Scattered pieces of the farmhouse phased through each other to join in unnatural amalgamations. Its foundation sank into the earth. An SS trooper melted into a door and stuck there. Another fell onto his back, then merged into the ground until blades of grass stuck out of his chest. Two more troopers ran into each other and became a hideous, writhing ball of flesh in a bulky SS uniform with eight limbs and two heads.

The chronoport hit with a mighty thud and the ground shock rippled through the earth with enough force to hurl Benjamin flat on his ass. The massive craft slid across the wheat field, chewing a path through the earth.

Screams erupted from the ruined farmhouse. The SS trooper merged with the ground let out a shriek that puffed dirt into the air. Blood trickled out around each blade of grass piercing his body. The one fused with the door flailed his hands and feet and opened his mouth in soundless terror. The creature formed from two SS troopers vomited blood and chunks of organs out of both mouths, then collapsed in a wet heap.

"*Mein Gott,*" Klaus-Wilhelm muttered and made the sign of the cross.

"Raibert?" Benjamin asked softly, horrified by what he was seeing.

"Yeah?"

"Are we the ones who *caused* the Knot? Are we creating it right now?"

"Don't even think about it." He scuttled over to Klaus-Wilhelm in a crouching run. "Sir, Admin troops are landing north of us on the far side of the woods!"

"Movement on the other side of the tracks!" Anton reported. "There are at least half a dozen vehicles driving across the field, headed for the bridge."

"The assassins see the confusion and are making their move," Klaus-Wilhelm said. "Anton, take your squad south over the tracks and engage them. Do *not* let them reach the bridge!"

"Sir!"

"The rest of you with me!" Klaus-Wilhelm moved out, and Benjamin, Raibert, and twelve of his men followed him north, back through the forest.

"Do you have any idea what you're charging into?" Raibert asked.

"That train *has* to get through," Klaus-Wilhelm answered. "Nothing else matters, and I'm not about to fight those things with it in sight."

They advanced through the woods in a skirmish line, fifteen against an unknown horde, then came to a rise with old growth trees and climbed to its crest.

"Here," Klaus-Wilhelm said quietly, and his men took up positions just behind the crestline, using it for cover.

"Drones coming in," Raibert whispered, his back against a moss-covered trunk. "Both aerial and on the surface. Be ready."

"We'll take them out from here," Klaus-Wilhelm said.

Benjamin cocked his MP40 and waited. Gunfire sounded off in the distance, and he wondered if Anton's squad had made contact with the assassins.

"Looks like they're moving aggressively through the forest," Raibert commented. Icons lit up in Benjamin's lenses to denote Raptor and Wolverine attack drones. "They either don't see us, which is doubtful, or they see us and take us for indigenes."

Benjamin allowed himself a thin smile and took aim.

A formation of eight aerial drones buzzed over the treetops, a gun slung under each main body. Variskin made them blend into the blue sky, but his mask highlighted each drone with a bright red outline. They swept forward, maintaining speed and formation, and their guns took aim at the soldiers on the hill.

"Fire!" Klaus-Wilhelm shouted.

His entire force opened up at once and thirtieth-century bullets fired from twentieth-century submachine guns devastated the enemy formation. Two of the drones simply fireballed out of existence. Others staggered, then spiraled out of the air, shedding bits and pieces before they smashed into the ground. Three of their fellows spun in place, concentrating their fire on one of Klaus-Wilhelm's men, and he fell back onto a bed of dead leaves. Benjamin and Raibert swung their submachine guns and a fire hose of bullets blotted them from the heavens.

The downed man shook his head, thumped the side of his helmet, and came back to his knees.

Another Raptor dipped beneath the crown of a massive beech tree, firing in savage bursts, blasting splinters off the trunk Benjamin crouched behind. He squeezed the trigger, and the drone shattered into a shower of scorched malmetal.

More bullets whizzed by his head, and one clipped his shoulder with enough force to knock his aim aside. He winced from the sting, clenched his teeth, recovered and fired, blasting the drone to bits. Another swooped down to take its place, and Benjamin swung his weapon toward it and squeezed the trigger. Two shots blasted from his muzzle . . . and then the bolt locked back on an empty magazine.

"Reloading!" he shouted, ducking behind the tree with his limbs squeezed in tight.

Splinters exploded off the tree like sawdust, and Raibert fired a burst through the cloud. The drone swerved drunkenly and clacked against a tree trunk hard enough to jam its propeller blades deep into the wood. Its gun spun in circles underneath as Benjamin shoved another magazine into his weapon and released the bolt. It slammed forward, chambered a round as the drone's spinning gun slowed. The immobilized Raptor brought its own weapon back under control, swinging it up to take aim.

He finished it off with a single shot.

"Wolverines!" Raibert shouted. "Watch the ground, too!"

Quadrupedal drones galloped up the hill, the guns in their faces firing as more splinters flew from the trees. Benjamin fired down the slope and blew the legs out from under the leader. Its body rolled back down the hill, but two more leapt over it and bounded up the incline.

A Wolverine reached the top and lunged, tackling one of Klaus-Wilhelm's men. The two fell back, and the weight of the drone slammed the air from the man's lungs when they hit the ground. Klaus-Wilhelm fired a burst into the drone's flank, then kicked the robot aside. He offered a hand, yanked, and the soldier came unsteadily back upright.

Another Wolverine raced over the hill and jumped Raibert. He grabbed it by the head, smashed it against a trunk—then again and again, until it stopped squirming. He fired two shots into its belly and hurled it back down the hill. It landed at the bottom and didn't get up.

A loud bang pierced the chaos, and one of Klaus-Wilhelm's men went down.

"Sniper!" the man shouted, clutching his side. When he pulled his hand away, the glove was covered in blood.

"Got it!" Raibert grabbed a red-striped potato masher off his belt and flung it overhand. The guided grenade lit its solid propellant booster and rocketed into the air. It flew upward at a steep diagonal and collided with a Condor sniper drone. The drone vanished in a flare of light, and pieces of it rained down through the lush canopy.

"Is it time to use that big gun of yours?" Benjamin shouted.

"Not nearly!" Raibert shouted back, raising his MP40 again.

More drones poured in, and bullets sparked against their malmetal carapaces. Benjamin raked his fire across a trio of Wolverines, and his shots gouged gaping holes through their backs.

"At least we've got their attention!" Raibert shouted.

"You *think*?" Benjamin replied, reloading, then stiffened.

"There's a STAND moving our—!"

Raibert's warning was cut off as a half-visible skeleton boosted into the woods at high speed. A red outline locked onto it in Benjamin's mask, and he swung his weapon toward it.

"STAND!" Raibert opened fire, but the machine dodged with quick burps of thrust. More gunfire blew the bark off trees and blasted divots in the dirt, but the STAND avoided every shot. It darted up the side of the hill and then skated at them from the side.

Benjamin tracked it with his weapon and squeezed the trigger. A quick string of detonations sent the STAND tumbling back, but it righted itself and dashed away before he could line up another shot. An enemy grenade zipped and curved through the woods, hit Benjamin's chest like a shotput, and exploded. The blast flung him through the air, his side slammed against a tree, and he collapsed to the ground, gasping for breath as stars danced across his vision.

He shook his head and struggled back upright. Gunfire chattered all around him, and more explosions wracked the line of men, stunning them as the STAND rushed them once more. But Raibert stood his ground, motionless as a statue, despite the flickers of flames at his feet and on the hem of his coat, and emptied a full magazine into the charging STAND.

The STAND's right arm blew off and an ugly gash yawned in its armor. The skeletal machine expanded part of its malmetal into a rectangular shield and covered the wound as it boosted around their position.

Benjamin grabbed a red-striped grenade and hurled it at the machine. It rocketed in, and the STAND swerved away, but the grenade arced after it and exploded against its remaining arm in a bright flash. The STAND tumbled end over end and smashed into a tree with enough force to uproot it. The machine crashed into the ground and struggled to its feet.

Klaus-Wilhelm hit it with another grenade that sent pieces of it flying through the canopy.

"Operators and drones coming after us!" Raibert reported. "And they've got at least *two* STANDs with them!"

"Oh, *wonderful!*" Benjamin replied.

CHAPTER THIRTY-SEVEN

Transtemporal Vehicle *Kleio*
non-congruent

"SEVEN CHRONOPORTS AT NEGATIVE SIX DAYS AND CLOSING," PHILO reported. "Main gun recharged, and I'm rearming the self-replicators. No need to worry about our shots polluting the 1940s anymore."

"Ready." Elzbietá spun the TTV around so that it was flying backward. Whole days flashed by at roughly one second intervals. The sun swooped by overhead, stars wheeled past, and then the sun returned once more. She dimmed the visuals around her so she could focus on both the temporal and physical positions of the chronoports trying to catch up. Seven murky nebulas wavered in the panoramic view, representing each chronoport's estimated physical location as it approached the TTV's *temporal* location.

"Chronoports at negative one day. Phase-lock imminent."

The temporal distance dropped to zero, and the chronoports materialized before her. Elzbietá aimed the bow at the nearest target, and Philo fired the main gun. The chronoports all banked in different directions, perhaps anticipating the attack, and the shot clipped the wing of their intended target.

"Minor damage to one chronoport," Philo reported. "Some microbot splash. They'll eat through its hull, but it's hard to tell how long they'll take."

"Too long," Elzbietá grunted.

Railgun slugs gonged at the *Kleio*'s armor, and yellow indicators flashed in one of her displays. She pulled the ship to the side, then up, then back down as the main gun recharged. The chronoports continued a relentless fusillade, and each small, individual hit began to add up. Friendly microbot swarms flowed underneath and over the TTV's hull to repair the damage, but even some of those were blasted off with each hit, weakening the *Kleio*'s ability to self-repair in the short term.

Missiles sprinkled out of the chronoports in a rain of death. Sharpened cones ignited their drives and dashed forward. Elzbietá pulled the TTV back, and Philo split open the gun pods. Streams of high-velocity rounds blazed out of them, and a few of the missiles disappeared.

The survivors swarmed in, powering forward at twenty gees, four times the TTV's maximum acceleration.

"The main gun?" she asked urgently.

"Twenty more seconds."

"Not soon enough!" She rolled her thumb over a knob on her omnidirectional throttle. The TTV's temporal direction flipped, and the cycle of day and night reversed. The missiles kept coming in, but they slipped out of phase and flew through the TTV without damaging it.

They fled backward through time, and the chronoports overshot them.

"Enemy at plus five days," Philo stated. "Plus ten. Plus twelve... distance stabilizing. Chronoports now reversing course. Temporal distance dropping. Plus eleven. Plus ten. Contact in thirty seconds, absolute."

"They're not letting up this time."

"From what Raibert and I saw earlier, that's almost their entire remaining force. Shigeki means to finish this."

"Well, right back at him."

"Main gun ready. They're coming in more aggressively this time."

"Yeah, I see that." Seven chronometric signals closed in until the glowing clouds representing their estimated locations overlapped the TTV. Her own temporal speed reduced the effectiveness of the *Kleio*'s array. She could probably pinpoint the chronoports if she stopped, but if she stopped, she died.

"Enemy at plus one day. Phase-lock imminent."

"Here they come again." She gripped the controls, and Philo dropped his helmet's visor with a loud *click*.

The chronoports formed a loose ring around them as they phased in, but the formation wasn't perfect. Clearly *they* couldn't pinpoint a target physically until they phased in, either, because the TTV was off center in the circle.

And dangerously close to one of the chronoports.

The entire formation cut loose with a swarm of missiles, and the collision warning warbled.

"Damn!" she pulled up on the throttle, and the TTV shot straight into the air.

One of the Admin missiles exploded against their hull almost instantly. Armor breached and the ship convulsed. Elzbietá fought the controls as microbot swarms rerouted from all nonessential tasks to close the tear in their armor. She brought the ship under control and swung the nose to face down, even as they accelerated upward.

"Philo!"

"I've got it!"

The main cannon discharged with a *whump* she heard in the abstraction, and the one-ton projectile punched clean through the top of the chronoport and broke it in half. A secondary explosion flared, and the two halves tumbled apart.

Another chronoport banked toward them, fusion thrusters blazing. Railguns fired, plinking away at their hull as it tried to maneuver around to their weakened flank.

The TTV's gun pods snapped open and the nearest missiles shattered into flaming streamers.

"That chronoport!" Elzbietá shouted, highlighting the closest threat with a mental command. "Focus it down!"

"Got it!"

Elzbietá reversed thrust and sent the TTV screaming down. The chronoport swooped up at them, and Philo brought their Gatling guns to bear. The two ships crossed, and over six hundred high-explosive armor-piercing rounds smashed into the enemy ship in four short, brutal seconds.

Malmetal bent, then tore open, and cannon fire savaged the interior. The two craft whisked apart as smoke and flame poured from the chronoport's hull.

"Take that!" Elzbietá declared viciously.

The collision warning sounded again as more missiles closed in around them, and she quickly switched the TTV's temporal vector. One of the missiles exploded prematurely while they were still in phase, and its shock wave buffeted them. The rest glided through without any effect.

Kloss screamed and tried to clutch his bleeding face through his pressure suit's bubble helmet. His seat broke off from the floor. It flew backward, and the chronoport's acceleration slammed him brutally against the rear of the bridge. Air exploded from his lungs, but the heavily padded seatback absorbed most of the shock.

The ship was still non-congruent, still not affected by Earth's gravity, and that meant the only acceleration came from the fusion thrusters.

He sucked in a breath and opened his eyes. Or tried to. Pain shot through every muscle in his face, but he saw nothing. He patted the helmet, searching frantically, and found a jagged piece of metal imbedded near his temple. He fumbled around with shaky fingers and found a tip jutting out on the other side. He tried to turn his head within the helmet, but the spike pinned him through the bridge of his nose.

And through both eyes.

He was blind.

"Help!" he cried.

No one responded.

"Help me! Anybody! I can't see!"

Was he the only one left alive? The only sound he heard was the hiss of air leaking from his breached helmet. The TTV's attack must have blown the compartment open, and with the ship still non-congruent, there was no air in phase with them beyond the hull. He was in a vacuum.

How much time did he have left before asphyxiation killed him?

Kloss gritted his teeth.

No, he thought savagely. *No, I am* not *going to die here! I refuse!*

He reached out through his PIN and accessed the ship's info-structure. His PIN couldn't contact anyone else, either because of damage to the ship or because everyone else really was dead. He had no way of knowing which, but he suspected he was, at the very least, the only person left alive on the bridge, and that meant no one was at the helm.

He tried to access the helm controls, but they required a

closed-circuit connection at a physical terminal. He cycled through less frequently used options. The menu kicked him out a few times due to the spotty connection, but he eventually drilled down to a 3D map of the ship's interior. He pulled up an abstraction of the ship and overlaid it based on his actual position.

An unblemished bridge appeared within his mind's eye. He could now "see" his surroundings, if only as a guestimate of what was actually there.

Perhaps that was for the best.

Acceleration pinned him against the back of the bridge, but the fusion thrusters weren't operating at full power. Gravity was close to one gee.

He could climb this.

He released his harness and stood up on the chronoport's rear bulkhead. Air whistled out of his helmet, and he began to feel lightheaded. Time was running out. He waved his arm through a virtual seatback and found the real one bent slightly downward. He clenched his fingers around the handholds built into each seatback for zero gee, and climbed.

The two pilot stations were at the front of the bridge, directly above him. If he could reach them, he could establish a direct interface and regain control of the chronoport.

He scaled one seatback, stood up with arms to his side for balance, then reached out quickly and grabbed hold of the next. He hooked an arm over the side and found something slick with rows of hard protrusions.

A ribcage.

Someone's ribs had been blasted open. He grimaced, found another spot to hold onto, and pulled himself up. It took him several minutes to scale the bridge, but he eventually reached the copilot's seat and the slack body still restrained there.

"Sorry," Kloss wheezed, then sucked in a labored breath.

He unstrapped the corpse, shoved her out of the seat, and pulled himself into it with a groan. He sighed with relief as the ship's primary functions lit up in his virtual vision. The top half of the chronoport flashed red and yellow, and the impeller shuddered worryingly as it maintained the ship's phase, but the fusion thrusters and weapon pods under the delta wing were undamaged.

"*Pathfinder-2* to *Pathfinder-Prime*," Kloss dictated for the telegraph. "Boss, can you hear me?"

"Kloss, is that you?" Shigeki's synthesized voice asked in his virtual hearing.

"Yeah, it's me." Kloss took a few deep breaths before continuing. "I've regained control of... the ship. Ready to assist."

"Hurry and join up with us. We're going to come at the TTV from two temporal directions at once."

"On my... way."

He located the other chronoports, swung the *Pathfinder-2* around, and sped to meet them.

"What do you mean they're not phase-locking with us?" Elzbietá demanded.

"Three of them flew right past us," Philo reported. "They're slowing now... matching speeds and holding position at plus one day. The other three are still at negative six days."

"What are they doing splitting up like that?" she asked.

"I wish I knew."

She glanced around, checking the estimated physical positions of each ship. Both groups of three had what might have been triangular formations that kept the TTV in the center. Were they trying to box her in?

Perhaps she'd used the trick of switching time-travel directions too often, and this was their counter. Admin impellers were faster; *they* chose when to phase-lock, not her. She'd been able to break away by quickly reversing directions, but not this time. It didn't matter which group she engaged first. When she reversed the impeller to flee, she'd run right into the *second* trio.

"Not good," she exhaled through clenched teeth. Microbots hadn't finished resealing the breached sections of the hull yet. She'd wanted to hold back until Kleio healed the gash in their side armor, but the Admin wasn't giving her that chance.

"Trio at plus one day decelerating," Philo stated. "They're coming for us."

"Get ready!"

Three chronoports flashed into existence around them, forming the points of an equidistant triangle with the TTV very close to the center. Railguns blared away, and hits stabbed into the *Kleio*'s hull.

"Graviton thruster three damaged!" Philo reported. "Compensating!"

"There!" She charged the closest chronoport, swinging the nose around as the TTV sped sideways, and Philo fired the mass driver. The shot punched a wicked channel down the seam where the hull blended into its wing, and then the payload exploded. The force of the blast shoved the chronoport down. Its wing supports cracked, and the craft folded in on itself.

Missiles sleeted in on her from its consorts, and she pulled at her controls. The TTV sped through rapidly moving cloud banks as it climbed steeply, but the controls responded only sluggishly and the missiles screamed in faster than before. More cannon fire struck the hull, and more indicators flashed yellow and red on her displays.

Philo swiveled the guns, and a rain of 45mm shells intercepted the incoming missiles. Some of them blew apart, but not enough.

She had to get out.

Elzbietá flipped their temporal velocity again. Explosions erupted from the closest missiles, and shrapnel rained against the hull before they completely phased out.

"Minor damage to the impeller!" Philo reported. "It should be okay, but those two chronoports are coming around!"

"I can't deal with them yet!"

The TTV raced backward through time, and the other three chronoports phase-locked with it. Like the first group, they formed a wide triangle, but they'd positioned themselves high above the TTV.

Right where she was heading.

"Damn it! Take the one to port, Philo!"

"On it!"

Gatling guns bellowed, their massed fire drawing a cone of flame across the heavens, and one of the trio above her staggered, then fireballed and fell off on one wingtip, but its companions fired back with equal fury. Twin streams of railgun slugs wracked the hull, and missiles sprinted out of their launchers as Elzbietá pulled back on the throttle and dived away from them. Philo worked his controls and kept the missiles at bay until one of his displays flashed urgently red.

"Gatling Two is down!" he reported. "Something's jamming the ammo feed!"

"Fix it! We're not going to last long without those guns!"

"Redirecting repair swarms now!"

Two chronoports phased in beneath her and launched their missiles. The collision warning sounded, and Elzbietá knew she couldn't phase out fast enough to avoid them entirely.

So instead she *closed* with them, angling just enough to cut inside the missiles' arc. One detonated from proximity as she overflew the chronoports, and the TTV shook as fragments battered its hull. She passed cleanly between them, then angled back and around until she was suddenly closing rapidly with one of them.

"Take it down!" she cried as she spun the TTV so their Gatling guns had a clear line of fire.

"Aiming!" Philo swung two 45mm and both 12mm Gatlings around. The top of the chronoport had been blasted open in a previous attack, and he manually set half the mix to incendiary before he issued the fire command.

The guns poured 167 rounds a second into the chronoport, and the entire top half blazed with self-immolation as tiny explosions tore the time machine apart.

Hellfire burned Kloss alive.

His helmet burst apart and he opened his mouth to scream, but all that did was set his lungs on fire. He convulsed and thrashed in his seat, flesh crisping until finally a piece of debris the size of a sharpened baseball bat impaled his skull.

Death came as a sweet, sweet mercy.

But Kloss had set one last navigational command before he died, and when the TTV reached the specified distance, the chronoport executed his final will. Safety parameters disengaged. Fusion thrusters blazed with suicidal power and the chronoport shot forward on a collision course.

The TTV darted to the side, but not before the chronoport's wing struck the nose and tore a deep gash through one whole side. The TTV spun away, falling out of control, and three other chronoports dove after their wounded prey.

CHAPTER THIRTY-EIGHT

─────── ⊗⊗⊗ ───────

Stendal, Germany
1940 CE

RAIBERT SNATCHED A RED-STRIPED MAGAZINE OFF THE CORPSE OF one of Klaus-Wilhelm's men and slotted it into his submachine gun. The wreckage of a second STAND spewed sparks and spurts of oily goo into the air next to him, and blood from special operators soaked the soil near the bottom of the hill. The Admin had pulled back, but he knew they were gathering for a decisive push on their position.

"Is it time yet to use that damned gun of yours *now*?" Benjamin shouted from behind a tree almost completely denuded of bark. He stabbed a medibot shot into the stomach of a wounded soldier, then tossed the empty tube aside and offered a hand to urge the man back to his feet. The soldier stumbled upright, and Benjamin caught him, then guided him to the tree's cover where he pressed his back against it, chest heaving as he fought for breath.

"Yeah, I'm thinking it's time." Raibert retrieved one of the rockets from his backpack, loaded it into the Panzerschreck, and raised the weapon to his shoulder. He spied a plume of smoke on the far side of the forest where two of the Admin's transports had crashed. Tiny outlined figures gathered ahead of the downed transports, their locations illustrated by data from remotes he'd deployed.

"What support do you need?" Klaus-Wilhelm growled, reloading his weapon.

"None. I'll move up and get off the best shot I can. Everyone else stay back."

"We'll hold this position as long as possible."

"Wish me luck." Raibert rose from cover, submachine gun in one hand and the rocket launcher in the other.

"Luck?" Benjamin replied. "What are you talking about? Schröders don't need luck!"

Raibert glanced his way, brow furrowed. "But I'm not a Schröder."

"The hell you say! I'm naming you an honorary Schröder right now, friend!"

"I like the sound of that." He flashed a lopsided grin beneath his mask. "Friend, huh?"

Benjamin waved him on. "Now go out there and kick ass like a Schröder!"

"All right, then."

He charged down the hill with long, powerful synthoid strides. His boots crunched through underbrush at the bottom, and he dashed forward through the thick forest, the red icons of his foes glowing ahead.

His feet pounded the ground, and he raced forward faster than the best natural athlete. He sliced through the trees like an earthbound comet, sidestepping trunks at the last possible moment, using them for cover as he sped through. He'd covered almost half the distance to the crash when a rail-rifle dart hit the side of his helmet and sent it spinning off his head.

He tripped forward, but managed to turn that into a lurching dive for cover behind a stump.

Two outlines of special operators materialized to his right. Another shot clipped his leg, and the rest blew splinters off the stump.

"Where did you two come from?" Raibert tucked his leg in and rose into a crouch.

The special operators split, flanking him. Another target split off from the forces near the downed transports and headed his way. *Fast.*

Faster than a drone or operator.

"Aw, hell!" he exclaimed and raised his submachine gun. He spun out of cover and sprayed one of the operators. The variskin illusion warped and vanished, and the armored man in black went down hard. Raibert kept firing, and tiny explosions severed the operator's leg and both arms in sprays of gore.

A hit thumped him in the chest, and he stuck out a leg to brace himself. His gun blasted in response, and the second operator's torso blew apart.

He'd just turned back to the downed transports when the STAND boosted into view, then sped past him. Its incinerator flicked on, and blue flame washed over Raibert.

"Won't work on me!" he shouted, firing his MP40 until it ran dry.

The STAND dashed out of the way, rounded the rotted remains of a fallen tree trunk, then darted deeper into the woods with precise spurts of thrust. Raibert, still on fire, pulled out a grenade, but the STAND shot first. Enemy grenades detonated around him, and he found himself flying through the air. He hit the ground, rolled, and quickly surged back to his feet. One of Klaus-Wilhelm's men would have been stunned by the blast—assuming it hadn't just knocked him out completely—but Raibert's onboard systems kept functioning. Parts of his coat's façade dropped off, revealing the gray prog-steel weave underneath.

He raised his arm and tossed his own grenade. The weapon ignited and tracked the STAND down. It boosted for cover, but the projectile swerved to hit it, and the two met with a loud, explosive crack that blasted the forest floor clean and stripped leaves off branches.

The STAND crashed to the ground and plowed a shallow groove. Variskin around its body failed, and one of its arms twitched erratically. It pushed itself up with the other and boosted away. One of its shoulder boosters burped loudly, then wheezed clear exhaust, and it tumbled to the ground again. The machine fired its arm and leg boosters and righted itself.

Raibert pulled out another grenade, then realized this one didn't have a red-stripe. He checked his belt for a replacement and realized it was all he had left.

"Oh, what the hell!" He didn't know how to arm the period grenade's fuse, so he simply tossed it at the STAND. The thirtieth-century killing machine boosted back, then spun around and fled from a weapon only *slightly* more threatening than a wooden stick.

"Ha!" Raibert used the short reprieve to sprint forward. He wormed his way through the forest, casting quick glances over his shoulder for the STAND's return, then came close enough to the crash site to see the gathered troops and drones through breaks in the trees.

His remotes counted fifty drones, thirty-one operators, and three STANDs in the vicinity.

"This'll do." He dropped to one knee and raised the Panzerschreck. A rail-rifle round whizzed by, then another chipped bark off a tree. He armed the replicators, set the dispersion and generational limits, then angled the launcher up and fired.

The rocket shot out of the barrel, spun rapidly as it powered upward, then arced gently down until its course straightened. It flew over the crash site, and its twentieth-century exterior split open to reveal an inner mechanism that resembled a bundle of oversized grapes. A powerful explosion flung the "grapes" away from the central shaft in a carefully designed dispersal pattern, the globes all burst at once, and weaponized self-replicators showered upon the Admin troops like rusty snow.

Raibert set the launcher aside and reloaded his submachine gun.

STANDs boosted clear, and Admin operators scattered. Their version of the thirtieth century was a rougher place than his own, and he suspected they'd encountered weapons like this before. Perhaps in armed combat, but more likely in terrorist strikes.

Their familiarity changed nothing. The touch of a single flake could kill, and the operators scrambled to remove infected armor or toss aside blighted weapons. Rust grew into fluidic beads that expanded hungrily wherever they landed. This wasn't some cocktail a terrorist cell had developed in isolation. These microbots had been developed for the armed forces of an entire planetary government—one that had openly scoffed at the Yanluo Restrictions—and their lethality showed.

Drones slumped into oozing puddles. Operators collapsed and frantically stripped their armor. A woman near the epicenter tripped and fell into a puddle. It splashed over her, engulfed her, consumed her, and then the vague shape of her dissolving corpse ballooned outward and burst open in a fountain of mutilated viscera. Rusty spray and spongy bits of meat splattered more people and equipment, and the cycle of consumption continued.

"Oh, God," Raibert breathed. "I hope I didn't set the number too high."

He had a strong desire to be somewhere else, so he picked up the launcher and turned to flee the scene of blood-soaked nano-blight.

The STAND he'd wounded boosted into view, and grenades

exploded underneath him. The blast sent him flying once more, and the Panzerschreck tumbled through the air with one of his arms still attached. His weapon and limb landed in a fold between tree roots. The STAND boosted over, picked up the launcher in one claw, then hurled it toward the crash site where the released microbots would undoubtedly consume it.

Raibert raised his submachine gun and sprayed the STAND with automatic fire. It dashed away, but its damaged boosters slowed it, and Raibert kept it in his sights. Bullets pummeled its armor, tore through it, and shredded vulnerable internal systems that caught fire.

The STAND flew out of control, crashed headfirst into a tree, and its head crunched under the impact. Boosters sputtered, and the wreckage collapsed into a sparking, fuming junk pile.

"Raibert, we need everyone at the downed chronoport!" Benjamin called in. "We're heading that way now!"

"Be right there!" He took one last look at the STAND as if expecting it to get back up. It didn't, and he turned and ran toward the railroad tracks.

Bullets perforated the armor of one of Klaus-Wilhelm's soldiers, and he fell back.

Benjamin swung out of cover and fired on the two Raptor drones. Shots sparked against their half-seen bodies, and they crashed into a dry leaf bed. He retrieved a medibot tube from his belt and bolted over to the downed soldier, then crouched down next to the man.

And then he stopped. Tiny explosions had torn the man's chest open, and shrapnel had scrambled his insides. Benjamin grimaced, slotted the tube back into his belt, and raised his weapon.

"Sir!" Anton signaled. "Half the assassins are dead and the rest are fleeing to the south."

"Excellent work," Klaus-Wilhelm replied evenly.

"However, sir, I am less pleased to report *why* they're fleeing. A lone STAND engaged them and did considerable damage, then attacked us. We managed to drive it off, but the enemy returned in force. They've occupied the crashed time machine—I believe in an attempt to secure their wounded.

"Sir, the train is nearly here, and a large enemy force is bunkered in the wreckage *directly* beside the tracks. We're currently stuck behind what's left of the farmhouse and can't get close! As trigger-happy as they are now, they're likely to open fire on the train as it passes!"

"Then we must drive them off," Klaus-Wilhelm said flatly. "We'll pull back and hit them from the other side."

Benjamin scanned the tree line. Half of Klaus-Wilhelm's men were dead or wounded.

"Are we really in a position to assault them?" he asked.

"We have no other choice. Move out, men! Back to the farmhouse!"

The soldiers took out the remaining drones in sight, then everyone turned and ran down the back of the hill.

"Raibert, we need everyone at the downed chronoport!" Benjamin said over a direct channel as he ran. "We're heading that way now!"

"Be right there!"

Benjamin sprinted through underbrush, leapt over a fallen log, and wove his way through the trees. The soldiers raced through the forest, and even the wounded men kept up with his and Klaus-Wilhelm's pace. Benjamin wondered if their energy came from the microbots in their bloodstream or their refusal to fail his grandfather.

Probably both, he concluded as they reached the tree line.

Fire ripped back and forth between the wreckage and the farmhouse's deformed remains. Drones and operators ducked in and out of cover along the chronoport's spine, while Anton's men did the same from the farmhouse. Three STANDs, one clearly damaged, sprinted back and forth behind the chronoport to take shots from different vantage points, and a dozen men and women in blue uniforms crouched down on the wing. None of them had weapons.

"*Three* of the bastards," Benjamin muttered, then turned as the sound of heavy footfalls drew his attention.

"Miss me?" Raibert asked, running up alongside the group.

"Raibert!" Benjamin exclaimed, then looked at the burnt remains of his coat and the strands of artificial muscle sticking out of one shoulder. "What happened to you?"

"You should see the other guy."

Benjamin nodded. "You okay?"

"I've been better." Raibert shrugged with one arm and raised his gun. "Reloading can be a pain."

"Anton, we're in position," Klaus-Wilhelm sent.

"Give the word, sir! We'll hit them at the same time!"

"Ready grenades!"

Benjamin grabbed his last red-striped potato masher, and three soldiers pulled out the only ones they had left.

"Throw!"

Benjamin and the soldiers tossed their grenades. Drives ignited, and the projectiles howled toward the chronoport from two directions. The STANDs were the first to notice, and the damaged one spun around, fired its rail-rifle, and managed to clip one of the grenades.

The other grenades sped in, some targeting drones, others going for operators.

And one rocketing straight at the unarmed crew.

The damaged STAND lit its boosters, dived in front of the chronoport crew, and expanded a malmetal shield. The grenade detonated and sent the STAND skidding back across the wing in a shower of sparks.

More grenades exploded amongst the Admin forces. Drones blew apart. Operators collapsed. One of the other STANDs took a direct hit against its back boosters and dropped heavily to the ground.

"CHARGE!" Klaus-Wilhelm bellowed, and they raced across the wheat field. Anton's squad erupted from the farmhouse, and everyone converged on the downed chronoport.

All three STANDs formed up in front of the crew, deployed shields that widened for additional cover, and slammed them down to form a phalanx. As one they opened fire with heavy rail-rifles. A headshot hammered one of Klaus-Wilhelm's soldiers to the ground with a dent in his helmet the size of a fist. More shots came in, and one blew a man's leg off at the knee.

"I'll draw their fire!" Raibert shouted, and raced ahead of the pack.

"Raibert!" Benjamin called out, but the big man wasn't listening. The synthoid emptied his gun, then tossed it aside and fired shots out of his palm that blew holes in the STAND shields. Incoming fire from the STANDs focused on him, but he kept charging straight at them.

Shot after shot pounded his armor, broke through, and blasted apart his synthoid body. He rushed onward, firing with each stride. One of the STANDs crumpled. The other two held their ground as the chronoport crew escaped to the side. Operators and drones formed a loose escort around them.

Rail-rifle shots pierced Raibert's mask, blew half his face off, tore a chunk out of his stomach, punched a hole through his upper chest, and wrecked his arm below the elbow. He stumbled forward, face-planted onto the chronoport's wing, and didn't get up.

Benjamin heard a primal scream...then realized, vaguely, that it had been his. His legs pumped, his heart pounded. They reached the edge of the wing, and he and Klaus-Wilhelm charged across it, spraying the STANDs with gunfire. One of them twirled back, then blew apart, and the final STAND survivor boosted away to join the retreating crew.

Anton's forces reached the chronoport's spine from the other side. They poured their own fire onto the retreating Admin forces, and Klaus-Wilhelm's men took up positions amongst the wreckage.

Benjamin spotted a jutting piece of a wing panel near where Raibert had gone down that would be perfect. He vaulted to it, raised his weapon...and the surviving STAND fired a rail-rifle shot into his gut.

The impact pierced his armor, shrapnel tore through his abdomen, and he slammed into the ground, clutching his stomach, as a train whistle sounded in the distance.

CHAPTER THIRTY-NINE

Transtemporal Vehicle *Kleio*
non-congruent

THE CHRONOPORT AND TTV SWUNG AROUND EACH OTHER, RAIL-guns and Gatlings exchanging fire at insanely short range. The *Kleio* shook with each impact, and warning icons flared as shot after shot punched through prog-steel to savage internal systems.

"Ready yet?" Elzbietá demanded.

"Twenty-two seconds!"

"Is there anything you can do to hurry it—"

More railgun slugs dug deep into the *Kleio*'s hull, and her mouth froze as sudden pain blossomed in her left leg and abdomen. Agony eclipsed rational thought, and she emptied her lungs in a shocked, silent wheeze, then sucked in a breath and screamed. The pain was worse than anything she'd ever experienced, worse even than the crash in her F-21. Searing needles tore through her body and mind, and she grabbed her thigh, curled forward, then collapsed out of the seat to roll across a clear floor.

"Oh, no!" Philo cried, and quickly pulled up new displays at his station. He navigated options with the speed of a machine, selected something, and the pain instantly vanished.

She lay on the invisible ground, gasping and sweating while her mind fought to catch up with what had just happened. The chronoport continued to wheel around them outside, and more hits shook the hull.

"What—" she began.

"It's fine! Everything's fine!" he replied, not sounding too confident. "You're going to be fine! Just keep piloting! I can't take them on alone!"

Elzbietá wiped the sheen of sweat off her virtual face, grabbed hold of an armrest, and pulled herself back into her seat. She took the controls once more and swerved the TTV above and behind the chronoport where its railguns couldn't track.

"Philo?" she demanded. "What happened to me?"

"A piece of debris reached your real body."

"Oh, God! How bad is it?"

"It's fine! You'll live!" he replied quickly, still not sounding sure of himself. "I'm flooding your casket with medibots! They'll patch you up! Your wetware just got disrupted when the debris hit and real pain reached the abstraction! That's all!"

"That didn't feel like something I'm just going to walk off! Are you—"

"Cannon recharged!" Philo interrupted.

Elzbietá snarled and swung their nose around, then pulled up and over the chronoport. The main gun fired down at a diagonal, hit the enemy time machine near the base of its spine, and tore through the interior. Gatling guns chattered, adding their own explosions and flames, and the craft became a blazing funeral pyre.

Secondary explosions blew out panels. The impeller juddered wildly. Exotic matter cracked, shattered, and the chronoport disintegrated into wheeling, glittering, see-through fragments.

"Two left! Both undamaged!" Philo looked over his shoulder and a section of the sky zoomed in to reveal a pair of dark manta rays diving toward them. "They're coming for us! Missiles inbound!"

Elzbietá jerked the throttle upward and spun them around. She shoved the throttle forward, and they rocketed straight at the enemy craft. Missiles streaked toward them, then shot past, unable to turn fast enough as she drove in under their line of flight.

More missiles spasmed out of the chronoports, and she yanked the controls to the side to keep them clear, even as she raced in. But something faltered within the ship. Red lights flashed on her displays, and the TTV lurched leadenly to the side.

"Graviton thruster three inoperable!" Philo warned.

"Damn it!"

She fought the controls, and the missiles homed in on her.

Philo sprayed them with cannon fire, but Elzbietá knew at least one would hit. She snapped the ship around, presenting a side that still had *relatively* intact armor, and a missile struck hard.

The explosion shattered armor and flung the ship aside.

"Mass driver offline!" Philo shouted as the TTV spun out of control.

"Can you get it back up?"

"The coolant lines have failed and the magnets are melting!"

"I'll take that as a no!"

She fought to regain control, finally righted the ship, and poured power into the surviving thrusters. The TTV surged ahead once more, and she closed in on the leftmost chronoport.

"Take it down!" she cried as they slipped underneath the craft, and she spun vertically beneath it to bring all of the *Kleio*'s Gatling guns to bear.

Philo focused everything they had left on the enemy time machine. A tsunami of 45mm and 12mm shells tore across its belly. Explosions blanketed its hull. Armor around its fusion thrusters breached, and plasma spewed out to sheer through the wing and main body. The long tail of the impeller split apart, and the chronoport exploded in a shower of winking stars.

"One left!" Philo reported. "It's backing off!"

"Not if I have anything to say about it," she hissed savagely and brought them around.

"Pull back!" Shigeki shouted. "Get us out of phase!"

The TTV opened fire on them. A few shots hit the hull, and then the chronoport phased backward down the timestream. The rest of the stream of rapid-fire metal flew straight through them without any effect as their temporal coordinates diverged.

"We're out of phase with the TTV, sir." Durantt's voice was hoarse, ragged, and his eyes were dark, shocked by the losses they'd taken.

"Proceed to negative five days, then match vectors," Shigeki grated.

"Pulling away, sir. Now at negative five and holding. The TTV is pursuing us, but distance is stable."

Shigeki took a deep breath and assessed the situation. He would *not* be beaten by this man!

He brought up a diagram of Kaminski's time machine and

turned it around. The ship had suffered extensive damage. They'd pounded it and pounded it and *pounded* it, and he was sure just a little more would destroy the damned thing.

But he had only one ship left. *Pathfinder-Prime* had yet to suffer any internal damage, but it was only *one* ship with a mere twenty-four missiles in its launchers. If they failed, then there was no one left to stop the TTV.

He needed to strike a decisive blow.

But how?

"Director," Vassal said. "I believe I have a solution to our current problem."

"Let's hear it."

"I have analyzed the enemy's attack patterns as well as our own actions during this engagement, and I have devised a new maneuver that should prove effective. It will allow us to attack the TTV while keeping us almost completely immune to reprisal."

"Sounds too good to be true," Durantt replied.

"You are not entirely wrong, Captain, because there is a significant downside. The maneuver will require extremely precise control of the ship's impeller. Human reflexes are insufficient for the task."

"Then what use is it to us?" Durantt demanded.

"The maneuver can still be performed, but it will require the precision of an AI."

Shigeki didn't respond immediately, merely closed his eyes as shocked silence fell over the bridge. The very notion of unboxing an AI and giving it control of a *time machine* was so repugnant he almost dismissed it out of hand. But the TTV *had* to be destroyed. Nothing else mattered, and he pushed aside his prejudices and gave Vassal's words serious consideration.

"Director," the AI finally continued. "Even in its damaged state, the TTV retains a significant realspace maneuverability advantage. However, it cannot keep up with us temporally. With your permission, I will leverage this advantage to its fullest and use it to destroy the enemy."

"You can't be serious!" Durantt blurted.

"As I said, Captain, this will require extremely precise control of the impeller. Your pilots lack the necessary reaction speed. Therefore, I am the only suitable candidate to execute this plan of attack."

"If we unbox you fully," Shigeki began in a slow, careful tone, "are you confident you can destroy the TTV?"

"Yes, Director. I estimate the chances of my success at over ninety-one percent."

"That will do."

"You aren't seriously considering this, sir?" Durantt demanded.

"I'm not considering anything." Shigeki released his restraints and floated out of his seat. "I'm doing it." He kicked off the seatback and floated to the PIN interfaces around Vassal's box at the front of the bridge.

"Sir, no!" Durantt pushed out of his seat and glided next to him. "You can't *do* this!"

"Florian," Shigeki put a hand on the man's shoulder. "We're all that's left. If we fail, the professor wins. Do you understand what that means? There will be no one left to stop him. We *have* to end this here. Nothing is more important than that. *Nothing.* Do you hear me? None of us will ever have *existed* if we fail to destroy that ship."

"But, sir..."

Shigeki gripped a handhold for leverage, then planted his free hand on the PIN interface.

"Authorization: Director Csaba Shigeki, Department of Temporal Investigation. *Full* AI unboxing requested. No interface restrictions." He held his palm against the interface and turned his head to meet Durantt's eyes with icy steadiness.

The man took a slow, shuddering breath and rubbed his hands nervously.

"Do it," Shigeki ordered.

Durantt swallowed, then nodded and placed his hand on the second PIN interface.

"Authorization: Captain Florian Durantt, Department of Temporal Investigation. F-f-f..." He squeezed his eyes closed. "F-full AI unboxing requested. No interface restrictions."

"Credentials accepted," the ship's nonsentient attendant said. "PIN integrity and noncoercion biometrics confirmed. Full AI unboxing will commence after a ten second countdown. You may pause or cancel the full unboxing at any time. Ten...nine... eight..."

For a moment, Shigeki thought Durantt would back down and pull his hand off. But the man only looked away as the attendant rattled off each number.

"Two...one...AI fully unboxed."

Every virtual station lit up with the warning FULLY UNBOXED. "I have control," Vassal stated.

A shiver ran through Shigeki as he heard those words. His expression never wavered as he floated back to his seat, but behind those steady eyes, he wondered what he'd done. Then the answer came to him, clear and simple.

He'd done what it would take to win...because nothing else mattered anymore.

"Vassal, engage and destroy the TTV," he ordered, strapping in.

"Yes, Director. Engaging the enemy...now."

"Chronoport's coming in again," Philo said.

"Right." Elzbietá wiped her hands together and settled them back on the controls. They had a more precise fix on the last chronoport since it now *was* the last and the *Kleio*'s array no longer had to sort through half a dozen signals all moving at rapid kilofactors, but the zone before her was still a rough estimate until the craft phased in.

"Negative one day. Phase-lock imminent."

Elzbietá positioned them near the edge of the chronoport's projected appearance.

The chronoport materialized almost directly ahead, and Philo cut loose with the Gatling guns as the Admin ship returned fire. Railgun slugs struck the hull, and four missiles shot out of its launchers. Forty-five-millimeter cannon fire reached the enemy craft and slipped through its hull.

"What?" Philo exclaimed.

The chronoport completely phased out, and the range of possible locations widened around them. He quickly retargeted the missiles and gunned down three of them, but the *Kleio*'s beleaguered systems failed to take down the fourth. It cracked against the hull, and graviton thruster two dropped offline.

"Philo!"

"It's bad! There's nothing left of the thruster to repair!"

"Not good!" Elzbietá gritted her teeth and pulled them away from the chronoport's range of positions, but *Kleio* was badly hurt. The TTV responded, yet the signal strength of the out-of-phase chronoport came slicing back in at them.

"Phase-lock imminent!"

The chronoport materialized again, and four missiles streaked out of its launchers. Railgun slugs slammed into their hull as Philo returned fire, but his shots slipped through a ghostly afterimage as enemy missiles zeroed in on the TTV. He took three out, and Elzbietá managed to pull the ship out of the path of the fourth, but its detonation pelted the *Kleio* with a scythe of shrapnel.

"Number two 12mm's out!" Philo reported. "Ammo feed's been cut!"

"We're in trouble!" Elzbietá flipped their temporal vector, but the signal from the chronoport held solid. The enemy pilot had changed vectors almost perfectly in sync with her.

"It's coming in again!"

"I can't get away from it!" she said.

The chronoport phase-locked once more. Missiles sprinted out of its launchers, and more slugs struck the hull.

Philo worked his controls, but the Gatling guns only took two out. One exploded near the *Kleio*, and most of its shrapnel missed, but the last one hit the nose dead on and the front third of the ship blew apart. They spun wildly away, and Elzbietá fired the remaining thrusters at full to bring them back under control. She steadied the ship and checked what they had left.

Two graviton thrusters, both showing yellow and small splashes of red, and two 45mm and one 12mm Gatling guns, both nearly out of ammo.

"What do we do?" Elzbietá turned to her copilot. "That thing is tearing us apart. We can't hit it, and we can't run away."

Philo sat in his seat like a statue, fingers hovering over the controls. The word STANDBY hovered over his head.

"Philo?"

The text vanished, and Viking started moving again.

"I've got it." He faced her. "Get in close."

"You want me to get *closer*?"

"Trust me. This is all we've got left. I'll hit them this time."

The signal from the chronoport grew stronger, and the range of potential locations narrowed.

"Get as close as you can before it phases back in!" Philo said. "Hurry!"

Elzbietá swung the joystick to the side, then shoved the throttle forward with a Valkyrie's scream, and the TTV sped into the heart of the chronoport's projected arrival.

✧　　✧　　✧

"Phase-lock complete," Vassal reported. "Firin—"

A hail of 45mm rounds—fired by Philo *before* the chronoport completely phased in—struck *Pathfinder-Prime*'s bow. They pounded through its front armor and drilled deep into the ship's interior.

Blasts opened the front of the bridge. Vassal's connection with the rest of the ship dropped out, and more explosions obliterated its box. The stream of high explosives tore through the interior, piercing people and seats as if they weren't there, and more explosions pulped Durantt and the crewmembers sitting in front of Shigeki.

He didn't even have time to recognize the totality of his failure. Before his synapses could form the first coherent thought, a 45mm round punched into the center of his forehead, the payload triggered, and his head and shoulders blew apart in a grisly spray.

Benjamin stabbed the tube into his stomach.

"Gah!" he cried as microbots flowed into the wound. He tossed the vial aside, and it clattered and rolled across the downed chronoport's wing. He collapsed on his back, arms and legs splayed around him, chest heaving with each labored breath.

"Get yourself up!" Klaus-Wilhelm grabbed his shoulder. Benjamin winced as his grandfather propped him up against an armor panel that bent sharply upward. He shoved Benjamin's gun back into his hands. "You with us?"

The train whistled, louder and coming closer.

"Yeah." Benjamin gasped and nodded. "I'm still here."

"Stay sharp." Klaus-Wilhelm clapped him on the shoulder, then pointed across the field. "Those bastards are coming back."

"Wonderful." Benjamin coughed and winced as he shifted himself around. His entire midsection burned, but he soldiered through it and slid his MP40's muzzle forward over the wing's cover. His mask outlined a large force of Admin gathered at the end of the forest. Special operators opened fire from the tree line, and a horde of drones charged out with two STANDs boosting up the flanks.

He ducked back down, and shots zinged off the bent armor plate.

"No one gives a centimeter!" Klaus-Wilhelm shouted. "This is where we hold! *Hold*, d'you hear me?"

A dozen MP40s chattered savagely, and drones burst apart.

More leapt or flew over the wreckage, and the STANDs boosted forward as they cut loose with guided grenades.

An explosion knocked Benjamin back, and he gasped as he hit the wing. He forced himself upright, the taste of iron filling his mouth, then raised his weapon and pulled the trigger. Drones exploded under his fire, and he hammered them until the clip ran dry, then yanked out the magazine.

He patted his belt, found another magazine, and raised it to the receiver. His vision darkened, his breath shortened, and he missed the slot. The magazine fumbled out of his fingers and slid away across the wing until it came to rest against Raibert's broken thigh.

He checked his belt again.

Nothing. He was out except for standard bullets.

A train whistle blared twice.

"They're too close to the tracks! Push the bastards back!" Klaus-Wilhelm ordered.

"We're trying, sir!" Anton shouted, spraying bullets.

Benjamin crawled behind cover until he reached the end of the upturned panel and was about to stretch out his arm for the magazine, but then stopped. The nose of the second self-replicator rocket peeked out of Raibert's torn backpack, its conical tip gleaming in the sun.

Aha!

Benjamin looked around frantically for the launcher, but didn't see it. Had Raibert even come back with it?

No. No he hadn't.

Damn.

"The train's at risk!" Klaus-Wilhelm barked. "Hit them with everything you've got! PUSH THEM BACK!"

The train whistled again, dangerously close now.

Benjamin steeled his nerve and reached for the rocket. A mag dart clipped the top of his sleeve, and he winced in fresh pain, but he grabbed hold and pulled the rocket back into cover. He cradled it against his chest, found the dial, and cranked it down to its lowest setting.

Fear of this weapon.

That's all he needed. Fear so deeply engrained in the Admin's collective psyche that they enshrined laws prohibiting its creation and waged wars to stamp out anyone who dared defy those laws.

Fear now ripe in their minds from the demonstration Raibert had so generously provided.

Fear would drive them back.

Benjamin's knuckles whitened as he clenched the rocket's shaft and pressed it against his chest. He nodded grimly, coming to terms with what he was about to do.

"It's not working!" Anton cried out, ducking behind cover. "I'm out of ammo!"

"Here!" Klaus-Wilhelm tossed Anton a magazine. "Make every shot count!"

Benjamin closed his eyes, made the sign of the cross, and sucked in a deep breath.

"EVERYONE!" he shouted at the top of his lungs. "COVER ME!"

He vaulted over the panel and sprinted toward the advancing Admin forces.

"What are you doing?" Klaus-Wilhelm barked. "Get back here!"

A STAND boosted across Benjamin's path. Its heavy rail-rifle fired, and two hits stabbed him in the chest. Blood sprayed from his mouth and nostrils, partially obscuring the inside of his mask, but he kept his balance and charged straight at the STAND with a berserker's fury.

Klaus-Wilhelm sprayed the combat frame with automatic fire, and its boosters faltered just enough for Benjamin to close the distance. He raised the rocket over his head two-handed, like a stubby spear, and the STAND swung its incinerator up.

The weapon ignited with a *whoosh*, and blue flame cooked his flesh through holes in the uniform's prog-steel weave. He screamed as he brought the nose of the rocket crashing down. The fuse struck the STAND's chest, the dispersion payload detonated, and Benjamin's hands and arms vanished as the explosion flung him back.

A rusty aerosol sprayed everywhere, coating the STAND, the ground, several nearby drones—

—and the front half of Benjamin.

He fell onto his back and gasped for air as replicators burrowed into his flesh through holes in his armor, through the bloody stumps that used to be his arms, and commandeered his own circulatory system to eat their way through his body.

The STAND stumbled back, boosters sputtering. Liquid rust

oozed out of its chest, internal systems caught fire, and it collapsed upon itself.

The Admin forces broke almost instantly. They knew the weapon they faced. They *feared* it, perhaps more than anything else they had ever faced, and they fled back toward the tree line, putting as much distance as possible between them and the blighted ground.

A black border encroached on Benjamin's vision. His body felt hot. So incredibly hot. And yet, for a moment he wondered if the replicators had stopped working because his pain slipped away and a strange lightness settled over him.

"No! Stay back, sir!" he heard someone say.

"Let go of me, damn it!" another man cried out. *"I'm not losing him, too!"*

Benjamin's last breath wheezed through pale lips as the train roared past, whistle blaring.

And the sword cut the knot.

CHAPTER FORTY

Denton, North Carolina
2017 CE

BENJAMIN SILENCED HIS ALARM CLOCK AND SMACKED HIS LIPS. He sat up in bed, rubbed the crusty sleep from his eyes, then blinked around at the bleary gloom of his bedroom.

The numbers on the alarm clock cast the queen-sized bed in a greenish hue, and he flashed a despondent frown at it. Today was not a day he'd been looking forward to. Today he had the privilege of attending his first of several gender awareness sessions.

Uuuuuuuuh . . .

Oh well, he thought. *No use putting it off. Let's get this over with.*

He shuffled into the bathroom, squeezed a glob of paste onto his sonic toothbrush and gave his teeth a thorough scrubbing. Then he flossed between each tooth, rinsed his mouth for one minute and spat, and shuffled over to his closet. Neat rows of button-down shirts hung organized from lightest to darkest. He selected one of his two gray shirts and a black bowtie and suspenders, avoiding all the cheerful colors. He was in a dark mood.

He put the shirt and a pair of black pants on the ironing board, rubbed his eyes again, and made his way to the kitchen counter. He opened the refrigerator, took out a plastic bag of fresh strawberries, and put four on the cutting board before returning the bag to the refrigerator. Then he cut each strawberry into quarters from tip to stem, raked the pieces into a bowl, and added milk and Cheerios.

Sitting at the counter, he curled his toes up for warmth and crunched down on the first spoonful. He chewed slowly, thoughtfully, and pondered the day to come, trying to remind himself that this was a critical step in his master plan. That stupid as this was going to be, O'Hearn was doing exactly what he wanted him to do.

It didn't help a lot.

"Gender-sensitivity training..." He stuffed another spoonful robotically into his mouth, then raised both eyebrows. "You know, it might not be as bad as I think."

Yeah. Right.

It'd probably be worse.

He finished his cereal, drank the milk, then rinsed off the bowl and put it into the dishwasher. He reclaimed his clothes from the ironing board, put them on, and checked his reflection in the mirror.

"I look like I'm going to a funeral," he muttered, then shrugged. "Oh well. They'll just have to deal with it."

He grabbed his wallet, phone, and keys, reached for the door—

And froze.

His mouth opened in a silent scream as the sudden shock clubbed him to his knees. His arms dropped limply at his side, hanging there as if they belonged to someone else, and then, slowly, his hands rose to his head. A torrent of thought roared through him with sledgehammer force, burning him, deafening him, scouring away reason and sanity, *consuming* him. He squeezed his eyes shut as if that could stop the flood, but it poured over him and through him. It tore him apart, stripping his mind layer by layer.

Alien thoughts crashed across his being, drowned out who he was. Memories he'd never had. People he'd never met. Places he'd never been. A big, crazy man knocking at his door. A Viking with an aviator helmet. His own *grandfather*, but younger than he'd ever seen him. Machines that couldn't possibly exist. SS troopers fighting the machines.

And a woman he loved with all his heart.

Two realities collided. Thoughts converged, swirled about, tore at each other, *fought* each other, and yet both were equally real. It was impossible. *It couldn't be true!* He was here, in his home, but he was also *dying*! How could that be? How could *any* of this be possible? His mind reeled as twin realities poured into a container that should only ever hold one.

His elbows hit the floor, his arms cradling his head in fragile self-defense as he collapsed completely. Phantom pain echoed through his chest and stomach, and he curled into a knot around the agony, gasping for breath that wouldn't come. What was happening to him? Was he dying right now?

But then the fog in his mind began to clear, and he realized the horrible truth.

He wasn't dying.

He was already *dead*.

He'd died in battle trying to save Adolf Hitler. Had *succeeded* in saving that monster's life. And he'd sacrificed an entire timeline with untold billions or even trillions of people to do it. He'd been *eaten alive* achieving those goals . . . and he'd done it *willingly*!

"No!" He writhed on the floor, the agony of that thought far worse than any physical pain, any fear of mere *death*.

He'd willingly participated in a temporal genocide greater than the most wretched monsters in human history could even have *imagined*, but that wasn't the worst of it. He'd made himself responsible for all the atrocities of World War II. For the Holocaust, the Chinese Revolution, Stalin's Russia, the Korean War, Pol Pot . . .

The horror crashed down on him, smashed him like the hammer of hell itself, and under the guilt for those billions of lives, behind it, slicing through it like Satan's own sword, was the memory of the single life he'd valued above all others.

And he'd killed *her*, too. Erased her from existence.

How could this be? How could any of this be true?

And yet he knew with absolute certainty that it was.

The chaos ripped and tore at him, the pandemonium screaming inside his skull, the conflicting memories desperate to escape. It went on and on and *on* as his mind tried—tried desperately—to reject the memories of the Benjamin Schröder who'd done those hideous things . . . and failed. He couldn't shut them off, couldn't deny them, and in their echoes, in that torrent of confusion and anguish, he saw the madness coming for him.

Knew he was *already* mad, because there could be no other explanation.

Yet somewhere in the midst of that maelstrom, there was an

echo of calm. A gestalt—fragile and fleeting—hovered just beyond his reach, and his agonized mind reached toward it. Reached and touched a moment of clarity. This other, alien, horrifying version of him had already experienced this. It had *already* been torn apart, shredded under the impact of *his* memories, and it had struggled long and hard to banish those memories, the memories of *this* universe. And for a time it had enjoyed some small measure of success. Yet that other Benjamin had known even then that his success could be only fleeting, and in the end he'd been made whole only through acceptance.

And that was because that other Benjamin, these memories, were a part of him. However much he might hate them, however terrible the pain, they were *part* of him. He couldn't escape them, couldn't will them out of existence. There was only one thing he *could* do, and so he opened himself to them, instead. He *let* them course through his mind, clinging by his fingernails to what sanity remained, and slowly—*so* slowly—they...settled. They echoed and reechoed at the heart of him, tearing him apart, yet even as they did, they made him...complete. He *felt* them fusing together, turning him into someone—something—neither of his realities had ever been, and his fists clenched as the torrent slowed from a tsunami to a flood, and then merely to a river, and then—

His breathing slowed. His muscles slackened. He flopped onto his back with his limbs spread wide and stared at the ceiling for minutes. Hours, maybe? The thoughts settled and congealed, piece by piece, and in the end, he sat up, whole again.

"God," he breathed. "What have I *done*?"

And then he wept. He buried his face in his knees and let the grief and agony take hold. He'd killed her. As surely as if he'd held a gun to her head and pulled the trigger. He shook his head as tears trickled down his cheeks. He rubbed his face against his knees as the long, shuddering sobs wracked him.

What kind of monster was he?

Benjamin drove up a gravel road on the outskirts of Denton and parked his car at the crest of the hill. He climbed out, closed the door, and stared across the field of barren dirt spotted with leprous clumps of weeds. It was the site of Irwin's Steak & Seafood restaurant. Or would have been, in another version of the timeline.

Here it was just a vacant lot.

He rounded the car, opened the passenger door, and took a narrow, white cylinder off the seat. He walked across the field, gravel and stubble crunching under his shoes, until he reached the center, then he dropped to his knees and picked up a handful of dirt. In his mind, he saw the drones bursting through the windows. Raibert shooting them down.

And Ella on the ground, bleeding, dying.

He tossed the dirt into the air, and the wind scattered it.

This was where he'd proposed to her. Before she ceased to exist...

He didn't know where he should do this. Her grandparents had died in the Holocaust, so there were no houses in Denton that belonged to her family. No gravestones either. All of it had been erased. The university had changed so much as well, so using that didn't feel right. A movie theater stood where her old apartment had been, and their favorite restaurant was now a landfill. None of those were suitable.

But this place was different. It was quiet here on the edge of town, and a barren patch of earth seemed fitting. This was where she'd been wounded by the Admin, where her blood had been spilled in the other universe. He popped the lid off the cylinder and took out three fresh roses he'd bought on the way over.

"I'm sorry," he whispered, and set the roses on the ground. His eyes teared once more, and he bowed his head. "I should have said no. I should have at least *tried* to save you."

A gust of wind kicked up dust. He smeared the tears running down his cheeks, bent over and wept. He couldn't even call it death. She simply...wasn't. All she'd been, all she would have become, had been swept away.

Because of me. Because I said yes to this madness.

He knelt before a grave with no body and no headstone. No one knew her name. No one existed to mourn her loss.

No one except the man who'd done far worse than merely kill her.

"You deserved better than this." He rose, eyes red with shame and grief. "Better than me."

He drove home feeling drained of life and purpose. He'd committed an unspeakable atrocity, one with consequences large and small, and a price had to be paid. No one here knew of his crime, and so it fell upon only one man to punish him.

He didn't bother locking the door when he returned home, only walked straight to the bedroom with limp steps and knelt before his gun safe. He unlocked it, took out his .45 USP, and retrieved a single cartridge from a box of ammo. He set it beside the gun on the dinner table, then sat down in front of them.

He stared at them for long, endless moments, feeling their rightness—their inevitability. Then he sighed, ejected the magazine, inserted that single, gleaming cartridge, and slid the mag back into the pistol's butt. He slapped it gently to be sure it was seated, chambered the round, and held the pistol in his hands. He never really knew how long he sat staring down at the familiar black polymer, wrestling with the rightness of his decision. But then, finally, he opened his mouth and slid the muzzle between his teeth.

He placed his thumb over the trigger and pressed his eyes shut.

The phone vibrated in his pocket.

He flinched at the sensation. His eyes started to open, but then his nostrils flared. He closed those eyes, more tightly even than before, and began to squeeze the trigger.

His phone vibrated again...and something happened. His eyes opened once more, bleak with a new and different sort of self-contempt, and he took the pistol from his mouth. He took his thumb out of the trigger guard, decocked the hammer, set the safety, and laid it back on the table. He stared down at it once more, feeling its whispered promise of release...and heard his father's voice in the back of his mind, knew what Klaus Schröder would have thought of *that* form of escape. Of *evading* the responsibilities of his life.

His phone vibrated again and again as those thoughts rolled through him, and he shuddered convulsively, then picked it slowly out of his pocket.

"Hello?" His voice was flat, wooden.

"I just wanted to check in and see how that gender-sensitivity crap's going," a cheerful voice said in his ear, bubbling with suppressed laughter. "You piss 'em all off yet, or are you waiting till tomorrow?"

"David?" he choked.

His brother was *alive*.

The realization crashed over him. The brother that other Benjamin had mourned without ever knowing was *alive*. The wonder of it washed through him, blazing in the darkness like some unhoped for star, and he swallowed hard.

"Hey," he whispered.

"Hey yourself." David's voice had changed, and Benjamin could see him in his mind's eyes, frowning, looking at Steven and raising one eyebrow as his big brother's ashen tone registered. "You doing okay? You sound a little . . . off."

"No, I'm not okay." His eyes moistened. "But I think I will be."

Some good had come from this madness after all, he thought, and latched on to that small glimmer of light, like a sailor clinging to a shattered spar after the shipwreck. David had been lost, but now he was alive again. Alive *because* of Benjamin's actions. He slid the gun away until it was almost on the other side of the table.

"Is now a good time?" David asked. "Sounds like you've got some heavy stuff on your mind."

"You could say that. In fact, I—"

Someone knocked on the front door—hard. The three, resounding knocks echoed through the house, and Benjamin shook his head with a tired sigh. The universe just wasn't going to let him kill himself today.

"Hey, Dave? Can I call you back?"

"Sure. Sure. We can talk later. You just take care of yourself, okay?"

"I will. Later."

He hung up, ejected the H&K's magazine, and stuffed the gun into a kitchen drawer.

Three more heavy knocks reverberated through the house.

"Coming!" he shouted. "Good grief, you're persistent."

Benjamin opened the door and came face to face with a towering fellow in a beautifully tailored gray-green uniform. That was a color that other Benjamin had seen very recently, the *feldgrau* of the German army, to be precise. The flash on its right shoulder was black, embroidered with a golden eye above a bared, horizontal sword. The letters "SYSPOL" formed an arch across the top of the flash, and the words "Gordian Division" curved around its bottom, turning that arch into a complete circle.

"Greetings, Doctor Schröder," the uniformed man began. "I hope I'm not intruding. May I have a moment of your ti—?"

Benjamin snarled and slammed the door in his face.

"I'm sorry?" Raibert Kaminski's voice was muffled by the closed door. "Was it something I said?"

"Get out of here! Get the *hell* out of here! I'm through helping you, you hear me?"

"Hold on. You know who I am?"

"Of *course* I do, you idiot!"

The door hinges ripped out of the wall.

"Damn it, Raibert! Doesn't anyone in the thirtieth century teach you people to respect closed doors?"

"Oh." He glanced at the dislodged door in his hands, then set it daintily aside. "Right. Sorry about that. Look, can we go back to the part where you know who I am?"

"Why are you acting so surprised? Of course I know who you are. You're the lunatic with the time machine that I never. *Ever. EVER!* Want to see again!"

"But that's not possible." Raibert crossed his arms, tilted his head to one side, and stared at him. "You shouldn't recognize me."

"And why wouldn't I?"

"Because this is the wrong universe unless..." His eyes went wide. "Oh. *Oh.*"

"What are you *oh*ing about?"

"We didn't consider this at all."

"Consider what?"

"But they clearly do. Now *that's* interesting! I've got to tell the others."

"Raibert, what the hell are you rambling about? No! Forget I said that! I don't want to know what you're rambling about. I want you to just go the hell away!"

"Right. Yes. Going away now." Raibert grabbed the door, stepped outside, and propped it against the outer wall. Then he raised one hand, index finger waving in a hold-that-thought sort of motion. "Just wait right there. I'll be back shortly."

"What part of 'never want to see you again' don't you understand?" Benjamin shouted after him, but Raibert had already dashed down the front walk to the street, reached the sidewalk, and disappeared. Benjamin glared after him, then exhaled an explosive sigh.

"Oh, what the hell," he muttered and picked up the door—not nearly so easily as Raibert had—and tried to fit it back into place.

But the doorframe had warped when Raibert broke off the hinges. He tried for several seconds before he finally gave up, leaned it back against the wall, and stalked across to the dining room. He sat back down at the table, glaring through the living room arch at the square of sunlight where his front door used to be, and his fingers drummed on the tabletop as he waited to discover what fresh madness Raibert thought he could visit upon his life.

Whatever it was, he was going to be disappointed. *Sadly* disappointed.

Several minutes passed, and he heard at least two pairs of footsteps approach the door. Someone other than Raibert tapped lightly on the doorframe.

"Come on in," Benjamin said nastily. "It's open, after all, isn't it?"

"Well, you heard him," Raibert said to someone else. "Go on!"

The synthoid stepped aside and someone stepped past him. It was a woman, wearing the same gray-green uniform, and Benjamin froze.

It couldn't be. It *couldn't!*

He stood there, unable to move, and she seemed just as frozen as he was. She stared at his face, her eyes huge and hungry... and afraid. And then she took another slow, tentative step into his home.

"*Ella?*" he whispered.

"You see?" Raibert said. "I told you."

"You really know it's me?" Her voice was soft, almost inaudible, and he shook his head violently.

"How could I *not?*" he demanded hoarsely.

Ella put a hand over her mouth and her eyes glistened, brimming with tears.

"It's you, isn't it?" she asked. "It's really *you?*"

"I—" He stared at her, unsure what to say, how to answer that question. Who *was* he, really, now? What sort of—

"Yes," he said, and in that moment, he knew it was the right answer. *Exactly* the right answer. "It's me, Ella...*both* of me."

"Oh, Ben!" The tears broke loose and she threw her arms around him. "Oh, Ben! I *lost* you! I thought I'd *lost* you!"

He held her close and shut his eyes, reveling in the familiar press of her body against his, the scent of her hair, the warmth of her cheek against the side of his neck. She was real. *Real!* Not some phantom from his other memories, not a hallucination. She was a real flesh-and-blood human being clinging to him with the urgency of someone who'd lost the most important person in the universe...and found out she'd been wrong.

He knew exactly how she felt, and his heart soared as he buried his face in her hair and whispered her name again and again.

He never knew exactly how long that moment of transcendent joy lasted. But the intensity eased—a little—at last, and they turned their heads as someone cleared his throat.

"Actually," Raibert said with all the insufferable perkiness Benjamin "remembered" only too well, "we *did* lose him. But now it seems we've found him again."

Benjamin glared at him, but then, despite himself, he laughed. He shook his head, then turned back to Elzbietá.

"I can't even begin to describe how happy I am to see you!" He kissed her hard, then held her out before him, hands on her shoulders. "But can someone *please* explain to me what's going on? How did you survive? Why are you here? What's up with these?" He motioned to the uniforms.

"Oh, wow, where to begin?" Raibert rubbed the back of his neck.

"The Knot," Benjamin asked. "What happened to the Knot?"

"Unraveled," Elzbietá said.

"With all those other universes accounted for and looking healthy," Raibert added.

"*All* of them?" Benjamin said quietly, looking at Elzbietá, and her face tightened for a moment. Then it smoothed.

"Fifteen out of sixteen isn't all that bad," she said, meeting his eyes levelly. He found his arms back around her, and she leaned into his shoulder.

"But...in that case..." He looked over her head at Raibert. "How can—?"

"The Knot didn't unravel instantly," the historian said. "It was fast, but not instantaneous. Elzbietá and Philo got back to 1940 in time to take out the rest of the Admin ground force and pick your grandfather and his men back up. And what was left of me, too. Luckily, those STAND bastards missed my case, so Kleio was able to put me back together—*with*, I might add, some improvements I don't think the Admin ever thought of... or would approve of if they knew about them—and we got out just in time."

"We would've picked you up, too," Elzbietá said, "but—"

"I was already dead," Benjamin finished for her. "Yeah, I remember."

Raibert and Elzbietá exchanged a look, and the synthoid shrugged.

"Apparently he remembers that, too."

"And why is that strange?" Benjamin asked.

"Because we didn't think the you in this universe would have dual memories," Raibert said. "And even if you did, we had no way of guessing you'd actually have *all* the memories up to the Knot unraveling. Don't take this the wrong way, but we thought you'd be...more normal."

"I'll try not to take offense...considering the source," Benjamin retorted. "But what's this 'got out just in time' about?"

"Elzbietá and Philo cut it really, really close," Raibert said, and his expression had turned grim. "We phased back out of 1940 less than five minutes before the Knot *did* unravel and the wave front hit us."

He shook his head, his eyes dark, but then he smiled suddenly.

"Turned out that handrail I had Kleio add on the bridge was a really good idea," he said far more cheerfully. "Elzbictá was still in her acceleration chamber, but your grandfather's boys would've gotten some broken bones—at least—without something solid to hang onto." He shook his head again. "The turbulence that overtook Philo and me on the way home from North Africa was *nothing* compared to this one, trust me! We damned near didn't make it this time."

"No. No, we didn't," Elzbietá agreed against the side of Benjamin's neck. "And I never want to experience anything that... horrible again." She paused to inhale deeply. "I was still tied into *Kleio*'s sensors. I saw an entire universe just...come apart. It just...*shredded*, Ben. You could see the chronotons peeling away like a sandstorm, disappearing..."

She shuddered, and Benjamin's arms tightened around her.

"That's exactly what happened," Raibert acknowledged, meeting his gaze steadily. "And the turbulence punched us—well, for want of a better term, it punched us laterally through the wall of Elzbietá's universe as it disintegrated. We, ah...acquired a lot of additional data in the process."

"That much I can believe!"

"Well, according to our new theories—which seem to be holding *so far*—Elzbietá and your grandfather and his men survived because they were protected inside *Kleio*'s phase state. Of course, if *Kleio* hadn't held together, that wouldn't have mattered in the long run."

Benjamin nodded, then pressed his face into Elzbietá's hair.

"I am *so* sorry, love," he said softly. "I lost everything I knew and loved in that universe, but...but there's still the me in *this* universe. But you...you and Granddad..." His nostrils flared. "I really did destroy everything you ever knew."

"Not...really," Raibert said, and Benjamin's head popped back up.

"But you just said—"

"Well...it turns out there was just a *teeny* mistake in our original models." Raibert shrugged. "Actually, given how little data we had and how far outside the Theory Of Everything we were operating at that point, I guess what *should* have surprised us would have been getting everything right. But it turns out Hitler's assassination wasn't the real causative effect at all."

"What?" Benjamin blinked, then stiffened. "Wait a minute! You're telling me that everything we did—everything we *went through*—didn't mean a damned—"

"No, that's not what he's saying...exactly," Elzbietá said in a soothing sort of tone. She gave him one more squeeze, then stepped back with an off-center smile. "But what happened is that you were the only map we had to where the event had occurred, and you remembered two different outcomes of the assassination attempt. So, *obviously*, that was the trigger. Only it wasn't, really. The real trigger was having that many chronoports—and *Kleio*, of course—disrupting the timestream in such a concentrated dose and in such a tight chronometric window. That's what really tore open a hole in the Admin universe and allowed all that chrono-metric energy to flood in from fifteen neighbors."

"So...so you're saying we *created* the event by going back and trying to *prevent* the event?"

"More or less," Raibert agreed. "Explaining what actually happened to you is going to require math you don't have yet, and honestly it's a theory I'm *still* trying to wrap my head around. You may recall we experienced two asynchronous temporal effects."

"We experienced what?" Benjamin asked in a pointed tone.

"First," Raibert held up a finger, "there's the Knot itself and how the temporal dogfight spawned it. And second, there's how we caused your original brain-melt. In both cases, effect *preceded* cause. From the absolute timeframe of the Edge of Existence, of course."

"Well, of *course*," Benjamin said with a frown.

"You see, the dogfight *followed* the Knot's formation, and likewise your episode *followed* us picking you up and then taking you back to 2018. According to the TOE that's not possible, which has pretty much every physicist in SysGov trying to sort out the missing theoretical pieces of our vaunted Theory Of *Everything*. Instead, it turns out these sorts of asynchronous events are only possible under *very* specific circumstances, such as within the bounds of the chronoton storm around the Knot."

"You've completely lost me."

"Well, the details don't really matter," Raibert dismissed with a wave. "What's important is you were the only guy we had with memories from two different universes, so we assumed—I still think logically, given what we knew—that the discrepancy between the two histories you remembered was the key event. But what it actually *was* was the focal point in time where the Admin universe separated from the SysGov universe. Only, it couldn't break free because of all the temporal mutilation we did fighting each other."

"My God. Then we didn't have to go at all!"

"Oh, we had to go," Elzbietá said. "The Knot existed, however it *came* into existence, and if we hadn't found a way to unknot it—if we hadn't found our sword—then it *would* have destroyed all of those universes. Including *this* one." She jabbed an index finger at the floor beneath her feet. "Never doubt that, Ben."

"All that concentrated chronometric energy actually *did* create the Admin universe," Raibert said. "By itself, that wouldn't have been a problem, since our new models predict that additional universes are coming into existence all the time. The problem was that *this* universe was mangled from the start. Our battle punched a hole in what you might call the 'outer wall' of the Admin universe, and that's where all of that energy was pouring into it and where all of it would eventually backlash into the universes it had come from initially. So it had to be undone. And the key to undoing it was to prevent Hitler's assassination, because that was the key event that formed that universe in the first place. It might only have happened originally because we went back, but when we prevented the assassination, we...restored just enough temporal consistency for the SysGov universe to break free from the Knot. And once it did, the rest soon followed. It didn't keep the original turbulence from having all the effects we observed and experienced, but it cut off the inflow of additional energy and the storm front dissipated well short of the Edge of Existence."

"And wiped out Elzbietá's universe," Benjamin said flatly.

"Wiped out *this* Elzbietá's universe," Elzbietá corrected very softly.

"What?"

"When we finally punched through the wall into a universe that still existed, guess where we found ourselves?" Raibert said. Benjamin looked at him, and the synthoid grinned. "Go on!" he urged. "Guess!"

"Oh, stop it, Raibert!" Elzbietá gave him a disgusted look, then turned back to Benjamin. "It turns out that my universe wasn't the only one in which Hitler was assassinated in 1940. Another iteration of that universe—all of it—existed. Turns out that the universe 'right next to' *my* universe is identical in every way so far as we can tell. There may be some divergences further downstream, but if so, we don't have anything to compare them to. And it doesn't really matter, because the point is that all of the people I lost with my universe *are still alive*, Ben. In some absolute sense, my universe, my family, my friends—they're all gone. But in every other sense, all the people I ever loved are alive and well...except for you. Because the Benjamin Schröder in that universe never remembered what you remembered. He never experienced what you experienced—what I experienced *with* you—and so...he's not you."

Her eyes softened, searching his face hungrily.

"But I don't belong there," she said quietly. "There's another Elzbietá in that universe, and she loves all those people—and they love her—just as much as I ever loved them. I can't just walk into her life, into their lives, and announce I'm also her. So in that sense, my universe *is* gone. I can't go home, but the thing is that thanks to you, I know 'home' is still *there*."

"Wait." Benjamin's eyes narrowed. "If that's true, then Yulia—"

"Yulia lived exactly as long as you remembered," she told him, laying a hand gently on his forearm, and smiled. "Your Aunt

Diana and Aunt Xristina are both still alive, for that matter! But," her smile faded, "your grandfather couldn't go home any more than I can. I think—I'm sure, from my own experience—that his grief has to have eased a lot, but he can't take that universe's Klaus-Wilhelm's place any more than I can take that Elzbietá's."

"Then it was worth it?" Benjamin asked.

"You better believe it was worth it. Although..." Raibert paused and grimaced. "You remember I said there was a *teeny* error in our original model?"

"Why do I get the feeling it was anything but 'teeny'?" Benjamin asked, his expression wary.

"*We-e-e-e-ll*, we did have this little problem. We just so happened to still be stuck in the wrong universe."

"Right. '*Little* problem.'" Benjamin rolled his eyes, and Raibert shrugged.

"Could've been worse," he said. Benjamin gave him a skeptical look. "Well, it *could* have!" he insisted.

"Okay, fine," Benjamin sighed. "You're stuck in another universe. Which 'another' universe? And how *did* you get back to SysGov?"

"Glad you asked." Raibert beamed. "You see, where we wound up when the Knot broke apart was the other Elzbietá's universe, and the TTV's chronometric array was still working when we punched through the wall. Like I said before, it recorded a *huge* amount of data that sheds a lot of light on how the multiverse is fundamentally structured. Philo and Kleio spent two whole months crunching the math and managed to come up with a modification for the impeller. We fixed the TTV, refitted the impeller, and we were finally able to phase back to this universe."

"So now you can hop from universe to universe?"

"Yep!" Raibert grinned. "For that matter, we can be certain we come and go in the *same* universe even on a temporal jump. We may still make changes, may still split off new universes, but we can phase back into the one where the change occurred instead of simply our own base line. The *Kleio* just keeps getting better and better."

"Once we were in the right universe, we headed for the thirtieth century," Elzbietá said. "Raibert's thirtieth century, not the Admin's. And, Ben, you should really see the place. SysGov is *incredible*."

"I can imagine." He smiled and reached out and stroked her hair. "And—" He paused, then shook his head. "I was about to say that you can't imagine how happy I am to see you, but fortunately I realized in time that you're probably the only person in the universe—in *all* the universes—who understands *exactly* how happy I am."

"You got that one right, Ben," she told him, reaching back to cup his face in her hands—both her hands—and kiss him thoroughly.

"Ahem!" Raibert said thirty or forty seconds later. Elzbietá turned her head to glare at him over her shoulder, and he coughed into his fist. "Moving right along?" he said helpfully.

"I guess that leads me to the next question I'll probably regret asking," Benjamin said. "Not that I'm not delighted to see you—well, to see *one* of you, anyway—but I have to wonder why you're here. Especially if you'd assumed that I wouldn't remember what happened any more than the Benjamin in the other Elzbietá's universe does?"

"Your grandfather sent us," Raibert replied, and Benjamin blinked.

"Why? And for that matter, since when did you start taking orders from my grandfather?"

"Hold that thought. We're getting a little ahead of ourselves here. First, we should tell you what happened when we got home."

"Okay." Benjamin raised both hands shoulder high. "Tell away."

"Well, Philo and I took our findings to the Ministry of Education as soon as we got home. A lot happened after that, and I mean a *lot*. Long story short, SysGov instituted the Gordian Protocol, a law code designed to regulate both time travel and transdimensional travel, since we just happened to have figured out how to do *that*, too. And also authorized SysPol—the police in my time, if you recall—to create a new division dedicated to enforcing the Protocol."

"Which we now work for." Elzbietá tapped the flash on her right shoulder. "SysPol, Gordian Division."

"'Gordian,' huh?" Benjamin nodded. "I like it."

"Actually," Raibert smirked and crossed his arms. "I was the one who suggested the name during my testimony."

"I like it less now."

Raibert gave him a dirty look, but Elzbietá chuckled. Raibert looked even more affronted for a moment, but then he began to smile himself.

"So how does my grandfather fit into all of this?" Benjamin pressed "Did you recruit him or something?"

"Recruit him?" Raibert laughed. "Are you kidding? He's our boss. *He* recruited *us*."

"How did *that* happen?"

"What can we say?" Elzbietá shrugged. "The man's like a force of nature."

"He may only have the Gordian Division for now," Raibert commented. "But give him time. I'll bet he ends up running *all* of SysPol before long."

"I suppose that explains the uniforms then," Benjamin remarked. "And he sent you back here to pick me up?"

"To offer you a job," the synthoid corrected. "We didn't think you'd have your memories, but a version of you *did* play a major role in saving this universe. The Gordian Division needs the very best, and your actions, my friend, impressed a lot of important people."

"Which is why Klaus-Wilhelm got this time-travel excursion approved and we came back here," Elzbietá said.

"*Soooooo.*" Raibert leaned casually against the wall. "Want the job?"

"If I take it, do I sign a one-way ticket to the future? I just got over losing Dave, Steve, and Mom and getting them back again. I don't want to lose them again!"

"Well, I'm not really sure," Raibert grimaced. "Like I said, we didn't expect you to be you, so yeah." He shrugged. "Haven't really considered this."

"But surely SysPol can make an exception in his case," Elzbietá pointed out, then reassured Benjamin with a smile. "Your grandfather got this trip approved, so I'm sure he can set up some sort of special arrangement for you. Perhaps a kind of periodic leave to this part of the timeline. You could even come back to the exact instant you left, so none of your family will even know you've been gone."

"Hmm." Raibert slowly began to nod. "Yeah. Could work."

"Klaus-Wilhelm *did* say 'make sure he says yes' before we left." Elzbietá winked at Benjamin. "He sounded quite adamant about that."

"Yeah," Raibert repeated with growing certainty. "Yeah, you're right. I'm sure he could get an exception like that approved. I mean, hell, look at everything *else* he's managed to ram through the Ministry. Plus, you did turn yourself into a puddle to save the day. That's got to count for something, right?"

"Great!" Benjamin exclaimed. "In that case—wait. There is one other thing."

"What?" Raibert demanded.

"Are there any gender-awareness classes I'll need to take?"

"Uhh, no. Why would you even ask?"

"No gender-awareness classes? Well why didn't you say so! We can leave right now!"

"Now that's more like it!" Raibert clapped his hands together. "The *Kleio* is right outside. Is there anything you want to bring?"

"That won't be necessary." He rested a hand on Elzbietá's shoulder. "I already have what matters most."

"Ahhh," Raibert sighed. "You two are so cute."

Elzbietá smacked Raibert on the arm, and the big man chuckled as he left the house.

"So what is it I'm getting myself into?" Benjamin asked as they followed Raibert out.

"I'll say this much about it." Elzbietá hooked her arm into his. "You won't be bored."

"But what if I'm in the mood for something boring?" he asked. "You know, just for a change of pace. I think I've completely forgotten what bored feels like."

"Well then." She patted his arm. "I'd say you're going into the wrong field. Having second thoughts?"

"Not a one."

They walked out onto his driveway, and the *Kleio* shed its metamaterial shroud and lowered the front cargo ramp. Its clean gunmetal hull gleamed in the sunlight, and the golden SysPol eye blazed high on the nose. The outer lines of the craft were bulkier—and meaner looking—than the last time he'd seen it.

"Good news is we're heading straight into your first assignment," Raibert stated as he walked the ramp. "We've identified three other time-traveling societies on different versions of Earth, and they're all blissfully going around wrecking this sector of the multiverse."

"Part of our job is to establish contact with those societies,"

Elzbietá said. "We hope to assemble pan-multiverse enforcement for the Gordian Protocol someday."

"That sounds ambitious," Benjamin noted.

"It is," Raibert groaned. "And two of those societies are going to be first contacts, so this might get interesting."

"I'll keep that in mind." Benjamin walked up the ramp, and the prog-steel sealed shut behind him. The other two continued across the cargo bay, but Benjamin stopped suddenly. "Wait a second."

Raibert turned back to face him. "Something wrong?"

"Yeah. You said only *two* of them are first contacts."

EPILOGUE

⊗⊗⊗

Department of Temporal Investigation
2979 CE

THE SCHEMATIC OF THE NEW *HAMMERHEAD*-CLASS HEAVY ASSAULT chronoport rotated over Csaba Shigeki's black glass desk. It bristled with weapons and armor, but he most assuredly did not drool over it.

Well, maybe a little.

He couldn't argue about the price either: just a few chronoports from Pathfinder Squadron placed under Cheryl First's command for an expedition to the Valley of the Kings. That and a carefully worded request to Chief Executor First, and now he had the budget to expand his squadrons with the best military hardware available.

Shigeki leaned back in his chair with a smug grin and placed his hands behind his head. Yes, today was going *quite* well. Quite well indeed.

The door chimed.

"Yes, come in."

He brought his chair back upright as the door split open, and a towering blond man in a gray-green uniform stepped in. Shigeki frowned at the unfamiliar face. He queried the man's identity with his PIN, but the only match the tower's infostructure could find was for an unassigned synthoid in DOI storage, which didn't make any sense at all.

"Hello again, Director," the big man said with a friendly smile.

"Excuse me? Have we met?" Shigeki asked pointedly.

"That depends on your point of view." He sat down and leaned back in the chair casually. "I'm Special Agent Raibert Kaminski, Consolidated System Police, Gordian Division."

"That certainly...sounds impressive," Shigeki admitted as he signaled for Nox to get the hell over here, "but I'm not familiar with your...organization. You seem to have me at a disadvantage."

"A refreshing change of pace, to be sure."

Shigeki's brow furrowed, and he waited for Raibert to continue. Nox and another security synthoid stepped in, but the big man seemed completely at ease despite their presence. Nox quickly approached the man from behind, but Shigeki held up a hand.

"All right, out with it. You clearly came into my office uninvited for a reason. What do you want?"

"I'm here on behalf of my government with a warning about your time-travel program."

"Is that so?"

"It is." Raibert leaned forward and flashed a satisfied smile. "And *this* time, Director, you're going to listen to me."